NEW Y

YEAR'S WISH

NEW YEAR'S WISH

KATHERINE GARBERA
SCARLET WILSON
ROBYN GRADY

First Published in Great Britain 2017
By Mills & Boon, an imprint of HarperCollins*Publishers*
1 London Bridge Street, London, SE1 9GF

NEW YEAR'S WISH © 2017 Harlequin Books S.A.

After Midnight © 2015 Katherine Garbera
The Prince She Never Forgot © 2015 Scarlet Wilson
Amnesiac Ex, Unforgettable Vows © 2011 Robyn Grady

ISBN: 978-0-263-93177-8

24-1117

AFTER MIDNIGHT

KATHERINE GARBERA

*This one is for Nancy Thompson
and Mary Louise Wells. Thank you
for the gift of your friendship.*

Katherine Garbera is a *USA TODAY* bestselling author of more than fifty books and has always believed in happy endings. She lives in England with her husband, children and their pampered pet, Godiva. Visit Katherine on the web at katherinegarbera.com, or catch up with her on Facebook and Twitter.

1

"HELLO, GORGEOUS."

Carter Shaw.

Bad boy, snowboarder and Lindsey Collins' worst nightmare. Carter was everything she wasn't, and if she was being totally honest, everything she sort of wished she could be.

"Hello, trouble."

He laughed in that husky deep-throated way of his.

She tried to ignore the fact that his eyes were a kind of blue-gray that reminded her of early mornings on the slope just after the sun came up. His dark hair was thick and curly on the top, but at this moment cut short on the back of his neck. She'd seen him wear it a lot longer, but this sportier cut called even more attention to his handsome, gorgeous face. He had that sexy stubble that made her fingers tingle with the urge to touch it each time she saw him. And it didn't help her libido that the guy had that relaxed vibe of someone who'd grown up in California. To her, he'd always looked as if he should be on a surfboard instead of a snowboard.

"Nice shindig," he said. "If you like glamour."

Briefly glancing away to check out their surroundings, she smiled despite herself. The club at the Lars
Usten Resort and Spa certainly did New Year's Eve in
a big way. Lots of champagne. Lots of partygoers. Hats
and horns for everyone. There was a large dance floor
in the middle and banquettes around the end, as well as
lots of high tables.

"I can do glamour," she replied.

"You sure can," he said with a wink.

"Are you hitting on me?" she asked. "You've always
said you'd rather kiss your snowboard than a Super G
skier."

"Well, you are looking a lot better than my snowboard at the moment."

Lindsey shook her head at the way he said it. There
was something different about him tonight. He wasn't
his usual cocky self. They were both here this evening
because of the wedding of their two friends, Elizabeth
and Bradley. The newlyweds had long since departed
and she had stayed behind because it seemed a little too
Bridget Jones to be sitting all alone in her barely furnished condo on New Year's Eve.

Up till now Lindsey had never been a big fan of staying up until midnight on New Year's Eve. What was the
point? Her entire life had been spent training to win an
international gold medal—and kissing someone at midnight really kind of paled in comparison to that goal. Or
at least it had. But tonight…she felt a little wild. A little
out of control. And if she was being completely honest,
she felt like doing something she'd never do otherwise.
Last year was supposed to have been *her* year, and she'd
crashed and burned playing by the rules and following
her plan. She'd suffered a humiliating fall in a practice

run in Sochi that had ended her career and changed her life. Instead of attacking the changes with her customary gusto, she'd settled into a sort of limbo here in Park City, Utah, at the Lars Usten lodge.

It had been so easy to do. The resort was cushy; her students at the lodge were cute and undemanding. The past six months or so had given her the chance to take it easy and slowly recover from more than knee surgery.

But this year... Well, this year all bets were off. Starting right here right now. The band was playing Van Morrison's signature hit, and she shot Carter a brazen look. "This is my song."

"Your song?"

She pointed to her eyes. Oh, God, was she really doing this? "'Brown Eyed Girl.'"

Yes, it seemed she was.

"Then let's dance," he said, grabbing her wrist and leading her onto the dance floor. He swung her around to face him, and she let go and pretended she didn't know all the things she knew about Carter.

That he played fast and loose with life and women. That he was a rebel risk taker who had caused more than one accident on the slopes. That he liked to put his hand on her hip and hold her close while they danced.

And he smelled good. A clean, crisp scent that reminded her of being outside and on the slopes.

She turned away from him.

She wasn't herself tonight. She should dance off the dance floor and out the door. Go home and forget about trying to be something and someone she wasn't.

Except she was lost.

Really lost...and she needed something to make her feel alive again. Something that going sixty miles per hour down the side of a mountain used to do but couldn't anymore.

"Gorgeous? You okay?"

No. Definitely *not* okay, but confessing that to Carter wasn't something she was going to do.

"Just thirsty."

"Let me get you a drink. Grab us some seats and we can chat."

"What would we possibly have to chat about?" she asked. "The charity event to get kids skiing that we're both working on. I know that's not until next November, but we are both playing a key role in it." His eyes gleamed with mischief. "*Or* the fact that, come midnight, I'm going to kiss you. I'll let you pick."

Suddenly tongue-tied, she watched him turn away and slowly weave his way through the crowd. He was popular, and everyone stopped him to chat or snap a quick selfie. And he smiled and acted as though he enjoyed it.

Heck, he probably did. She'd heard her coach say he loved the spotlight and the spotlight loved him. And she'd never seen any evidence to the contrary. How did he do it?

She wished there was some way she could claim his confidence for herself. To make herself into the invincible badass that Carter was. But the truth was she wasn't that type of girl, and no matter how much she tried, she wasn't going to change overnight.

Part of the problem was that she'd just come from an incredibly romantic winter wedding that seemed to emphasize that she was alone. Added to that, the bride's maid of honor, Penny, had recently hooked up with Will, her handsome vacation fling, which was quickly turning into something that was bound to last a lot longer.

And she was alone.

Lonely.

Desperate...

No. Not desperate. Though it did feel that way until Carter came back with a lemon-drop martini for her and some kind of mixed drink for himself. He slid in next to her at the high table instead of across from her and draped his arm along the back of the seat.

He canted his body toward hers and she thought, *What the hell.* She wasn't going to start another year the way she had all the rest. This year was going to be different, and Carter Shaw would be hers tonight.

CARTER HAD WANTED Lindsey since the first time he'd seen her. They'd both been two hotshot seventeen-year-olds being interviewed on ESPN, and when she'd looked straight at him with her pretty chocolate-brown eyes, he'd felt that spark shoot through his body.

But she'd always been the ultimate ice queen. Too cool for someone as wild and risky as he'd always been. But he'd gotten to know her better now. More than ten years later, he still wanted her, but he saw her through the eyes of a man and not a lusty boy.

Though, in all honesty, gazing at her now, looking like a gorgeous goddess, she still made him horny as hell.

And it was New Year's Eve. He'd spent more of them than he wanted to admit higher than the Rocky Mountains and with people whose names he couldn't recall.

He knew he'd changed over the course of the past year. The winter games had given him a check in the last box of his goals list. And it had been a sobering wake-up call when he'd witnessed Lindsey crash and realized his Nordic angel had feet of clay. Seeing her career end so quickly and unexpectedly had made him understand that he needed to look at his own life. He wasn't going to be able to snowboard forever at the top level of his event.

So he'd come here to Park City… Okay, in part to be closer to her. To see if maybe she'd be interested in him now that she wasn't so focused on training 24/7. But she still looked straight through him, as if he was just another man in the room. He wanted to be the *only* man in the room she saw.

Especially tonight.

"So, gorgeous, have you been thinking about that kiss?" he asked smoothly.

He sure had. It was hard to think of anything else when he was standing so close to her. Tonight she had her long, pale hair pulled back into an elegant updo. Tendrils framed her heart-shaped face and accentuated her long neck. Her mouth was full and sensuous, and she'd coated it with a sparkly lip gloss, which made it so hard for him to tear his gaze away. He leaned in closer. Almost kissed her before he pulled back.

He was waiting for midnight.

Besides, he had more control than that. He didn't give in to his baser instincts. Not anymore.

"I can tell it's been on *your* mind," she purred, lifting her hand and running her finger over his lower lip, back and forth, before spreading her fingers out and rubbing them over the stubble on his jaw.

She closed her eyes as she touched him for just a second, nibbling at her bottom lip before her hand dropped away.

"I have. You know I've been interested in you forever."

"Forever?" she said. "That's a bit of an exaggeration."

Not really. But admitting to her that she'd been his obsession for the better part of ten years wasn't something he planned to do tonight.

The band had switched to contemporary dance hits, and the loud, infectious beat pumped through the room. Lindsey swayed to it as she took a sip of her lemon-drop martini. It was sad that he knew what she liked to drink. But in a way she'd always been his safe fantasy. The one thing in his life, however distant, that was good and always just out of reach.

Until now.

He wrapped a wispy tendril of straight blond hair that was hanging along the nape of her neck around his finger. Her locks were exquisitely soft. Her skin, showed off by the stunning emerald-green dress she wore, so pale and creamy.

"Not an exaggeration. When we met at ESPN, I knew I wanted to kiss you."

She pursed her lips and tipped her head subtly away from him. "You were a player even then. And we both know you were attempting to throw me off my game. I almost let you."

"Why didn't you?"

"My parents. They had sacrificed a lot for me to get where I was, and no hotshot snowboarder with a tattoo was going to change that."

"*With a tattoo.* Is this a mark against me?" he asked, rubbing the side of his neck at the site of his first tattoo. It was a courage symbol that he'd seen in Japan when his father, an international businessman, had taken him there for a trip. Carter had been sixteen at the time and had snowboarded in Nagano while his father had worked. The tattoo had been his way of getting his father's attention while also proving to himself that he hadn't needed it. What could he say? He'd been a teenager.

She traced the design with her long, sparkly painted fingernail. "Not now. But back then you seemed wild and reckless. Too much for me. I needed to concentrate on my skiing."

"You were the fast one," he said with a wink. He knew that a lot of people thought what he did was dangerous—the flips and the 360s—but Lindsey had thrown her body down the mountain at speeds in excess of sixty miles per hour. Something that never failed to turn him on.

She scraped her finger down the column of his neck, sending delicious shivers through his body, and his cock stirred. Seeing his reaction, she leaned in closer, closed her eyes and released a sigh.

"Why is it that you are always racing ahead of me, then?" she asked in a soft whisper spoken right in his ear.

His ability to think was gone. Her breath was warm and her finger kept stroking his neck. All he could think about was her mouth. And how close it was to his. He turned his head to kiss her. Needed to feel her lips under his. But a waitress bumped into their table, jostling the drinks, and Lindsey pulled back.

Carter cursed under his breath but put on a smile for the cocktail waitress, who looked stricken. "No worries."

"These are for you," she said, setting down two cards and handing them Lars Usten Resort and Spa pens before walking away.

IT WAS ONE THING to decide she was going to spend the night with Carter, but she was finding it altogether more unnerving than she would have expected. In movies she'd seen the woman go after the guy, and then there would be a montage of kisses or dancing that ended up with the couple in bed. But she'd always been awkward at this stage.

There was something about Carter that for her was irresistible. His tattoo had fascinated her for a long time, and that stubble of his was just as a soft as she'd imagined it would be. She was letting the martini power her courage tonight…and she had to admit she liked it.

A lot.

"What is this?" She pulled the card the waitress had dropped on their table toward her. He'd been about to kiss her, and though she wanted that kiss, she was glad for the reprieve. She only needed a kiss at midnight. Not a public make-out session before that.

"Some sort of resolutions form," he said. "So, gorgeous, what do you want for this New Year?"

She arched a brow. "Why do you keep calling me that?"

"Because you are gorgeous," he said with another sly wink. "Plus, I'm sort of afraid if I say your name, you'll remember you don't like me."

"Ah, I wouldn't say I don't *like* you," she demurred. He was a little too wild and too out of control to be someone she felt comfortable with most of the time, but tonight that appealed to her. She wanted to forget who she was. Forget the past year had happened and wake up on January 1 as someone else.

That was pitiful, she thought. She should stop drinking. She'd had two martinis, and while she wasn't drunk, she did have that nice little buzz. But it was the maudlin thoughts that bothered her.

"Okay. What would you say about me, then?"

"I like that tattoo," she admitted. "And your stubble. How do you get it so soft?"

He laughed. "I've got more tattoos if you like that one."

"You do?" she asked. "Where?"

"I'll show you if you play your cards right."

She flushed a little. Not as bold as she wanted to be, but she wasn't backing away. She *was* doing this. She was going to be impulsive. And daring. Not Lindsey-like.

Needing a distraction, she glanced down at the resolution list on the card. "Do you do resolutions?"

"Seriously?" he asked with a mocking look. "Do I look like someone who wants to better myself?"

She shook her head, but realized in that instant that he was playing at being the bad-boy snowboarder she'd always thought he was. "I'm not sure about that. I think there is a big part of Carter Shaw the world never gets to see."

He shook his head. "Nah. I mean, there are those tattoos, but otherwise, what you see is what you get."

She doubted that. She was on to him. Why did he work so hard to be something he wasn't? For that matter, why did *she*? Because it was easier than letting the world see who she truly was.

"What food do you want to try next year?" she asked, reading from the list and hoping that she could keep her courage until midnight. Only another fifteen minutes. She wanted him. She wanted this New Year's Eve to be different from all the rest.

"Food, eh?" He wrinkled his forehead. "Not sure. I'm going with one of my cousins on a trip in Iceland to see a reindeer farm. So maybe reindeer?"

"I bet it doesn't taste like chicken," she said with a half smile. "When is that trip?"

"In the fall. It's a Northern Lights trip. We spend three weeks up close to the Arctic Circle living with the locals and watching each night for the aurora borealis."

That sounded…cold, but intriguing. "Have you done anything like that before?"

"Nah. This is the first year that I'm not competing anymore."

She looked at him in surprise. "What? Why not?" If not for her reconstructed knee, she'd still be training and focusing on four years from now. The next winter games.

"I have gold medals and more titles that one man could ask for. It's time to set my sights on something else."

"Such as…?" she asked, leaning closer. This is what she was searching for. *What* came after competing the way they had for most of their life? It was different for Carter because he'd been born with a silver spoon in his mouth. A little rich kid who got whatever he wanted. But that had only carried him so far. She knew that he'd worked as hard as she had to get to the winter games.

"Not sure. But this is my year of adventure. My year to find out. I'm working on that charity you're involved with to help kids get started in winter sports, because that's new for me. The old man is glad to see me giving back. Can you believe he said that to me?" Carter scowled. "I've given back a lot over the years."

For a moment she caught a glimpse of the real Carter.

"You have. I've heard about the board you developed. It changed snowboarding."

"Yeah, that was nothing," he said, flashing a grin at her. And the real man disappeared behind that flirty facade. "So what new food are you going to try?"

"Nothing exotic like you. I have a thing about dairy and have usually not eaten cheese. I know that sounds silly but this year I think I'll give it a try."

He lifted a brow. "Cheese?"

"Yes."

"You seriously don't eat cheese?" he asked.

She had friends who acted the same way when she mentioned it. "I don't like dairy stuff usually."

"Cheeseburgers?"

"Nope."

"Pizza?" he prodded.

"Pesto-based pizza with fresh tomatoes. No cheese."

"Weirdo," he said.

"Like *you're* normal!"

"Who wants to be normal?" he scoffed. "Okay...all kidding aside, what new thing are you really going to try?"

She looked at him for a long minute before the two lemon-drop martinis and her courage finally caught up with her mouth. "You."

2

"ME?"

"Yes, you. Remember all those times you badgered me for a kiss?" she asked.

He did. It had been a game for him since that first meeting. He'd wanted her, but she was out of his league. A classy woman—even at seventeen—who wouldn't give him a second glance. Of course, that hadn't stopped him. He'd teased her relentlessly, invaded her personal space and kept clamoring for a kiss.

"The last time I asked I thought I spooked you," he said, getting to the heart of the reason why he was really sitting with Lindsey Collins, who, despite her request for a kiss, would more than likely not end up in his bed this evening. He'd pushed her in Sochi. Had goaded her into agreeing that she'd kiss him if he beat his world-record time, and still she hadn't.

Not that he'd ever really expected her to fulfill her end of the bargain.

To him it had seemed like a simple little bet. Something to push her, because it had been ten years of flirting and it had seemed ridiculous to continue playing that game. And he'd been feeling trapped by his coach and sponsors, who'd wanted him to sign a new deal to keep doing the same thing he'd always done. So instead of acting like a man, he'd done what he always did and sought out Lindsey before her run to demand what he'd always wanted from her.

"It wasn't you. God, please, don't think that crash had anything to do with you," she said, reaching over to put her hand on his.

She leaned in, and the scent of her perfume filled the air around him. Her brown eyes were sincere as they met his. She squeezed his hand. "My crash was… I'm not sure what, but it wasn't you. I've been over the footage a million times. I wish that was an exaggeration, but it's not. I've watched it over and over again, trying to figure out what I could have done differently. Did you see how smooth I was at the top?"

"I did." He'd watched her run like everyone else. But for him, he'd felt that sense of pride he always did in her. He'd thought this time she'd beat him, and maybe that would put an end to his pursuit of her. Because she'd told him if she won that was the end of his kissing taunts.

But instead she'd crashed midway through her run. Her body and skis tumbling over each other. His heart had stopped beating for a second. She'd looked small and fragile as she'd crashed into the bright orange safety webbing. Guilt and fear had warred inside him.

"Well, it wasn't you. I think I hit the snow wrong out of the gate. My coach has a couple of theories, as well. But, honestly, I'm not so scared of being kissed that I'd crash.

"Kissed lots of guys, have you?"

She made a face. "A lady doesn't tell."

"Apologies."

"But I don't mind telling you that the anticipation with you has been killing me. I want to believe when you do kiss me it will be spectacular. However, given that it's been ten years of waiting, I can't rule out the possibility that it might be a dud."

He laughed. Threw his head back and just forgot everything else in this moment except for Lindsey. She was as nutty as he was but just covered it up better.

"It might. Or it could be the best damned thing either of us ever experiences."

She let go of his hand and settled back against the seat. "I guess that's why I've made you my resolution."

There was something different about her tonight. The wedding earlier had made him start thinking about things that he usually ignored. That and the fact that beginning tomorrow he was no longer only an athlete. He didn't have to train every day; he was going to chart a new path.

"Champagne or sparkling grape juice?" the cocktail waitress asked as she approached their table with a tray of drinks.

The Lars Usten Resort knew the party was going strong. Behind her was another waitress with hats with the year marked out in glitter and some kind of horn.

"Juice for me," Carter said. He didn't want to dull a single moment of the night with Lindsey, and although he liked to believe he could handle whatever life had thrown at him, he did it better when he was sober.

"Juice?" Lindsey asked, arching one eyebrow. "Champagne for me."

The waitress set their drinks in front of them, and then they were each given a hat. For him a top hat. For her a tiara. She promptly put it on her head and turned to bat her eyelashes at him. "Do I look like a princess now?"

"The queen should be afraid you're after her title," he murmured.

"As if. I'm not after anything. You're lucky, Carter. Lucky that you still have snowboarding. Life is very strange when you don't have to get up every day and train," she said, taking a sip of her champagne.

Not exactly what he'd been hoping to hear. "I think you're supposed to wait for the toast to drink that."

She smiled mischievously. "Going to tell on me?"

He shook his head. "Your secret's safe with me, Linds." How could he possibly deny this woman anything? She enchanted him. And he had to admit, she was a total mystery. He'd teased and cajoled her for his own amusement but had never really taken the time to get to know her. Tonight was showing him that all the preconceived notions he'd had were wrong.

She wasn't the ice queen she'd always been on the snow. She was real and fragile and so damned tempting...

LINDSEY HAD NEVER worn a tiara before. Even though this one was plastic with fake gems, she was still thrilled to be wearing it. It made her feel girlie. "This is my first real New Year's Eve party. Pitiful, isn't it?"

"Not really. Your life was focused in a different direction."

"Yeah, but you were training and still found time to party," she said.

"I'm good at multitasking," he replied.

"Most men really aren't."

He gave her a cynical look. "Really? You want to do the whole 'battle of the sexes' thing? Tonight?"

She didn't. She wanted to enjoy the fact that she felt like a normal girl instead of someone apart from the mainstream. The Ice Queen, the media had labeled her. But the truth was, she had gotten so used to keeping her feelings hidden it was hard for her to actually show them.

"Of course not. I had no idea your ego was so thin," she teased.

"It's not. But you should know if you throw down what you're going up against."

"What? That you're the boss?" she asked, trying not to smile. Carter had been flouting rules and tradition since the moment she'd met him. She found it really hard to believe that he'd have some hard set-in-stone ideas about anything. But she did believe that if he got into a fight, he'd go full-out and leave nothing.

She was used to winning and knew how to get what she wanted on the slopes but, one-on-one, she had a gut feeling he'd beat her every time. Hard as it was to admit, she just didn't know how to play a game like this.

She sighed.

Who was she trying to kid here? She wasn't going to be any different in the New Year than she'd been before. When had she ever been anything other than a stick-in-the-mud, tall, outdoorsy girl who would rather talk about skiing than anything else? Even her own family found her boring at times. Though they were kind about it and would listen to her talk about a new position or when she liked to shift her weight, she'd known they probably weren't really all that interested.

"Want to dance?" Carter asked, bringing her back

to the present. "One last spin around the dance floor to ring out the old year."

She nodded. "I'd like that. And *I'm* kissing *you* at midnight."

"Should I be on guard?" he murmured, stepping down from the high table and offering her his hand.

She took it and stumbled a little in her high heels. Bracing one hand on his chest, she whispered, "Not really. I know you want to kiss me."

His blue-gray gaze slowly drifted over her lips before he locked eyes with her once again. "I'm having performance anxiety now that you mentioned it. It might not be that great."

"I doubt that," she said. "You never have that."

"I wish I was as confident as you seem to think I am."

"Aren't you?" she breathed, reveling once again in his brisk masculine scent. They were pressed close together due to the crowds streaming in to hear the last song of the year. "You walked into a boardroom filled with executives you ticked off by campaigning to make them let you snowboard on their slopes, and then convinced them to back your charity event. You've got *nerve*, Shaw."

He had more than that. He seemed to embrace his life in a way she only had when she'd left the gate and started down the slope. She knew people thought what she'd done was dangerous, but to her it had just felt natural. It was a tightly controlled run down the mountain, and she'd spent her lifetime training. So she didn't credit that for anything other than being something she was good at.

She wanted to throw herself out of the gate of life, too. But she was getting a little nervous now that midnight was approaching. Carter had kissed lots of women; she knew that for a fact from all the gossip in the athlete's village at the winter games, and from firsthand accounts from other Alpine skiers over the years. As for her... Well, she hadn't kissed that many men. And the few sexual encounters she'd had were hurried affairs that had left her feeling cold and wanting more.

She didn't want Carter to be the same. She'd sort of set him on the sex-god pedestal in her mind a long time ago. *What if he wasn't?*

Or worse yet, what if he was great and she was the dud?

Ugh! This was what happened when she stepped outside her nice, safe, little zone. Carter stared down at her with those intense eyes of his, and she hoped she looked intriguing or inviting but was afraid she might just seem confused.

"What?"

"We don't have to dance," he said softly.

"I want to." She had in her head an image of New Year's Eve, and it involved her looking glamorous, which, thanks to the beautiful dress she wore, ticked that box. And she had a very handsome, sexy man who'd just asked her to dance.

She took his hand in hers. It would be too much for the band to play "The Way You Look Tonight," but in her mind she wanted them to. Instead they danced to "Wrecking Ball." Something that didn't speak well for love.

But this wasn't about love.

This thing between her and Carter had always been about pure lust. And tonight she was finally going to cross the finish line. Get the kiss he'd been taunting her with since they'd met.

The funny thing was, she was just as scared about that today as she had been when she was seventeen. He held her close, and for just a second she rested her head on his strong shoulder. Pretended they were that couple in her mind. The couple who could gaze lovingly into each other's eyes at midnight and share a kiss so profound it would rock both their worlds.

But then Carter squeezed her hip and slid his hand up the middle of her back.

She tipped her head back to look up at him.

"The countdown is starting."

It had already begun, Lindsey thought. It had started ten long years ago, and now it came down to this moment.

She licked her lips and couldn't help but focus on his mouth. Those chiseled, full lips nestled in that closely shorn stubble.

"Ten. Nine. Eight. Seven. Six. Five…"

"Ready?"

"Three. Two. One."

She went up on tiptoe, wrapped her arms around his neck and met his mouth with hers. His lips were soft, surprising her into parting hers. His breath was warm and minty, and he held her loosely, but she was rooted to the spot.

Around her people were kissing and celebrating, but her world had narrowed to just Carter. *Carter Shaw.*

Of course, he kissed like a dream. He was the kind of man who'd had lots of practice, but this didn't feel routine, like something he'd done a million times before. To her it felt special and it awakened the passion she'd tucked away after her crash. It felt as though she was finally able to relax again as he kissed her.

She held his shoulders, and his hands on her waist

tightened as he pulled her closer into the curve of his body. His chest was firm against hers. Solid. He held her as if he wasn't going to let her fall. Or let her crash. And that was exactly what she needed.

She framed his face with her hands. Ran her fingers over that soft stubble of his and then pulled back. But he followed her. Kissing her again, dropping soft and tantalizing kisses along the line of her jaw before he lifted his head to look down at her.

"Not a dud," he said.

"Not at all. That was…"

"Unexpected?" he suggested in a smooth, sexy voice.

His hands on her waist caressed her. She noticed that as the music changed to "Auld Lang Syne" and he pulled her closer, swayed with her to the music. She didn't want him to let go. Maybe it was the drinks she'd had tonight or the fact that this was a new year. A new slate for her. But something made this moment with Carter seem almost perfect.

The rational part of her brain tried to say it wasn't, but she shushed it. For just one night she wanted to be like every other person and not analyze her actions to death. She wanted to live.

She grabbed Carter's shoulders and pulled him toward her. Caught his mouth with hers and kissed him the way she'd seen it done in the movies. The way she'd tried in the past. She'd found reality and movie kisses didn't deliver in the same way; they'd always ended up tasting not quite right. But this time, as her tongue slid past his lips and into his mouth, everything felt different. Carter tasted good. His kiss was warm and…yes, perfect. Absolutely, profoundly perfect. He leaned over her and bent her back the slightest bit, angling his head to deepen the kiss. Her pulse was racing, and little tingles shot down her body. He twisted and moved them a few steps off the dance floor.

She felt the hard wall at her back and Carter's warmth pressed into her. He pulled his mouth from hers, but only went as far as her neck, where he suckled at the skin as his hands roamed up and down her body.

She skimmed her own hands down the strong muscles of his back to his lean hips and tugged him closer. Felt the shaft of his erection against her and knew he wanted more.

She needed more. So much more from him at this moment.

"Want to get out of here?" she asked.

"I've got a room at the lodge." He exhaled roughly. "Is that what you want?"

She nodded.

She didn't want to talk about it or to discuss it too much or she might change her mind.

And tonight she was being impulsive.

"Yes, I want you."

"I want you, too. I have for a long time," he said, taking her hand and leading her out of the dance club. The lobby was quiet, almost shockingly so after the noise in the club. But there were a few staff members who smiled at them and wished them a happy New Year.

She kept her hand laced tightly with Carter's; trusted him to lead her through this night. This new beginning. The one she'd wanted for so long but hadn't been sure how to find.

They were alone in the elevator car, and Carter dropped her hand and stood a few inches from her. "Are you sure about this? I don't want you to have any regrets."

"I promise you I won't." That much she knew was true. She'd regret it more if she walked away from him. If she let this moment pass.

Suddenly she realized that it had been fear holding her here. Fear that had motivated everything she'd done since the crash. The crash that had taken her career and could have taken her life.

She'd been lucky.

Now she wanted to make up for lost time, wanted to make the most of her life, but had been struggling to get over the hump and actually do it.

Figured it would be Carter Shaw who'd push her and get her moving again.

She cupped his butt and squeezed. "Are you having doubts?"

He turned around, and she hadn't realized how turned on he was by her until that moment. He moved toward her, backed her up against the side of the elevator car and kissed her full-on, his entire body pressing provocatively against hers.

His chest rubbed over her breasts, his hips canted in toward her and she felt the brush of his erection at her center. His hands went to the back of her head as his mouth hungrily claimed hers. He kissed her with a long, deep kiss that left her trembling and wanting so much more.

The bell dinged and the elevator doors slid open. But still he kissed her as if he couldn't let her go. The doors started to slide shut, and he pulled back and cursed. He shoved his foot out to stop them from closing and tugged her behind him as he stepped into the hallway.

"I'm not changing my mind, gorgeous. I can promise you that."

3

CARTER LED HER into his suite. He'd left the light on over the bed because he had never been a fan of a dark room. Kissing Lindsey was like the first time he'd hopped in the half-pipe and had the ride of his life.

She'd awakened something inside him that was so much more than physical. It was easy to say the affection and lust roiling through him right now was due to the day he'd spent with her. They'd both been in the bridal party. Lindsey as a bridesmaid and Carter as a grooms-man. The other couple standing up for Elizabeth and Bradley was a real couple, so she and Carter had sort of been forced together. In spite of all his faults, he'd never been a big fan of lying, even to himself.

She cupped his butt again and groaned. He wanted to take this slow, but if she kept fondling him it was going to be a wham-bam-thank-you-ma'am encounter up against the wall of his hotel room.

Even the thought of that made him shiver. God, he wanted her.

"Want a drink?" he asked, forcing himself to take a few steps from her. He hoped the distance would clear his head and maybe penetrate the red haze of lust that was surrounding him. Make him remember he'd wanted her for a long time. Their first time should be epic.

"There is only one thing in this room that I want, Carter Shaw, and I'm looking straight at him."

She kicked off her high heels as she sauntered toward him, her hand under her arm. For a moment it looked as if she was cupping her own breast. He groaned as she slowly dragged her hand down the side of her own body. The dress gaped and he realized she was getting naked.

"Slow down, gorgeous, we have all night," he said, toeing off his shoes as she closed the distance he'd put between them.

"It's midnight, Carter, which means we only have six more hours until morning. Until the cold light of day. I don't want to waste a second of it."

She was different. He wanted to be, too. He wanted to just go with it and pretend that this was the real Lindsey. Except he knew it wasn't.

Was she playing a game tonight?

She placed her palm flat on his chest, and then leaned into him. The scent of her perfume once again surrounding him, inundating his senses. Pressing even closer, she went up on tiptoe to kiss his neck, just above his tattoo, as her hands pushed his jacket off his shoulders and down his arms.

He let the jacket fall to the floor, then slipped one of his hands into the gap in her unzipped dress. Her skin was cool and satiny smooth. He felt his way over her ribs toward her breasts. Her breath hitched, and she caught the lobe of his ear between her teeth and bit down lightly.

"I'm curious where those other tattoos of yours are,"

she said, her fingers moving between them and undoing the buttons at the front of his shirt.

Her breath brushed over his neck and made him throb even more. Shivers spread down his body; blood pooled in all the right places, making his skin sensitive and cock rock hard. He stopped thinking of how he wanted this to be and just followed her lead.

Lindsey wasn't going to let him put her off her goal. And as she'd said downstairs, her resolution for the year was him. He'd never been anyone's anything special before. Fun time, sure, but that wasn't all he intended to be for Lindsey tonight.

He pushed his hand farther into her dress, up her back, and found the clasp of her bra. Undoing it with one hand and then rubbing his hand between her shoulder blades, pulling her closer to him as he lowered his head to take her mouth with his.

She tasted like the promise of a night he'd never forget. Her mouth was both languid and passionate under his. Her tongue tangled against his in a slow, sensuous dance that felt as though it would never end. As though it didn't have to end tonight.

Her hands slid under his shirt, her fingers cool against the fabric of his T-shirt, and he felt the bite of her nails into his pecs. "Where is your skin? How am I going to see these rumored tattoos of I can't get to you?"

A laugh rumbled through him. "Sit on the bed."

"No."

"I thought you wanted to see me?"

"I do, but that doesn't mean you get to be bossy," she said.

Lindsey slipped her hands up over his shoulders again

and pushed his dress shirt down his arms. "You forgot my cuffs."

"No, I didn't," she drawled. "I think you'll see that you are trapped. And I am in charge."

He wasn't trapped at all. He might not have a full range of motion, but he could still hold on to her waist, which he did. But she stepped back and put her finger right in the center of his chest. "Why don't you go sit on the bed?"

He laughed again, that jolt of lust and joy taking him by surprise. And he did what she asked, slowly working his hands to free them as he sat. As soon as his hands were free, he leaned back on his elbows and arched one eyebrow as he looked over at her. "Okay, now what?"

"Hmm…let me see." She moved forward, straddled him on the bed and brought her mouth down hard on his. She sucked his tongue into her mouth, and everything inside him came to attention as she nipped his tongue and then abruptly stood. "Take off your T-shirt."

"Take off your dress. I'm dying to see what you look like without it."

"Can I keep my tiara on?" she asked impishly.

"Definitely. I think the Ice Queen should always wear her crown."

She stepped away, shimmied out of her dress and then let her bra slowly slide down her torso, pulling first one arm free and then the other and dangling it from one finger. She stood there with that cool Nordic beauty. His gorgeous ice queen, very sure of herself and her appeal.

He started to get up, but she wagged her finger at him. "Did I say you could move?"

"I think you're going to want me to move," he told her.

"Not yet."

He sank back on the bed and grimaced as his slacks cut into his erection. He shifted and then thought, *To hell with it,* and unzipped his pants, pushing them down his legs.

"You look good, Carter. You could be an underwear model."

He'd done a few ads in his day, but lately he preferred to keep some things for himself and his lovers. His body was one of them. He stood and slowly pulled the hem of his T-shirt up past his abdomen as he closed the gap between them. She reached out and traced the tattoo on his left side. Her fingers were warm and seeking as they moved over him.

The design disappeared into the top of his boxer briefs, and she pulled the elastic waistband away from his skin, pushing the side of the briefs down so she could see the entire thing.

"Is this a mountain?"

"Yes. Nagano."

"Why Nagano?"

He let out a groan. "*Now?* You want to talk now?" he asked, painfully aware that he could barely string together two words as she leaned lower to examine his ink. Her beautiful, lush breasts swayed forward and her breath brushed over his hip. She was so close to his cock, he could only think of twisting his hips so that he could feel her touch where he desired it most.

"I guess not. But later," she said, "I want to know more about it."

"Later," he growled, cupping her breasts, rubbing his palm over the center of her nipples and gently fondling them.

She caressed his upper body and pushed the T-shirt

up and over his head. He stopped stroking her as she tossed it aside. Again she put her hand in the center of his chest and pushed against him. He walked backward until he felt the edge of the bed at the back of his thighs, and put his arm around her waist, dragging her forward with him as he sat. Inhaling her sweet, womanly scent, he pulled her onto his lap so she straddled him.

She reached up and did something with her hair, letting it fall around her shoulders as she leaned forward. Staring at him with passion-glazed eyes, she cupped his face, rubbed her fingers through his short stubble and then leaned down to kiss him. Not a dominating one, as earlier, but one that promised that the games were over. He held her close to him with one hand on her hip, and let his other hand caress her, starting at the back of her neck and then slowly moving down the back of her spine. He felt her shiver as he traced his way around the tiny indentation right above her buttocks.

He caressed her hips, and she rocked forward against him, then winced. Her knee. He'd forgotten that she'd injured it a year ago. He scooted back on the bed and rolled them onto their sides so they were facing each other.

"Sorry," she whispered.

"Hey, gorgeous," he said, lightly running his hand down the side of her body over her curves. "It's okay. How's the knee?"

"Fine. It was just the angle."

"Then let's find a better angle," he suggested. "One where we don't have to think about anything but each other."

She nodded. But the confidence that had been driving her had waned. He could read it in her eyes. "I guess I'm in charge now."

Just as he suspected, the thought of the power shift was enough to nudge any embarrassment Lindsey had over her knee out of her subconscious. She gave him an arched look, raised herself up onto her elbow and put her finger to the middle of his chest again.

"Not so fast." She leaned over him, slowly following the pattern of his chest hair as it narrowed down his belly and disappeared into the top of his boxer briefs. Then she dipped her finger under the elastic and brushed the tip of his cock, and his hips jerked forward.

He breathed in and out, struggling to stay in control. Then he reached for her and mimicked her caress. He started in the middle of her chest and traced his finger down around each of her breasts, and then lower to her belly button. He drew a small circle around it and then leaned over to trace the path with his mouth. But he lingered at her breasts, catching her nipple in his mouth and sucking as he continued to fondle her belly button.

She pushed her hand into his underwear and slid her hand up and down his shaft. He shivered in response, felt as though he was going to lose it, but instead rocked himself against her touch. He liked it. Her fingers were long, and she wrapped them around his length, stroking up and down within the confines of his underwear.

He lifted his lips from her breast to move lower, kissing each of her ribs, and her hand slid off him as he did so. She let her fingers drift up his body and around to his back. Caressing the area near his tattoo, her fingers moved gently over the imprint as he tongued her belly button and then dipped his head lower. He peeled her underwear over her hips and down her long legs, stopping to kiss the scars at her knee, and then tossed them to the floor.

He shoved his own briefs off, ready to be totally naked.

"Are you on the pill?" he asked.

"What?" She seemed dazed, and he realized that he'd jarred her.

"Are you protected from pregnancy?"

She nodded. "Are you clean?"

Fair question, given his reputation, but still… "Yes. Are you?"

"Of course," she said.

"Good."

He moved so that he could take her ankles in his hands to raise her legs. He smiled as she propped herself up on her elbows.

She was spread out in front of him, her tousled blond hair falling around her shoulders, her pink-tipped breasts rising and falling with each breath she took. His eyes traced her nipped-in waist and the soft blond curls at the apex of her thighs. The long smooth legs that he'd admired often when she'd worn snow pants.

She had a great ass, but he'd save that for next time. Tonight was special. It was the first time, and he wanted it to be just right. Wanted to see her face, so that in his mind he'd always have this image of Lindsey.

Naked. Wanting. Completely his.

He brought her foot to his chest and caressed her leg, starting at the ankle and working his way to her thigh, stopping just short of her center. Then he did the same with her other leg, lingering over the scars on her fully healed knee. Next he used his mouth on the same path, and when he got to the apex of her thighs, she sighed and tangled her hands in his hair as he parted her and kissed her most intimate flesh.

She shifted under him, her heels pushing down on the bed as she lifted her hips toward his mouth. He flicked his tongue over her and then moved lower to taste her. She slipped her hands across his back, her nails digging into his shoulders as his mouth took full possession of her. Her thighs came up on either side of his face as she thrashed underneath him.

She tried to pull him up over her, but the taste of her was addicting and he couldn't get enough of it. His cock was hard and he wanted to be buried deep inside her, but he didn't want to have to stop tasting her, either.

He swirled his tongue around the little pink bud at the center of her and felt it swell under him. Her nails dug into his shoulders, and she made a breathy sort of moaning noise that let him know she liked it. He slipped his finger inside, stroking her. He kept it up until she tugged at his hair, and he lifted his head.

"Carter."

"Yes, gorgeous?"

"I want you inside me."

"I am inside you," he said.

She sighed and shifted on the bed, bending at the waist, finding his cock first with her hand and then with her mouth. He felt her tongue feather down the side of his shaft as her fingers lightly caressed his balls. She squeezed him as she took the tip of him inside her mouth, her tongue swirling all around it.

A drop left him, and he pulled back. This first time he wanted to come inside her body. Wanted to see her face as they both climaxed.

His hips jerked, and he realized that if she kept this up, he wasn't going to last at all. He pulled his hips back, sitting up and noticing the very satisfied look on her face. Evidently she'd gotten what she wanted. She was a minx, and seeing this side of her made him wonder what else he thought he knew about Lindsey that he didn't.

But he didn't mind, because he was getting what he wanted, too. He took her hands in his, stretching them above her head as he levered his body over hers, shifting his hips until he felt the opening of her body.

"Got your way," he rasped. "I hope you're ready for me."

"I am." She lifted her hips as she wrapped her legs around him, and he slid into her. She held him tight to her and moved her hips to bring him closer each time. Cupping his buttocks, she pulled him.

She was tight and felt so good that he drove all the way home and immediately pulled back to do it again. She wrapped her arms around his shoulders, lifting herself up to whisper hot words of need and desire in his ear. She told him how much she wanted him. How she needed him deeper and deeper.

And he did exactly what she asked. Drove himself into her again and again, deeper each time. He felt shivers run down his spine. Reached between them to caress her clit because he knew he wasn't going to make it much longer. He was going to come and he wanted—needed—to make sure she did, as well.

She moaned his name, bit his neck and arched her body frantically underneath him and then cried out. He felt her body tighten around him, her inner walls gripping his cock and urging him on. Pounding into her, harder and faster than before, he gazed down into those big chocolate-brown eyes as he felt his orgasm rush through him.

He emptied himself inside her and then collapsed,

careful to support his weight with his arms. He dragged one of his hands from where he'd held hers, caressing her arm and shoulder, and then rolled to his side, keeping their bodies joined as he cuddled her close.

She rested her head on his shoulder and ran her fingers over his chest. He felt each exhalation of her breath against his skin, and she sighed a little.

Did she regret this?

"I guess that proves it."

"Proves what, gorgeous?" he asked, almost afraid of her answer. He wanted to lie here with her in his arms and just pretend for a moment that he didn't have to let her go.

"That you're not a dud," she said.

4

HER BODY TINGLED, and she felt more alive than she had in the past year. She pushed herself from Carter and leaned back on her elbow so she could watch him. God, a man shouldn't look like this. Not when he was lying next to her in bed. He was all sinew and muscle and, despite his reputation for being debauched, he was in very good shape.

He'd said he was retiring from snowboarding but there was no evidence of that in his lean, hard body.

His eyes were half-closed; he had one hand on her waist, idly gliding up and down her side. His hands were large but sort of soft when he touched her. The confidence and the courage that had brought her up to his room and into his bed were still there. Buzzing around in her mind, which was a little fuzzy from the drinks she'd had and the sex.

God, she'd had no idea sex could be like that. Could be that good. She understood now why so many people were tempted to miss their training schedules for it.

"Was it a surprise for you?" she asked a bit tentatively. Maybe this was the way it always was for him.

He fully opened his eyes, turning his blue-gray gaze on her. "What?"

"The sex. Or is it always like that for you?"

"Damn, gorgeous, the things you ask," he said. Scrubbing a hand over his eyes, he grabbing a pillow from the head of the bed and bunched it up under his head.

"If I don't ask I'll never know. And you *are* a player," she reminded him.

He arched one dark eyebrow at her.

"Not going to try to deny it, are you? I heard about many of your hook-ups over the years."

"Why would I when you wouldn't believe me anyway?"

"I don't know. Actually, I really don't know you," she admitted. She traced the tattoo of Nagano on his hip. She'd skied there at a world-cup competition twice. She traced the path down his hip and noticed that he let her, just kept still while she ran her finger over his skin.

She didn't know what to do next. She hadn't been kidding when she'd said this wasn't her kind of situation. And let's face it, most etiquette books didn't cover what to do when a woman ended up in bed with a bad-boy snowboarder. In fact, her mom would have probably said don't end up there. She was practical like that.

He sat up and caught her hand in his, bringing it ever so slowly to his lips. He kissed her palm and then looked her straight in the eye. She saw the sincerity his gaze and something else. Something she couldn't really define.

He leaned closer. She closed her eyes because it felt too intense. The room smelled of sex and Carter. That spicy aftershave she'd noticed that lingered in the air after they'd had a conversation.

"It was special for me, too."

"Why do you think that is?" she asked, opening her eyes and almost smiling. She wanted to hear that she was different from the other women. Carter had exceeded her wildest expectations and made her realize that the safe dates and bed partners she'd had in the past weren't the norm.

He laughed again. "Give me a minute to wash up, and then we can continue this conversation."

He got out of the bed and padded naked to the bathroom, returning a moment later with a warm washcloth for her to use. He took it back into the bathroom, and while she was alone, she glanced around the room and caught a glimpse of herself in the mirror over the desk. She notice her tiara with the year on it on its side near the bed.

She placed it on the nightstand before scooting up and getting under the covers. As she leaned back against the headboard, she realized he might not want her to stay.

This would have been easier if she'd taken him to her place. Then she maybe she wouldn't feel so awkward.

He strode back into the room with all the grace and elegance of a tiger.

She forced a smile and what she liked to think of as her game face. The expression she used in the press room after a bad run, or when she'd had to go in front of the media and act as though it hadn't mattered that her career in skiing was over after her fall.

Watching his muscles moving with each step he took, she realized he was a perfect specimen. Not like her body, which was broken and bore fresh scars. She envied him his healthy body. Tamping down her roiling emotions, she shook her head. She wasn't going down that path tonight.

Instead, the sheet falling to her waist, she drank him in. "Dammit."

"What's wrong?" she asked in alarm.

"You make me want to start all over again."

"Start what?" She wasn't following him.

"Sex," he said. "I've just had you but I want you again. Want to take my time and make sure that I haven't missed one glorious spot on your body."

She arched one eyebrow at him. "I don't think you did. But first I want to hear why you think I'm special."

He rubbed a hand over his chest and came to sit next to her on the bed. "Gorgeous, you've always been special to me."

That was a nonanswer if she ever heard it, but it was New Year's Day. He was her little gift to start out a fabulous year, and she guessed from his tone that discussing their past wasn't exactly what he had in mind.

She sighed, but the drinks and her emotions were catching up with her. She traced his tattoo and thought of all the risks she'd taken in her life and how they'd paid off for her. Carter Shaw was the biggest one. She'd come to his room for a night of pleasure and hopefully to jar herself out of the sameness that her life had taken on.

That was it.

It was hard, though, because she was a planner, and to face any situation knowing that she didn't have a proved strategy made her edgy and scared.

IF SHE'D BEEN any other woman, he would have been happy to climb back into that bed and have another round of mind-numbing sex. But this was Lindsey. His gorgeous Nordic angel who'd always been different. And tonight was no exception.

She kept touching him in that innocent way of hers that turned him on, but more than that, she seemed to touch him as if she wasn't thinking about it.

"Tell me about this tattoo."

That she'd changed the subject kind of let him off the hook and also disappointed him the tiniest bit. He wanted her to demand some answers from him, not let him keep skating by on the surface. But she saw him the way every other woman did. She was different to him but he wasn't different to her.

It hurt for a split second before he shrugged it aside and shifted to lie next to her. He pulled a couple of pillows closer and propped them under his head.

"What about it?"

"When did you get it?"

"On a trip to Japan with my dad when I was a teenager."

"How on earth did you convince them to give you a tattoo…or did your dad okay it?" she asked with a smile.

Carter thought of his old man and how, back then, he'd been sort of his enemy. Now that he was an adult they got on well, but growing up, his dad had seemed like this guy who had never really lived or ever done anything daring. The exact opposite of everything that Carter wanted to be. His mom had died in childbirth, and his dad had never recovered.

"No, he didn't approve. But I was on my own, spoke decent Japanese and looked like I was eighteen. I knew from the moment I'd seen the mountain that I wanted it. I wanted to snowboard down it, learn its paths and twists and turns. Try to capture some of its wildness."

He lifted his head and stared down into her pretty

brown eyes. She smiled in response. "That's almost poetic. Watch it, Shaw, your badass image is slipping."

"I got ink at sixteen. That's pretty badass," he retorted, trying to push aside the feelings she called easily to the surface. He wasn't one of those guys who spent much time thinking heavy thoughts. So he could only blame Lindsey and this evening for stirring up those old memories.

"And now you're twenty-seven and retiring? Time flies, doesn't it?" she said, rolling onto her back and lifting her arms up above her head.

The movement forced her breasts into prominence, and he reached over and feathered his fingers across them. Slowly stroking her skin, which was very smooth and very warm. Addicting almost. He never wanted to stop touching her.

She turned over again, facing him. "I don't want to talk about the past."

"Me, either."

The present was way more interesting than the things he'd done in the past. For instance, this was the first time he was close enough to hold Lindsey in his arms. Close enough to notice that on her rib cage just below her breast she had a small birthmark. He leaned in to kiss it.

"What are you doing?"

"Memorizing you. Trying to make sure I know every inch of you."

"I thought it took guys a while to recover after sex," she said.

He shook his head and laughed. "Some guys. Some of the time. I think it depends on the woman and man. It's not taking me any time with you."

"Why do you think that is?" she asked curiously. "Is it back to me being special?"

He caressed her side, starting at her shoulder and working his way slowly down to her hip. "I don't know why. It's not something I've ever analyzed. Why would I? Sex is supposed to be fun, not figures put in a spreadsheet."

"Is it?" she mused. "That hasn't always been my experience, but then I haven't done the amount of experimenting you have."

"Gorgeous, you're pushing me. I'm not sure why."

"I'm scared," she admitted. "This seemed like fun in the bar, but now that I'm up here, I don't know how to act or what to do next. I'm not used to that."

He sighed. "There is no right or wrong action here. We make up our own rules, okay?"

He wanted her to be different, and she was. She made him feel alive in a way that only snowboarding had before. Something he'd never found in any of his personal relationships. Maybe it was just the novelty of sleeping with a girl he'd wanted since he was seventeen. Or maybe it was just the place he was in at this moment in his life.

But he didn't want her to think they had to behave in a certain way. With other woman he'd been different— happy for the sex, but not wanting anything more. It had been casual and friendly with no feelings getting hurt. But this was Lindsey, and he needed more.

More? How much more, he had no idea. This was all new to him, too.

"Okay, so what kind of rules should we have?" she asked. "Are we going to do this again?"

"Um…I thought that was obvious," he said, gesturing to his erection.

She laughed, and the sound washed over him like a warm bit of sunshine on a cold day.

A moment later she reached for him, stroked her hand up and down his cock, and then leaned down to kiss him. "Okay, so after that—then what?"

"We'll figure it out. This is one thing we don't have to train for or have a rigorous schedule about." She nodded, and he saw that something was going on inside her head, but he had no idea what it was. What was it she was thinking? He thought maybe he shouldn't let himself get distracted, but for tonight he'd had enough conversation.

He had a naked Lindsey in his bed and he intended to enjoy her.

THEY FELL ASLEEP in each other's arms after making love the second time, and when Lindsey woke, it was to the soft snores coming from Carter. He was turned on his side, facing her, and their fingers were linked together. She was riveted by the sight of him, but had a little bit of a headache and was thirsty.

Really thirsty.

She carefully pulled her hand from his and made her way quietly across the bedroom into the bathroom, where she closed the door, letting just the illumination from the night-light break the darkness. She saw herself in the mirror, but avoided eye contact as she filled a glass with water and slowly drank it.

Lost in thought, she closed the lid on the toilet and sat on it.

She was no closer now to knowing what to do next

than she had been six hours earlier. She noticed she had a little bit of razor burn on her neck, remembered the feel of him in her arms and shivered. Carter Shaw. Who'd have guessed?

She finished her water and then stood to lean in over the sink.

Her previous sexual experiences had been less than stellar. Did she look different now that she'd had an orgasm with a man rather than by her own hand? She searched her face for some sign, but there wasn't one. She still looked like Lindsey. Like herself. But inside something had awakened. Something was changing, and she had no clue what she was going to do next.

She bit her lip. Staying here and waiting for Carter to wake up sounded like a bad idea. She knew that last night was only one night. It had been fun and frivolous, two things she'd never embraced in her entire life. But she'd liked it. No regrets.

You only live once, right? But now it was a new day and time for making plans.

No matter how incredible it had been, there was no denying that this thing between her and Carter wasn't going to last. They had nothing in common aside from sports, and skiers and snowboarders were very different. Frankly, they didn't really even know each other that well.

Something that she intended to ensure didn't change. Because there was no need for it to. He was going back to his wandering ways, and though she'd cross paths with him once in a while on the committee for the charity event, she doubted she'd really see that much of him.

She felt a little pang and ignored it. Of course, the thought of going back to the adversarial strangers they'd been hurt after last night. After sharing something with him she'd experienced with no other man. But it wasn't going to happen again. Carter was a bad boy and not at all the kind of guy she was interested in trying to date. Besides, her life was a big-ass mess right now.

Lindsey sighed. Her clothes were scattered in the other room, and she needed to collect them, get dressed and beat a hasty retreat before he woke. But first she grabbed one of the robes from behind the door...because in the cold light of day walking around naked didn't feel right.

She opened the door cautiously and heard the low rumble of Carter's voice.

"Thank you very much."

He was awake.

He was sitting on the edge of the bed, his back to her, his brown hair tousled and sticking up a little on the left side. He tossed the cordless phone onto the bed and stood. "I ordered breakfast."

"I actually should probably be going," she said hastily. "I feel like I've—"

"Where do you have to go? I know you're not working today."

"You do?" Her eyes widened. "How do you know that?"

"Because you were drinking and partying last night. I know you aren't the type of person to ski after a night like that," he said. "Take it from me, your concentration won't be that great."

"Have you done that? Snowboarded in that condition?"

"I have. I don't recommend it." There was a long

pause. "Let me grab a robe and we can have breakfast, okay?"

She didn't want to get to know Carter any better. Sure, she knew how that sounded, but the truth was, the more she knew him the bigger the chance of her starting to like him was. She didn't want to change the dynamic between them that had worked so well for so long. She had figured out a way to manage him.

"I'm not sure."

"Really? *Now* you're running scared?" Crossing his arms over his bare chest, he flashed a taunting smile her way. "After all that we did to each other last night, this morning you want to retreat?"

She gave him the hardest stare she could muster. Given her headache she suspected it wasn't as steely as she'd like. "I'm not a child to be swayed by a petty dare."

"It wasn't petty, gorgeous. It was a flat-out challenge. Prove you're not a coward and stay."

She rolled her eyes. This was the guy she had no chance of ever falling for… The one who needled her and tried to make her— "Fine. I'll stay for breakfast."

He nodded. "I'll be right back."

She walked over to the table set up in a corner of the suite with chairs that faced the plate-glass windows that provided a perfect panoramic view of the Wasatch Range. The mountains she knew like the palm of her hand. She'd skied all the different runs down that mountain. It was a constant to her. In fact, she'd trained there for so long it was like her home.

But it wasn't anymore. And she knew that it wasn't Carter she was angry with this morning. It wasn't the mountain, either, although that big majestic thing did play a part in it. She was angry with herself. For falling and for failing. She'd never realized how much she'd let herself down. Hadn't wanted to admit that to herself. As a matter of fact, she hadn't been able to let those emotions out until this morning.

Coffee and breakfast weren't going to sweeten her mood now. *That* she understood, so she got dressed as quickly as she could, gathered her clutch and her tiara and walked out the door before Carter came out of the bathroom.

She needed time and distance. Not the distraction that he provided.

5

It DIDN'T TAKE a Stephen Hawking–level genius to figure out that Lindsey wanted to be left alone. But Carter hadn't achieved all he had in the world of snowboarding, or in life, by not going after what he wanted. And after last night, it was pretty damned clear to him that he still wanted more from her.

He took a shower, got dressed, ate the breakfast he'd ordered and then went out to find her. She worked at the lodge, and he suspected she must live pretty close to it. They'd both been serious athletes for the majority of their lives—if Lindsey was anything like him, she'd want to be close enough to the mountains to spend all her free time on the slopes.

He texted Will Spalding, the other groomsman from the wedding, whose girlfriend, Penny, was friends with Lindsey, asking if he knew how to get in touch with Lindsey.

He put his head on the steering wheel, feeling like a complete and utter fool.

This was nuts.

Will texted back that he'd ask Penny. A few seconds later he texted a phone number and the word *why*.

Yeah, Shaw, why do you need her number? he asked himself.

He texted that he wanted to talk to Lindsey about the event they were working on at the lodge and wished Will and Penny safe travels as they headed home later in the day.

He was still sitting in his rented SUV, trying to figure out which of the many slopes she'd been taking a run on this morning, when he caught a glimpse of her walking from her car to the lodge. She was wearing a pair of dark pink ski bibs and a cream-colored puffy jacket. Her Nordic blond hair had been pulled back into a ponytail, her hair held back by a ski band around her head.

She looked for all the world as she always had. As if nothing had changed.

He rubbed the back of his neck, thinking that maybe for her nothing had.

It hadn't occurred to him until that moment that prim-and-proper Lindsey Collins, darling of the Alpine ski community, might have used him to get her rocks off on New Year's Eve. It wasn't the first time he'd been a woman's illicit thrill, but on every other occasion he'd known what he was getting into. And he'd been prepared for it.

He'd thought Lindsey was different. He shut off his SUV, got out and followed her across the parking lot and up to the ski lodge and the après ski café. She sat at one of the tables nestled near the big fireplace and facing the slopes. The expression on her face wasn't peaceful or serene.

She looked angry and lost.

Why was Lindsey upset?

Maybe he'd screwed things up when he'd taken her to his bed last night. Another sin to add to his list where this woman was concerned. He walked over to the bar, ordered two hot chocolates and then went to her table.

He set one down in front of her and took the seat next to her so he, too, could look up at the mountain.

"Carter."

"Lindsey."

She pulled the mug closer to her and wrapped her fingers around it, staring down into the whipped cream on the top like a fortune-teller searching for answers.

"What's this for?"

"I'm not sure." He raked a hand through his hair and sighed. "I think I might need to apologize."

"For what? I know *I* should for walking out. But my head's not in the right place this morning. I might do or say something stupid, so I figured I better clear out until…"

He got it. This he understood. He'd spent most of his life clearing out and searching for answers that he still hadn't found.

"No need. I get that. Let's start over," he said.

"How? Do we pretend we never met at seventeen? Or do we act like last night never happened?"

"None of that. Let's just start the morning over." He reached over and clasped her hand in his. "I'm dying to get up on the slopes. You want to go with me?"

"I… Really? I thought you'd want to take it easy."

"I didn't anger all the resort owners here by taking them on and demanding they let snowboarders on the slopes just to be a douchebag. I did it because when I look at that mountain I see something I wanted to conquer. Besides, it was elitist to try to keep us out."

"I never saw it that way," she admitted, staring down at their entwined fingers. "But then, Alpine skiing is accepted everywhere."

"So want to take on the slopes? We can race for real this time," he said. "Not against the clock but against each other."

She slowly withdrew her hand and took a sip of cocoa. "I can't."

He leaned back in his chair and glanced at her. She wasn't watching him but was staring at the mountains again. "I'll go easy on you."

"It doesn't matter. I can't go down the mountain."

"Why not?"

She shook her head. "You were my bit of fun last night, Carter. We're not friends and I—"

"I don't see that you have any friends here right now. Not trying to be mean, but it's obvious—even to this *bit of fun*—that you need someone." He clenched his jaw, trying to keep his temper in check. "I'd like to think over the years I've at least showed you I'm not a total loser."

"I never think of you that way," she said, turning to face him.

He saw something in her expression that he'd never glimpsed there before. It was something more than fear, and if he had to define it, he'd say it looked a lot like disappointment.

"I'm scared, Carter. I can't go down that damned mountain, because every time I've taken the ski lift up there I freeze. I'm fine showing kids what to do in their lessons, but I can't go down a big slope."

His anger instantly cooled. That wasn't what he'd been expecting. Lindsey was afraid? It didn't jive with the bold, fearless woman he'd always known. She'd been throwing herself down the toughest, fastest runs since she'd been ten, or something. She'd gone over sixty miles per hour routinely, and now she was afraid?

"Okay, fair enough," he said. "But we're going to get you over your fear."

She shook her head and took another slip of her hot chocolate. "I don't think so. You're sweet to suggest it, but let's face it, the only thing we've ever had between us is an adversarial—"

"We have more now. We spent the night in each other's arms."

"That was sex," she reminded him. "You always act like sex is just a physical thing. Nothing emotional there."

"Was it for you?" he asked in a low, deceptively calm voice.

"Wasn't it for you?" she countered.

She gave nothing away. Why was he surprised? This was Lindsey Collins, and she never let him have an inch.

LINDSEY DIDN'T WANT to talk about her fears with Carter. In fact, the only thing she wanted was a distraction. God knew he provided her with that.

"I'm sorry I feel like I'm not myself this morning. That's why I left. I can't explain it very well, not even to myself."

"What can't you explain?" he asked, pinning her with his penetrating blue-gray gaze.

"Last night, until the moment you arrived at my table, I was looking at my future and trying to figure out what my next move would be." She sighed. "Last year at this time I was gearing up for a gold medal and setting my future, you know?"

"I do know. But things changed."

"They did, and I ended up here in the bosom of some good friends and in the valley where I first learned to ski and started my world-champion path. I thought this was the place to press the reset button, but it didn't work out that way. I couldn't handle the slopes... I mean, not even the kiddie ones at first. Even now they still scare me."

She tried to stop talking, but the words were just flowing out of her as though they wouldn't be stopped. She'd needed to share this with someone, and Carter, as unlikely as it seemed, was the one person she was finally able to do it with.

"So the reset didn't work," he said, tracing the rim of his mug with his finger.

An image of him doing that exact same thing to her nipple popped into her head and made her squirm in her chair. Dammit. She never thought of sex this way. But Carter had changed her.

"No, it didn't. I have seen a therapist and he suggested it was because reset means I can go back to where I was and that maybe somewhere in my brain is the thought that I don't want to go back there."

He nodded. "My therapist has often said that, for me, I have to keep moving forward. Once I master a skill, I need to find a new one."

"That's interesting... Does he have a theory why?" Maybe there was a clue in Carter's problems that could lead her to a solution of her own.

"He does, but it's very personal." There was a glimpse of the real man. The one he kept hidden behind a curtain of sexy charm and outrageous dares.

"Sorry," she said quietly. "Didn't mean to pry."

"I brought it up. Just throwing it out as an option."

Resting an elbow on the table, he turned to face her. "I want to help you get back on the slopes. It will be a way for me to make up for any part of your crash."

"I told you that wasn't your fault."

"I know, but I need to do this. Plus, and if you repeat this to *anyone* I'll deny it, but when you ski it's like magic. I love watching you on the slopes, and I'd hate to never see you ski again."

"Why would you deny that?" she asked, touched more than she wanted to be.

"Because I'm a bad-boy snowboarder and I've got a reputation to preserve," he said with a wink.

"Well, far be it from me to ruin that for you," she quipped. But deep down inside the freedom she'd felt last night was starting to fade. It made her wistful and wonder how she was going to achieve what had seemed so possible last night. How could she change her life?

"You won't," he said slyly. "So let's see… How's the knee? Have you taken any runs?"

Lindsey shook her head. She thought of how she sometimes brought her skis here and sat as though she'd just taken a run, even though she clearly hadn't.

Who the heck was she trying to fool?

"My knee is fine. No runs. I mean, I'm teaching the classes, so I am on the bunny slopes with my kids, but that's not really skiing."

"Not for you," he said.

"No, not for me. But why do you care? I mean, really. Not that BS about feeling guilty about my crash—the real story."

He leaned in close and shrugged. "Maybe I sense that's the only way you'll let me see you again."

He was right, but she wasn't about to admit it to him.

"We're on a committee together, Carter. We will have to see each other again."

He took a sip of his hot chocolate. "I expected better—more from you than this."

She held the same high expectation for herself. "I'm sorry. I think the combo of too much to drink, a very sexy encounter and confusion left over from last night are making this morning difficult."

"You think too much," he said softly. "I've had more mornings-after than you. Take it from me, you have to just shake it off."

She didn't want to shake it off. A part of her wanted to be the woman she'd been last night. That bold, self-assured, confident woman she'd been with Carter, the woman who'd believed in herself. Surely that hadn't just been the champagne talking. The seeds of that woman had to be inside her.

She just had to figure out how to sow them.

Carter was offering her something by saying he wanted to see her ski again. He'd always been that devilish rogue who could needle her into doing things she'd otherwise pass on.

"Were you serious about helping me ski again?"

"Yes. Thinking of taking me up on it?" he asked, leaning back and giving her a cocky smile. "I knew you would. Women can't resist me."

That was part of her problem. She didn't want to be one of the masses that had been in Carter's life. She wanted to be important and special. And she couldn't. Not right now, because she hardly knew herself anymore.

CARTER REALIZED THAT Lindsey saw him as a bit of fun. And after all the women he'd played around with over the years, a part of him got that it was payback. But another part, the bit where he'd actually thought she was different than all the lovers he'd been with before, bristled. She was looking at him as if he were a stranger. The kind of man that she didn't know or trust.

"What do you say, gorgeous? Want to give it a shot?"

"I do. I'm just not sure that I should be committing to doing anything more with you because you're a bad influence."

He looked at her, amused despite himself by her adorably earnest expression. "How do you figure?"

"Kissing dares. Sex twice in one night… Skiing again."

He noted that she'd started with the light stuff and ended with what was really worrying her. "I'm not going to push you down the slope, Linds. I just want a chance to help you remember what you loved so much about the sport."

She cocked her head to one side, her blond ponytail swinging behind her head, and he remembered the feel of her silky-smooth hair against his body. His blood heated, and he realized that he was working so hard to find a reason to stay in her good graces because he wanted her back in his bed.

He hadn't been finished with her when she'd walked away, and now he had to do whatever was necessary to get her back.

"What do you know about my love of the sport?"

"Only that if I fell and couldn't snowboard for six months, I'd be devastated. And though I'm retiring from amateur competition, I know I still want to be on the board. I can't define myself without it."

She gave him a hard stare. "I hate that you actually get me."

He laughed, but inside a part of him was hurt by that. "Why?"

"You're not a serious person. You think dares and games are the way to get what you want—"

"It's worked for me in the past, hasn't it?"

"You have a point." She sighed. "Maybe this *is* what I need. So what do you recommend?"

"You have to get to the root of your fear."

"How do you know that?" she asked. "Do you have something you're afraid of?"

Of course he did, he thought. But he liked the fact that she saw only the confidence he'd worked so hard at projecting. If she saw him as the man he wanted to be, he was good with that. He wasn't about to start confessing to things that he couldn't do and the secrets he protected.

"Just being walked out on by women like you, gorgeous," he said smoothly.

She nibbled on her lower lip, and he remembered how her mouth had felt under his the night before. He had thought he'd had enough time to exorcise the lust demons that had been plaguing him for years, but realized now he hadn't come close.

Would he ever be able to sate his thirst for Lindsey?

He'd sort of believed that her elusiveness was all that kept him still wanting her. It had been a while, and each time they were apart he'd try to forget her. Those big brown eyes and the pretty blond hair.

The media had dubbed her the Ice Queen for her cool persona before each of her runs. Other skiers smiled and joked, but Lindsey had held herself aloof and had come down the mountain as though she owned it. Now he realized that he had wanted to be the man to melt that icy exterior.

He'd done it once, but that wasn't enough.

Why wasn't it enough?

It seemed to him that having waited so long to claim her in his bed, he should be happy, or at least content. But he wasn't.

He wanted something more.

But as was par for him, he had no way to define it and could only say that it involved Lindsey.

"I am sorry again for leaving so abruptly," she said softly. "I wanted to see if I could take a run this morning... Well, that's not entirely true." She fixed her gaze squarely on his. "You scared me, Carter. I've never been the way I was with you last night. I'm not sure I recognize that part of myself."

"Good," he said. "The old you has been hiding. Frozen in some sort of limbo. I'm glad you don't recognize yourself, because that means you are finally thawing."

"Thawing? Wow, I thought I'd proved last night that there is nothing icy about me," she said in a slightly breathless voice.

"You did, but then you retreated behind your wall of ice," he said.

"Fair enough."

"Let's go," he said, standing and holding out his hand to her.

"Where?"

"Trust me?"

She reached for his hand and gave him a forced smile. "No. But I'll follow you anyway."

He'd take what he could get with her. She stood and he led the way to the parking lot and his SUV.

"Where are we going?"

"You'll see." He smiled mysteriously. "I have an idea."

She got into the vehicle without another word, and he drove them away from the lodge to a path he'd found about a week ago when he'd needed to get away from everyone and everything. He parked the SUV on the side of the road and came around to Lindsey's side of the SUV. She had her door open and had hopped out before he got there.

"This is your big idea?"

"Stop with the doubt and follow me."

He led the way to the tree line over the snow-covered ground, and she followed him. Her boots were good and sturdy, as were his, and he kept walking until he found what he was looking for: a small clearing in the copse of trees. Icicles hung from the branches, and in the center was a mound of snow that he suspected some local kids had built.

"This is it?"

"Yup," he said.

"How'd you find it?" she asked, looking at the steep snow mound, which was large enough to slide down. In the middle was a trench big enough for a sled.

"I don't know, but I think it will work perfectly for us."

She walked over to it and then looked back at him. "Thank you."

Seeing her quiet, contemplative expression as she continued to look at the snow mound made it easy for him to believe that he'd done the right thing. But deep inside he knew that helping her ski wasn't what he really wanted.

6

THE STEEP MOUND of snow might look like a bit of fun to anyone else, but to Lindsey it looked huge. As she stood at the base of it, she realized that Carter had found her the ideal place to test her own limits.

"I have a sled in the SUV," he said. "Let me go and get it."

She nodded.

Words were inadequate while fear was tightening her throat, but really her fear had to do with the public way she'd fallen. She knew everyone had seen it, and now when she put on her skis she was always aware of people watching her. In truth, they might not be, but her fear was that they were.

She noticed some foot holes had been dug in the snow and put her boots in, slowly climbing to the top of the mound. When she got to the top, she simply stood there. Her pulse was racing, and she was sweating inside her snow wear even though it was freezing.

She licked her dry lips and tipped her head back to look up at the sky. This height was so small compared to the mountains she'd skied in her career, yet it felt bigger. Felt scarier somehow, and she knew she didn't want Carter to see her this way.

It was one thing to admit she was afraid to ski but something else entirely to actually let him see a glimpse of what that fear looked like. She turned to climb down and saw him standing there, the trees behind him, their limbs heavy with snow. The small sled in one hand and the most serious look she'd ever seen in Carter Shaw's blue-gray eyes.

He knew.

She hated that he was witnessing this moment of horrible weakness.

He didn't say anything, just continued to watch her. Inside her fear a small bubble of rebellion formed. Carter was the last person on earth she wanted to witness this meltdown.

"Great...I'm glad you have that sled. I was going to give it a try without one but thought I'd wait for you."

"You don't have to do this," he told her. "Baby steps are the way forward."

"I have no idea what you are talking about. This little mound is nothing," she said airily. *God, please let me get off this damned mound, and quickly.*

"Okay." He pointed into the distance. "See that drift over there?"

She glanced all the way across the clearing to the large drift that had been reinforced probably by the same people who'd built this mound. That had to be where the sled would stop. It seemed huge. Farther than anything she'd gone down before.

But she knew that was fear talking.

"Great."

"Great?" he repeated. "I know it's not great, gorgeous."

She knew it, too. But she wasn't about to let him once again see her weak and vulnerable. Man, was that what this was all about? Was that why she couldn't ski? Vulnerability?

Whatever it was, she was going to have to sled down this mound to prove a point to herself—and to Carter. She'd expected him to hand her the sled, but this was Carter, so instead he climbed up next to her.

"Not so bad from up here," he said. "Reminds me of the first time I stood at the mouth of the half-pipe."

"Is this really how high it is?"

"Nah, it's a bit higher, but I was strung out on nerves waiting to take my first run. Excited, scared and so full of ideas of how I wanted it to go I couldn't stand it."

Her hands were shaking, and she wove them together to keep Carter from seeing, but he put one of his big hands over hers. Held them for a minute, and she looked up to see his face close to hers. So close she could see the flecks of silver in his blue-gray eyes and notice how thick his eyelashes were.

He had incredible eyes.

She wanted to do something crazy, like kiss him. *If* she kissed him, then passion could sweep them away and she wouldn't have to go down the mound. Hell, she'd strip down naked in the cold with the wind blowing the snow from the tree branches if it meant she didn't have to go down this small mound of snow.

Realizing that made tears burn at the back of her eyes. Dammit. If she couldn't sled down this freakin' mound, how was she ever going to ski again?

"I'm scared," she whispered.

"I know," he whispered back. He lifted his free hand and cupped the side of her face. "But you are the bravest woman I've ever met."

"Liar."

"I wish. I know that no matter what, you will conquer this mound and then get back on the expert slope. I believe that with every fiber of my being."

His eyes burned into hers, and she could feel the sheer force of his will radiate through her.

But how could he have such unwavering faith in her when she was riddled with so many doubts and fears? She appreciated what he was trying to do here, but a part of her—a huge part—wasn't sure it could really come true.

"I—"

"No, don't say anything else. Just sit your sweet ass on this sled and take the run you've been thinking about."

The run she'd been thinking about was down the Wasatch Back Range, but she had to do this to get there. His strength was there all around her. His breath was warm against her cheek. His hands, which held her so solidly, reminded her that he was virile and strong.

She leaned up and pressed her mouth to his. Angled her lips over his and thrust her tongue into his mouth. Surprised, he opened his mouth, and in her mind she pretended she could borrow his courage just by kissing him. She pulled her head back, took the sled from him and sat before she could think anymore about where she was and what she was about to do.

She put her hands in the snow and shoved with all her might. She wanted to close her eyes as she flew down the mound, but kept them open. Wind whipped past her cheeks as she skidded across the flat snow-packed ground into the drift, and she started laughing.

CARTER HAD ALWAYS been a gambling man. Reaching for things and willing to play the risks, but this was the first time he'd gambled on someone else.

He'd felt as if he'd failed miserably as he'd stood at the bottom and saw Lindsey standing up there literally shaking with fear. It was more than fear or pride or even vulnerability. If he'd had to define it, he would have admitted she was lost. He never wanted to be responsible for that look he'd seen on her face again. So, heart hammering in his chest, he'd climbed up there with her, told her he believed in her. And then, just like that, she'd kissed him and thrown herself down that snow mound as though it was the gate to a Super G course. And when her laughter rang out around the clearing, he'd felt justified, and more than a little bit relieved, if he were being honest.

The risk had paid off.

They spent the next hour sliding down the snow mound. Each time he watched her carefully, and he noticed it wasn't getting easier for her, but she had made up her mind that she would do it.

And she did.

He felt like a jumble of nerves. A mess. This wasn't like him. He was the guy who felt nothing. Why did Lindsey change all that?

And he was beginning to believe that his desire for more of her in his bed wasn't the only thing he wanted.

"Thank you for this."

"You're welcome," he said.

She put the sled on the ground next to him. "Your turn."

He didn't want another turn with anything but her. "Will you go with me?"

"Go with you?" she asked. "Are you asking me to date you?"

Not a bad idea, but they were too old to be dating like that. Weren't they?

"Maybe. But for now I want to take a run down with you."

She nodded.

Picking up the sled, he led her back to the mound and then stood behind her as she climbed up. The woman had a first-class ass, and when she got to the top she glanced over her shoulder and caught him staring at her butt.

"I think you just wanted another chance to ogle me."

"No denying that, gorgeous. I do like your body."

"I like yours, too," she confessed. He climbed up after her and set the sled on the top of the mound. He sat on it and anchored himself in place by stomping his boot into the snow.

"Come on," he said.

Lindsey carefully sat in front of him, scooting back until her buttocks were pressed firmly up against him. He wrapped one of his arms around her waist. She smelled of snow and the pine trees that surrounded the clearing.

"Ready?"

She put her hands together over his arm, holding him as she nodded. He lifted his boot from the place where it was anchoring them in the snow and pushed off with one hand. He leaned in close, holding her to him, and then pivoted his body so they slid sideways into the snow. He fell off the sled and pulled her with him, making sure she was on top of him.

She rested her arms on his chest and looked down at him, and for the first time this morning he saw something close to happiness shining in her big brown eyes. She smiled, and he arched his eyebrow at her. "You must be messing with my mojo."

"I must be," she said. "I've never seen you fall."

"I usually don't," he admitted. But he'd wanted her to see what would happen if she did. Wanted her to experience a fall and maybe in some way show her that this time it wouldn't be as bad as it had been before.

He was messed up. He knew it. He was trying to make her see him in a different light, but the truth was he was too flawed to really want her to see the man behind the bluster. He knew that, but at the same time he sort of wanted her to be the one person who knew the real guy under that cocky facade.

"I imagine this is just one of your seduction techniques. The way you get woman to kiss you."

"Nah, it's how I get women to *let* me kiss them," he said, going along with her. He traced the bottom curve of her lip and held her to him with his arm around her waist. The ground was cold, but he didn't feel it through his snow pants. He looked up at the cloudy sky and saw the first snowflakes falling toward them. One of them landed on the end of Lindsey's nose, and he caught it on his finger and brought it to his lips to lick it off.

She leaned down as another flake landed on his lips, and kissed him. The chilled snowflake melted under the heat of her kiss, and he felt the warmth spread from her mouth to every cell of his body. Slowly working over him until he wrapped both arms around her and kissed her as if nothing mattered except the two of them.

As if there wasn't anything else in the universe but him and her and this snowy clearing. Nothing but her lips moving over hers, her hands on his face and her body pressed intimately to his. Nothing except the taste of her happiness and the cold chill that couldn't penetrate the heat they were generating.

Nothing but he and Lindsey and this outdoor world that they'd both called home for so long.

LYING ON TOP of Carter with the snow gently falling around her was the perfect end to this crazy first day of the year. She had been running on empty, she realized, until he'd pushed her to go down the mound. She wasn't perfect. It was silly to think one man would make that big of a change in her, but this was Carter.

The bad boy who'd been teasing and cajoling her since the moment they'd met. But damn, could he kiss.

Lindsey forgot about everything but how soft his lips were under hers. How right his tongue felt as it tangled with hers. And his taste. It was minty but earthy...and she couldn't get enough of it. Of *him*. His hands were moving up and down her back, cupping her butt and pulling her more fully against him.

Despite the cold, his erection was strong and solid between them, awakening an answering ache deep inside her. She wasn't a sexual person, so this desire so quick on the heels of last night was new. She wasn't sure she wanted to be this lusty. Not with Carter. He had already proved to her that he was different, or rather that *she* was different when he was around.

He made everything she felt seem bigger somehow,

but he also called to the parts of her soul she preferred to keep hidden from the world. She pulled her head back and gazed down into those blue-gray eyes of his. There was something almost harsh about his features, and she recognized the look on his face as smoldering desire. Last night had given her a glimpse into how passion changed him from that sort of mischievous badass into a man who knew how to seduce.

"Let's go back to my room," he said, shifting her so he could sit up.

She shook her head.

"Why not? It's not like—"

Lindsey put her finger over his lips, rubbed it back and forth for a second. Then she brought her finger to her own lips and kissed it. She wanted to be able to dismiss him as easily as she always had. But she couldn't. She thought about how awkward she'd felt this morning and how electrified she felt right now. She wanted him. Wanted to feel his muscled body moving against hers and over hers again. Not again. If she had sex with him again she had to be in control.

"You have to stop thinking that you are the boss," she said, lifting her finger from his lips.

"I'm not?"

"No, you're not."

He swept an errant lock of hair off her cheek. "Then you aren't on fire for me? You don't burn when you think of both of us naked in each other's arms?" His words fanned the flames that were already coursing through her. Of course she wanted that. Just wanted it on her terms. "We'll go to my place. When I say."

"When *you* say?" he asked, quirking one eyebrow at her.

"Yes," she said.

He tightened his arms around her, and she felt him shift before he stood with her in his arms. "I don't think so."

He brought his mouth down on hers, and unlike the last time there was no doubt that he was in charge of this kiss. Her body, which felt as though it wasn't hers anymore, stirred to life. She moaned as he angled his head and deepened the kiss. He held her as if she weighed nothing, but she kept her arms locked around his shoulders. Held on to him.

The only solid thing she could find in a world that she was losing her grip on. A world where all she could see was Carter. She couldn't let him mean that much to her. She knew better than that. He was her sexy midnight man. That was all.

She thought being confused about what to do next was a problem, but dealing with this attraction to Carter was turning into something much harder to handle. She wasn't used to lust or the feelings that coursed through her body. Her skin was so sensitive; her breasts felt full, her nipples tight. She throbbed for him. Needed him between her legs, and she didn't care that they were in this clearing exposed to anyone who happened along. She had to have him now.

That wasn't her.

She didn't need Carter Shaw.

She loosened her hold on him. Startled, she felt his release as she sort of slid down his body and stepped back from him. She didn't like the fever that had engulfed her.

He watched her with narrowed eyes, a flush on his cheekbones, his breath rasping in and out of his body rapidly. She put her hand out and took another step backward, stumbling in the snow and falling, and he stood there watching her. He stretched a hand down to help her up.

"Sorry if that got out of hand. My control disappears around you. I've never wanted a woman the way I want you, gorgeous."

He was getting himself back under control. Giving her that rueful smile of his that made her heart soften and her fears sort of melt away. "Me, either. You make me forget everything I thought I knew about you."

"That's because you didn't know me at all."

She was beginning to believe that. But who was the real man? Did she really want to know? Could she handle him now when she was just barely able to limp forward toward finding herself again?

And could she live with herself if she didn't? He had shown her a world and an experience she'd never found with another man. She really wanted to believe that it was better because she'd experienced it with him.

After all, this morning he'd given her back a piece of the winter world she'd used to love so much. While sledding down the slope wasn't nearly as fast as hitting the Super G course on two skis, it felt like a huge step back to her old self.

7

LINDSEY'S CONDO WAS a little embarrassing now that she saw it through Carter's eyes. She'd always lived sparsely mainly because she and one of her parents—usually her mom—had stayed in this sort of temporary housing during her years of training. Once she'd turned eighteen and started to live on her own, she'd sort of just kept it sparse.

But now as she led him into the two-story condo, she realized how plain and boring it might seem. Carter was surely used to more luxurious accommodations. And this entire bring-him-back-to-her-place-for-sex thing seemed to be backfiring.

"Nice place," he said. "I'm a fan of the Nordic open-air interior design, too."

She couldn't tell if he was serious or having fun at her expense. But she let it go. "Want a drink? Maybe something hot?"

"The only hot thing I'm interested in is you."

"Really? I don't feel hot," she said. Unless being a big, fat, hot mess counted, and she was pretty sure it didn't. But for right now she shoved that aside. She wasn't going to be able to get what she wanted from him if she let her doubts and fears plague her. And unlike standing on all that freshly packed snow earlier, this fear was a lot easier to conquer.

She heard the sound of the television next door coming on. The walls in this place weren't exactly thick. "Sorry about that."

"I have lived in apartments before, so I know what it's like. Why'd you choose this place?" he asked, coming into the room and taking off his coat. He sat on the ottoman to remove his boots.

He was getting comfortable and acting normal. It made her realize how out of sync she felt. She took off her coat and picked his up, hanging them both on hooks by her front door. Her father had put them up when her parents had visited over the holidays.

She kicked her boots off and set them under her coat. Carter came over and did the same with his.

"So why do you live here?" he asked again.

"It's close to the lodge. When I was cleared to ski again, I came back here thinking I'd go straight into training. My coach—do you know Peter Martin?"

"I do. Not sure he likes me very much," Carter said with a huge grin.

"Why does that not surprise me?" she replied. "You do tend to annoy a lot of people."

"I know. I like it."

She knew he did. That had been obvious from the first. "Anyway, I got to the top and couldn't ski down, and he suggested that maybe I stay here and teach classes so I'd be on skis every day as a way of getting used to it again. But so far it hasn't worked."

"Yet it did today. You went down a slope—"

"A tiny one. That hardly counts."

He gave her a chiding look. "But you did it. And we crashed—"

"You did that on purpose," she said.

"You're right," he admitted, taking her hand in his and lifting it to his mouth. He kissed her palm and then placed her hand on his chest. "Guilty as charged. But I had enough of waiting to hold you in my arms. I don't think you can appreciate how much I want you."

She thought that maybe she could. She wanted him, as well. With each aching breath she took she wanted to feel his naked body pressed to hers again. She wanted to see if in the cold light of day he'd been as sexy as he'd been the night before.

Had it been the night and the champagne that had made it seem magical? Surely it had. No man could make her feel so alive. A mountain, maybe. Taking a run down a dangerous slope, definitely. But Carter Shaw—surely she was remembering it wrong.

She felt her pulse beating a little more quickly, and her lips felt dry thinking about his mouth pressed to hers. A slow burning heat brushed over her from head to toe, and her clothes felt too restrictive and she wanted… just wanted things that she'd never thought she would.

He watched her with that uncanny gaze of his and she felt as though he could see all the way through her fears and her doubts. Straight to the heart of her, where she questioned everything she'd experienced with him the night before.

"Gorgeous, what am I going to do with you?" he asked.

A tingle of anticipation swept through her, and she guessed that this was her chance to try out all the risqué things she'd always sort of wanted to try but had never had the right guy to do it with. But this was Carter. The live-for-the-moment poster boy and her chance to do all the things she'd always deemed too dangerous.

"Kiss me?"

He smiled and then lifted one of his hands, pulling the ponytail holder from her hair very carefully so he didn't snag even one strand. He ran his fingers through her hair, fanning it out and pulling it forward over her shoulders. Then he tunneled his fingers through it, tipping her head back, and very slowly lowered his head toward hers.

She kept her eyes open this time. This kiss, she wanted to see his emotions, ascertain what he felt and try to figure out if she was doing this right. Because if she'd learned anything from watching Carter over the years, it was that he knew how to roll with the punches. He moved effortlessly through life and didn't get slowed down by emotional entanglements. Something she knew she had to master before she started to like him any more than she did at this moment.

It could be just sex. Sex was healthy and something she'd never denied herself, but any other kind of attachment wasn't. She'd been focused on skiing and being the best in the world. There hadn't been time for a relationship when she'd eaten, drank and even dreamed about her downhill runs. She had to remember that.

But as his lips moved over hers, just rubbing lightly, and he dropped nibbling kisses along the line of her jaw to her ear, all the while whispering hot promises about all the places he wanted to ravish her, she knew she was in very real danger of forgetting.

LINDSEY KEPT HIM on his toes, always dancing just out of his reach, which normally was exactly what he wanted and needed. But today he didn't. Today he wanted to hold the woman who was so brave and strong but didn't see those qualities in herself. Today he wanted a few moments where he didn't feel as if he had to chase her. And now that they were at her condo—her sparse, nondescript home—he had hoped he'd be able to relax.

But this was Lindsey and she surprised him. Never more so then when he held her in his arms. She wanted him. That was obvious from the flush of her skin and how she kept coming back into his arms when normally she would have been running for the hills.

Last night he'd taken it nice and slow; savored each and every delectable inch of her. But he wasn't sure he could take his time right now. He kept feeling that the harder he tried to keep her by his side the more easily she slipped away from him. And it hit him that the reason was that she saw him the way everyone else did.

As the careless playboy who'd taken too many women to his bed. And for once, he was with a woman that he wanted to be different with, and it wasn't going to happen.

He kissed her, and he meant for it to be a sort of sweet extension of everything that had gone on before, but his control slipped and he plunged his tongue deep into her mouth. His hands tangled in her hair as he urged her head back so that he could get even deeper.

He rested one arm on the wall and leaned in over her, surrounding her yet at the same time keeping some small distance between them. He needed to do that or he was going to rip her clothes off and be on her like a man who hadn't had a woman in years. Instead of just a few hours.

Dammit.

He'd never been this close to the edge of his control.

But Lindsey, with her wide-open, chocolate-brown eyes that gazed up him, searching his face for something—almost daring him to try to make this about something other than sex—goaded him on.

It made him struggle to find a balance between what she expected and what he wanted. That was the key. He knew what he wanted and he had to figure out how to walk that fine edge without revealing to her how desperately he desired her. Not just for this afternoon but for...

How long?

He tore his mouth from hers, reaching for the top of her snow bib and sliding the shoulder straps down. Then he pulled the sweater she wore underneath up and over her head. He tossed it to the floor and stepped back to look at her.

She stood there with the bib folded down from her waist with just a simple cream-colored bra covering her. Her skin was soft; he knew that from the night before. And he remembered how much he'd enjoyed caressing her. She stood there staring at him with that intense gaze that made him harden.

Lindsey took a step forward, grabbed the hem of his shirt and pulled him back to her. She went up on her tiptoes to kiss him as she tugged the fabric up over his chest. He felt her fingers on him. Her nails scraping over his nipples and digging into his pectorals.

"Why do I want you?" she asked under her breath as she pulled her head back. "Why you?"

"There was always something between us, Linds. We both knew that."

He unhooked her bra with one hand and pulled the fabric from her torso. Tossed it on the floor and then leaned down to kiss one nipple. He'd barely had time last night to taste them. They were pinkish red and hardened under his lips. He skimmed his hands over her ribs and down to her narrow waist.

Carter spanned it with both of his hands, pulling her from the wall and more firmly toward him. Then he turned so he could lean against the wall. Her hands roamed up and down, bringing every nerve in his body to red alert.

He wanted her now.

But he was trying to...

Why? Why was he taking this slow when he knew that Lindsey was a sixty-miles-per-hour girl? She liked the exhilaration of speeding through life. But he wanted it to take longer. Needed to tease it out for his as much as her pleasure.

This morning had showed him just how fragile his hold on her was, and he knew that every time he took her in his arms it might be his last.

He lifted his head from her tempting body and looked up at her. Her eyes were half-closed and her skin had a pretty rose-colored blush to it. She was lightly skimming her hands over his skin as she chewed her lower lip.

A moment later she pushed her hands into the waistband of his pants and shoved them toward his feet. He stepped out of them. Then she pushed his boxer briefs down, as well. Standing naked in her hallway, Carter realized he was where he wanted to be. She took his erection in her hand and stroked him up and down while he frantically shoved her clothes out of the way. Then, groaning low in his throat, he lifted her into his arms and turned so that her back was braced against the wall as he thrust into her.

He pushed himself all the way inside her and then

rested his head on her shoulder. He took several deep breaths, but her fingers moving up and down his spine and then lower to cup his buttocks urged him on.

"Take me," she said, whispering the words directly into his ear.

He was already there, moving his hips as she lifted her legs and wrapped them around him, forcing him farther inside her. She tipped her head back, her silky blond hair sliding over his shoulders as he plunged in and out of her.

His world narrowed to just her, and he couldn't think beyond the urge to go deeper, to take her so completely that there wouldn't be a Lindsey and Carter when he stopped, but just one being.

He felt his orgasm at the base of his spine and cursed as he tried to slow it or stop it. But it was too late. He was too close to the edge, and she dug her heels into his thighs, arching up against him as he came inside her. Realizing she wasn't there yet, he reached between their bodies, finding her clit and stroking it while he kept moving in and out of her body.

She felt so good. He felt her tighten around him, and she called his name as she came. He sank to the cold, tiled floor, cradling her in his arms as they fought to catch their breaths. He rubbed his hands up and down her back, and she scooted closer to him, resting her head on his shoulder as his blood pounded in his ears.

"Wow," she said.

Wow. Was that good? He had a feeling as quick as he was, he might not have given his best showing, but he was tired and he'd had that feeling all day that he might never have all he wanted from her.

"That good?" he asked gruffly.

"Yeah. I had no idea... My sexual experience isn't as diverse as yours. I mean, mission-style, lights off is my usual thing." He would've laughed if he'd thought that was what she wanted from him. "We've had the lights on every time."

"Yes we have. You make me feel so comfortable in my skin," she murmured. "Other guys seemed to just..."

Jealousy shot through him. The last thing he wanted to talk about were other guys she'd been with. But he was glad she felt comfortable around him. "I'm glad I didn't disappoint you."

"Me, too. So what now? I invited you back here so I wouldn't have to feel awkward and wonder if I should leave, but to be honest, I still feel weird."

He shook his head. Lindsey was never going to react the way he thought she would. She surprised him yet again, but really that was proving to just be her way. "I'll take that hot drink you offered, and then we can figure out what to do—or I can leave." Turning toward her, he slowly searched her face. "What do you want?"

She hesitated, and at that moment he knew she was going to send him on his way. Disappointment churned inside him, but he kept his game face on. "Okay. Let me clean up and then I'll head out."

Lindsey stood. She smelled of sex and regret, he thought. But then she offered him her hand. "Silly boy. I'm not done with you yet."

He took her hand and got to his feet, making sure his body brushed against hers. Felt her shiver, saw her lick her lips. God, was he really willing to be her boy toy? Because that was how this felt.

"A hot bath would be perfect after all that playing,

but my tub is smallish. What do you say to sharing a shower?"

"I say hells to the yeah."

"Good. That's one of the things I meant to put on my resolutions list from last night," she said.

"I actually have it right here," he told her, bending to pick up his pants and pull out the card he'd shoved in there before he'd left his hotel room.

She reached out to take it from him. "I have a lot of blanks."

"So do I," he admitted ruefully. But in his mind he'd already started filling them in.

"Shower first, and then we can fill them in together and order pizza because I'm hungry. Then you can head home. Is that okay?" she asked after a moment.

He nodded. "It's your show, lady."

"It is?" She blew out a breath, biting down on her lush lower lip. "It's not easy to believe that. I'm totally winging it here."

"So am I. This is different for me, too."

She took his resolution card from him and glanced down at it, wrinkling her brow as she read the few words he'd jotted down.

Crap. He wasn't good with words or spelling. He had dyslexia, which was something he didn't share with the world. And something he certainly hoped she hadn't picked up on. He'd brought her list because he wanted to know what she expected from her year.

He should have left his at home.

But there was no point in worrying about that now. He scooped her up in his arms. Taking the stairs two at a time, he paused on the landing. "Which way?"

"Second door on the right," she said. Nodding, he

carried her into her room. This space seemed more like Lindsey—there was a bright floral-patterned comforter and a large stack of pillows at the head of the bed. The walls had been painted a pale blue color that reminded him of the reflection of the snow and sky first thing in the morning. He saw her medals hanging on the wall under a photo of her with the president.

Carter set her on her feet, and she put the cards on her dark-finished, solid-oak dresser as she led the way to her bathroom. She bent to get some towels from the cabinet, and he realized that there was something about Lindsey that would always leave him wanting more. That being here with her now wasn't doing anything but making him crave her more intensely.

He wondered if he'd ever get his fill of her, but then she turned, held her hand out to him, and he stopped thinking and questioning. At least for now, he was exactly where he needed to be.

8

It's a bad idea. She knew she had to say it as soon as they were done eating the pizza they'd ordered. They weren't going to be a couple or start dating. She was a mess and he had to know it.

But she liked him. He was fun and he made her feel as though she was a fun person, too. Except that she was also acutely aware that she wasn't really the woman she acted like around him.

She'd had more sex in the past twenty-four hours than she'd had in the previous ten years; which was both great and confusing. She couldn't keep the compartments she needed Carter to stay in straight in her mind.

"Stay or hit?" he asked.

They were playing poker...well, blackjack or twenty-one, at her kitchen table. She wore her flannel pajamas and Carter had on just his boxer briefs. It felt intimate and cozy and would be if she'd just let it be. But she couldn't.

She glanced at her cards, trying to recall the rule that Carter had shared with her for taking cards. She had an eight and a three. She needed twenty-one and had eleven. Seemed pretty safe for a hit.

"Hit."

He turned a card up in front of her. *Ace.*

"Damn."

He laughed. "I'm guessing you want to stay?"

She shook her head. Had she given the game away? She hated to lose, so she needed to pay better attention, but the truth was Carter was a distraction with his naked chest and tattoos sitting across from her. The light from the kitchen shone down on him, his face hidden by the shadows cast on him.

"No," she said. No guts, no glory had always been her motto. "Hit."

He gave her another card. It was a seven. A nice, safe little seven card that kept her from going over twenty-one.

"Stay."

"Think you can beat me?"

He had a face card showing, so chances were he might have a twenty but... What? She'd just said no guts... "You bet I do."

He took a card and got another face card.

"Ooh, that's twenty. Did you bust?" she asked.

He flipped up his card to reveal a two. "Why, yes, I did, gorgeous. That means you win."

"That's right, I win," she said, smiling. This was good. Competing against Carter reminded her of all the things that were usually between them.

"Now you have to tell me the one habit you are hoping to break this year," she said. They'd been playing loser-tells-all for their resolutions.

"Fair enough, but I'm going to ask you about sexual positions. Sure you don't want to know about them?"

"I don't have to win a game to get you to tell me about them," she said. "Now, what habit is it that you want to quit?"

He scratched his chin. "I think I'd like to quit… Wait—does it have to be a vice?"

"Not at all. You get to choose."

"Well, then, I will quit answering these questions," he said insolently.

She narrowed her eyes at him. "That's *already* your habit. And we both agreed to the terms. You have to answer." He leaned back in the chair so his expression was visible now. She looked over at him, trying to figure out what was going on behind his handsome face. He was too sexy for his own good. It would have been better if he'd been average looking with that personality of his. He was used to charming anyone—man or woman—into doing whatever he wanted. She was determined to be different.

Hell, that had been her attitude from the beginning. Had she been attracted to him all this time?

"Well, if you must know…" he said. "I'm going to give up pulling all-nighters. I think I'm past the point where I can keep drifting through life."

She almost laughed, but she knew he was being sincere. He was one of the top athletes in winter sports and he thought he was drifting through life. She kind of got it because that was how she felt now that skiing had been taken from her.

"So what does a serious Carter Shaw look like?" she asked.

"Ah, that, gorgeous, is a second question, and I'm

afraid you've only earned one," he said with that half grin of his that she found way too irresistible. "Besides, that's not on the resolutions list. I might answer it if you win again."

"So deal," she said. Now that she was getting the hang of the game and she'd won, she was ready to keep winning. It was a sort of safe way for her to find out more about Carter. Learn all the intimate details about him while keeping her own secrets safe.

"Don't forget there is a little thing called beginners luck," he warned as he dealt her two cards.

"I've never relied on luck. Just skill and grit. Something that I guess a drifter like you wouldn't understand."

"Touché."

Her cards weren't so good this time. A five and a nine. Fourteen. It almost felt as if she should stay, but she wanted to win again.

Carter had a three showing.

"Hit me."

He flipped a card up in front of her. A three. Not what she'd been hoping for, but she smiled as if it was the only thing standing between her and twenty-one and gestured that she'd stay.

"That good, eh?"

She shrugged. "Like I said…no luck needed here."

It was funny, but she'd forgotten how often she'd had to use her press face with people in the real world to mask what she was really feeling. And now she was doing it playing cards. She'd never tell him, but Carter was giving her back little pieces of herself she hadn't even realized she'd lost when she'd stopped skiing.

Things such as bluffing, which didn't seem to have much in common with her skiing life but actually did.

He took a card and got a nine. "I'll stay. What have you got, gorgeous?"

She flipped up her cards. "Seventeen."

"Aw, that might be enough to beat me if I didn't have…"

He flipped his card over. An eight.

An eight!

"Looks like I win."

"Looks like you do," she agreed. "What are you going to ask me?"

He leaned forward, that blue-gray gaze of his intense—so intense she couldn't look away—as he took her hand in his. "Will you give me a shot, or is this just a one-night stand?"

HE HADN'T MEANT to ask her that, but now that he had, he knew that was exactly the only thing he wanted an answer for. Today had been one of the best of his life. But there was a part of him that realized she had pegged him into the casual category and he knew he wanted more.

He had to know what he was up against. Just like each time he stood at the lip of the half-pipe and took a breath before taking his run. Each half-pipe was different. Each run unique. And he prepared for the different mountains and the different events as if he'd never taken a run at it before.

Lindsey was like an unfamiliar run. This was his first time with a woman who mattered. *She* mattered. The words echoed around in his brain as he sat at the table trying to be cool. Or as cool as a guy could be wearing just his underwear while playing cards.

It had felt right until this moment when he'd laid everything out in front of her. He saw in her eyes the moment she thought she'd come up with an answer. She tipped her head to the side and gave him that smile he'd seen on her face in photographs a million times.

"What kind of shot?" she asked coyly.

"One where you don't wear a fake smile," he said.

Sure, he loved games, but not with her. Or at least not with her at this moment.

"I honestly don't know what to say." She released a breath. "I think it's a bad idea to take this any further. Because like I already told you when I left your hotel room this morning, I'm dealing with some stuff. It's not fair to get involved with anyone at this moment."

He nodded and leaned back in his chair. "Fair enough." He wanted to argue but he knew that he wasn't going to change her mind. Not right now anyway.

"That's it? I was expecting an argument or some passionate plea to give you a shot," she said.

"Do I look like I have to beg a woman to be with me?" he asked. But that was pride making him stupid. He shouldn't have said it and knew it the moment the words had left his mouth.

"No, you look like a guy who has too many women saying yes… I think I've had enough of games for today. Why don't we call it a night?"

Damn. He should say something—apologize—but she'd slammed him hard in the ego and he wasn't ready to let her know that. Doubted he ever truly would be.

"Good idea," he said.

Carter left her kitchen and went to the hallway, where his clothes sat in a pile, and got dressed. He'd pushed too hard, he knew it, but could see no way to back out of this without admitting he was an ass.

He heard her in the hallway and looked up to see her hovering in the doorway. The expression on her face was unreadable, and he wondered if there was anything he could say. He wished he was better at interacting with people, would give up his ability to do a 360 for the chance to make this right.

"I— Thank you, for today," she said quietly. "Thanks for the fun in the snow and…everything else. I needed it. You've helped me kick off this year with a great start."

She was classy. He had to admit even when showing him the door, she did it in such a way that he almost didn't mind. He had sensed from the first moment they'd met that there was something different about her and now he knew what it was.

She had a kind, beautiful heart.

Lindsey had that innate goodness that he'd never been able to find. Even when he wanted to be nice, it usually came off as self-serving. He'd tried, but around her it was easy to see that he would continue to fail.

"What can I say? It's all a part of the Carter Shaw package." He bent to tie his boots, and then straightened to face her.

"Don't do that," she said.

"Do what?"

"Make it sound like you don't feel things like I do." Their gazes met and held, and he could see a depth of emotion glimmering in her beautiful brown eyes.

"What makes you believe that I could?"

"I spent the day with you, Carter. I saw a side of you that few people ever do, and I'm so glad I did." She reached up and gently squeezed his biceps. "I like you."

But she was still kicking him out. "Gosh, thanks."

"Stop it. You know what I mean. I had no idea that behind that big braggart and awesome talent was a man who could see past his own ego and help me try to conquer my fears. I really can't thank you enough."

His jaw flexed and he swallowed hard. That was nothing. He hated that he might be even the tiniest bit responsible for her not skiing anymore, and he didn't want to think of the winter sports without her. For him the two things were inexorably tied together. So even his unselfish move of trying to get her back on skis had turned out to be for him.

"You're welcome," he said at last, because he really didn't know what else to say. There was a part of him that knew if he was an eloquent man, maybe more like his old man, he'd come up with just the right sentiment to express.

But he wasn't that guy.

He was a tattooed snowboarder who'd been searching all his life for the next big thrill. The next adrenaline-fueled high he could find. He'd never have guessed that he'd find it in this cool Nordic blond, Alpine Super G skier who always seemed to look right through him.

"Goodbye," he said.

He turned, opened the door and forced himself to walk away without looking back. But he wanted to see if she watched him as he left. Wanted to know if he'd had an impact on her the way she had him. But was afraid to see the truth: that he might need her more than she wanted him.

LINDSEY STEPPED INTO the boardroom at the Lars Usten lodge with more than a little trepidation. It had been two weeks since she'd sent Carter away, and she wasn't sure if he'd be at this meeting or not. She'd been back to that little snow mound three more times.

The first time she hadn't been able to go down the hill on her sled. The second time she'd gotten mad, climbed to the top and stood there shaking until she'd forced herself to slide down. It had been hard, but she'd forced herself to do it three more times before going home, and then yesterday she'd gone and just did it. The fear was still there, but she was finding her strength again.

This weekend she hoped to get back on her skis and actually go down one of the easier runs in the Wasatch Range. But today she had to get through a corporate meeting.

She just didn't like having to dress up and sit in a stuffy boardroom. The lodge itself was rustic and homey. First-class luxury. She loved the large patios that over-looked the picturesque mountain vistas and the pris-tine ski trails.

"You're one of the first to arrive," Elizabeth Anders said, coming over to give her a hug. "I'm glad. I have missed our breakfasts and was hoping you'd have time for a coffee before we get started."

Her friend was the general manager of the lodge and had recently—as in on New Year's Eve—married her best friend, Bradley. Lindsey had been one of the brides-maids at the ceremony.

"I didn't know exactly when you were getting back from your honeymoon today," Lindsey said. "I've missed our breakfasts, too. Too much time alone with myself and my thoughts."

"Like what?" Elizabeth asked as she led the way down the hall to where a coffee service was set up.

"Nothing. Just some crazy decisions I made on New Year's Eve," she said as she made herself a cup of coffee. No way was she going to elaborate on what had gone down with Carter. But it was nice to have her friend back, so maybe for a little while she didn't have to keep thinking about it.

"How was your honeymoon?"

"Fab. The Lars Usten Resort in the Caribbean was really nice. And it was a change of pace to be a guest and not have to always be watching for things that might go wrong."

Lindsey laughed. Elizabeth looked polished from head to toe, like someone who had everything all together. Even when she was going through the ups and downs of falling in love with Bradley she'd still done it with panache.

Something that Lindsey never felt she had.

"That's great."

"Are you okay?" Elizabeth asked, her brow in concern. "You don't seem yourself today."

Lindsey nodded. "Just nervous about this meeting. I know what the event is supposed to be but I've never been on a committee before."

"You'll do fine. It's nothing like skiing sixty miles per hour."

Lindsey gave Elizabeth the smile she was sure her friend was looking for. But she knew that skiing wasn't easy, and this meeting wouldn't be, either. Of course, she could contribute and she'd do whatever she had to to make the charity ski event a success.

The event had been proposed by Carter and had taken a lot of the resort owners in the area by surprise. The last time he had proposed something it had been to allow snowboarders on the runs in the valley; something that had gone against the resort owners' policies. He'd won them over, and now skiers and snowboarders were welcome on the mountain, but he hadn't exactly endeared himself to the owners with that move.

So the charity event, which would bring world-class athletes and young kids interested in winter sports together, had initially caught the higher-ups off guard. Lindsey smiled to herself at the thought of how shocked the owners had been to see their old nemesis in a different light.

Not unlike the way she was. Carter had changed, and he'd sort of changed her. She missed having him around, but wouldn't admit it to herself or to anyone else. She figured if she had a few restless nights plagued with dreams of making love on her kitchen table with Carter, that was the price she had to pay for peace of mind.

"Hello, ladies," he said, walking up to her and Elizabeth. Seeming to appear from out of nowhere.

She took a sip of her coffee and burned her tongue. He looked good. Polished in that roguish way of his. Elizabeth and he were chatting, but all she could do was watch him and acknowledge to herself that her dream-induced fantasies fell far short of the real man. She missed him.

No denying that.

"Well, Linds, how's the skiing going?" he asked after Elizabeth excused herself to greet some of the other committee members.

"Great," she said. No use telling him she still hadn't made it up the mountain. That was her personal struggle. "How long are you here for?"

"For the next six months."

Her eyes widened. "What? Why that long?"

"This charity event is my number one priority right now," he said. "And I told you I was going to get you back on skis. I can't do that from California, now, can I?"

"I think you've done enough. Feel free to go back to Cali."

He leaned in close to her and the spicy scent of his aftershave wrapped around her, reminding her of how strong the scent had been when she'd rested her head on his shoulder after making love.

"I promise you I haven't done nearly enough."

9

CARTER SAT ACROSS from Lindsey in the meeting. He was excited for the event and when he'd originally come up with the idea had known it was going to be a hard sell. Truth was, he'd never really played up to the resort owners in Park City, Utah, and the surrounding valley. They had sort of always looked down on snowboarders, but he wasn't Houston Shaw's son for nothing, and had learned from his father that turning adversaries into business partners made for some interesting and profitable ventures.

But this wasn't about profit. This was about bringing snowboarding and skiing to kids who couldn't afford it otherwise. Giving them the chance to have what he'd always had. To be honest, he hadn't realized how much of a financial struggle competing at the world-class level could be, since he'd had the benefit of his father's money.

Lindsey understood that. She spoke eloquently on the fact that it wasn't just inner-city kids or those at the lowest economic level who needed help, but also middle-class families who were getting by—as her family had when her talent had been spotted.

"I think we're all on board now," Lars Usten, the namesake and owner of the resort, said. "We just need to figure out what the event will look like."

"I see it as a three- or four-day event," Carter told them. "Starting on a Thursday with events for the kids who've maybe signed up through our program to have lessons."

"What program?" Elizabeth asked. "Is this something new to the agenda?"

"Yes," Carter said. He passed around some folders that outlined his idea. "Since we're not doing the event until the fall, I propose we start getting local kids involved in training sessions now. I'd like to see each of your resorts offer up your facilities, and maybe we can have teams to compete against each other."

Everyone had opened the folder and was skimming the contents. He had done a lot of work.

"Bradley Hunt of FreshSno is donating the gear for the kids, and Thunderbolt, my energy drink sponsor, will give the kids the clothing they need," he said finally. "Ski pants, jackets and a T-shirt. All I really need now is your resorts and time on the slopes."

"That's great, but who's going to teach the kids? We all have full-time jobs," Lindsey reminded him. "Not everyone is a man of leisure like you."

"Well, I'm going to teach snowboarding. It's what I'm good at and, as you've pointed out, I do have the time. I'm sure there must be a few former world champs who wouldn't mind teaching the next generation."

"I didn't say I minded," Lindsey said, bristling at his insinuation. "Of course I'll do it on my days off. These will just have to be needs based and when I'm not teaching the kids from the resort."

"Good. So now we've got Alpine skiing and snow-boarding," Carter replied.

"I've got an idea," Bradley said. "Watching you two square off... What if we put together two teams, captained by each of you, to raise funds? Anyone who follows winter sports knows that you are adversaries—the Ice Queen versus the Bad Boy." He smiled broadly. "It's classic and fun. We can have people from the committee and other resort staff members on the teams as well as the kids. What do you think?"

Carter liked it. It was an innovative idea and would give him a chance to spend more time with Lindsey. A legitimate reason that she wouldn't be able to back out of. "Sure. I think it's got some merit. Plus, it's for charity. I want to see it be a success."

Lindsey glared at him from across the table. He wasn't sure what it was he was doing today, but he seemed to be getting on her nerves. *Perfect.* He wanted her to be aware of him and to be bothered by him. It seemed only fair, since she was bothering him.

He was here because of a cause that was dear to him. He'd seen a lot of talented kids over his years in the sport that'd had to quit because they couldn't afford gear. That wasn't right.

But then, as he stared back at Lindsey, a telltale smirk suddenly tugged at his lips. Okay, if he was being *totally* honest, his reasons for being here weren't entirely altruistic. It was also because he'd wanted to see her again and this was the only way he'd been able to do it. She'd shut him out. He'd thought about calling, but he wasn't going to keep chasing her. At least not in an obvious way.

"I want it to be a success, too. I'd be happy to captain a team," Lindsey said, her fake smile firmly in place.

"Okay, then. How are we going to choose teams?" Elizabeth asked. "We have two representatives from all the resorts and other participants here, so we could do it that way. One from each?"

There was some discussion around the table of the different skills, but soon the teams were established and Carter thought he'd made out pretty well. Most of the owners and executives from the resorts were passionate skiers.

"We'll need to come up with events. And they should be pretty standard but not risky," Lindsey said.

"It should be fun, too. We want to bring new people to the sport and make it something the kids will want to do. In fact, maybe we can use our teams as mentors," Carter suggested.

"That's a great idea," Lars said. "I'll be in charge of the events for our competition. I think we should hold it in February to kick off our announcement for the fall event. Use it to encourage kids to sign up."

There was agreement around the table. Lars asked each of them to jot down one or two ideas for events for the kickoff to be held in February. A meeting was set for the following week and everyone left the boardroom.

Carter gathered his papers and followed Lindsey down the hall and out onto the patio that led to the ski rental and lesson building.

"Wait up."

"Sure," she said, whirling around to face him. "Think of something else you wanted to challenge me on?"

"Not at all. I told you I wasn't done with you," he warned.

"I know that. I'm not done with you now, either."

She wasn't really angry with him. On the contrary,

he could see worry and maybe a little bit of fear on her face. She couldn't ski, and she'd just been put in charge of a ski team for a major public event.

Crap.

SHE HADN'T MEANT to talk to Carter. She'd meant to exit the lodge, get into her ski clothing and then… What? She had no real idea. Obviously she couldn't lead a team down the slopes in February considering that just sledding down a little snow mound took all of her courage.

But she had to. Everything had changed thanks to this guy and his damned argumentative streak. She had a hunch that he'd originally started sparring with her in front of everyone as a sort of payback for the way she'd kicked him out of her place on New Year's Day, and frankly, she hadn't blamed him.

But this… She put her arm around her waist.

"Okay, this is serious. I already offered to help you and I'm not going to let this go," he said.

"Carter, thanks, but you can't make that fear I feel when I strap on a pair of skis go away. I mean, you seem to be able to charm anyone into doing anything, but this is something I don't think even you can simply force under your control."

She dropped her arm as she realized how defensive that might look to him. Then she spun on her heel and started walking again. As she moved across the resort grounds, she paused to look around her. It was the kind of day she used to love. The snow was thick, perfect for a fresh run, and the sky looked clear and endless. This was her favorite sort of winter.

"I know that," he said, quickly catching up with

her. "I'm just saying every time I dare you to do something—"

"It backfires," she retorted. The bet on a kiss that had started all of this hadn't spurred her on to greater skiing glory. Or had it? She'd kept her head down and trained harder to prove he didn't bother her. That his flirting couldn't shake her. Maybe that was what she needed to do now. Put her head down and pretend he couldn't affect her.

"I've got this."

"You know," he said, "it wouldn't hurt you to admit that you can't do it all on your own."

"I don't need an entourage to remind me— What is it exactly that they do for you?" she asked sweetly.

"Nothing. They are friends, not an entourage. Something that seems foreign to you." He reached out and gripped her arm. "You have people who care for you, but you are always so afraid to let them in."

"Let *you* in," she said, jerking away. "That's what you really mean."

"True. Why is that?"

She stopped walking and looked over at him. He had put on a pair of sunglasses so she couldn't see his eyes. "You scare me. You make me confused. I don't really like it."

"I don't like it, either, but we are going to have to work together."

"Why?" she asked.

"I'm the only person who knows you haven't skied since your surgery, aren't I?"

She nodded. When she got home she was taking that damned resolutions list off the fridge and adding "no drinking champagne" to it. Maybe if she hadn't been drinking she wouldn't have found him as attractive and confessed all sorts of things she should have kept to herself.

"Carter, please. Just let this go. I'll figure it out and no one will have to know anything," she said.

"I can't."

She sighed in frustration. "Why not?"

"Because you made me your New Year's resolution and I'm determined to give you a year you won't forget."

"I was drunk when I said that," she said. But despite her annoyance with him, his words made her feel warm like the sunshine on her face. There was more to Carter Shaw than she wanted to admit. Mainly because if she didn't keep him at arm's length she might do something foolish, like fall for him.

And it was foolish. Though she hadn't seen him in person for the past two weeks, she'd seen him online on the gossip websites with a bevy of women at the Thunderbolt Energy Drink Extreme Winter Games as he'd promoted his upcoming professional debut in California. She knew that he was a player.

She had to seem like a novelty to him. And while she got that to him she was different, a challenge of sorts, how long would it take for that to wear off and for him to move on? She wasn't being down on herself. She had plenty to offer a man, but not one like Carter. His expectations were based on a model of woman and a lifestyle that made hers seem boring.

"You weren't drunk. If you want to pretend you were, then fine," he said tersely. "I don't know why I keep chasing after you."

She didn't know, either, and she wasn't foolish enough

to guess. "Thank you. I guess I'll see you next week at our meeting."

"Yes, you will."

She walked away and admitted to herself that she was disappointed he'd let her go. She'd hoped that maybe he'd follow her. But she knew she'd have shut him down if he had.

She got changed in the locker room and, as usual, putting on her ski clothes brought out that little bit of sadness and fear. But she had a class to teach, and letting down her students wasn't something she'd do.

Her first lesson went well, and instead of just holding her skis, this time she put them on and skied around a little bit while the kids met their parents for lunch. She was going to try to take a run after lunch.

The clock was ticking and she wasn't about to let anyone else know her secret. It was time she conquered that fear and moved on. Then maybe she could figure out what to do about her attraction to Carter.

10

LINDSEY SURVEYED HER TEAM. She had Bradley Hunt, Lars Usten, Stan Poirier from Thunderbolt and two other executives from other resorts in the area. She had been practicing sledding every day on her little snow mound, as well as getting used to standing at the top of a slope and going down.

But she was nowhere near as ready to take on a downhill race as she'd need to be if her team was going to win. Beating Carter was important to her. She needed it. He had seen her flustered and flawed and she wanted to wow him.

"Okay, team, welcome to our first practice. I thought we'd talk a little about the skills each of you has and then decide how to proceed."

"I'll go first," Lars said. The former world champion still skied every day, and he was in pretty good shape despite a health scare back in November. "I'm probably the biggest liability on the team since my heart attack at Thanksgiving, but I want you all to know I've been skiing every day and my runs are getting faster and smoother."

"I don't think anyone doubted you, Lars," she reassured him. "I've always been in awe of your control while you're on skis."

"Thank you, Lindsey. Coming from you, that's a compliment I'll treasure," he said with a smile.

He reminded her of her grandfather in a lot of ways. Except hers didn't really like to ski. Lars was the kind of grandfather she would like to have.

"I'm more into sponsoring crazy athletes than actually doing the crazy stuff myself."

"Sponsoring athletes is what you are good at," Lindsey said.

"I've already sent an email to the committee agreeing to that." Bradley grinned. "Oh, and by the way, I have a feeling my wife is going to want to compete against me."

Lindsey rolled her eyes. "That would hardly be fair, since you just started skiing."

"I know. I think that's why she keen on it," Bradley said with a laugh.

Clearing his throat, Stan added, "My wife, Georgina, is better than I am. She might want to go against someone like you, Lars."

"This is all good to get out in the open, but let's face it, we have to train to do our best times," Lindsey informed the group. "Now, I suspect that Carter is going to want to go down on his snowboard, and I think the committee has agreed to let him. Does anyone else snowboard?" Tim and Paul raised their hands. She talked to them briefly, but frankly she didn't snowboard so couldn't really "coach" them.

Bradley left to take a call, and during the hour-long practice that followed, Lindsey spent most of her time writing down the times of the others and waiting for them to finish with various business calls. It was obvious this wasn't going to be like training for an international event.

In addition to practicing, they'd sell tickets to the event, and each member of the team was to fund-raise. The group was breaking up when Bradley returned. Whistling under his breath, he was obviously in a good mood. Lindsey wished she felt the same. She was upset with herself that she hadn't taken a run. Deep down she wasn't even sure she could do it, but she knew she was going to have to. Either that or admit to everyone in this microcosm that she wasn't the skier she used to be.

"Hey, I just got off the phone with a college buddy of mine who is an orthopedic surgeon for the military," Bradley announced. "He mentioned that some of the vets who've been wounded overseas and lost limbs have a winter sports team." He paused. "I was wondering what your thoughts were about getting them involved. He gave me the number of their team captain."

"I love this idea," Lindsey said.

Everyone else agreed, too, so Bradley sent a group email to the other committee members.

"Once we get everyone's acceptance, maybe you could liaise with him, Lindsey?" Lars asked. "I think we've all proved you can take the executive out of his office but you can't make him stop working."

She laughed, as she was sure he'd intended. "No problem. I have time between classes to make a few calls."

"Perfect. Let's meet back here next week, and if anyone needs any pointers or one-on-one coaching, I'm available."

The group left, and she walked to her office at the back of the ski rental office aware of the fact that she was a total fraud. She wondered how she was going to get over this. How was she going to make herself ski when it was the last thing she thought she could do?

Right now, sitting in her office, looking up at the mountain, she felt dread and fear. She should just confess and stop trying to be something she used to be.

"Knock, knock," Carter said from the doorway. "Got a minute?"

Definitely. Her breath hitched as their eyes met and held. She'd rather spar with him than dwell on her own inadequacies. "Sure. Come to tell me that your team isn't up to snuff? Mine is great."

"Ha. Mine is pretty good, too. Elizabeth can really ski, and I was surprised that Georgina could, as well. Don't tell either of them. It's just that they never talked about skiing."

"I know what you mean. I've got two snowboarders and I'm not really sure how to handle them. But they are pretty good. Not you good, of course, but still, they've got some skills."

"It's hard to be as good as me," he said with that big sexy grin of his.

A shiver of awareness skittered down her spine as she gazed into his blue-gray eyes. It had been days since she'd been alone with him, and instead it felt like years. Everything about him turned her on. His disheveled hair, his baggy snowboarding pants, the spicy scent of his aftershave. New Year's Eve had whetted her appetite, and she wanted more of Carter Shaw. And right now flirting and playing with him felt safe.

CARTER FOUND IT harder and harder to keep up the casual pretense he'd cultivated around Lindsey. He missed her.

He physically ached for her and wanted to do whatever he could to get her back into his bed, but she was setting the limits, and right now that meant taking it slow.

Sitting in the small office and smiling when what he really wanted to do was to pull her into his arms, run his fingers through her long, silky blond hair and kiss her until she was panting. But that wasn't going to happen. He was pursuing her but didn't want her to know it. He needed to keep up appearances. And that was exactly what he intended to do.

"It is hard to be as big as your ego," she said glibly. "I wish I had a tenth of it."

"What do you need it for?"

"I have to ski at our event in the middle of February, Carter. I haven't done anything but slide down a mound of snow since I crashed last year in Sochi. What am I going to do?" she asked.

Looking as though she had the weight of the world on her shoulders, she walked around her desk and sat on the edge of it, right in front of him. He saw a hint of vulnerability in her eyes. She needed him. It felt good. Stroked his ego. And she'd probably never let him live it down if he let her know.

"Take a run with me."

"I don't even know if I can. You saw me on the snow pile. I was shaking like an idiot up there. If I was on skis—"

"I've got an idea," he said.

"I doubt it would work."

"My last one did," he said, bragging just a little, but also making a challenge out of it. He knew how she was. She'd rise to the challenge.

Lindsey sighed impatiently. "Fine. What's your idea?"

"Just a ride down the mountain in a toboggan."

"I don't know."

"I'll be with you," he said gently. "You know, like I was at the snow mound."

She watched him with wary eyes, and he ached that she had lost her faith in herself. He vowed he'd do whatever he had to do to help her get it back.

"Would we go here at the lodge?" she asked.

"Yes. We could even say we are checking it out for an event for our nonskiers. I've got two of them."

"I didn't get one. Maybe we can swap one of my snowboarders for your nonskier. It's always weird to me when people live and work this near the Wasatch Range and they don't ski."

"Me, too," he admitted. "I can see it in Cali because there are so many other sports that people can do, but here? It's pretty much ski or snowboard. Or, at the very least, ice skate. Speaking of which…you ever try that?"

She shook her head. "I'm not that good at it. Plus, my coach used to like me to focus on my sport."

"Good idea. My coach said something similar but I did it anyway."

"Rebel."

"You know it," he said.

Lindsey bit her lip, then turned to stare out the window before finally looking back over at him. "I wish I had your courage."

"You do have it. But in your own way. You are a rebel when you need to be. I've seen you when you pass through the gates for the downhill. You look very fierce."

He had never mentioned it, but the first time he'd noticed Lindsey was after her run. She'd broken the world-record time. He'd been so turned on by her he hadn't known what to do. She hadn't been his kind of woman, but then suddenly his body had been, like, hell yeah, she is.

"Thank you, Carter. You know, for an egomaniac, you say some really nice things," she said, tipping her head to the side to study him.

"I'm not as ego driven as you think I am."

"Really? You're not going to convince me." She checked her watch. "But I can probably take off in about an hour if you want to try the tobogganing idea."

"Great." He was shameless where she was concerned, using her love of skiing and her need to be back on her skis as a way to keep him by her side. He wondered if she would still be talking to him after their night together if it wasn't for the fact that she couldn't get back on her skis.

It was humbling, and he didn't like the way it made him feel, so he treated those feelings the way he usually did. He shoved them so far down he could pretend they didn't exist.

"I'll go to the concierge and make sure we can get on there and then come back in an hour," he said. It would probably be a good idea to give her some space so she could miss him.

"Okay. Thanks, Carter," she said.

"For?"

"Just being a friend."

Friend. Ugh. He wasn't about to let her relegate him there. Glancing over his shoulder to make sure no one was nearby, he closed the gap between them and pulled her into his arms. Then he gave her a hot, hard kiss. "We're more than friends, gorgeous, and don't you forget it."

He strode out of her office without looking back, mainly because he didn't want to seem as if he wanted to know how that kiss had affected her when it had shaken him to his core.

Carter knew he was playing a dangerous game with her. That he wanted something from her that she might give him, but he was trying to keep her from even knowing he wanted. He shook his head and thought of what a sap he was. He wanted to be more than friends and more than lovers, but had never in his life been successful at making any kind of relationship work.

Even his coaches had been short-term before they'd thrown their hands up and walked away. He just wasn't good at making things last. Usually that didn't bother him, but the thought of being short-term in Lindsey's life simply wasn't acceptable.

CARTER SENT HER a text telling her he'd meet her at the top of the toboggan run just after lunch. She had one more call to make, to the staff sergeant from Marietta, Montana, that Bradley had told her about.

Lane Scott was one of the men who had been part of the paraplegic ski squad. She'd heard he had recovered and was now running his family's ranch with his brothers.

"Hello, ma'am," he said, his voice deep and strong.

"Good afternoon, sir. I'm Lindsey Collins, the ski pro at the Lars Usten Resort in Park City, Utah."

"The same Lindsey Collins who broke two world records?" he asked.

No, she thought, not anymore. But she couldn't say that to him. "Yes, I am. I'm calling today because the resorts in Park City are participating in a charity event to get more kids out on the slopes, especially those who can't afford it. We're doing a kickoff event in mid-February and we were hoping some of you military guys might want to join us in the exhibition event."

"Mid-February? I think I can make it. It's not like I have to be in Marietta on Valentine's Day," he said good-naturedly. "What kind of event is it?"

"Well, I'm captaining one team and snowboarder Carter Shaw is the captain of the other one. We have local celebs and executives from the different resorts on our teams and we are each raising money for the fall event as well as getting some press for it."

"Sounds interesting. Where do my men and I fit in?"

She took a breath. "Well, your team was brought up because we know there are some kids in your situation that might not be aware they can still participate in sports. No offense. I hope you understand how I meant that..." She was feeling flustered because she wasn't sure if she'd phrased her comments right.

He chuckled. "I get it. A lot of people see losing a limb or two as the end of their outdoor life. I'd love to participate, and I think I can get one or two others to do it, as well. If it's okay with you, we'll just be a part of your two established teams. No need for us to be singled out."

"That sounds great. I'll text you my email address. Just send me your details and I'll get you all set up with the committee so you can be up-to-date on the plans. They'll assign you to a team."

"I hope I get to ski with you," Lane said.

"Me, too. I'll put in a good word. Thanks, Lane."

"Thank you for thinking of us," he said.

Lindsey hung up the phone and was moved by the

fact that Lane and his buddies hadn't let an injury slow them down. She was going to use their courage to motivate herself. And in all honesty, she was fine. So why was she struggling so hard to get back on the snow?

Once Lane's information came through, she forwarded it to the committee and then headed out to meet Carter. As she walked up the trail to the toboggan course, she put on her sunglasses and applied the lip balm of the company that used to sponsor her.

In the summer the lodge used the course, as well. It was one of the many year-round attractions that made Park City so perfect for families. But today she wasn't thinking about the fact that she had a job. Today she was thinking about her flaws. Her own shortcomings, and why other people had been able to get back on the snow and she hadn't. Her coach had sent one of his newest talents to meet with her over the Christmas break, and she suspected he'd meant it to motivate her, but all it had done was make it even harder for her to get back out there.

She wasn't young and untried. She had broken two world records and still held one of them. But she was afraid that was all in her past. It was hard to stare at your life when you were almost thirty and think that the best may have already happened. She'd always looked to each New Year as a chance to do better, to achieve more.

She saw Carter chatting with Nate Pearson, one of the guys who ran the toboggan course. Nate had been on one of the US teams at the winter games last year, so it wasn't surprising that he knew Carter.

"Hey, Lindsey," Nate said, smirking. "Couldn't believe it when this player said you were meeting him."

Lindsey rolled her eyes. Well, what could she say

in her defense? Carter *was* a player. That was why she was struggling so hard to make sure that she didn't attach too much importance to their one night together. Maybe if she was able to keep it to just that one night it might be okay. They could flirt and tease each other outside the bedroom and she could pretend that nothing had changed between them. Even though she knew that everything had.

"You're preaching to the choir, Nate. I know better than to get serious with a guy like Carter."

"I'm standing right here, you know," Carter said.

She winked at him. "I guess you are sort of charming and cute. That's why all the girls like you."

"We can't all be the Ice Queen," he muttered under his breath. "So are you ready for this?"

"Let me get you guys set up," Nate said.

He walked away, leaving them alone for a minute, and Lindsey noticed that Carter looked a bit ticked off.

"You okay?"

"Yes," he said after a long silence. "I just don't like you thinking of me as a player. That's not what I am with you."

She smiled, because he sounded so sincere. "I don't believe it's something you get to choose. You are just naturally the kind of man that all women are drawn to."

"Even you?" he asked.

Especially her. "Of course."

11

CARTER CHECKED INTO one of the residences at the resort that was away from the main building but still close enough that he could drop in when he needed to. It had been five days since he'd seen Lindsey and gone tobogganing with her. He'd contemplated buying a condo in Lindsey's development. It would have been an investment, and he did like having his own place to stay. But he had opted not to. He didn't want to push her too much. He'd been flying back and forth between professional engagements, his home in California and Park City.

He changed into some casual boarding clothes, grabbed his snowboard and headed out. He was dying to get on the slopes. He'd taken a few runs over the past few days. Not tricked-out ones as he did on the half-pipe but runs down the mountain. God, there was nothing like that feeling as he barreled down it.

He was almost to the ski lifts when he stopped and thought about Lindsey again. As if she was ever far from his mind. He knew she loved skiing the way he did snowboarding. So he went to the rental shop, stowed his board and got himself a pair of skis. He'd tried skiing maybe twice and decided he'd liked the solidness of the board beneath his feet better.

But he was going to have to sacrifice that to make sure Lindsey knew he was serious about helping her. He'd signed up for her afternoon lesson, which had already started, so he had to hurry to join the group.

He saw the look on her face when he showed up.

She forced a smile onto her face, saying, "Looks like we have a star in our midst. This is world champ Carter Shaw."

The kids all turned in his direction, and one boy, who was about eight, grinned up at him. "I wanted to snowboard, but my mom said no."

"Mom said you had to do the same thing as me and Kylie." The girl who spoke looked about two years older than the boy and, if he had to guess, Carter would have said she was his sister.

"Yeah, you're right."

"I like snowboarding but I'm a novice at skiing," he said to the kid. "We can learn together."

"Cool. I'm Jackson," the boy replied.

"Jackson, do you want to show Carter what we've learned so far?" Lindsey asked.

"Sure."

Jackson was an enthusiastic teacher for someone who wasn't sure he wanted to learn how to ski. For the duration of the class, he was Carter's shadow. Not that he minded. He followed the kid and caught up with him.

When they were all set to take their first runs down the very small slope they'd been practicing on, Carter noticed that Lindsey looked a little pale.

Was she going to ski?

Jackson went first and looked over at him, showing

off a bit as he slid down the slope and fell on his back-side. One of his sisters rushed over to help him up but he pushed her hands away.

"I'm fine."

Carter used his poles and skied over to Jackson. "Dude, you did great."

"I didn't. I fell."

"Everyone falls," Lindsey said. "I crashed big time. The key is getting back up."

Carter looked at Lindsey, realizing again how brave she was. "It's not easy to do, but I bet next time your run will be even better."

Jackson nodded. Another kid called for Lindsey and she turned away to talk to the student. "Not everyone gets it the first time," he told the boy.

"The other kids seem to," Jackson grumbled.

"I'm going to let you in on a little secret, Jackson," Carter said, leaning down to look the kid straight in the eye. "I'm a slow learner. I have to practice something ten times more than other people before I finally master it."

"Really? But you've got gold medals and X-Energy girls hanging around you. Doesn't seem like you have any problems," Jackson said.

"Dude, those girls get paid to hang around me," Carter replied, realizing that the women might attract older men to the sport but were sending the wrong mes-sage to younger ones. "There are a lot of things in life, not just skiing or snowboarding, that are hard. Some of them are going to be a breeze for you and other things will be a breeze for your friends or your sister and will take you longer to master."

Carter put his poles in one hand and held his other out to Jackson. The kid reached up, and Carter pulled him to his feet. "I'm a little worried about my first run down the slope."

"We can go together," Jackson offered.

"Deal," Carter said. He glanced over Jackson's head and noticed Lindsey watching him. He winked at her.

She shook her head at him, but mouthed her thanks. "You guys ready to take your run?"

"We are," Jackson said.

Carter stayed close to Jackson as they got to the top of the slope. Lindsey skied up next to them and smiled, but he noticed the tension around her mouth. He wondered if just being on the skis was rattling her.

"Give yourself a minute to look down the slope," Lindsey said. "Remember where you fell?"

"Yeah."

"This time in your mind picture yourself going straight past there," she said.

"I will. Ready, Carter?"

"I am."

Together they took off down the slope, and it didn't really take Carter any time to adjust to having two skis under him instead of his snowboard. Lindsey had given them the basics, but more than that, just knowing the kid and Lindsey were watching was enough to make him want to do a little better.

The entire class was at the bottom of the small slope, and he looked back up at Lindsey. He was scared for her, and wondered if she'd be able to ski down it. But he saw her take a breath and come sailing down.

Her form was shaky to his eyes, but he'd seen her at her best, and today it was fear driving her—not the need to win. The smile on her face as she joined their little group, though… That was real.

THE CLASS BROKE UP and all the kids were reconnected with their parents. Jackson waved happily at Carter. Lindsey shook her head. Was there anyone who Carter *couldn't* relate to?

She sat and took off her skis, and then stood there for a minute. Her first run in the better part of a year. It was a big deal and she didn't downplay it. She'd been scared, but as usual letting Carter see any vulnerability had pushed her to just do it. And now she had. She was tempted to take another run. Down the little slope again? Or maybe something more moderate. Maybe one of the bunny slopes.

"Great class," Carter said, coming up to her.

"Yeah? Well, you were certainly a big hit. What are you even doing here?" she asked. "Ski lessons? Just doesn't seem to be your style."

"When are you going to learn that I don't fit the little mold you keep trying to shove me into?" he asked. "I'm here because if I'm going to lead a team with skiers on it, I have to at least be able to participate in a few of their events."

"Crap. Do you think I'll have to snowboard?" she asked. She didn't even want to begin to think about that. Not now. "I might give it a go on one of those indoor places. It's all virtual."

"I've seen them. In fact, I have one that is branded in my name," he said.

She laughed. Of course he did. That was really a Carter sort of thing. From the beginning he'd took to the press and to advertising as though born to it. He was photogenic, that went without saying, but he also really liked the spotlight. Almost as much as he liked snowboarding—or at least that was the impression she'd always had.

"Well, then, I guess you know what I'm talking about."

"I do," he said. "The kids in your class were great, by the way."

"You caught a good class. Some of them aren't so great. Jackson sure took to you." Lindsey looked up at him. "Don't take this the wrong way, but you were really encouraging."

"Shocked you, didn't it?" he asked with a rueful grin. "Don't let the word get out or all my rivalries will look like shams."

"As one of your biggest adversaries, I'd never let the cat out of the bag." She studied him for a long moment. "Have you ever thought about coaching?"

"It's really not my thing. I mean, helping Jackson over a learning curve is one thing, but day in, day out, keeping up that kind of energy… I'm not sure I could do it."

That was too bad. He'd sounded as though he really got the difficulties that came along with participating in a sport. Well, duh. She shook her head.

"I saw that look on your face after the run. You liked it, didn't you?" he asked.

"Sort of. When I got to the bottom, I was elated that I'd done it. But if you and the class hadn't been at the bottom, I might have walked away."

"I don't think so. You've turned a corner, Linds. You're not walking away from anything anymore."

He was right—she wasn't. She didn't know how she was going to take a big run, but from now on she wasn't going to let her fear dominate her. She'd sort of turned a corner, and she knew exactly who to thank for it.

The only problem she could see was that she'd sort of tried shoving him out of her life, but here he was again. He was one determined fellow, as her granny would say.

"Why do you keep showing up?"

"Why do you keep pushing me away?" he countered. "That's the real question. What is it about me that makes you do that?"

She could feel the heat rising to her cheeks. "I just need to sort through my stuff. And this job… I have to make some decisions, and I've always believed the best time to get involved with a man—"

"Wait. Are you actually contemplating getting involved with me? I thought I was your dirty secret. Your booty call."

She shook her head in exasperation. "I don't know why I try to talk to you. You look like a normal human being but inside you're just one big ass."

"I am. I really am," he said. "But let's both agree that you have been treating me as though I have the plague."

"You like to exaggerate, don't you?"

"Just a tad." A wicked gleam flared in his eyes. "Seriously, you *are* thinking of a relationship?"

"I don't know. Not now," she said, but that was her own pride talking. She knew that she was infatuated with him. She'd typed his name into internet search engines, read every article on him and spent hours looking at pictures of him. Especially the one of him for the famous underwear designer. It'd be dumb to pretend she wasn't already attached to him in some way.

"I can be too much," he admitted. "But it's only when I'm nervous. When I was a kid, before I found snowboarding, I used to drive my nanny crazy. Sometimes she'd have to take a day off just to keep me in line."

That was interesting. "How'd that work?"

"I wanted her to come back. She was my companion whenever we travelled and I was homeschooled for a while so I missed her."

"Why were you homeschooled?"

"I was a late reader," he said. "Isn't it funny how there is a PC term for anything that's wrong with you?"

"I bet you were too physical to actually sit still and read," she said. "Nothing wrong with that. And I'll take PC over Ice Queen any day. I can't believe Bradley called me that."

"Well, it is sort of what the media calls you. But if you want me to defend your honor, I'll challenge him on the slopes and humiliate him for you," Carter said, reaching out and tucking a lock of hair behind her ear. "Just say the word."

"I think we're good," she said with an uneasy laugh. She noticed that it was starting to get a little dark and she knew it was time to go, but she didn't want to leave Carter. Not in the punch-drunk-love way but more in a tired-of-spending-all-her-nights-alone way.

CHASING HER WASN'T working exactly the way he'd planned, but Carter wasn't going to argue with the results. Who knew that skiing would be the thing to bring them closer? In a way, that made perfect sense to him because it was the sport that had always been between them and it still was.

She'd been so focused on her skiing when they'd first met and now that she couldn't ski anymore... Well, that hadn't brought them any closer together.

"A group of people from Thunderbolt are in town and hitting a few of the bars tonight. Want to come?" he asked.

She gave him a long, level look. "Dang it. That's on my resolutions list. I guess I'm going to have to."

He knew she hadn't put *bar crawl* on her list. It was the exact opposite of everything he knew to be true about Lindsey, but he also guessed she was tired of the space between them. Or maybe that was just wishful thinking on his part. He wanted her to need him.

Almost as much as he wanted her in his bed.

"I'll pick you up at eight," he said. He knew he should go, but instead he reached for her skis and put them over his shoulder with his own. "I have to return these... unless you want to take another run."

"I was actually thinking about it. But I have to do it on my own."

"I get it," he said. "Let me trade these skis for my board and I'll catch a ride up with you and then meet you at the bottom?"

She chewed her lower lip. For a minute he understood what she'd been trying to say to him earlier. She wasn't in any position to think clearly about her future. In a way that was why he thought he had to strike now. She wasn't going to want him when everything in her life was neatly sorted into boxes. He wasn't going to fit, but he did now.

"Okay. Where's your board?"

"I left it with your staff. Someone named Jeff," Carter informed her as they walked to the main ski-rental building.

"He is a huge fan," Lindsey teased. "He probably set up an altar and lit a candle around it."

Carter had to laugh. "I doubt it."

"I don't. He talks about you and the half-pipe all the time. I guess your latest stunt has really gotten him. He'd probably love some pointers."

It always floored him when he heard someone talking about his accomplishments as though they were special. He wasn't being funny, but the stuff he did came naturally to him and always seemed just that little bit not good enough. "Maybe I'll see if he wants to meet up."

"He'd love that," Lindsey said as they entered the building. Unfortunately the kid wasn't there.

"Hey, is Jeff here? I need to get my board," Carter said as Lindsey went behind the counter to talk to the other ski instructor.

"He's going to be bummed you came back while he was gone."

"Tell him I'll stop by tomorrow... When does he work?" Carter asked. He found out and made a note in his phone to stop by. It wouldn't hurt him to chat with the guy. He worked with Lindsey, so it might even help her to see that he was so much more than his bad-boy image.

"Ready?" he asked Lindsey when he noticed she was standing by herself with her skis.

"As I'll ever be," she said.

They walked to the ski lift and waited in line to take it to the top. He could tell she was nervous because she kept looking up at the mountain. All he really wanted to do was to hold her in his arms and tell her everything would be okay. But since this probably wasn't the time or place, he searched his mind for something to distract her.

Then he grinned to himself. Humor. It worked every time.

"Oh, guess what, gorgeous? I've added a few things to my resolutions list. I might have to write a thank-you note to the resort for all the ways they are helping me improve."

She rolled her eyes at him. "What did you add?"

"Kiss Lindsey on the ski lift."

She wrinkled her nose at him. "That's too bad, because I just don't see that happening."

"That's odd. I totally do."

She laughed, but as they got closer he noted she didn't look worried anymore. When it was their turn, they both got on the lift.

"What was your best ski-lift ride?" he asked curiously.

"First time I was going up for a world event. I was so excited. I'd run the course in my mind and was so ready for it. You?" she asked.

This one. But he didn't say it. There hadn't been many times in his life that he'd done something without wondering what was in it for him. But this thing with Lindsey? Sure, it brought him closer to her and gave him a chance to tease her about kissing and intimacy, but it really was for her. She needed to be skiing, not teaching kids at a resort.

He knew that and had a feeling that she knew it, as well.

"Same. Right after I had this interview with a pretty girl and she gave me the cold shoulder."

"I guess that was a common reaction to you back in the day," she said with a grin.

"Only your reaction. I was determined to get to the top and then wow you with my skills."

She smiled. "You did when you hit the half-pipe. I've seen you run moguls, and you are good."

"Good enough to let me steal a kiss?" he asked, waggling his brows at her.

"Not today, Carter. Maybe if I make it to the bottom

of the hill, I'll *think* about kissing you good-night after we hit the clubs."

"That's a long time," he grumbled. "I'm not sure I can wait."

"I think you'll do just fine."

They'd reached the top and got off the lift. She looked over at him, and he remembered his promise. He'd had no idea it would be so hard to leave her. Especially not with that look in her eyes.

"I'm out of here," he said, but walked over to her and kissed her quickly on the lips before stepping back and putting his boots in his board. He clicked the buckles and pushed off with a grin. "You'll have to catch me to yell at me."

LINDSEY TOOK HER time getting her booted feet into her skis. The kiss from Carter... It had been nice and really not much of a surprise. His confession that he'd wanted to impress her hadn't been, either. They'd been doing that since they'd met.

She'd counted on her own feelings of not wanting to let him see her freak out to get her down the mountain. She thought of all the runs she'd taken in her life, and this one wasn't nearly the hardest or most dangerous but it was in her head.

She took a deep breath when she realized she'd been breathing in and out too quickly. She remembered New Year's Eve when he'd sat at her table and she had felt that tingle of excitement. She wanted to be that woman again.

The one who could take on anything and beat it.

She closed her eyes and offered up her little prayer, and then pushed her sticks in the ground at the same moment as she opened her eyes. She froze and forgot to crouch and was kind of awkwardly bumbling along down the slope until everything sort of clicked together.

She felt the wind on her face, and the poles started to feel right in her hands as she adjusted her stance and leaned into her run. She was skiing. *Oh. My. God.* She was on skis again and taking a run.

She didn't do anything fancy, just kept her wits about her and tried not to think of all the possibilities that were opening up to her after this. This was one of the major things keeping her in limbo, and she felt as if she'd just ripped off her last bandage and found that she didn't have a scar.

She reached the bottom of the run and skied to a stop next to Carter, who was standing there with his goggles pushed up on his head. Then she pushed hers up, too, and launched herself at him.

She caught him off guard, and he fell back onto the snow as she kissed him. Heart thudding wildly in her chest, she feathered kisses all over his face and then lifted herself up to look down into that intense blue-gray gaze of his.

"I skied."

"I saw you," he said, his voice husky.

He hugged her close, and she realized without Carter she might not be here. She looked down at him again and saw the man she'd known for all of her adult life, but she also had the feeling she was seeing him for the first time.

She'd had sex with this man, but lying in the snow on top of him after taking a run that she'd never thought she'd be able to again, she finally realized that she'd had him pegged all wrong. This was intimacy. This sharing of something that went beyond the physical.

It scared her, but it also exhilarated her, and there

was no way she was going to keep him at arm's length after this. She wasn't sure how long the magic of having Carter with her was going to last, but she intended to ride it for as long as she could.

She lowered her head and brushed her lips against his—a soft sort of thank-you to the man who'd pushed her and forced his way past all of her barriers until he got her to do the very thing that had been scaring her for way too long.

He smiled up at her, looking smug, as though he knew that he'd done something for her that she couldn't have done for herself.

"Caught ya," she said at last, reaching past him and scooping up a handful of snow.

"Dang it. Now I'm going to have to put up with more kisses," he complained.

"Not just kisses, Carter. I'm afraid you stepped over the line. I did warn you," she said, rolling over and shoving the handful of snow into the crook between his neck and shoulder.

He yelped and scooted back from her. He grabbed a handful of snow and lobbed it at her. She laughed as she unbuckled her skis and gathered more ammo to hurl at him. She kept throwing snowballs and ducking his until he rushed her. Scooping her up into his arms, he kissed her, and this time it felt real. Not a dare, not a thank-you, but that red-hot lust that always lurked beneath the surface whenever he was around.

"Enough, gorgeous," he said, letting her slide down his body and lacing his fingers through hers. "I'm proud of you. I knew you could do it, and you proved yourself."

She swallowed hard. "I didn't know I could. Thank

you, Carter. You always know just what to do to nudge me out of my comfort zone."

"I intend to do a lot more nudging tonight when we are out with my friends," he warned her softly. "I think you've been the Ice Queen for too long and you're over-due for a thaw."

She arched a brow. "I think you know that I'm not always icy."

"I do, and I like it."

They walked back to the rental building and Carter said goodbye to her. She watched him walk away, and this time he glanced back over his shoulder and winked at her before he disappeared around the corner.

12

THERE WAS ONE more week of the Sundance Film Festival in Park City, so the bars were crowded with some celebrities and a lot of film industry insiders. There were a few people she had met at the big winter games last year but Lindsey mostly avoided them. Instead she sat nestled on a high bar stool at a table jammed with people. Carter sat next to her with his arm casually draped over her shoulder.

She tried to be cool and casual, but this wasn't her kind of place and she felt uncomfortable. Plus, Carter was different here. It was as if he was aware of an image he had to project, or maybe a person he had to be, and he wasn't acting like himself.

If she'd been aware of that, she would have turned him down when he'd invited her to come along with him today.

Oh, who was she kidding? She would have been here anyway, because this afternoon after she'd skied she would have said yes to anything. There had been such a rush of adrenaline flooding through her, making her feel lighter than air.

That she could do anything.

"Another drink?" the cocktail waitress asked.

"Manhattan, please," Lindsey said.

"Vodka and Thunderbolt," Carter said. "A round for the table."

The waitress nodded and moved away. She turned to look at Carter, who wore an Oxford shirt with some sort of graffiti-style art on the left side of a snowboarder doing a "crippler"—an inverted 540 spin. He hadn't shaved, but that little bit of stubble on his jaw made him look roguish, and his hair was styled in that messy, casual way he always wore it.

"We have to show the sponsors some love," he said.

"I'm not drinking an energy drink and vodka. That kind of thing makes me feel weird. I mean inside."

He leaned in close to her. In his eyes she saw a hint of the guy who'd sat in her kitchen and played cards with her, but it was just a glimpse. "Don't tell, but me, too. I just order them and then leave mine on the table."

"Why?" she asked.

He tugged her to him as he leaned back from the table. It was as if they were cocooned together with the cacophony of noise around them.

"I have to order them. It's my image."

"But kids might buy into it. And they think you love those drinks, so they try it…"

"Damn. You're right." He winced. "But I can't change who I am now."

"Why not?"

"Because Stan and his company pay me a lot of money to do what I do. And I like it."

"So money makes it okay?" She was pushing because she was uncomfortable, she knew that. Maybe she should just let it go. Smile and be like the scantily clad energy drink girls, but she couldn't.

"Do you get off on being a buzz kill?" he asked.

"No. Sorry if my pointing out the truth is messing with your fun." She huffed.

"It's not," he said. "I'm just having a hard time being my usual self tonight."

She rubbed her finger over his stubble, liking the way it abraded her skin. She sat there thinking about her life and this year. Three weeks into January and already it felt as though things were changing.

"Maybe that's not a bad thing," she murmured. "I wasn't trying to slam your choices, Carter. Lord knows I've made a few of them that haven't been the best. I guess I'm feeling out of place so I'm not being my nicest."

He had the prettiest eyes, she thought. Especially when he leaned even closer and she noticed those little blue flecks in his irises.

"I like it when you're not all nicey-nice," he admitted. "And when have you ever made a bad choice? My entire amateur career I've heard how perfect Lindsey Collins is."

She doubted that. Her coach had pointed out every little flaw she had on every run she'd ever taken. Her mother thought her hair was too long. Her sponsor—a manufacturer of a beeswax-based lip balm—thought she needed to look Nordic and had asked her to wear blue contacts for her last photo shoot.

"Well, I'm far from perfect," she informed him. "And I have many regrets."

"Like what? Name one."

She sighed. "The things I regret most are maybe not

living as much as I should have. I mean, I'm almost thirty, and my twenties were spent training every day."

"I can't believe you regret that. Maybe because of the way your career ended you think you should have done something different..." Carter said.

Their conversation was just starting to get interesting, but their drinks arrived and he got pulled into a conversation with a Thunderbolt energy drink representative.

"Carter Shaw is hot, isn't he?" a tall, svelte redhead said as she sat next to her at the table.

"Yeah, he is. He knows it, too," Lindsey replied, turning toward the other woman. "You're Georgina Poirier, right? Stan's wife? I'm Lindsey, by the way. I saw you with Stan earlier but you and I haven't had a chance to meet."

They shook hands. "Nice to finally meet you," Georgina said. "And you're right—Carter does know how good-looking he is. I think that's part of his appeal."

Lindsey had to agree. Confidence was very attractive.

The rest of their group filed in, and Georgina left to chat with one of the Hollywood starlets who'd had the lead in the film screened at the film festival earlier today.

Lindsey slowly sipped her cocktail, feeling oddly out of sorts. Truth was, she wasn't enjoying this party as much as she had the one on New Year's Eve. It suddenly dawned on her that the reason was that she didn't have Carter's undivided attention. Then the band started playing, and the song was that catchy Pharrell Williams' tune "Happy."

She grabbed Carter's hand before she could think twice about it. "Dance with me."

He smiled at her and followed her out onto the dance floor. Moments later, when he pulled her close and they swayed to the music, moving their bodies together, Lindsey finally knew why she was here tonight. Finally, she admitted to herself that this was what she'd missed and what she craved.

She wrapped her arms around his broad shoulders and told herself that it was the only the music and the nighttime influencing her, but she had a feeling that she was lying to herself. Knew that she wanted Carter all the time, not just after midnight.

CARTER WAS FLYING HIGH on energy, and not the kind supplied by the Thunderbolt energy drink company. Stan and Georgina had left and he was free to do whatever he wanted. Lindsey was in his arms, the club was jumping and, as far as he was concerned, life was about as good as it could be.

He thought of what she'd said earlier about missing out on her twenties. In a way he'd done the same thing, but he wouldn't trade it for anything. Without that decade of really hard work he wouldn't know Lindsey and wouldn't be holding her tantalizingly close at this moment.

And she felt so good.

The music played on, and the two of them stayed on the dance floor for most of the night. She seemed lost in the music, and the moment they gyrated to the hip-hop beat until he couldn't resist her for another second. He pulled her off the dance floor and into the first quiet corner he could find.

He trapped her between the wall and his body. She wrapped her arms around his neck and pulled him closer to her until they were pressed together. Her breasts rubbed his chest; her thigh twisted around his leg. Her mouth under his, she kissed him in a way that made every other high he'd experienced in his life pale in comparison.

There was magic in her kiss, and he felt caught under her spell. She was tall, so he didn't have to bend to meet her mouth, and she never left any doubt that this embrace was hers. To the world it might seem as though he was surrounding her, but she'd been invading him body and soul. She'd taken up residence in those empty places inside him and he didn't question it.

Only wanted to let her have her way with him. Not just physically but emotionally, too. She made him want to be a better man. The kind of man that she'd be proud to call her own.

He knew they weren't close to being a couple, but he also knew that until he made a few changes she'd never want him to be her man.

But for tonight he was happy enough to let that go. To just let his hands slide up and down her torso, caressing her through the blouse she wore. She moaned and bit his lip with delicate force.

He groaned as all of his blood rushed to his groin, and he knew that every shred of logical thought was gone. Gone for the night at least, but maybe longer because this was Lindsey and all she had to do was to crook her little finger and he would follow her wherever she led.

That was dangerous. But it didn't matter. All he wanted to do was to keep kissing and caressing her. To do whatever he had to do to stay right there in her arms.

He lifted his mouth from hers, buried his fingers in her soft, silky hair and dropped kisses on her neck. He felt her fingers moving over the tattoo on his neck, and then her mouth was there, her tongue tracing the lines, and then she suckled at the base of his neck as she arched her body against his.

He thrust back before realizing that things were getting out of hand. This was Lindsey, not the kind of girl he wanted to screw in the hallway of a bar. He pulled back but she held on to him.

"Let's get out of here," he said.

She seemed startled when she realized they were still in the club. She nodded, and they went back to the table to grab their coats before weaving through the crowd to get outside. He thought the cold January air would help cool him down, but it didn't.

Not for Lindsey, either. As soon as they were out of the doorway and in the puddle of darkness between the streetlamps, she pulled him back into her arms.

He went willingly, holding her to him with his hands on her butt, anchoring her firmly to his growing erection. Her mouth moved over his, her tongue rubbing over him, and he couldn't help but rub sinuously against her in the same motion.

These weeks without Lindsey had been too long. He was trying to remember his plan. He wanted to be more than a hot lay for her, but right now his body didn't care and his mind was outvoted.

He braced his hands on the wall on either side of her head and seduced her slowly with his mouth. She pushed her hands inside his coat, caressing his chest and moving lower. She stroked him through the fabric of his jeans, her hand moving up and down, and she tore her mouth from his to look up at him with eyes dilated with passion.

"I want you," she said. "You make me forget everything except what you feel like inside me."

He shuddered and almost came right then. He needed

her desperately. But not out here on the street. He stepped
back, grabbed her hand and led her to the parking lot
where he'd left his SUV. He opened the door and lifted
her onto the seat. She pulled him into her arms, wrapped
her legs around his hips, and he thrust against her once.

"Get your seat belt on, gorgeous. We need to get home
in record time."

She nodded and he closed the door, going around to
the driver's side as quickly as he could. He stood there
for a minute, looking up at the stars as he took several
calming breaths. But the fire she'd started in him wasn't
about to be abated.

He got behind the wheel and she put her hand on
his thigh, moving closer to his erection. Pulsating with
need, he let her caress him as he drove through the town,
thankful the traffic was light.

LINDSEY FOLLOWED CARTER into his hotel room. He held
her hand loosely, but the drive from the town to the lodge
hadn't lessened her passion. Today had been another one
of those points where she knew there was no going back
to her old life. They'd happened at different times—the
first when she'd been invited to train with the national
team and had move out of her family home at twelve.

But this was different. This was Carter and that hot,
hard sexy body of his. She wanted to make it about sex.
To balance out the developing feelings she had with him
and try to manage it. To lessen the impact of what he
was coming to mean to her.

He dropped his keys on a table near the door and
hauled her against him. She stopped thinking. Instead
she felt as though she was right back in his arms with
the electric pulse of the music surrounding them. She

grabbed the sides of his shirt and pulled him closer to her, arched her body against his as she had earlier and lifted her head to meet his mouth, which was coming down to claim hers.

He let her take control just as he had before, and she felt a trickle of warmth flow inside her. Felt everything feminine that had once been buried beneath being an athlete now rising up and taking over. She devoured his mouth as she rubbed her hands over his chest and found the buttons of his shirt. She had it undone and pushed off his shoulders in less than a minute.

She caressed his shoulders and down his arms, feeling them flex as he wrapped an arm around her waist and lifted her off her feet. He was strong. Stronger than she'd expected him to be. She wrapped her fingers around his biceps as he set her on her feet and flexed his muscles again.

"Like my guns?"

She nodded. She continued caressing his bare chest as he flicked on a lamp on the nightstand and she realized they were in his bedroom. She undid his jeans and pushed them down his legs, wanting him naked. Needing to keep this in the context that she'd tried to assign it. She didn't want to notice the picture on his nightstand of the two of them from New Year's Eve. Didn't want to admit that this was so much more than just sex.

But it was too late. A flood of emotion washed over her. Gratitude for how he'd seen past her ice-queen facade and lust at seeing his face harden with desire for her. He wanted her. He made her feel as if she was the only girl in the world. And that shouldn't make her heart feel fuller…but somehow it did.

She pushed him backward and he fell onto the bed.

She pulled her shirt up over her head and tossed it aside, then shimmied out of her jeans and underwear. He lay on the bed naked and staring at her. There was something on his face; a quiet emotion that she couldn't identify. She knew that he was used to women.

The way he'd driven here at that high speed worried her, dimmed a little of her joy. But she pushed that aside. He wasn't a saint. He was a man.

Human, with all the faults that went with that. And he wanted her.

"Are you going to just stand there?"

"For a minute. It's not often that I can enjoy you naked and quiet. Totally at my mercy."

"Gorgeous, you've got about three seconds before I'm going to lose it and have my way with you."

She smiled at him and climbed onto the bed, straddling his lean body. She sat on top of his thighs. "Is this better? More what you had in mind?"

"Hell," he growled. "It's better and it's not."

He reached up for her breasts, cupping them in both of his hands, and she arched her back, thrusting them at him. Then she slid up his body until she could rub her moist center over his long, hard erection. It felt good as she rocked against him, and he shifted his hips, thrusting up toward her.

Pulse fluttering in her throat, she leaned over him and fused her lips with his. He pushed his tongue into her mouth, and she sucked hard on it as she rocked her hips and felt the tip of his cock at the entrance of her body. She slipped down just a bit so that he was barely inside her and moaned at the feeling. At the anticipation of being filled by him. And then she spread her thighs and glided all the way down on him until he was deeply seated inside her.

His hands slid to her waist, and he lifted his back off the bed, finding her nipple with his mouth as she moved on him. Pulled them both deeper into the web of lust and arousal. She leaned back, bracing her hands on his thighs as she continued to move.

He suckled harder at her breast and then bit lightly at her nipple, and she felt the first fingers of her orgasm shivering down her spine. She arched more frantically against him. Trying to take him deeper until everything inside her clenched and she climaxed hard. He pulled his mouth from her breast and thrust up into her three more times before she felt the warmth of him fill her.

She wrapped her arms around his shoulders, still moving her hips against his as they both slowly came down. He held her close, his hands tangling in her hair as he kissed her until their breathing slowed and they both returned to themselves.

Falling on his side, he cuddled her close. "I've missed you."

13

THE ADMISSION SLIPPED OUT, but Carter didn't want to take the words back. Deep down he had missed her and the realness he experienced when he was with her. He knew that it would be easy to say he could be himself around her, but that wasn't exactly true. With Lindsey he could be the man he wanted to be. He didn't have to be on his guard with her.

True, they competed, but with her it felt good. As though they were both doing it from a kind place, unlike some other people in his life.

"You have?" she asked.

"Never mind," he said, getting up from the bed and going into the bathroom. When he came back a few minutes later, she was sitting on the side of the bed looking at the picture of the two them.

"Where did you get this?"

"The hotel gave it to me," he said. "If you'd stuck around that morning you would have seen it."

She pursed her lips. "True. Why is it on your nightstand?"

"Because I like it," he said curtly. He'd already said

he missed her—what else did she want from him? To admit that he felt something for her he'd never experienced in any of his other relationships? He knew that was the truth, but telling her wasn't exactly something he fancied doing.

"Fair enough. And I'm sorry for what I said, Carter. I've…missed you, too. I think you scared me when you said it," she admitted. "Because the truth is, I've been thinking about you too much."

"And why's that a bad thing?" he asked, moving to sit next to her. Nothing was easy with her. And a part of him thought that was probably the way it should be. His father had always espoused the fact that value was only placed on the things he had to work hard to have. But just this once, he wanted Lindsey and him to have something easy.

"It just is," she said. "Like I've said before, I'm figuring out a bunch of stuff. Each day, even over these past two weeks, I can feel myself changing. And you're part of it. But none of it is real. It's that discovery of a life I'd thought I'd lost. But I'm also trying to find a new path."

When she gazed up at him, he could see a glimmer of uncertainty. Yet he saw hope and tenderness, too.

"And what I feel for you is strong. I meant it when I said I've spent a lot of time thinking about you."

"Me, too. That's why we can take this one moment at a time. Pretending we don't want each other or that this is never going to happen again is ridiculous. And if I know one thing about us, it's that we don't make dumb decisions."

"Speak for yourself," she said with a grin. "I'm not sure about being a team. You and me. I'm so used to being on my own."

"We wouldn't be a team per se, we'd be dating. We'd be a sort of couple."

"*Sort* of couple?" she asked. "How does that work?"

"However we want it to," Carter said. He knew himself well enough to know that he didn't do well with rules. He always wanted to break them. But with Lindsey he wanted to take things slow. No rushing in and just jumping. That was why he'd been careful about keeping his distance when he'd needed to and being himself around her.

"Okay, but just know that I might have to put distance between us. Skiing has always been my main focus, and I'm close to getting that back. I don't know how to balance anything with skiing."

He understood that. He'd known her for a long time, and she'd always been one of those people not distracted by the spectacle of international games or tempted to cavort with athletes from other countries. She'd gone to bed early, eaten well-balanced meals and skied.

That was it.

"I thought you wanted to maybe change that. Remember how you mentioned that your twenties were a blur?"

She nodded. "I do, Carter. But it has to be for me. If I figured out anything over the past year, it's that trying things for other people doesn't make me happy. And it's also not real." She blew out a breath. "I have to figure out skiing for myself, but I want you, too. I like this hot little thing we have and I don't want to lose it. Can you be okay with that?"

No. Hell no. "Sure. Whatever you need. I'm not a serious kind of guy anyway."

Liar.

He had turned into the biggest fraud…and why? She

had just said she didn't want anything serious. He knew this was karma. This was payback for all the times when he'd played fast and loose with a woman's feelings. And it sucked.

He was tired of talking, and would love for just a few moments to hold her in his arms and pretend that the facts he knew weren't real. Pretend that she was his and he could be with her all the time, not just in this unique little sliver of time when her guard was lowered and he was so desperate he'd say anything to keep her.

So he gave in to temptation.

He pulled her into his arms, tucked them under the covers, and she turned on her side to cuddle close to him. He stroked his hand over her hair as she rested her head over his heart and he felt the minute exhalation of her breath over his skin.

He knew this wasn't real. That it was a chimera of the one thing he craved most in the world at this moment, but he didn't give a damn.

She tipped her head and he looked into her sleepy brown eyes.

"I've missed you, too," she whispered. Then she lifted her head, dropped a quick kiss on his chest and went to sleep.

He lay awake until dawn crept in with its pinky-pearl color. In a way he felt as though he had everything he wanted in his arms, but at the same time she felt farther away than ever.

CARTER ASKED HER to put on the mask and get into his SUV. Given that he liked to play little bedroom games, she wasn't too sure what to expect.

"Are you going to ask me to take my clothes off?"

"Not yet," he said with a chuckle.

She felt his hands on her waist, and then he leaned over her, pulling the seat belt into position around her. She heard the door close, but all of her senses were hyperalert. She felt the breeze wrap around her the moment he opened the driver's door, heard the sound of the cloth of his jeans against the leather seats.

"No peeking," he warned softly.

"What are you doing?"

"I'm kidnapping you."

"Will there be a ransom note? My folks already think you are something of a bad boy."

He laughed, and she was reminded of how much she liked the deep timbre of his voice.

"No note. This is just between you and me. I'm sure we can come up with something for you to do in order to achieve your freedom."

"I'm not sure where you are going with this, Shaw, but I'm game," she said. And she was. She'd checked her inhibitions at the door when, almost a week and a half ago, she'd gone with Carter back to his place from the bar. Ever since then, they'd played sexy games with each other, trained with their teams for the big charity event kickoff and pretty much lived in limbo the way she had been for the better part of the past year.

The only difference was that Carter was with her now.

He put the SUV in gear, and at first she tried to keep up with the turns he made but soon realized she didn't know Park City or its surrounding area as well as she thought she did. He had some blues music playing on the radio, and the heat was cranked up, so she wasn't cold.

"Can I get a hint about this place?"

"You're going to be cold at first, but then you'll warm up and be hot and wet," he said in a deep, husky voice.

The images that came into her head were of the two of them kissing and making out in the little clearing where he'd taken her on New Year's Day. She still remembered that kiss in the snow and how it had changed everything for her.

"I get the cold, but hot and wet? Give me another hint."

"It'll feel like the Caribbean," he said. "But we're not flying anywhere."

He really wasn't helping her to figure out where they were going. "I guess I'll have to wait and see. What will we be doing there?"

"Something daring from your resolutions list," he teased.

"I hope it's not a cheese tasting," she said, wrinkling her nose. "I told you I'd start eating cheese when I'm ready."

He laughed. "No, not at all. That's one thing I'm happy to let you explore on your own."

Not cheese. She had put "try something new" on her list, but she had no idea what it would be. She racked her brain, thinking hard...then inspiration struck. It was something Elizabeth had mentioned just the other day. So why not borrow a page from her book?

"Carter, have you ever heard of picking a word for the year?" she asked. "Kind of a resolution, but more an attitude thing."

"I haven't, but it sounds intriguing," Carter said. "What word would you pick?"

"Something about returning to myself. But that sounds lame-o, doesn't it? Something better—maybe *rejuvenate*? Great, now I sound like a spa. What about you?" she asked. Surely he'd have an idea of something that might help her come up with a better word.

"Different," he said.

"Different? How?" She couldn't see how he'd done anything different this year from the years before. Except that he had retired from amateur snowboarding and had entered the professional realm.

"Just my attitude. Experiencing things that I wouldn't have before," he said. "I'm not sure how else to explain it."

She reached out and fumbled until she found his thigh and squeezed it. "I like it when you let me see the vulnerability behind that big ego of yours."

He put his hand over hers and squeezed. "That's your imagination, gorgeous. I'm always confident."

"Really?" she asked, but then chided herself. Of course he was. He hadn't fallen. He wasn't flawed and scared the way she was. He was decorated with his tattoos and his badass, can't-be-stopped attitude. In a way she resented him for that strength, but she knew that really she wanted it for her own. She wanted to claim it and find her way back to the top of the mountain instead of being on the bottom in a crumpled heap.

"Yes, really. If I feel myself slipping and doubt starts creeping in, I immediately push it out. I do the same with most of my emotions." There was a pause. "Well, the ones I can't control," he qualified.

She realized she was asking him questions she never would have if she wasn't wearing the blindfold. There was a freedom at not being able to see. It kind of made her forget her fears. In the dark she could divulge her secrets and ask him about his.

"What kind of emotions?" she asked softly. "I mean, I'm the Ice Queen, but even I can't keep my emotions locked up forever. That's why I don't usually get involved with anyone."

"That makes sense. It's easier to control them when you just don't experience it. But I have a quick temper and am passionate about a lot of things, so every day if I'm not careful I can be up and down." He tightened his grip on her hand. "That's one thing I like about you, by the way," he said.

"That I make you calm?" she quipped. "Must be my icy powers spreading."

"Nah, you make me want to impress you, so controlling my emotions is easier when I'm around you."

She liked that. Liked that she had an influence over him. Seemed only fair, since had a huge influence over her. She wasn't sure when it had happened but suspected it was that first day he'd taken her to the sledding hill. It made her feel as though, despite the way their relationship had started, it might have the seeds of something that could last. Ah, she hadn't seen that coming, but she did want this to last.

More than she dared to admit.

CARTER PULLED INTO the parking lot of the Homestead Crater near Park City. He'd seen this place on the internet a few weeks ago and had decided it would be a nice surprise for Lindsey. The past several days with her had been great, but most of the time he'd felt as if they were both working on getting her back on the slopes or training their teams. There was no time to just hang out and enjoy each other.

And he really wanted the chance to do that.

He turned off the engine and leaned over to kiss her. She'd been sitting there with the blindfold on, boldly asking him questions and sharing bits of herself that she normally wouldn't have. He had to remember that the blindfold seemed to work like some sort of truth serum where she was concerned.

"We're here, Linds."

"Great," she said, reaching for her blindfold.

She pulled it up over her eyes, and he was close enough that he saw her pupils dilate in the light. "Where's here?"

"Homestead Crater."

"I've never heard of it," she said, looking around the parking lot. "Looks like a hotel."

"It is. We're going to snowshoe to the crater, where they advertise ninety-five-degree water."

"Sounds like fun, but I don't have a bathing suit," she said.

"I brought one for you. I don't suppose you feel like changing in the front seat?" he asked casually. "I won't look."

"Somehow I'm not buying that. I'm sure they have a facility in the hotel.'

"It won't be as much fun," he said. "What if you put the blindfold back on? Would you do it, then?"

She laughed, and he bit his lip to keep from smiling. He liked seeing her forget about all the troubles of the past year. She seemed a lot like the woman he used to know before her crash.

"No. I'm not going to get naked in the front of your SUV, Shaw, so stop asking."

"Fine, be that way," he grumbled. "Just so you know, I was willing to do it, too."

"I bet. You are willing to get naked anywhere." She narrowed her eyes at him. "I saw some of those photos on the internet."

"What photos? Did you Google me?"

She clapped a hand over her mouth and shook her head.

"You did. Why did you do that?"

She shrugged. "Those two weeks I didn't see you I sort of missed you."

"Missed me? Well, I never thought I'd see the day," he said. "Tell me more."

She scooted back toward the door. "I thought we were over. I'm used to seeing more of you, and I just typed your name in once."

"Once? Surely more than that," he said, taunting her.

"Stop it, your ego can't take much more inflation. It was interesting reading the articles about you. I've never read that much of my own press. Have you read yours?" she asked.

He shook his head. He didn't mind press interviews and the like because it was the only way to get his sport more into the public consciousness, which they needed if it was going to continue to grow. But he never read it. When he'd first started, he'd read a few articles where they'd twisted his words totally out of context. He couldn't get them to change what they'd printed and had made a conscious decision to stop reading the stuff after that.

"I haven't. But I have read the articles about 'Skiing's Favorite Ice Queen,'" he said.

She flushed and shifted on her seat to put more distance between them. "I'm not anyone's favorite this year."

He put his hand on her shoulder and used his other hand to tip her face up toward his. "You're my favorite, gorgeous."

"You're just saying that because you think it might soften me up and maybe I'll get naked in your SUV," she said.

He laughed as though he could tell she wanted him to. But he knew he'd been serious. She was his favorite. He who'd never allowed himself to hold on to anything— or anyone—wanted her. Desperately. He'd always had the feeling that his life was like quicksilver, always changing, and he'd gone with the flow. But right now he wanted to pull her into his arms and never let her go.

He needed her with him, but that made him weak, and he wasn't going to be weak. There had to be a way to keep her close without losing himself. He shoved his feelings down as he always did and smiled.

Then he kissed her. A soft, slow, sweet kiss that he hoped showed her the emotions he'd never admit he had. But he wanted to. Not for the first time, he wished he was a different kind of man. Someone who would easily be able to share what was in his heart.

But he wasn't. He never had been. That just wasn't his style. And he had the feeling it might never be.

"We should go in and get changed so we're not late," he said after finally releasing her. "The person I spoke to said the guide left for the crater promptly." He opened his door, grabbed the bags from the back he'd put in earlier and handed one to Lindsey as she came around to his side. They walked into the hotel and he watched her enter the change room.

A few minutes later as they snowshoed out to the

crater, he wondered if they looked like a couple to the other people on the tour.

She didn't say much and neither did he. Part of him wanted to believe they were both just enjoying the majesty of the Utah winter, but another part knew that too much had been said.

He wasn't good at sharing, because every time he did, it ended up this way; further away from Lindsey than he had been before.

14

WHEN THEY GOT to the crater, Lindsey caught her breath. It was spectacular. The water was actually about seventy-five feet from the opening in the crater, and getting down to the water had been tricky. But now that they were here and the instructor was explaining the diving safety information, she couldn't contain her excitement.

She looked over at Carter and he smiled back at her. They were both treading water, and it was warm. Almost hot. It felt surreal being here with him.

They spent the next hour diving in the crater, and she saw some of the most spectacular sights of her life. Carter stayed next to her. A few times he reached out to tap her arm to point out the sunken wagon wheel and fake mermaid she might have missed.

While there weren't any fish due to the high calcium content, the dome over the cavern filled it with light. The crater was in the shape of an hourglass, and Lindsey followed the rugged arc of the walls. As she dived beneath the surface, she saw the chunky white surface of the wall that jutted out.

Finally they surfaced to sit on the edge of the pool

while the rest of their group finished diving. She looked over at Carter. His hair was rakishly slicked back, eyelashes thick and dark from the water, his body long and lean; she felt a spear of desire go straight through her.

If they were alone, she'd be tempted to climb onto his lap and start kissing him and not stop until he was buried deep inside her and she was riding him to completion. She blushed at the thought and felt the heat move up her neck and face.

"What are you thinking?"

"Nothing," she said. "This was a great idea."

"Thanks, but I'm pretty sure you have something on your mind besides diving," he drawled.

"I might, but it will have to wait. Unlike you, I'm not into exhibitionism."

"Who said I was?"

"*GQ* winter issue two years ago. It was on your turn-ons," she said.

He cocked a brow. "You read that?"

"I did. How else would I know that fact?"

"I just said that because the reporter was irritating me," he admitted. "I'd had a big fight with my board sponsor and it was pretty public and he kept trying to get me to bad-mouth them, which I wasn't going to do, so I said that instead."

She put her hands back on the tile behind her. Their worlds were weird. In one way they spent all their time training and trying to be the best in their sport, and then had to deal with sponsors and media. It was hard to balance it all, and she envied how Carter had always seemed to manage it.

"That was a clever way of keeping him from asking

about it. Plus, it probably got a bunch of new women to watch your sport," she said.

"Well, it didn't hurt," he responded. "Our sport has been like the bastard of winter sports for so long I'll do whatever I have to do to get more people interested in it."

"You're very outspoken. I remember when you first showed up at the training center and all the coaches weren't sure how to take you guys," she said. "You snowboarders were a group of really young athletes and coaches. No one really knew what you'd be doing." She paused. "But you've been a vital member of the winter sport family and have even brought some new events like ski moguls into the sport."

"It has been a long, hard fight," he agreed, "trying to get some respect."

"Why'd you do it?" she asked curiously.

"I like recognition as much as the next guy. My dad was impressed when I got my gold medal," he said. "Plus, I liked being part of the team that represented our country."

"Me, too. Most of the time I don't think about being from the US, but when we walked into the opening games and the anthem played, I really felt it. I wanted to win not just for me but for everyone back home."

He smiled at her. In that moment she realized there was a lot more to Carter Shaw than he wanted the world to see. He seemed like this tough badass, but in truth he was a softie just like her.

Their tour guide gathered them together for the hike back to the hotel. This time Lindsey didn't seem as distant from Carter as she had been on the way down. She reached for his hand and held it in hers as they walked back.

After they'd changed and she headed out to meet him

in the lobby, she noticed he was talking to a group of people but stopped when he saw her.

He waved goodbye to the group and walked over to her. He made her feel special. As though, despite her flaws and scars, she was enough for him.

IN THE WEEKS that followed their diving at the crater, Lindsey felt they'd fallen into a safe routine. She got up each morning and took a run down the bunny slope. Each time she felt paralyzed with fear at the top, but when she got to the bottom she felt exhilarated. She often met her friend Elizabeth for breakfast and then worked her shift at the school.

Carter was always in one of her classes. She wouldn't admit it to anyone, but she was starting to really care for him, and that worried her. This new life where she could only ski the easiest slope and where Carter was part of her joy was odd, but she liked it.

It was time for her last class of the day, and she skied out to meet the kids, a little disappointed when Carter wasn't there. Though he hadn't said he'd be at the class, this would be the first day he'd missed. These kids had been taking lessons for a while, and most them already had the skills they needed to ski. They were ready for something more advanced, as was she. She felt nervous, but made the decision after checking with their parents to take them to the ski lift for a moderate run.

This would be her first chance to try out something other than the bunny slope. She was nervous, of course, but having the kids along made her focus on them and not herself.

"This kind of thing must seem pretty tame to you,"

Courtney said as they got off the ski lift and readied to take their run down the mountain.

"Not at all. I love skiing, and when I'm on the snow I'm just happy to be there," she said. The words were press friendly and sound-bite worthy, but she realized that she meant them. This was what she'd needed.

And she didn't need Carter Shaw to do it. Not that she ever had, but she realized she'd sort of been leaning on him as a crutch.

Dan, one of the other instructors, had come along for the run and taken the first group of kids down the slope. The ski patrol was nearby and always on alert, so she wasn't worried. These kids were good skiers. She was more concerned her nerves might snap, but her fear of embarrassment was greater than her fear of a fall, and as she led the last group down the mountain, she felt a little of her old confidence returning.

She hadn't realized how much she'd missed it until this very moment. And when she got to the bottom, she knew that something significant had changed inside her. Everything was telling her to go to the top and take a run.

Lindsey released a sigh. She was a little freaked out that she hadn't heard from Carter all day. And there had been no answer to the texts she'd sent earlier. She wanted to take her run, but now she was worried about Carter.

This just wasn't like him.

Something had to be seriously wrong for him not to show up or to return her texts.

She stowed her skies and signed out at work. Changing out of her ski gear into a pair of faded jeans, a thick sweater and her Ugg boots, she decided to swing by his place to check on him.

But as she walked into the lodge and up the patio, she noticed a large group around the pools and hot tubs. Looked like a camera crew, even. They were probably filming a new commercial for the resort, but as she looked closer she recognized a couple of Thunderbolt women from the shindig at the bar a while back.

She started for the group, thinking maybe they knew where Carter was, when she saw him. Sitting in the middle of the hot steaming water with his arms around two bikini-wearing hotties. Her heart sank. She'd heard that expression before, but this was the first time she'd actually experienced it.

She felt light-headed, as though she wasn't all there, and then she felt her face turning red. This was so embarrassing. She'd been worried about him. She'd given up skiing to come find him because she'd thought that surely something must really be wrong.

And he was sitting in a hot tub with a bunch of women!

His laughter rang out over the pool area, and she clenched her fingers together. She felt stupid. As though she should have known this would happen. As though the relationship she'd thought they were building was just a thought on her side.

She almost went to confront him, but then Georgina caught her eye, and the look of sympathy on her face made Lindsey feel so small she just turned and walked away.

She didn't want to think about Carter Shaw. She got as far as the lobby where Elizabeth was talking to one of the front-desk staff. Her friend waved, but something on Lindsey's face must have showed her inner turmoil because Elizabeth rushed over.

"Are you okay?"

"I'm great," she said through clenched teeth.

"Uh, let's go get a drink and talk." Elizabeth wrapped her arm around Lindsey and led her to the bar.

Lindsey could only nod. She needed someone to talk to, and hadn't realized how much until this moment. She was used to keeping everything inside. Had made her reputation in skiing by being the Ice Queen... Maybe it was those months when she'd been here working and not practicing, but suddenly it felt as if she had no control over her emotions anymore.

She didn't like it, but she couldn't change it.

"What's up?" Elizabeth said once they had secured two empty seats in a corner of the cocktail lounge. "You look like... Well, if it was anyone else I'd say you look pissed off."

Lindsey nodded tersely. "I am."

"At who?"

"Carter Shaw."

CARTER HAD HAD a really long day, and when he was finally free of the corporate people his first thought was to go find Lindsey. She'd become his touchstone. The calmness in his crazy world. He'd hoped to make it to one of her ski lessons today but was disappointed he'd missed out on it.

"Hey, Carter, you got a minute?"

Georgina was one of Thunderbolt girls, though calling her a girl was a bit of a misnomer. She was his age and had been married to Stan Poirier, the owner of the Thunderbolt energy drink company, for a few years now. He liked her—she was nice enough and had always sort of had a way of making the overtly sexy ads he shot for her husband's company seem almost okay.

She also must have the temperament of a saint to put up with Stan's flirting. But there was some real love between those two, and somehow they must have figured out something that worked for them.

Carter wanted that with Lindsey. But he was honest enough to admit that he had no idea how to get it. He wasn't good at the normal days. He could do nights of sex and fun adventures, but the everyday living was harder.

"Actually, I was just on my way out," he said. He was anxious to find Lindsey. And, if he was honest, to wash away a bit of the fake attitude he'd had to step into to be the spokesman for Thunderbolt.

"It won't take long," she promised, leading him away from the others to a cozy couch set up in one of the alcoves in the long hallway in the lodge.

"What's up?" he asked as she sat and gestured for him to sit next to her. Sitting would mean this wasn't going to be as quick as he had hoped, but he complied.

"That woman you were with at the nightclub, Lindsey... I think she's an Alpine skier," Georgina started.

"Yes, she is. What about her?"

"She saw you filming. She didn't look too happy and I wanted to let you know before you went charging off to see her."

Ah, hell. That was the last thing he'd expected. "Thanks."

He started to stand, but she stopped him. "Do you want some advice?"

He just looked at her, and she smiled.

"Probably not, right? Who wants to listen to another

person when it comes to relationships? But I'm going to tell you about Stan and me. He's always interviewing those gorgeous girls. You know how they look at him, and he likes it. He likes that they fawn all over him."

"It's not like that for me," Carter said. "Lindsey makes all the rest of them pale in comparison."

"Good. Make sure you tell her that."

He studied Georgina for a moment. "Does Stan tell you that?"

"Not often enough," she confessed. "But I know he loves me."

"How?" Carter asked curiously. Women had sometimes mentioned the *L* word around him, but the truth was he'd never experienced it in a relationship. He loved his dad, but then the old man had been his only constant in his life. His mom had died giving birth to him, and it had always been just him and his dad. A part of him thought maybe the fear that gripped him when he thought of not having Lindsey in his life might be love.

Or maybe it was something else. He just had no idea.

"Stan shows me every day," Georgina explained. "Does special little things that he knows I like, and he always makes me feel like I'm the most beautiful woman in the world. I don't know if that will work for Lindsey, but it does for me." Leaning closer, Georgina reached out and patted him on the shoulder. "Every year those girls seem younger, and I feel... Well, that doesn't matter. I just wanted you to be aware of what she'd seen. I like her."

"I do, too. I'll explain that I had to do the photo shoot today."

She arched a brow. "You've known about it for weeks."

"I...I'm not really good with the relationship stuff," Carter admitted, releasing a frustrated breath.

"Don't try to pull that kind of BS with her."

It was funny that Georgina could see through it; most people just shrugged and assigned it to his snowboarder, live-free attitude. But she knew that it wasn't. He didn't like the fact that she could read him, and wondered if his mask was slipping now that he was spending so much time with Lindsey.

With her he felt as though he could be himself. But he didn't feel that way with the rest of the world. Certainly not with the Thunderbolt energy drink company. He needed to keep his guard up.

"I won't. Thanks," he said, standing.

He walked away from Georgina, but the farther he moved into the lodge, the slower his steps became. Talking to Lindsey wasn't going to be easy. He knew it. He should have mentioned it earlier, but he'd felt silly saying he was going to be in a hot tub with a bevy of twenty-somethings.

"Dude, you don't want to go to the bar," Bradley said, coming up behind him.

"Why not?"

"Lindsey is pissed about what happened earlier, and Elizabeth texted me to find you."

Great. "It was just a job."

"I get it, man, believe me, I do. But apparently Lindsey thought there was something wrong with you because you missed a class. She went from worrying for your safety to seeing you cavorting in a hot tub."

"Damn. I didn't think of it that way."

"Or maybe you did," Bradley said. "I know for me there are times when I need to know that I'm at least as

important to Elizabeth as the resort is. So I do stuff to
get her attention."

Was that what he'd been doing?

He knew each day she was getting more confident on
her skis and needed him just a little bit less. That was
something he couldn't tolerate.

15

"I'M SORRY," CARTER said as she opened the door to her condo. He'd texted her that he'd had to work and had just gotten her message. Then he'd asked if he could stop by her place and she'd said yes.

Lindsey was over her earlier upset and realized that if she was going to be involved with Carter she'd have to get used to seeing him with other woman. His biggest sponsor had a lot of those scantily clad girls. But she also knew that it was more complicated than that.

"It's okay. I was foolishly worried something had happened to you," she said. But it wasn't as if they'd had a standing appointment or anything like that, so a part of her felt that maybe she shouldn't have been so freaked out.

"I know. I should have mentioned the photo shoot but I just didn't… I felt like we were starting to feel too settled and that I had to tell you, so I didn't."

"It's fine. I get it." She gave him a cavalier smile. "Remember, we said we'd make up our own rules. So we don't have to share everything if you don't want to."

He stepped inside her condo, and she closed the door behind him. "The thing is, I think I want to."

Lindsey didn't believe him. She wasn't even going to pretend that his idea of being a sort-of couple could work for her anymore. He'd made it pretty plain that he wanted to sleep with her, and she liked that, but she knew that moving forward she was going to have to make sure she didn't start thinking of him as anything other than a lover.

"It's cool."

He shook his head, and she could see his jaw tighten "It's anything but cool. I was playing a game and it feels like I might have lost."

"We both did. We were both pretending that for the past weeks we lived in some sort of world where it was just the two of us. But the truth is, you still have a pro career and you need to dedicate a certain amount of time to it."

"I can see you've thought this through," he said quietly.

He leaned against the wall, and she couldn't keep the image from flashing through her mind of the last time he'd held her in his arms in a hallway. The way his mouth had moved over her lips, trailing hot, molten kisses down her neck before travelling slowly lower. How she'd lifted her arms above her head and stopped thinking.

That might have been dangerous.

She needed her wits to deal with Carter. To ensure she didn't forget the truth of who he was. Of who *she* was. While this was fun, that was all it would ever be, and she had to remember it.

She had to stop looking for him at her ski lessons and wanting to share her little successes with him. He was already putting her in one section of his life, and she needed to stay there.

"I have thought it through. I'm starting to ski a lot more. Today the class and I went down a moderate run, and I've called my coach to tell him I think I'm ready to get back to training. I don't know what the future holds for me, but I know I have to try skiing again."

"What about your other commitments?" he asked. "Your job at the resort and the charity event?"

She licked her lips and tipped her head to the side. "I'm going to take a part-time role at the resort and I'm still captaining the team. Lars thinks my return to the training should help boost our team's chances of beating yours."

He shoved his hands through his hair and exhaled roughly. "I don't want this to end."

"It's not. I'm sure there will still be moments of weakness on my part where I call you and ask you to stop by."

"Weakness?" His eyes flicked to her face.

"Yeah, weakness. I felt so upset seeing you today with those women. I get that it's your job and you're going to keep on doing it…but you didn't say anything to me about it. Didn't mention it, even though every night I talk to you all about my students."

"That's different."

"See, until today I didn't realize that." She swallowed a lump in her throat. "To me it felt like I was building toward something. Slowly pulling my life back out of the abyss where it had fallen, but then I had a wake-up call."

He moved closer to her and she stood her ground, not backing up or turning away, because this was too important. She'd hidden away from life when she'd lost her ability to ski, and Carter hadn't taken anything from her, but today she'd had a glimpse of what he could take, and she simply couldn't allow that to happen. Not again.

"What wake-up call?"

"That I'm more involved than you are," she accused. "It made me feel silly, especially when I'd thought that something must be wrong, that you'd had an accident or something. If it had been me, I would have let you know."

He cursed under his breath and turned away from her.

"Why are *you* so pissed?"

"Because you have it all wrong, Linds. I've been struggling this entire time to keep from letting you see how much you mean to me. How much I need you in my life." He turned back to her, reached for her, but she recoiled.

"What the hell…?" he asked.

"I can't think when you touch me, and I need to make sure I'm clearheaded."

"Fine. I haven't wanted to crowd you, and I guess that maybe I thought of today as a chance to see how much I mean to you," he said brusquely. "I shouldn't have done it, but I'm tired of always guessing where I stand with you."

He should have been better prepared for this but knew he had been hoping this would all blow over. It hadn't. And, in hindsight, it was probably for the best. This had been lurking under the surface for a while now for him. It had felt too unsettled. He knew that he was going to have leave Park City after the February event to kick off the charity to fulfill his Thunderbolt Extreme Winter Games duties, but he'd be coming back and forth for the next six months. He hadn't known how to ask Lindsey if she still wanted to see him.

"I'm not a coward," he said. "You're the one who's been afraid and hiding here. Not at the training center, but at a resort teaching little kids to ski."

"There's nothing wrong with what I've been doing. It takes time to recover from the kind of injury I had."

He knew that. He was just being mean because she'd cut a little too close to the truth with her comment. The fact was, he was scared. Scared of having his heart broken. He'd known he was in danger ever since they'd started sleeping together. She'd known it, too. He could tell by the way she had wrapped her arms around her waist.

"I know. That was horrible, and I have no idea how long it would take me to come back. You're sort of my hero for getting back on skis as quickly as you did," he said, shoving his hands through his hair again. "I don't want to fight with you, gorgeous."

"Me, either," she admitted. "I like you, Carter, but you've never really been serious about anything but snowboarding. Today, when I was searching for you, I realized how much you've come to mean to me."

"How much?" he asked, staring at her intently. He had to know. And he wanted her to go first and tell him that she cared so he'd feel that much safer admitting he felt the same.

"A lot. Too much," she whispered. "So much so, in fact, that somehow in my mind you and skiing have become intertwined. And that's dangerous."

He inhaled deeply. "It's like that for me, too. But I didn't want to admit it. I like all the time we've spent together and I'm scared of what will happen when I leave Park City."

He took a step toward her, and this time she didn't back away. And when he wrapped his arms around her and pressed his lips to her forehead, she didn't resist. Finally he had her where he needed her. He hugged her close and let out a small breath of relief. This was one of those little hiccoughs that couples went through. They'd get through this.

"When are you leaving?"

"Not until after our charity competition. I have other commitments that I have to fulfill…but I don't want this to end."

"Are you sure?"

"More sure than I've ever been of anything in a long time." Holding her close, he gently threaded his fingers through her hair. "It's ironic that it was me wanting to keep my professional life away from you that caused this. I've never had someone in my life that I've shared so much with before."

"Me, either," she said in that quiet way of hers.

"Can we start again?" he asked. "Third time might be the charm for us."

"How do you figure we had three times?"

"Seventeen, when I was a jerk. New Year's Eve, when you were…well, fabulous. And now this time when we are both ready."

"Okay," she said. "How about we grab dinner and talk?"

"I was hoping for something more physical."

"Sex?" she asked.

The way she said it let him know that if he said yes, it wouldn't be his smartest move.

"Not right now. I know a nice place where we can do some snowshoeing. It's not too far from here and might be perfect for tonight."

"Why?"

"Because we can forget about all the fears that are making a relationship such a struggle for us."

"Sounds perfect. Where is it?"

He pulled out his smartphone and glanced at the screen. "Not too far from here. One of these places groomed by the Mountain Trails Foundation. Ever heard of it?"

She took the phone from him and studied the screen, and he almost felt as if they might be okay. But he'd never had anyone in his life he feared losing the way he did with Lindsey. She was more than a lover.

That was hard for him to admit, but he knew it was the truth.

"I haven't. But it sounds like fun."

Suddenly his stomach growled. "Have you arranged for dinner?" he asked.

"I have a pizza on the way," she said, leading the way into her kitchen.

She got out drinks for them while he called to make an appointment. "Can you go tomorrow night?"

"I can," she said.

He finished the arrangements and the pizza arrived. They sat at her table eating and he realized that she wasn't talking. That maybe just because he'd thought everything was okay, it wasn't.

"Tell me about your lessons," he said. "I had planned to make the last one but then the shooting ran over."

Her eyes lit up. "That class was awesome. Some of the kids were getting restless—you know they are more advanced than some of my other ones—so I decided to take them on a run."

"You did? Which one?"

She gave him a smile that cut him all the way to his soul. So much joy and pride in her look that he knew he was falling for her. That her joy could be his was the first indication. But it wasn't the only one. How he'd planned to stay here until he could get back in her good graces was another one.

"A moderate one. Not a world-class trail, but it was close, and I wasn't scared this time. I mean, I was at the top, but once I started skiing it was like old times. I got into my stance and just sort of felt everything fade away."

"Gorgeous, that's great! Tomorrow morning we're going up the mountain."

LINDSEY LEFT A note for Carter to meet her and left early to meet Elizabeth for breakfast. They'd started the tradition when Lindsey had first started working at the resort and had kept it up even through the holidays and new relationships. Last night in the bar, she'd been so out of control with her feelings that she hadn't really been able to talk.

They sat in the main dining room at the lodge, the Wasatch Range standing majestically in the distance. Lindsey was playing with her food more than eating it.

"I don't think a night's sleep has helped you," Elizabeth said.

"It hasn't. If anything I'm more confused now than ever," she admitted. It was hard to talk about her feelings. She just wasn't the kind of woman who had ever done a lot of sharing.

On the team where she'd spent most of her life, everyone had been focused on their own goals. Sure, they'd discussed good runs or new products, but they'd never really talked about their real lives. Elizabeth reached over and squeezed her hand. "What's on your mind?"

"Stuff," Lindsey said. "Honestly, I can't make any sense of it. There's a part of me that wants to believe that Carter has changed, and I've changed enough to give him a shot, but then there's this other part that's too afraid to believe it. And I'm stuck not knowing which is right."

Elizabeth took a sip of her coffee. "I'm betting the truth is somewhere in between all of that. Maybe you are looking for an easy answer where there isn't one. I'm far from an expert on relationships—believe me, Bradley would be the first to say that—but I have discovered that you have to be honest with yourself, with your heart. Otherwise you will be miserable."

Lindsey took a bite of her omelet and wondered what her heart wanted. She knew she cared for Carter. She couldn't deny it after the blind panic she'd felt the day before when she couldn't find him. But love? She was afraid to admit to it. In her life she'd loved two things: her family and skiing.

Right now she was struggling to find her way back to skiing and felt as though she was on the right path. What she felt for Carter wasn't really like that. She had no idea how to define it or him. She just knew that when he'd showed up at her place last night, she'd felt a sense of relief mixed with joy.

"How do you know what the heart wants?" she asked Elizabeth. If there was one woman in the world who seemed to have it all, it was her friend. She needed some guidance here. Because she'd been out of the game of love for too long.

"Only you can say. When Bradley called me, even before we were dating, I'd get really excited. I couldn't wait to talk to him, and I pretended we were just friends and that was all I wanted, but I knew I needed more from him."

It was different for her and Carter. She'd never felt anything toward him except for faint amusement and a little bit of irritation before New Year's Eve. She'd needed this year to be different. Vastly different from last year, which, if she was completely honest, she could say was happening.

The problem was, as much as she wanted to change, she kept getting tripped up on the fact that she had no idea how to really handle it. How to handle Carter. Jealousy would have been easier to deal with, but the truth was that it had been more than jealousy she'd felt at those other women. Something deep inside her had been awakened and she'd wanted to claim him. To tell those girls and everyone else that he was hers.

And that was far from the truth.

"Thanks," she said.

"I didn't help, did I?" Elizabeth replied with a very kind smile.

"No. But I'm beginning to believe this is something that I have to figure out for myself."

"The toughest decisions are. But that's the way it should be, since you're the one who has to live with the consequences."

Consequences. She had left him this morning, and it had been hard. He was leaving soon to get back to his touring schedule and his new professional life. He'd said last night that he didn't want to lose her, but she knew him better than that.

Eventually he would move on.

And where would that leave her?

Lindsey took a sip of orange juice to wash away the parched feeling in her throat. She should put some distance between them now, instead of skiing with him and asking him to stay the night at her place.

"I guess you must really like him," Elizabeth said, "if you are that confused about what to do."

She did like him. A lot. But as with all the other things in her life that she wanted, he was right out of her grasp. He wasn't like skiing, something she could train for and master. He was always going to keep her guessing and trying to keep up with her own feelings.

She had to cut her ties to him, and she had to start doing it now.

"Sure, what's not to like? Carter is sexy, charming and just the sort of guy a woman uses as a distraction."

_16_

CARTER WOKE UP feeling pretty good. He'd done just enough to get Lindsey back in his bed where he wanted her. Or, as it was in this case, his bed. He saw her note and swung by his place to shower, change and collect his snowboard. Hitting the slopes with Lindsey was going to be fun.

It felt right in his bones to be doing this with her, and after yesterday's setback, he was ready to move forward. He hoped that he didn't have to talk about his emotions ever again.

That had easily been the scariest moment of his life. He smiled at the valet as he tossed his keys to him and stopped by the little counter-service café off the lobby for a coffee before heading into the main dining room to find Lindsey.

He saw her sitting with Elizabeth near one of the windows. They were talking intently, and he felt something shift and settle in his soul. She was his. Lindsey looked pretty with her long blond hair hanging loose around her shoulders. She wore a pair of leggings and a long sweater, and when she talked she gestured with her hands.

He stood there in the shadows, just watching her, almost afraid to believe that he'd somehow convinced her to take a chance on him. The guy that the world saw as never serious about anything had a very serious crush on her.

His ice queen.

He'd melted her, and in return found that she had melted him. A part of that would never be the same again.

He took a sip of his coffee as the maître d' came over to see if he wanted breakfast.

"Nah, I'm fine. I'm going to surprise those ladies."

The other man nodded, and slowly Carter made his way through the tables. There weren't that many people in the restaurant this morning. He noticed Georgina and Stan were sitting quietly together, and he thought of how it took all types of relationships. That there wasn't just one kind of relationship or one answer to how they worked.

Maybe even someone like him could find true happiness with Lindsey.

"He was a distraction," Lindsey said.

He paused. Was she talking about him?

"Are you talking about me?"

She glanced over her shoulder; all the color left her face and she bit her lower lip.

"Carter, how nice to see you this morning," Elizabeth said quickly.

But he wasn't interested in being sociable or pleasant right now. Unless he was wrong—and let's face it, he wasn't—Lindsey had pretty much just relegated him to booty-call status. Well, hell. He'd been thinking they were something special and she was getting ready to show him the door?

"We're you talking about me, Lindsey?" he asked again.

She turned her face down and wouldn't meet his gaze. "Yes, Carter, I was."

He didn't know what else to say to that. And he hadn't been expecting her to admit it—especially not in front of Elizabeth.

"I thought we were past that." He gritted the words out. "Didn't last night mean anything to you?"

She stood. "I don't want to talk about this now."

"That's too bad," he said, blocking her path. "Your *distraction* isn't going to be just brushed aside as easily as that."

"Carter, please. I don't think this is the right time."

"Too bad. I'm tired of running after you and never feeling like I'm good enough. You know that you can't keep me dancing to your tune forever."

"You haven't been dancing to anyone's tune except your own," she said, her temper flaring. There was a red flush on her cheeks as she stepped forward, pushing her finger at his chest. "We aren't normal couple material. You have a life that takes you around the world, I don't. I'm here working and trying to figure out—"

"Figure out what? How to not be afraid of the one thing that makes you special?" Sure, he had weaknesses, but she did, too. How could she not see that with her, he was different? With Lindsey he had a shot at being the man he'd always wanted to be but had never been able to figure out how.

As soon as the words left his mouth, he knew he'd

gone too far. She shoved her way past him. He wanted to take it all back. To pull her into his arms and apologize, but he couldn't. He knew he should, but he wasn't built that way. And the farther out of his grasp she moved, the meaner his thoughts became.

"Don't walk away like that," he said.

She shook her head, and he saw the sheen of tears in her big brown eyes…but she didn't let them fall. "At least I have something that makes me special and I'm not afraid to admit it."

What the hell did she mean by that? "I'm not hiding."

"Yes, you are hiding. Everything you do is another barrier to keep everyone from seeing the real man. The boy I met at seventeen already had those barriers in place, so I wonder if you even know who you really are anymore."

She'd cut a little too close to the bone with that observation, and later on he'd feel the bruising, not just to his ego but also to his soul. But right now he was too busy trying to even the score and make sure she walked away as deeply hurt as he was.

"You're not seventeen anymore, either, and maybe hiding away in Park City isn't the solution for you," he said harshly. "You fell. So what? A lot of skiers fall. You were injured and now you're better. It's time you stopped hiding."

He'd gone too far again, and this time she didn't look as if she was going to cry. Instead it seemed she might actually hit him. "Congratulations, Carter, you've ceased being a distraction and become an irritant. And one I'm happy that I am able to walk away from."

"Just like you walk away from everything else in life whenever it doesn't come easily to you," he said.

"At some point, gorgeous, you're going to have to stop running scared."

"Screw you, Carter."

LINDSEY WAS HUMILIATED, angry and hurt. She strode out of the restaurant and away from Carter and all the people who'd witnessed their argument. God knew no one was going to refer to her as the Ice Queen after that outburst.

She was shaking and felt as though she might be sick, so she sat on one of the chairs dotted along the hallway. She put her head in her hands and felt as if she wanted to cry, but the tears wouldn't come.

There were a lot of times when she had cried. The day they'd told her she'd need surgery. The day she'd gone back and found out she'd need a second surgery and a long recovery period. But this was the first time a man had made her feel this way. She wondered if she'd started the fight and pushed him away because it was easier to be alone than to figure out how to be with him.

In one preemptive strike she'd made sure she didn't have to worry about him or who he was with when he was away from her. She'd pretty much made sure she'd never have to see him or talk to him again.

It was difficult for her to clear away the anger. But once she did, she knew that if she hadn't been trying to save face with Elizabeth and called him a distraction, none of this would have happened.

She also knew that it had needed to happen. There wasn't any path for the two of them. She knew that now.

She was flawed…but that wasn't why she'd started the fight with him. She should have just been comfortable enough to tell him how she felt. That she was riddled with uncertainty, but admitting that she didn't know what she was doing still wasn't easy for her.

Especially with Carter.

She heard footsteps, and looked up to see one of the families from her ski lessons.

"Morning, Miss Lindsey," Jeremy said.

Oh, crapola. Had they witnessed her fight with Carter? She forced a smile, grateful to have an excuse to slip behind her iron wall once again. "Morning, Jeremy. Mr. and Mrs. Smith. How are you today? Looking forward to our lesson?"

"I'm good. We are going for a toboggan ride this morning," the boy said.

"Jeremy loves your lessons," Mrs. Smith said. "I know you probably get asked this all the time, but can he take a picture with you?"

"Sure," Lindsey said.

Jeremy came over to her, and she wrapped her arm around his little shoulders and leaned in and smiled. The same fake smile she'd used for years after defeats at world-champion events. And it seemed to fool them as they smiled and waved goodbye.

She sat back in the chair and realized that if she could find away to slip back into that persona as her normal, everyday self, she'd be fine.

Yeah, right.

"So, um, maybe you were right about not talking in the restaurant," Carter said from where he stood across the hallway.

She'd been too caught up in Jeremy and his family to notice that he'd arrived. She hated that she'd said those mean things, but she knew under her anger there was a kernel of truth. For him as well, she thought.

"I'm sorry," she whispered.

"I'm not," he retorted, flashing that familiar smirk. "I put 'big embarrassing fight with Lindsey' on my resolutions list."

She shook her head. "Glad I could help. I'm good at that."

"Just like I like being a distraction," he said, coming over to sit next to her. "That hurt."

"I know. I'm sorry," she said. "It's not something I would have said to you."

He lifted a dark brow. "Then why did you say it to Elizabeth? She's my friend, too."

She knew that. She'd said it because… Those reasons didn't matter to her right now. "I don't know. I just felt it was one more thing in my life that I had no control over and I hated it." She took a breath, let it out. "It's hard to deal with the way I feel for you. I know we hashed things out last night, but this morning it feels even more messed up than ever. I like sex with you. That part feels safe and okay, but the emotions and how tied you are to my skiing… I don't like it."

"What are we going to do?" he asked.

"You could maybe not always seem like everything works out for you. You act like nothing that happens between us fazes you," she said.

"Of course it does," he admitted. "I'm always running and trying to catch you, Linds, and you are always just out of my reach."

She didn't believe that for a minute. He had been there when she needed him, seen her at her worst, and always seemed so with it and cool. As if he was rolling on through life just as he had planned.

"It doesn't seem that way," she told him quietly. "I wish you had some flaws like me."

"I have more flaws than you, gorgeous," he said. "Everyone knows that."

"You still have your career. You seem great at everything you try—even skiing—and I have to admit I was sort of hoping you wouldn't be."

"What can I say? I've always been good on the snow. You know…" Carter shrugged. "'The cold never bothered me anyway.'" He sang the line from the Disney movie with a smile. "That's why I've always been drawn to you."

He was playing again. Trying to lighten the mood…to distract her from her very real fears. She knew that was why she'd started the fight today. He wasn't just a distraction to her anymore. He hadn't been for a while, and she was afraid to admit to herself how much she needed Carter. She was serious—too serious about her life and about having him in it. Her biggest fear was that to him she was a temporary stopover. And once he moved on, she'd be left alone again.

He FELT THAT he was losing again. Last night he'd dodged the bullet and hadn't had to bare his soul, and now it felt as if he might have shortchanged himself by not doing that. But her doubts were spurring on his, and he no longer felt as confident as he had when he'd woken this morning in her bed.

Alone in her bed.

Maybe that had been some sort of sign that he was too blind to see. He stretched his arm along the back of the seat and released a ragged breath. He wanted to hold her. To pull her into his arms, kiss her until she was aching for more and somehow fix everything that was broken between them. But he was afraid that he couldn't.

That maybe there was no way for things to be fixed between them.

"Singing isn't your strong suit," she said at last in that quiet way of hers that really revealed nothing of her inner thoughts.

His lips twisted ruefully. "I guess it wouldn't be fair if I could sing when I've got all this going on."

"Probably," she said, slouching back against the arm of the seat and looking over at him. "What are we going to do now?"

"I don't know," he admitted. "I want to shrug this off and pretend that nothing happened, but we are both wounded by what we said. I'm sorry, too, by the way. Is there a way we can move forward from this?"

She tipped her head to the side, studying him. "Only if you are honest with me. You said that life isn't as easy for you as it seems. Show me the real Carter."

The real Carter. Did that man even exist? He had been pretending for so long that he almost thought that this guy was the real man. But he knew that he wasn't. He knew from the way he'd been chasing after Lindsey, that each time she walked away from him he wanted something more.

"What's real? I want you in my life," he said.

"I know that. Why?"

How to put into words what he could barely understand as emotion. It was almost beyond him, and as he sat there in the quiet hallway he understood for the first time the real meaning of fear. He'd thought he'd experienced it before, but it paled compared with this. "You know how everyone in the world has an image of you?"

She nodded.

"Well, for me, I've always seen that beyond that you were this girl who wanted something more. You weren't icy because you thought yourself above everybody." He looked into her eyes. "You were cold because unless an endeavor improved your skiing, you didn't bother with it. I liked that."

"Why?"

He sighed. "You know how everyone thinks that nothing bothers me and I just keep rolling on?"

"Yes. That's why I want to know what you feel," she said.

"Well, I am the same as you. Underneath that, I do what I have to do to get back to the important stuff. I've always thought if we ever both dropped our guard, we'd have a lot in common and be a powerful pair. I've never told anyone, but I have dyslexia. It was hard for me to overcome."

"But we can't be," she said sadly. "We'd both have to change to do that."

"Change?"

"Yes, you can't give up your persona and I can't give up mine." She sighed. "I realized that when I saw you yesterday in that hot tub."

"*That* again? I thought we had settled it."

"We did. I understand that you aren't really interested in those other women, but that's your persona. Nevertheless, I can't be in a relationship with someone like that," she told him.

"Careful, you're starting to sound like I'm a distraction again," he said. He had that sinking feeling in his gut that no matter what he said, Lindsey was slipping further and further away from him.

"You are one. You have been great for motivating me to get back on my skis, and I'm not going to pretend I'd be as close to contemplating the Super G again without you, but at the same time we just don't fit together."

"We fit together just fine when you stop worrying and just let us enjoy our time together." He reached down and brushed his thumb over her lips, then clasped her chin in his palm. "What was it that spooked you this morning?"

She jerked away, as if his touch had singed her. "I'm not going to fight about this. I don't want to say anything else that is mean to you."

"Why not? Clearly you are okay with thinking them. So let's be clear here," he said, narrowing his eyes at her. "You are pushing me away for nothing other than your ego. Because you don't want to be the woman who is confident enough in herself and in her man to be with me. Be with that public image of me."

She nodded. "You're right. I'm not. Ego isn't my thing the way it is yours. I have tried to do this every way possible, but I keep coming back to the fact that you and I make no sense."

Except in his heart. "Lindsey, please. I can give up my sponsorship if it will make you stay with me."

She smiled at him, and his heart really almost broke. "No. That's not what I want. My fears stem from my own insecurities. I thought that maybe I could change that, but I can see now I haven't."

"You are that way because you've never let yourself care about another man before. Are you going to deny it?"

"No, because it would be a lie," she said stubbornly.

He thought it stemmed from his lack of a mother and how his father had never settled down. When Carter thought of forever— He didn't think of forever. The future was always changing, and as much as he thought at this moment that he needed Lindsey by his side, he was afraid he might be wrong.

_17_

WATCHING CARTER WALK away was the hardest thing she'd done in a long time. She was tempted to go after him and bring him back to her. In the end she knew she needed more from him than he could give.

But Carter had given her back something she'd lost. That confidence she'd used to be able to rely on. She grabbed her skis and went to the top of the Wasatch Range. The most difficult run serviced by the resort and the one she'd be skiing in two weeks' time for the charity event.

When she got to the top, she felt all of the crazy emotions that Carter inspired in her drop away. She stood at the top of the biggest run she'd dared to take since crashing out in Russia last year. Carter had made her realize a lot of things about herself, not the least of which was that she was no longer the woman she used to be.

But pieces of her still remained. She buckled her skis, pulled down her goggles and felt the breeze stir around her. The mountain was cold and very wintry today. Not the best day for a run, but she'd come up here, and nothing was going to stop her from taking it.

"Lindsey?"

She turned and saw that Carter was there. He'd followed her up the mountain. His hair was windblown, his shoulders broad as ever, and she had to turn away to keep from staring at him.

"What are you doing here? I thought we'd said all that we needed to." She was secretly thrilled to see him.

"We have, but I promised you I'd see you back on the slopes, and last night we said we'd take this run together. Despite what you think about me, I'm a man of my word."

She knew that. Maybe that was why she'd been pushing so hard for some sort of emotional commitment from him. She wanted some security in her life, and she had fallen in love with the one guy who was known for just drifting along.

"Thank you."

"You're welcome. It's a crap day, but I checked the mountain reports and there's nothing too dangerous. Are you ready for it?"

She wrinkled her nose. She wanted to say yes. Hell, she was going to say yes. "Of course. This is what I do."

"I'm glad," he said.

"This is part of who I am," she added, tilting her head up to meet his gaze. And she wanted to prove it to him. Downhill skiing was in her blood, part of her DNA at this point in her life. She'd spent more time on skis than off them.

"I thought you weren't sure anymore," he said wryly.

"I'm going to prove that I'm not only still a skier, but that I can beat you down the mountain."

He put his snowboard down and buckled his boots.

"I'd love to see you try. Hardly seems like a fair competition, though."

She knew what he was doing, but she didn't care. Driven by the need to prove him wrong, she put her poles in the ground and stumbled as a rush of fear swept through her body. It clouded her vision, and then all of a sudden images of her last tumble began playing through her mind. The crash that had left her broken and so flawed.

Not physically, she realized. No, she was hurting from the flaws the crash had revealed were inside her. The emptiness that was buried deep inside that she hadn't even been aware of until Carter had started to fill it up.

She looked at him. He had his goggles on as well, but he was watching her with that keen gaze of his, and she wanted so desperately to believe that he was scared for her because he loved her. But she didn't think for a second that was true. If she couldn't find the courage to say those words to him, how was the man who had more women running after him than anyone else going to say them?

"You okay?" he asked.

"No," she said. "I'm just realizing how not okay I am."

"I'll call the mountain patrol and we'll get down off the mountain," he said. "No shame in that."

She shook her head. "I have to do this, Carter. If I can't ski with you now, how am I going to be able to do it at the event?" Why had she even signed up for that stupid event? She should have run the other way instead of working with the team and acting as if she was okay. She wasn't.

"I'll just say that I'm not going to do it," he said. "You can say it wouldn't be fair for you to ski if I don't."

She looked at him, and all at once it hit her how much she loved him and how the words she wanted to hear might not mean anything when she was presented with the truth of his feelings. He did care for her. And the fact that he'd be the one to take the blame, make it seem like it wasn't her and her fear that was responsible, made her want to stop running.

And face life and her fears.

Fear number one: skiing. She had to do this, or she'd never be able to find happiness anywhere else in her life.

"Carter Shaw, you're a great guy. I'll have words with anyone who says different," she said. "But I have to do this. I have to stop hiding and running away from what I am."

"Are you sure?"

She nodded and turned back to look down the mountain. The breeze blew once again around her, and this time it swept away those doubts that had been lingering. She had her eyes wide-open, and the trail in front of her was one she'd taken many times before her crash. And had studied just as many times after it. She could do this.

Not only because she had to get back to doing what she loved, but because without taking this run, she had absolutely no shot at future happiness.

CARTER WATCHED LINDSEY take off down the mountain and let out the breath he'd been holding. In his life he'd never been afraid of a mountain. It just wasn't in his nature to see it as something to fear, but rather as something to conquer. But as he'd seen Lindsey on the precipice of taking her run, his heart had somehow climbed into his throat.

Talons of fear wrapped around him, and though he

knew she had the skills to safely make it down the mountain, he couldn't shake that fear. And it was at that moment that he realized he loved her.

He'd been "chasing" her from a distance, trying to protect his pride and safeguard his heart. Not because of any of the reasons he'd given himself before but because with Lindsey he knew his feelings were genuine. He had been giving her distance, hoping to keep himself safe, and now he was coming to realize how foolish that had been.

He should have held her closer to him while he'd had the chance. He should have held his tongue instead of pointing out her flaws to cover up his own. He should have told her he loved her instead of letting her believe that he didn't.

He jumped and swiveled and started his own run down the mountain. He knew as he did it that he needed to figure out how to get Lindsey back into his arms. Back into his life, where he'd really missed her. Because without her, he saw a future of more faceless women who were nice for a night but not forever.

It didn't take a genius to figure out that for him there was only Lindsey. And it had always been that way. She was the only woman that he'd ever really wanted, but he hadn't been ready for her until Sochi. And when she'd crashed, when she'd taken that devastating fall, everything had changed. He'd had no idea how to get back into her life until now.

She was ahead of him on the run, and as he watched her crouch low to increase her speed, he admitted to himself that her form was better than ever. She was good. Maybe better than she had been before because there was a new core of strength inside her from having lost it all and come back.

He wondered if while he'd been falling in love with her he had been giving her the very key to what she'd needed to move away from him. To go back to her old life where she wasn't surrounded by scantily clad energy drink girls or a man who couldn't control his temper.

It frightened him, but he pushed it aside as he hit a rough patch and barely caught his balance. He'd almost crashed out as she had last year. That shook him to the core. Was this how Lindsey had felt?

At the bottom of the run, he found Lindsey with her goggles pushed up on her head and a sheen of tears in her eyes as she looked up at the Wasatch Range. He got it. She'd reclaimed a part of herself that she'd thought was lost forever.

He hoped he'd made up for the teasing he'd done in Russia. She'd said he had nothing to do with her fall, but he'd never been able to shake his guilt. Not until this moment.

She was back. She'd ski again, and unless he'd completely lost his gut instinct when it came to other athletes, he was pretty sure she'd eventually be back to her old form. It was what she was meant to do. Not teach ski lessons to little kids at a luxury resort.

"Nice run," he said.

"Noticed you couldn't keep up."

"I gave you your space so that this victory could be all yours," he said.

She gave him a smile that cut through all the layers he'd been using to protect himself from her charms. It simply confirmed what he'd already figured out for himself. That he loved her.

"Still can't admit that I'm better on the snow," she teased.

"I can. I just don't like to," he retorted. "There's a big difference."

"I know." She hitched in a breath. "I'm sorry again for what I said earlier. I know that without you, I probably wouldn't have had the guts to do this."

"It's fine—I get it. We're oil and water, aren't we? We've never really been able to mix."

"I guess we are. So one more big battle and then you can go back to your life," she said.

"That's right. Back to California and training," he said. "Unless you want to try again?"

"Try again?" she asked, but he heard in her voice that she wasn't going to accept it. Perhaps it was his words spoken in anger but resonating still in her mind. And he understood that, because he knew he couldn't shake what *she*'d said.

He was a distraction. Distractions weren't welcome. God, how many times was he going to have to learn that?

"As a couple," he said, offering her an olive branch.

She shook her head. "I care about you, Carter, but it hurts too much to try to find a place for myself in your life."

"I could make room." For her he'd do it. Change whatever he had to.

"You'd resent me," she said. "I'd probably resent myself, too. I can't ask you to do that. Today as I was coming down the mountain I realized that I couldn't separate my skiing from my life, and I know it's the same for you and snowboarding."

Gazing down at her, he exhaled slowly and then trailed a finger down her cheek. "I guess I'm still just a distraction after all," he said. He knew he should tell her that he loved her. More than anything, he wanted to, but the words were stuck in the back of his throat. Fear was riding him hard, and he suddenly realized that he'd never felt afraid before because he'd never really had anyone that he didn't want to lose.

"You were never just that," she replied, stepping back. Then she took her skis and walked away.

He let her go, knowing that there was still unfinished business between them.

LINDSEY'S TEAM WAS in the best shape they'd been in since they'd started training. Lane Scott, the disabled American vet who was skiing on their team, was funny and inspiring. He was in his late twenties, maybe early thirties, and from his attitude it was hard to guess he'd lost both his lower legs to an IED in Afghanistan.

"I'm not sure that Tim should go before me. He's always flirting with the ladies and then they might miss my run," Lane said.

Tim, the fifty-five-year-old balding executive from one of the Park City resorts, just smiled over at them. "He's jealous."

"We all are," Bradley said. "But I agree with Lane. You should take the run after his and then we'll wrap it up with Lindsey. Carter's team been talking smack about beating our team, especially my wife, so I want to see them lose."

Lindsey hadn't realized how competitive Elizabeth was until the competition had gotten closer. At their daily breakfasts she'd listened to all sorts of good-natured ribbing from her friend. And to be honest, Lindsey had just been glad that Elizabeth hadn't brought up the argument with Carter. She'd asked one time if Lindsey wanted to talk and then let the subject drop when she had declined.

"Okay. Bradley, do you want to liaise with the other team and make sure we have all of our pairings in order?" Lindsey asked. "I'll be at the bottom when you come off your run and will radio up any changes in the slope to you guys at the top. That way you'll have up-to-date information before you take your run."

Everyone nodded. "Let's take our practice runs and do it like we will tomorrow. Since our regular guy isn't here today to man the radio at the top we will all take turns."

"I can't wait," Tim said. "My kids are going to be here tomorrow. My son got everyone in his school to donate."

"I'm really excited about the way the entire community has gotten behind us. I saw the poster in FreshSno, Bradley, that your graphic artists designed."

"Thanks. Those kids are awesome. Hard to believe they were wasting their talents painting graffiti on buildings."

Lindsey had heard about the kids Bradley had taken under his wing and turned from a life of punishable offenses into lucrative artistic careers. Speaking of changes… She'd given her notice at the resort, and at the end of the ski season, she'd be going back to training full-time. Her coach had wanted her to start right away, but she'd wanted to honor her commitment to the resort first. They'd given her a safe place to recover and now she wanted to pay them back with a win.

Plus, concentrating on winning had given her something to pour all of her emotions into over the past weeks. Never having been in love before, she'd had no idea how much it could hurt to care so deeply for Carter and know he was forever out of her reach. She missed him. He'd kept his distance since she'd walked away from him.

She didn't blame him for that. Because, in all honesty, she'd done the same thing. And it was easier to not see him than to catch small glimpses and be reminded that he wasn't hers anymore. Not that he ever really had been.

But she knew for a short while she'd had a good time pretending he could be hers. She had a selfie of the two of them on her phone from the day they'd gone diving in the crater, and she looked at it way too often. She'd almost deleted it but had been unable to because she wanted these small connections to him.

A part of her was tempted to go to him, to force him to see her because she knew that physically they still had that bond. But she had decided she wanted more from him than that. She knew if it was just sex, that bond would fade over time.

But it wasn't just sex. At least not where she was concerned.

But it was hard. She wanted to call and talk to her mother about it, but really, what would she say? Finally, she had a problem that had nothing to do with skiing. Even the joy she found at being able to ski wasn't enough to dull the ache left by Carter's absence in her life.

"Skier number one is in position."

The voice over the radio was deep and rich, and for a second she hoped it was Carter but then recognized it as TJ, one of the mountain patrol guys volunteering as a helper for their team on his day off.

"Thank you," she said.

"Go."

She hit the button on her stopwatch and waited for

Georgina to complete her run, but her mind wasn't on winning. It was on the feeling that dominated her thoughts whenever she was awake anymore. Where was Carter?

What was he doing?

Could she ever make him realize that he wasn't distracting her from her problems, but helping her to solve them? Because she knew that he had. Without Carter's quiet, steadfast support—taking her to places that weren't familiar, pushing her and challenging her at every turn, encouraging her to find her feet again—she would never have taken that run. And she just wanted one more chance to tell him that.

If she could get back on skis after that horrible crash, then why couldn't she do the same in their relationship? She'd been wrong to give in to her fears, and she wanted him back.

Now she knew she had to go and get him.

But winning back a man was something she had no clue about. She had an idea that her friend Penny would have some answers. She'd been a guest at the resort for two weeks during Christmas and had turned her holiday affair into happily-ever-after. If anyone could help her win Carter back, it was Penny.

At this level Carter noticed that Benji had a hearing aid in one ear. "She's saying that you have to remember the skis are an extension of your leg. And that when you have them on you are gliding over the snow."

"How do you know?" Benji asked suspiciously.

"I've taken her class before."

"She mustn't be very good if you're back here again," Russ pointed out.

"She's very good," Carter said with a wink. "I like coming back because of her."

Russ scrunched up his face. "Girls are gross."

"Sometimes they are," Carter agreed. "Why do you keep shoving your brother?"

"He pushed me first," Russ said, looking up at him with wide blue eyes.

"Fair enough. But how about you two stop fighting and we learn how to ski?"

"I'm done pushing him now," Russ said.

Benji nodded in agreement. "Me, too."

Lindsey demonstrated a basic move. The kids slowly took turns doing it, going to the front of the group where Lindsey would watch them and give individual feedback. Carter moved around so he could go last. When he got up there she looked at him.

God, he'd missed her. She seemed tired, but happy. That made sense to him because he knew she was taking a lot of runs down the mountain to get ready to go back into training. He wasn't too proud to admit he'd asked Elizabeth about her.

"So you're going back to the team after the winter season is over," he said.

"I am. I figured out what I wanted for the rest of the year," she said.

18

CARTER HAD BEEN avoiding Lindsey, but being a coward wasn't his style so he'd decided to show up for her late-afternoon ski class. He liked the fact that he rattled her. He could tell by the way she kept losing her concentration with the kids. It wouldn't have been obvious to anyone who didn't know her as well as he did.

He was at the end of the line with two twin boys who looked like trouble and were barely old enough to be in school. They had freckles and matching bright red hair. Standing precariously on their skis, as though they were learning how to walk for the first time, they kept slipping back and forth and shoving each other whenever Lindsey's back was turned.

"Hello, boys," Carter said, stepping between the two of them to keep them from shoving each other. "I'm Carter."

"I'm Benji and this is Russ."

"Do you like skiing?" he asked, crouching to their level.

"No. I might if Russ would stop talking all the time. I can't hear what she's saying."

"You did?"

"Yes."

"Care to tell me?" he asked softly. "I kind of have a vested interest since I started this year with you."

She looked at the kids who were watching them, waiting for Carter to take his practice time. "Not right now."

"And not later, either," he said, one corner of his mouth quirking up. "We both know that we're avoiding each other."

"We were until you showed up," she reminded him. "I can't talk right now."

It went against his nature to back down, so when the class went to the bunny slope he left, turned his skis in and went up to the lodge looking for a distraction. Something that would help him understand why he wanted that woman and why she kept freezing him out.

Granted, he knew that he hadn't shared his feelings with her and that it was hard to admit to falling in love. She acted as though it was a bad thing, but he knew she might find it hard to believe in him, especially since he hadn't admitted his feelings out loud.

"Hey, Carter! How's it going?"

He was surprised to see Will Spalding back at the resort. The dude had come over Christmastime and fallen in love with one of the other resort guests. They'd both been groomsmen in Elizabeth and Bradley's wedding.

"Not bad. What you are doing here?" he asked, shaking the other man's hand and sitting next to him at one of the lobby conversation areas.

"Penny wanted to spend our first Valentine's Day here and Elizabeth asked her to help plan the after-party for the charity event tomorrow."

"It's not too late for you to get in on it if you want to," Carter said.

"Get in on what?" Will asked.

Lindsey entered the lobby and walked over to the concierge desk with one of her young students.

Carter stared at her. That woman made him crazy. He wanted her—*loved* her—but he was hopeless at how to tell her. In his entire life there had never been anything he'd encountered that frustrated him more.

"You seem preoccupied," Will said.

"I'm just… Dude, I'm a mess. That woman is driving me nuts," Carter muttered. His snowboarding friends didn't get it. Had never had someone like Lindsey in their lives or they were still young and new to the sport so women weren't important to them. But Carter had moved on.

When he'd moved from amateur sports last year he'd signaled that he was ready to start his life after sports. And he was just now realizing it. He needed Lindsey in ways he'd never thought possible before, because it wasn't until he saw her standing by that kid in the lobby that he was struck with an image of her with *their* kid.

And that was precisely why he'd been running scared. It was time to stop running.

He started to get up to go over to her, but she was gone. She'd left the lobby. He looked around for her.

"Where'd she go?"

"I wasn't paying attention," Will said. "But I think she's having dinner with Penny and Elizabeth tonight. You could crash that."

Carter shook his head. He'd had enough of doing things with an audience.

DINNER WITH THE girls had seemed like a good idea when Elizabeth had first suggested it, but as she entered Elizabeth's house and noticed that Bradley and Will were nowhere in sight, she wasn't sure. The last time she'd been here had been when Elizabeth had tried on wedding dresses sent from California by Lindsey's dress designer cousin.

It was funny that her cousin had gotten all the romance genes and she'd gotten none of them. She should have flirted with Carter today, or heck, at least given him some sign that she still wanted him in her life. But instead she'd acted true to form, gotten scared and frozen him out.

She was like that ice queen in the Disney movie who always hurt the ones she loved by keeping them away. Her parents were a good example of that. She loved them, but they weren't close. Once she'd turned eighteen, she'd started living near her coach and never had time off to visit with them.

Her relationship skills were sadly lacking, and dinner tonight confirmed that until she had her second glass of wine and Penny turned to her.

"Rumor has it you've been hooking up with Carter Shaw," Penny said as she arched her eyebrows.

"Rumor?"

"Well, *Elizabeth.* But I want to know all the dirt," Penny replied. "You're pretty quiet for someone in the midst of a red-hot affair."

That was because, as usual, she'd doused the flames and there was nothing to tell. "I screwed up."

"What?" Elizabeth said, coming into the living room with a new bottle of wine. "What did you screw up?"

"Everything with Carter," Lindsey lamented. "I love

him but I can't find the words to tell him. He was at my class this afternoon and I just acted like I always do. Focused on skiing and pretended that I wasn't excited to see him."

Penny patted her hand. "Why did you do that?"

She glanced at Elizabeth. Her friend took sympathy on her and poured more wine into her glass.

"She called him a distraction and got into a huge fight with him in the restaurant," Elizabeth said, filling their friend in. "It wasn't pretty."

"No, it wasn't. But we sort of talked afterward and I realized that I'm not sure *I* wasn't a distraction for him. I'm just not good at relationships." She took a sip of wine, then went on, "Before this thing with Carter, I hadn't really had time for one, and now... Well, as I said, I screwed up and have no idea how to fix it."

"Sexy lingerie," Penny said, her eyes sparkling with mischief. "That will get his attention, and then afterward you just tell him all of that stuff you just told us."

Penny's idea had some merit. She could do the seduction thing. That part was easy between the two of them. "What if he doesn't feel the same way about me?"

"That's the risk you have to take when you fall in love," Elizabeth said gently.

Taking a sip of her own wine, Penny added, "And if he doesn't feel the same, isn't it better to know than to stay in the agony of what-if?" Penny had another valid point.

"Is that what you did?"

"No way. I just kept my guard up until Will stepped up and proved himself. I knew I loved him, but I had pretty much resigned myself to living with heartbreak for a while. But he made a big gesture," Penny explained.

"The dog? Everyone knows it was Fifi," Elizabeth said, poking her friend in the ribs.

"Well, not every guy has two great artists working for him so they can make a mural and hang it up for the world to see," Penny fired back, referring to the gesture that Bradley had made.

Was that what she wanted? A big romantic gesture so she knew it was safe to fall for him? Safe to tell him how she really felt?

She wasn't sure. Even if he did something like that, how would she be able to believe it? How would he believe it?

"Maybe I *should* do something to get his attention," Lindsey said, biting her lip.

"Lingerie," Penny reiterated. "Believe me, it works. Men can be brought around to your way of thinking once you have their undivided attention."

Lindsey swallowed, remembering New Year's Eve and how that night had worked out exactly the way she'd wanted it to. But since then she'd been struggling to figure out how to get him where she wanted him and not have to risk showing him any more of her weaknesses.

"It's different with us. Sex is easy. He thinks I was using him as a booty call and he's got all those scantily clad girls hanging around him," Lindsey said. But deep down she knew that wasn't true. She felt closest to him when he held her in his arms after they made love.

"Well, whatever the gesture, you better get moving. He told Will he's heading back to California on our flight in two days' time. And you've got the ski event and then my awesome party between now and then," Penny said.

"Maybe I could do something at the party?"

"Like what?" Elizabeth asked. "Given that the last

time you two interacted in public it felt like a nuclear meltdown, I think you need a plan."

"I do need a plan. I need something that shows him that I've finally figured out that we belong together."

"How?"

"Now, that's the million-dollar question, isn't it?"

She put her wineglass down and thought again of all the things Carter had done for her and how he'd taken time to help her learn to ski again when he was so busy… But he'd never been too busy for her. Carter had been there for her when she needed him most, and he had been there to catch her when she'd felt like she'd been stumbling around in the dark. Now it was her turn.

It was time to take the ultimate risk. To prove to Carter Shaw, once and for all, that she wanted only one thing for this year, and it was him.

CARTER AND HIS team were in high spirits, wearing the trademark green-and-gold Thunderbolt colors. The other team had gold with green accents, since Georgina and Stan had sponsored all the events. They were at breakfast in one of the ballrooms set up with two long tables on either side of the room. In the middle of the room were big, round tables draped in green or gold, depending on which team they had sponsored.

The tables in the middle were for the other big sponsors—resorts donating their instructors and their teams to help staff the event—and those tables were slowly filling. Carter stood to one side, smiling and joking with his team. Thunderbolt girls were moving around the room posing for pictures with the attendees.

They had their branded charity event logo on a big drape in the corner. It was set up with a backdrop of the

Wasatch Range so that guests could pose for a picture to appear as if they were skiing.

The wounded vets were very popular. Carter was pretty sure that Lane, Duke, Marsalis and Wynn hadn't had a minute to themselves all morning. Georgina and Stan were making the rounds, with Thunderbolt girls handing out beverages. Lars Usten had invited some of his old ski team cronies and they were all sitting at the head table.

Carter kept watching the room and knew that there was only one person he was looking for: Lindsey. But she had yet to show.

He worried about her, wondering if all the practice runs she'd taken had prepared her for this big run with so many people watching. Granted, it was nowhere near the pressure of the winter games, but this was the first time she'd be skiing in an event. It would bring back memories, he was sure of it.

"Hiya, Carter," Will said, coming up to him. He was wearing a pair of chinos and a button-down shirt. He looked as though he should be in the office instead of waiting to go out on the mountain.

"Morning. Nice event your— What is Penny?" Carter asked. He wasn't sure how to refer to her, but once people got out of high school it was hard to keep a straight face when calling them boyfriend or girlfriend.

"Well, girlfriend now," Will said. "But I have a surprise for her on Valentine's Day that should change that status."

Carter smiled and nodded at him. "Glad to hear it. I like you two."

"Thanks, buddy. You any closer to getting back in your lady's good graces?"

"Hopefully by the end of the day I'll have some good news for you," Carter said. "If not you can find me in the bar."

Will laughed as Carter had intended him to. Playing at being normal when he wasn't. He didn't have Lindsey and he didn't have a broken heart. He was still hopeful he'd win her back, but if he didn't, this would turn out to be the worst day of his life.

Yet he still was trying to play it cool so that no one could figure out how desperately he wanted and needed Lindsey in his life. He knew that nothing would be quite as good without her by his side.

He knew it. At the same time that knowledge paralyzed him. Made him unsure of what to do next.

But telling her was still a difficult thing. The words were hard, and he was so used to acting as though nothing mattered that now that something did he wasn't sure how to proceed. He had a plan, however, even though he had no idea if it would work.

He'd called his dad to ask for advice, but the old man had told him that if he'd had the answer to what women wanted he wouldn't have been married and divorced five times. But there had been no bitterness in his father's voice. And Carter had realized that every man had to find the path that worked for him. For Carter he couldn't see a path without Lindsey in it, which was why he was waiting for the right moment to show her what she meant to him instead of just finding out what he meant to her.

He had figured that out at three in the morning. Why was it that all the answers to his craziest ideas came to him then? He knew that tricking her into falling for him wasn't the answer, but it might be the vehicle to the answer.

Like the blindfold he'd used when they'd gone to the crater. It had turned out to be a sort of magic elixir to getting her to talk about all the things she usually kept locked away.

"You keep watching the door like you can make her appear," Will said, dragging him out of his thoughts.

"If only," Carter grumbled. "Life would be so much easier if she'd just do what I wanted her to."

"Really?" Will asked. "I've found that I don't always know what I want when it comes to Penny. She always surprises me, and it's better than whatever I planned."

He looked at the other man. There was an element of truth in his words. "I just want her to be here so I can make sure she's okay."

That was part of it. And then he was afraid he'd probably embarrass himself by going to her and pulling her into his arms. But that was what he wanted to do. He wanted to admit that he'd had enough of chasing her from a distance. To tell her that nothing was insurmountable when they were together. To say he should never have let anger motivate him into walking away from her.

Because he knew better than to let his temper control his actions. He was all prepared to say that…and more…but then Lindsey walked into the room with her long blond hair braided to one side and hung over her shoulder.

19

"I'VE GOT A new rule," Lindsey said as Penny led the way to the small stage that had been set up on the far end of the kickoff breakfast. The room was full, and she saw her teammates as well as the corporate sponsors... and Carter.

He stood by his team's table talking to Penny's boyfriend, Will. Penny had been sweet last night when she'd shared stories of how she'd been unsure of Will and how he'd overcome it. Elizabeth had bared her soul, as well. It had been humbling to realize that the other women had been in her shoes. She'd felt so isolated by her doubts.

"What rule?" Penny asked.

"No making important life decisions when I've had two glasses of wine," Lindsey said. Last night when she'd been trying to come up with the right gesture to show Carter how much he meant to her, it had seemed a good idea. But this morning, as she'd had her hair braided to match the Ice Queen image that was often used in the media to go along with articles about her, she'd started to have second thoughts.

"Do you want to spend the rest of your life in agony?" Penny said.

She noticed the pretty event planner wasn't afraid to go for over-the-top drama at times.

"Or without Carter?" Elizabeth asked, coming up on her other side.

"No, I don't. But this seemed like it would be a lot of fun last night and this morning... I'm scared."

Penny threaded her arm through Lindsey's left one, and Elizabeth did the same on her right. "We're here with you."

She smiled. She'd made good friends. It was one thing that she'd gotten from the past year. The time she'd thought was lost because she hadn't been skiing turned out to be very valuable.

"Okay, I guess I'm as ready as I'll ever be," Lindsey said, bracing herself for whatever was about to come next.

"That's good, because it looks as if Carter has noticed you," Penny said. "Let's get this show on the road."

"What?"

"My mom used to say that every morning when it was time to leave," Penny said. "I don't get to quote her often enough."

Lindsey allowed herself to be distracted for a moment by Penny, but then searched out Carter. She found him, wearing his snowboarding outfit from the winter games last year, standing by his team table. And when their eyes met, she felt the courage that had been lacking in her until this moment.

She realized that once again she was drawing strength from him, and it felt right. He was her strength, and she needed to prove to him that he was more than a distraction. More than she'd labeled him, and that she was willing to take the risk and admit that she'd fallen for him.

Because she had fallen big-time for the bad-boy snowboarder.

And it was time to stop running from that love the way she'd stopped running from her fear of going down the mountain. She followed her friends through the crowded room, pausing to greet her team and tell them that she thought they'd win today.

The closer they got to the stage, the more her nerves almost got the better of her. But she had realized that nothing—not skiing again, not embarrassment—*nothing* scared her more than not telling Carter how she felt.

They got to the stage and Lars smiled at her and gave her the thumbs-up. She'd decided to take the entire big gesture thing and make it pretty gigantic. She glanced around the room and saw that everyone she'd talked to was in place, too. Bradley was standing by the sound system in the back of the room as she climbed up onto the stage dressed in her ski outfit looking like the ice queen as she took off her coat.

Penny and Elizabeth climbed the stage, too, and stood behind her. She cleared her throat as one of the techs handed her a microphone.

"Good morning, everyone," she said. The talking slowly died down and everyone turned toward where she stood at the front of the ballroom.

"First of all, thank you for participating in today's event and for volunteering your time and services for our event this coming November."

There was a round of applause and Lindsey took a deep breath.

"What many of you might not know is that this event was the brainchild of Carter Shaw."

She pointed to the corner where Carter stood. "There is probably a lot about Carter that you don't know, but the most important thing from my point of view is that he's…um…*not* a distraction to me."

She signaled to Bradley and heard the single drum beat before Cher started singing "The Shoop Shoop Song" and she lip-synched, "'Does he love me?'"

With Penny and Elizabeth dancing and shooping behind her, she met Carter's blue-gray gaze from across the room. Slowly she sang and danced her way over to him, weaving a path through the crowd as everyone clapped and turned to look at him, too.

She was more nervous about what he was going to do once she got to his side, but she felt alive and so in love with him at that moment that it really didn't matter. She wasn't going to be able to tell herself that he didn't know how she felt after this moment.

She stopped in front of Carter as the song ended with "It's in his kiss." She stood there for a minute and looked into his eyes.

"I wanna know if you love me so," she said quietly. She lifted her hands to his face, curving them against his cheeks as she went up on tiptoe and kissed him.

He stood there, his mouth rigid under hers for a moment, and she feared she'd made a huge mistake. But then she felt his arms come around her as he lifted her off her feet and spun her around in his arms.

"I do love you," he whispered into her neck. "I hope you felt it in my kiss."

CARTER FELT HUMBLED and happy and so damned glad that Lindsey had more courage than he did when it came to showing how much she loved him. He held her closely to him and never wanted to let go.

"Gorgeous, I loved that," he said with a big grin. Then he realized that everyone in the room was still staring at them. And if he'd learned anything from their last public discussion, it was that she preferred privacy.

He led her out of the room and down the hall to one of those little conversation nooks. He set her on her feet and gazed into her big brown eyes.

"Did you mean it?" he asked. He'd been alone so long. Felt so unattached to everyone else in the world that it was hard to believe she'd connected to him. That she loved him. Love wasn't something he'd ever prized until he thought he'd never have hers.

"Yes, I meant it. Would I sing that song and dance around the ballroom if I didn't?" she asked, still clutching his hand tightly.

She seemed to need his strength now that she'd made her confession, and he was more than happy to give it to her. "You do like the spotlight."

"Ha. You know I don't. Listen, I wore this outfit today because last year when I had my crash I felt like I lost everything. That my life was over. I retreated here and recovered physically, but mentally I had no idea how to fix myself.

"And then you showed up, teasing me and flirting and making me think about things that had nothing to do with skiing, but you woke me up. Shook me out of my icy state, and I'm not the Ice Queen anymore. You've made it so I can't be again. I really do love you, Carter." Tears shimmered in her eyes as she reached up and gently brushed a lock of hair off his forehead.

He brought his mouth down on hers, kissing her with all the emotion that he'd shoved deep down for so long. To hear her say those words and confess to loving him.

"Do you feel it in my kiss?" he murmured as he lifted his head. "I love you, Lindsey. I have never in my life been afraid of anything. I've never needed anyone. I'm happy to look for my next big challenge and move on, but the thought of leaving here without you by my side was unbearable." He cupped her face in his hands, one thumb gently caressing her cheek. "I wanted you to see me and know that last year when I dared and tried to claim a kiss, I was really coming after you.

"I was ready for our lives to stop being about competing on the snow and to make them more intimate. I can't live without you, gorgeous. I love you."

She smiled at him. "I was so nervous. But I wanted to prove how much you meant to me. I'm sorry for all the things I said. And how I acted at the ski lesson yesterday."

He sat on the couch and pulled her onto his lap, cradling her close to him as he stroked his hand down her back. He could hardly believe that she was his. At last, after all these years, he had the one woman he'd always been afraid to admit he wanted.

"I was pushing you, too. I didn't want to leave myself vulnerable. Admit I loved you before you did," he said. "Damn, gorgeous, you beat me to it today. I was planning to confess at the end of the events."

"Once again you are eating my dust," she said with a huge grin. "I couldn't wait. Skiing is important, of

course, but I needed to know where you fit in my life…
Well, that you'd be in my life at the end of the race."

He looked into those big beautiful brown eyes of hers
and felt a sense of rightness settle over him. "You have
me."

"Good. That doesn't mean I'm still not going to beat
you at everything we do."

"Uh, how do you figure you've done that?" he asked
drily.

"Um, poker, I won. World records—I've got two.
Your heart, I won again."

He'd won, as well…at poker and with her heart.

He cuddled her close and traced the line of her neck
down her arm and lifted her hand to his mouth to kiss
her palm before placing it over his heart. "You have my
heart, that is true. I have a world record, and I only compete in one event so that pretty much makes us even.
And…poker? I let you win."

She threw her head back and laughed. The joyous
sound echoing through the hall and through his empty
soul. "You let me?"

"That's my story, and I'm sticking to it," he said.

"If that's what you want to believe," she murmured.
"I want the man I love to be happy."

"I am."

She'd made him the happiest man in the world today.
Where he'd had doubt and fear and bottled-up emotion,
he now had Lindsey and her love. He knew that the
road for them wouldn't be traditional or smooth—that
just wasn't their way. But having her by his side was all
he'd wanted, and he could admit now that he was very
happy to have her by his side.

They both went back to their teams and competed in

their events. Carter felt a little nervous when Lindsey got ready for her run, but she did it like the pro she was and even beat him down the mountain.

But winning didn't seem as important now that he'd won her heart and had her by his side for today and the rest of their lives.

* * * * *

THE PRINCE SHE
NEVER FORGOT

SCARLET WILSON

Scarlet Wilson wrote her first story aged eight and has never stopped. She's worked in the health service for twenty years, trained as a nurse and a health visitor. Scarlet now works in public health and lives on the West Coast of Scotland with her fiancé and their two sons. Writing medical romances and contemporary romances is a dream come true for her.

PROLOGUE

Ten years earlier

SHE COULD FEEL the electricity in the air, feel the excitement. It seemed as if everyone in the world had decided to celebrate New Year's Eve in Paris.

She was jostled along with the crowd, being practically carried off her feet on the route from the Champs-élysées towards the Eiffel Tower.

'Aren't you glad you came?' her friend Polly screamed in her ear, sloshing wine over her sleeve. 'This is the best place in the world right now.'

'Yes, it is,' murmured Ruby.

It certainly beat sitting at home in her flat, brooding over the job that wasn't to be or the boyfriend who never should have been.

Polly gave a squeal. 'The fireworks will be starting in an hour. Let's try and get near the front!'

Ruby nodded as she was shouldered from behind. There were ten in their group but it was getting harder and harder to stick together. 'I need to find a bathroom before we head to the fireworks,' she whispered to Polly. 'Give me five minutes.'

There were cafés and bars open all the way along the Champs-élysées, but unfortunately for her just about every female in the city seemed to have the same idea that she had.

She waved to Polly, 'Go on without me. I'll meet you at the sign we saw earlier.'

The group had already planned their night with precision. Dinner on a riverboat. Drinks in the hotel. A walk along the Champs-élysées and rendezvous at the Eiffel Tower for the fireworks. They'd already picked the spot they planned to stand at in case anyone got lost—which on a night like tonight was a certainty.

She stood in a queue for an eternity before finally heading back out to the thronging crowds. In the thirty minutes it had taken to get access to a bathroom it seemed the whole of Paris had started to congregate in the streets.

The crowds were sweeping along the Avenue George V, carrying along anyone who happened to be standing close enough. It was one part terrifying, one part exhilarating.

The crowd was even thicker at the Rue de l'Université. The street was packed, with everyone heading directly to the base of the Eiffel Tower. Ruby glanced at her watch. Visiting the bathroom hadn't been such a good idea. There was no way she was going to be able to find her friends in this crowd.

But she wasn't too worried. The mood of the crowd was jubilant. People were drinking wine and singing. The atmosphere and heavy police presence made her feel safe—even if she was alone.

Around her she heard dozens of different accents: snatches of English, Italian and Japanese all mixed in with French. The streets were lit with multi-coloured lights and a variety of decorations and garlands left over from Christmas. She unfastened the buttons on her red wool coat. She'd expected Paris to be cold in December, but the heat from the people around her meant the temperature was rising.

She clutched tightly onto the bag strung diagonally in front of her, keeping her hand clasped over the zipper. Pickpockets were rife in Paris at New Year's. They'd all been warned to keep a close hold of their belongings.

Her phone beeped just as she was in sight of the Eiffel Tower and she struggled to move out of the thronging crowd. It had practically ground to a halt, with people from behind still pressing ahead. The streets were packed. There was no way forward.

She moved sideways, unzipping her bag and pulling out her phone.

Where are you?

It was from Polly. Her friends were obviously waiting at their designated meeting point.

She typed quickly. Not sure if I can get to you, but I'll try. She pressed Send just as someone bumped her from behind and the phone skittered from her hand.

'Oh, no!'

It was kicked one way, then another, quickly going out of sight. She tried to push her way through the crowd sideways, but that proved impossible. It was a sea of people. And she was heading in the wrong direction.

'Hey, watch out. Ouch!'

Her feet were trampled, her ribs elbowed and the wind knocked from her. It was impossible. She looked up for a few seconds, to try and make her way through the crowd, then looked down again amongst the stampeding feet, trying to track down her phone.

A thud to her shoulder sent her flying into a group of rowdy Germans.

'Sorry…sorry.'

They were laughing and joking and smelling of beer. She tried to find her way through but it was virtually impossible. There seemed to be nowhere to go.

Her chest started to tighten. They weren't doing or saying anything untoward, but the sheer amount of people meant they'd started to crowd around her, closing in. She tried to take a deep breath and lifted her elbows up, edging her way to the side. But the only place she seemed to be moving was closer and closer.

There was a waft of beer-soaked breath on her cheek. Too close. Too invasive. A hand at her back, someone pressing against her hip.

'Let me out. Let me through. Move, please!'

A hand reached down between her shoulders, grabbing her coat and pulling her upwards. The air left her lungs momentarily and her feet were still stuck amongst the crowd. A strong arm wound around her waist and pulled her clear. Her feet stopped unsteadily on a wall at shoulder height to the throng.

'Are you okay?'

She was teetering on the wall. The hand and arm that had steadied her had pulled away the instant she was free. She reached and grabbed hold of the dark sleeve in front of her, trying to regain her balance.

The voice sounded again. 'Are you okay? Are you drunk?' There was a slight edge of disappointment to the voice.

She steadied herself on the wall, taking a deep breath of relief before turning around to speak to her rescuer. How dared he accuse her of being drunk?

But the words died in her throat. Bright blue eyes and a broad chest obstructed her view.

Even on a dark Paris night those blue eyes would have attracted her attention. He was tall, dark-haired, with a broad chest, wearing a simple white T-shirt and jeans with a dark wool coat on top. Trust her to find the best-looking guy in Paris and have no reliable witnesses. No one would believe her.

She automatically lifted her hands. 'No. No, I'm not drunk. I just got stuck in a crowd going in the opposite direction from me.'

His demeanour changed. The skin around his eyes

creased as he smiled. 'What? You're going home already? You don't want to see the fireworks?'

His accent sent tingles across her skin. He sounded French, with a little something else.

He was teasing her, and now she could actually breathe she could take a little teasing.

She sighed. 'No. I'm not going home. Not tonight anyway. Of course I want to see the fireworks.' She held out her hands to the bodies pressed below. 'Just not like this.' The crowd had ground to a halt. She stared across at the sea of people. 'I was supposed to be meeting my friends.'

'You are lost?' He sounded concerned.

'Not exactly.' She turned back to face him, getting a whiff of woody aftershave. 'We were meeting at a sign near the Eiffel Tower.' She shook her head. 'I have absolutely no chance of getting there now.'

She had no intention of leaving the safety of this wall any time soon. She only hoped his friends weren't all about to join them and there'd be no room for her to stay here.

He smiled as he looked down at all the people below. 'You could be right. I'm sorry if I startled you but you looked frightened. I thought you were beginning to panic in the crowd.'

Her heart had stopped fluttering in her chest and her breathing was settling down. It had been an odd feeling, and so not like her. Ruby Wetherspoon didn't tend to panic.

'I was. Thank you. I've never really been in a crowd like that before.

It had definitely been a bit claustrophobic.' She shook her coat free, letting some air circulate around her, and pulled her red hat from her hair.

'There—that's much better.'

'It certainly is.'

He was smiling appreciatively at her and for a second she was unnerved. But, no. There was nothing predatory about her rescuer. He had kind eyes, even if the man exuded sex appeal from twenty paces. If her up-close-and-personal alarm was going off it wasn't because she was scared—it was because it had been jolted back into life. About time too.

He nodded slowly. 'Crowds can be…difficult.'

It was an odd choice of words, but then again her hesitant French would sound much poorer than his English.

'And you'd know?' She was curious.

His face crinkled. It seemed her half-inquisitive, half-sarcastic question was lost on him.

She held out her hand towards him. 'Ruby. Ruby Wetherspoon from England.'

His warm hand closed around hers. 'Alex,' he said simply.

Her eyes glanced up and down his body. White T-shirt, blue jeans and black boots. But the dark wool coat seemed a little strange for a young guy—a little formal.

'Are you from here?'

The corners of his lips turned upwards. 'Close enough.'

Mystery. She liked it. Perfect for New Year's Eve.

Under normal circumstances she might have felt a little nervous, a little wary around a mysterious stranger. But Alex didn't give her those kind of vibes.

Trust your instincts. That was what her gran had always told her. And she should have. Because if she had she probably wouldn't have found her boyfriend in bed with her ex-best friend. Truth was, she couldn't wait to see the end of this stinker of a year.

She glanced around. For the moment they were the only two people perched on this precarious wall. 'Well, Alex from "close enough", where are your friends? Am I about to get trampled and thrown back to the crowd when they all want a place on this wall?'

She sent a silent prayer upwards. What was the betting they were all gorgeous and female?

He shrugged. 'I lost them too. I climbed up here to look for them. Then I decided I liked the view.'

She turned to face where he was looking. Of course. A perfect view of the Eiffel Tower. For now it had a row of white lights running up the outside of its edges. The sun had set a few hours ago and it stood out like a beacon in the dark sky.

She'd been so busy fighting her way through the crowd that she hadn't really had time to stop and take in the sight.

'Wow. I just remembered why I came here,' she breathed.

A few people shouldered past beneath them, knocking into her feet, and she wobbled again. His arm rested around her waist to steady her, and he didn't move it once she'd regained her balance.

'So, why is an English girl in Paris for New Year's Eve?'

Why, indeed? She was still asking herself that question. And Mr Gorgeous Mysterious Stranger didn't really need the whole truth. Maybe just a tiny part.

'Visiting a boyfriend?' he added.

It was a loaded question. Was he really testing to see if she was taken?

She sucked in a deep breath and tried not to let the idiot smile that was whooping and dancing around in her brain actually appear. 'My flatmate Polly persuaded me it was time to try something new. We usually spend every New Year's in London. We did try a Scottish lodge once, but that was a disaster. Snowed in with no power and no booze.'

He was laughing at her now.

She held out her hands. 'What girl would say no to Paris on New Year's? This place is just amazing...' Her voice tailed off. 'And, to be honest, I'm not sorry to see this year go.'

'You've had a bad year?'

'Somewhere between a wrecking ball and a demolition derby.'

She could almost see his brain trying to make sense of her words.

'Ahh. You sound sad. But surely not everything about this year can have been bad?'

Perfect. Her own Pollyanna.

He was right. Of course he was right. She'd just needed someone to remind her.

She gave a little nod. 'Of course not. There have been a few good things. I qualified this year.'

'As what?'

'A speech and language therapist.'

'Well, that sounds great. Congratulations.'

She nodded. 'Yeah. Yes, it is.'

Three years doing a course she'd absolutely loved. Her placements had been fabulous, letting her practice all her skills and making her realise exactly what she wanted to do.

'So why aren't you jumping for joy? You'll get to do the job that you want. Some people would give anything for that.'

His voice sounded a little wistful.

Wow. She must sound an ungrateful misery-guts. But there was something easy about talking to a perfect stranger. Someone who didn't know all the people or personalities involved. Someone completely independent.

'I should be. I know. It's just that I really, really wanted to work in one area. I did two training stints there, but by the time I'd qualified there was only one job and they gave it to someone with more experience.' She shrugged. It still stung. She'd had her heart set on working there.

'Where was it?'

'In London. A specialist speech and language unit attached to the biggest children's hospital. I loved it there. The staff were really special and the kids…they just made my heart melt.'

'What kind of things did you do there?'

He seemed genuinely interested.

'I worked with children with specific language impairment and language disorders. Those kids made progress every day.' She held up her finger and thumb. 'Even if it was just in the tiniest way.' She smiled again, caught up in the memories. 'I even worked with children with hearing problems. Seeing the look on their faces when they got a cochlear implant and heard for the first time...' She shook her head. 'It was magical. It was exactly what I wanted to do.' She lifted her eyes to meet his. 'These things stay with you for ever.'

He was looking at her with such intensity, such sincerity, that it took her breath away. Here, in a city with over two million people, he was looking only at her.

She couldn't imagine how she'd done it, but she seemed to have completely captured his attention—just as he'd captured hers.

His voice was low and deep. 'So you don't have a job now?'

Even the timbre of his voice sent butterflies along her skin. Those two glasses of wine earlier seemed to have finally hit her system. Any minute now she was going to have to find some food before her brain was truly addled. No guy could have this kind of effect on a girl? Not in real life anyway.

She shook her head in an attempt to find some clear thoughts. 'I do. And I don't mean to sound ungrateful. I've got a job at a stroke unit, working with patients who've suffered a stroke and are having trouble with speech.'

He kept smiling at her—one minute looking serious, the next as if she amused him. Those teeth were perfect. Too perfect. He must be a model. He probably advertised toothpaste.

He raised his eyebrows. 'But that sounds just as important as the other job.'

Clear, rational thought. Easy when you didn't dream about the place where you wanted to work every night.

She cringed. 'I know. I *know*. I don't mean to sound like that. I'm lucky to have a job. Not everyone on my course got one. And once I get there I know that'll love it.' She gave a sad smile. 'It's just not what I'd hoped for, that's all.'

She heard him suck in a deep breath. 'We don't always get what we hope for, Ruby.'

His voice was serious. It made her curious.

He couldn't possibly have any idea of the kind of thoughts that were circulating in her head right now. Her imagination was running riot. Handsome mysterious Frenchman. Gorgeous, smelling good enough to eat. Polly wouldn't believe a word of this. Any minute now someone would pinch her and she'd wake up.

Time to get back to reality. Time to get a little nosey.

'So, Alex. What do *you* do? Do you work around here?'

He shook his head. 'I'm like you—just visiting for New Year. I'm in business. Boring things. Investment banking.'

Smash. The first dream broken. Not a model. But what interested her most was how he'd described his job. This guy gave very little away.

'Why do you do it if it's boring?'

'Because I'm expected to. It's a job.'

Another tell-nothing answer. The less he said, the more she was curious.

His phone buzzed and he pulled it from his pocket and frowned.

'Is it your friends? Are they looking for you?' She looked through the crowd, expecting to see a bunch of Amazonian blondes charging in to steal their prize back.

He shook his head. 'Nothing like that.' He stuffed the phone back in his pocket.

Ruby bent forward and peered into the crowd below. 'I dropped my phone. It's probably smashed to smithereens.'

'Smithereens? What is that?

He wrinkled his nose. It made him even cuter, if that was humanly possible.

'You know—broken into lots and lots of tiny pieces. Irreparable.'

He nodded. 'Aha. Can't be fixed?'

She smiled. 'You got it.'

His hand tightened on her waist, edging her a little closer, and she didn't object. She liked his hand there. She was happy standing next to his shoulder with his arm anchored around her.

'So, your friends… The ones you're here with. Will they be looking for you?'

He gazed across the crowd. 'I'm quite sure they are.' He shrugged. 'But I don't always want to be found.'

Hmmm… More mystery. He was so good at deflecting questions. It was almost an art form.

He turned towards her, pulling her so they were face to face. 'Are you comfortable without *your* friends, Ruby Wetherspoon? Are you happy to watch the Paris fireworks with some strange man who pulled you from the crowd?'

It was the way he said it. The way he looked at her. The gentle smile on his face and the twinkle in his eyes. For a second she didn't want to breathe.

The wind caught her curls and blew them across his face. He laughed and took her hair in his hand, smoothing it down and tucking it behind her ear. She lifted her hand and put it on his chest. She could feel his warm skin on her palm through his thin T-shirt. She could feel the curling hairs on his chest.

The man just oozed sex appeal. If anyone had told her this time last year that she would be standing here, now, like this, she would have shaken her head in disbelief.

But right now there wasn't any place else she'd rather be. 'You're not a stranger,' she said simply. 'You're Alex.'

The countdown started around them.

Dix…neuf…huit…sept…

'Yes,' he murmured. 'Tonight I'm just Alex.'

The world around them exploded. Multi-coloured lights flickered up and down the outside of the Eiffel Tower. And Alex bent to kiss her.

The fireworks around her were nothing to the ones exploding in her brain. She didn't do this. She didn't do any of this. But everything about it felt right.

This was the kind of thing she could tell her grandkids about when she was an old woman. *I once kissed a gorgeous Frenchman in Paris on New Year's Eve*.

Because this *was* a fairytale. This wasn't real life.

Except Alex's kiss was more than a fairytale. It was right up there with an award-winning movie.

Tingles were going to places that tingles hadn't been in a long time. One of his hands was resting gently on her lower back—the other was holding the back of her head. Except it wasn't *holding* the back of her head…it was *caressing* the back of her head. His fingers tangled through her hair, gently moving with tantalising softness to the side of her face.

If she could capture this moment and stuff it in a jar she would keep it for ever.

His lips finally pulled free and she had to stop herself reaching out for more. When her eyes finally opened his blue gaze was on her, his fingers still on her cheek. She'd thought the moment would be gone. But it wasn't.

It was still exploding in the stars all around.

He smiled at her. People were still shouting in the street beneath their feet, jumping up and down, and a million mobile phones were being held aloft to capture the last few seconds of the firework display.

'Happy New Year,' he whispered.

'Happy New Year,' she murmured. She couldn't wipe the smile off her face. It would probably last for eternity.

They stood for a little while as the firework display

came to an end and the lights on the Eiffel Tower finally finished.

He grabbed her hand in his. 'What say we get away from all this? Do you want to find something to eat? To drink?'

Her eyes flickered towards the far-off sign where she was to meet her friends. People were still tightly packed around it. There was no way she would be able to find her friends, then fight her way back through the crowd to Alex. The choice was simple.

'Food sounds good.'

The crowd around their feet had dispersed a little. The excitement of the countdown and the end of the fireworks display had sent people dispersing into the surrounding streets.

He jumped down and reached his arms up to catch her around her waist as she sat on the top of the wall, and he placed her gently on the ground.

Getting through the crowd was much easier with Alex in charge. No one seemed to argue with a broad-shouldered, six-foot-four man. He swept her along easily, pulling her behind until most of the crowd was behind them.

For a few seconds she thought there was a strange group of men behind her—all in black, with earpieces. But seconds later they'd vanished and she forgot about them.

By the time they reached Avenue George V the street was still busy but the crowd was gradually beginning to thin out. There were a number of open restaurants and cafés still serving customers. Alex hesitated a second outside of the door of the Four Seasons, then pulled her over to one of the other nearby restaurants with tables on the street.

He pulled out a chair and gestured for her to sit down. She rubbed her hands together and smiled at his good manners. It had been a while since she'd met anyone who'd pull out a chair for her.

'Are you cold? We can sit inside.' He pointed at her fingers.

'No, it's fine.' The restaurant looked claustrophobic, packed with people. It was strange, but outside seemed more private.

A waiter appeared quickly and nodded to Alex.

'What would you like, Ruby? Wine? coffee?' He picked up a menu. 'Food?'

She smiled. 'I'll have a cocktail.' Her eyes scanned the menu. 'I'll have a Royal Pink Circus—and the biggest piece of cake they've got.'

Alex grinned and reached forward and grabbed the menu. 'What *is* that? Hmm…vodka, champagne, raspberries and violet syrup. Interesting choice.'

He turned and spoke in rapid French to the waiter.

Under the warm light from the restaurant she got a clear view of the man she'd just kissed. Under dim lights he'd been gorgeous. Under street lights…*wow*.

She couldn't help but smile. No phone. No camera to record the moment. Typical. Her friends would never believe this. His blue eyes stood out even from across the table, complemented by the lightly tanned skin she hadn't noticed before and the shadow along his chin.

'So, what plans do you have?'

She shrugged. 'I don't have my phone so I can't contact my friends.' She waved her arm. 'But it's fine. I know where I am from here. I can find my way back to my hotel.'

She gestured towards the Four Seasons.

'For a second I thought you were going to take me in there.' She glanced down at her red wool coat, jeans and boots. 'Somehow I don't think I would have got inside.'

He gave a little shake of his head. 'Oh, you would have got inside.' He reached over and took her hand. 'But I wasn't talking about right now. How long are you in Paris?'

Mysterious Alex was getting better by the second. He actually wanted to know if she was staying.

'Just another two days. We go home on Friday. What about you?'

'I don't really have a fixed timetable. I can go home any time. Do you want to do some sightseeing for the next two days? See a little more of Paris before you go home?'

Her heart gave a little leap. She was here with a group of friends, but Polly wouldn't mind if she spent some time with a sexy French guy—in fact after this last year she'd probably encourage her.

She nodded as the waiter appeared. 'That sounds fun.'

He set down the raspberry cocktail in a sugar-frosted glass. She took a tiny sip. The alcohol was stronger than she'd expected and the bubbles from the champagne flew up her nose. She choked and laughed.

'Wow|! This Royal Pink Circus is a doozy!'

'What does that mean?' asked Alex as he took a sip of his beer.

'You know—extraordinary, spectacular. A doozy.'

Next came the cake. If it could even be described as that. This was no delicate *petit-four*. This was honest-to-goodness the biggest piece of cake in the universe. Seven layers of sponge, cream, raspberries and sauce.

She picked up her fork and took a bite. 'Oh, wow…' She leaned back in the chair. It had been hours since she'd had dinner. Alex was smiling at her again, with a twinkle in his eye. 'Would you like a piece? This is to die for.'

He shook his head. 'Don't let me deprive you. I'm getting enough pleasure seeing the look on your face.'

'Didn't you order anything?' She waved at the empty space in front of him, poising her fork above the cake again.

'I did, but I asked the waiter to bring your cake first.'

She swallowed another heavenly spoonful, 'I could get used to this kind of consideration, you know.'

Something flickered across his face that made her wonder if she'd made some kind of dreadful *faux pas*.

But Alex just nodded in agreement. 'And I think I could get used to Ruby Wetherspoon, who knows how to eat a piece of cake.'

She licked her fork. 'What? Do the people around you not eat?'

He lifted his eyebrows as the waiter reappeared and put a plate down in front of him, with the biggest BLT and portion of French fries she'd seen in a long time. She reached over and grabbed a fry.

'Not like you,' came his amused reply.

She shrugged. 'They certainly don't skimp on portions here. I'll need to remember this place. What's it called?' She looked at the name and screwed up her face. 'Too difficult. I'll just need to remember it's next to the fairytale hotel.'

'The fairytale hotel?' He'd started to eat and was making short work of the fries.

She nodded her head sideways. 'Yeah, next door. Isn't that the hotel every little girl wants to stay in when she comes to Paris?'

'I thought that was Cinderella's Castle at Disneyland?'

'Yeah, well. I'm older now. Tastes change.' She eyed her cocktail again. 'You know, you're going to hate me. But this is going straight to my head. Do you think I could order a coffee instead?'

He gave a wave of his hand and ordered her a coffee.

The cocktail might be a little strong, but the cake was perfect. The restaurant was perfect. The ambience in the street was perfect. And Alex…? Even more perfect.

'Have you been up the Eiffel Tower yet?' he asked.

She nodded, then leaned across the table and whispered, 'Don't tell anyone, but I thought I was going to be sick. It was okay looking into the distance, but when I looked down…' She made a swaying motion in her seat and shook her head. 'Bad idea.'

He laughed. 'And have you been to Versailles and the Louvre?'

She nodded. 'I queued for ever to see the Mona Lisa.'

He raised his eyebrows. 'What did you think?'

She wrinkled her nose. 'Honestly? Smaller than I expected—and a bit dark. But do you know the strangest thing? I still wanted to reach out and touch it.'

'She mesmerised you. Just like she did Leonardo. What about Notre Dame? Have you been there yet?'

She nodded again.

He held up his knife and fork. 'How long have you been here?'

'Just a few days. We've tried to cram in as much as possible.'

'Is there anywhere you'd still like to see?'

'Of course! This is Paris.' She counted off on her fingers, 'I still want to visit the Sacré Coeur and Montmartre—oh, and the Père Lachaise cemetery.'

He took a drink of his beer. 'So, I offer to take you sightseeing and you want to visit dead people?'

He slid down in his chair a little—he seemed to be relaxing more and more as their conversation continued.

'Well, I guess I bring out the best in you.'

She laughed. 'It's supposed to be beautiful—enchanting. Haven't you ever walked around a cemetery before? In the summer it can be so peaceful. I actually quite like wandering around and looking at the inscriptions in the gravestones. There's a few in our local church that have a skull and crossbones on them, showing that people had the plague. It's fascinating.'

His smile spread from ear to ear. 'Ruby, every time I think I might know you a little you say something else that surprises me.'

'Is that bad?'

He shook his head. 'No, it's good. *Very* good.' He reached over and took her hand. 'I'm sure I can find some things in the next two days for us to visit.'

'But today's New Year's Day. Everywhere will be closed.'

'Don't worry about that. I'll work something out.'

She was so wrapped up in him—in the way he was smiling at her, the way he was flirting with her—that she almost didn't notice the men in long black coats until they were almost on top of them.

One of them put a black-gloved hand sternly on Alex's shoulder, bent down and spoke quietly in his ear. She couldn't make out a word.

'Alex? What's wrong? Who is this?'

The expression on his face changed instantly. First it was a flare of anger, then it was a pure panic. He stood up, sending his chair flying.

'Alex?'

The black-coated man barely even acknowledged her presence.

'Ruby, I'm sorry—I have to go.' He fumbled in his coat for his phone. 'Give me your number. I'll call you.'

Her hands went automatically to her bag. No phone. She'd lost it.

'I don't have my phone, and I can't remember what my number is.'

She felt like an idiot. Everyone should know their mobile number. And she did—she had it written down at home—but right now she couldn't tell him if her life depended on it.

'What's wrong, Alex?'

He shook his head. He wasn't focused on her any more. He looked shocked.

'It's my family. Tell me where you're staying. I'll send you a message.'

She rattled off the name of the low-budget hotel where they were staying. He mumbled something to the man behind him.

'I'm sorry. I need to go. I'll send you a message later.'

He walked around to her side of the table and bent to kiss her. It was the briefest moment, but his lips came into contact with hers in the lightest of kisses. A brush like a butterfly's wings.

And then he was gone.

Surrounded by black coats, disappearing down the street.

The fairytale was over.

January

Ruby crashed through the door with her shopping bags, work folders and uniform over her arm.

Polly was sitting cross-legged on the sofa, eating a plate of noodles. She nodded towards the kitchen. 'Come and sit down, Ms Misery. Noodles in the pot and wine in the fridge.'

She was knackered. Honestly and truly exhausted. Between the long hours and the killer commute every day, this job was proving tougher than she'd ever thought. But today had been a winner. Today she'd finally believed that her work had helped a patient regain a little part of his speech. 'No' had been the finest word she'd heard in a while.

She poured the wine and tipped the rest of the noodles into a bowl, kicking off her shoes and thudding down sofa next to Polly. 'What are you watching?'

'Just the news. How was your day?'

She put the first spoonful of noodles into her mouth. It was like a chilli explosion. Polly had a penchant for spicy foods, and as she was the cook in the house Ruby was getting used to it. She took a few quick gulps of wine to try and quell the burn.

Her eyes flickered to the screen and she inhaled quickly, coughing and spluttering as her noodles went down the wrong way.

Polly turned and laughed, leaning over and slapping her hand on Ruby's back. 'Was the chilli kick that strong?'

But Ruby couldn't answer. Her eyes were streaming.

She swallowed as best she could. 'Turn that up,' she said, pointing at the screen.

'What?' Polly mumbled, her mouth still full of food.

'Turn it up!'

She started throwing cushions and newspapers around, searching for the TV remote, which seemed to have an innate ability to hide whenever she left the house. Finally she spied it, hiding part-way under the sofa. She pointed it at the TV and pressed the volume button hard.

Polly just stared at her open-mouthed.

'There are unconfirmed reports that King Leopold of Euronia is seriously unwell.

'The normally quiet principality has seen a flurry of activity in the last few days as private jets have been seen landing at the state airport. Crown Prince Alexander has returned home after a recent sojourn in the US, where he was apparently working with MIT and Harvard University.

'Prince Alexander, the only child of widowed King Leopold, is rarely seen. He is an astute businessman who is passionate about his country. Rumours have circulated in the last few years about King Leopold's declining health and his lessening public engagements.

'Crown Prince Alexander was seen returning in a private jet in the early hours of New Year's morning, quickly followed by dignitaries from the surrounding area. We've been told to expect a statement in the next few minutes.'

'It's him,' Ruby croaked, pointing at the screen. 'It's Alex.'

It was almost as if an elephant had sat on her chest, stopping her breathing.

Polly dropped her fork and bowl on the table. 'What?' She glanced from Ruby to the TV and back again. 'Him? *He's* your Alex? Crown Prince...whatever?'

'Apparently.'

Her throat had dried like an arid desert. She picked up

the wine and gulped it down as if it were a glass of water, grimacing as it hit her tastebuds.

Her brain was in overdrive. Tiny words, tiny phrases, looks that had fleeted across his face and disappeared in an instant. Tiny pieces of a jigsaw puzzle she'd had no idea even existed.

A close-up picture of Alex emerging from a plane appeared on the screen and she gasped. He looked awful. He was still handsome, but his tanned skin was pale and there were lines around his eyes—even their blueness had dimmed.

He hadn't called. He hadn't left a message at all. At first she'd been irritated. Then, she'd been angry. Finally, she'd admitted to herself she was devastated.

But this was something else entirely. Her fairytale in Paris had never included a real live prince.

Polly started chattering in her ear. 'No wonder you were miserable. What a catch. Ruby—you kissed a *prince*!' She stared back at the screen. 'I wonder what's going on.'

The newsreader interrupted the next report mid-story. 'We're going to cross live now to Euronia for an announcement.'

A sombre-faced grey-haired, black-suited man stood on a podium. A sign appeared beneath him: 'Palace Principale'.

'What does that mean?' asked Polly.

'I have no idea.' Ruby shook her head.

The man started speaking. 'After consultation with the Crown Council, the principality of Euronia would like to announce that, with immediate effect, Crown Prince Alexander de Castellane will be taking over as Regent of Euronia as His Majesty King Leopold is no longer able to exercise his royal functions. The Crown Prince Alexander will now be known as Prince Regent.'

The picture cut back to the newsreader as he glanced up from reading the piece of paper in his hands. 'There are unconfirmed reports that King Leopold has suffered a catastrophic stroke, but no one at the palace is willing to comment on his medical condition. We'll bring you an update whenever we get one.'

Polly turned to face Ruby. 'Wow. Just...*wow.*'

Ruby felt sick. Her heart had squeezed when she'd seen the expression on Alex's face. How on earth must he be feeling?

She wanted to be angry with him—she really did. Why couldn't he have told her who he really was?

But deep down she knew the answer to that.

A real live prince wouldn't be looking for a girl like her.

Not in this lifetime anyway.

CHAPTER ONE

Ten years later

'RUBY?' THE DEPARTMENT receptionist shouted at her again.

Too many things were circulating in her brain. She needed to refer one child to someone else, another to an oral surgeon, and speak to the dietician about another.

She turned round and was nearly knocked over by a giant flower display. Her stomach tied itself up in little knots.

Rena smiled as she tried to hold up the giant display. 'You've got flowers again. Even more gorgeous than the last time. And, oh, *so* expensive.' She looked thoughtful for a moment. 'It's been a little while since the last bunch. Do you realise that, on and off, it's been six years you've been getting these mysterious flowers? Right from when you started here. Surely you must have guessed by now who they're from?'

Ruby shook her head. 'I have no idea. The cards never say anything specific.' She pulled out the latest one. 'See? *"Thinking of you and wishing you well."*'

Rena frowned at the card in her hands. 'Have you tried phoning the florist to find out who sent them?' She was a regular amateur detective and could usually find a missing set of case notes in less than five minutes.

'Of course I have. But these places are used to things like this. They don't give anything away.'

'Well, whoever it is, money certainly isn't an object. These must have cost a fortune.' Rena reached up and touched one of the coloured petals. 'They smell gorgeous.' She frowned. 'Who have you seen lately that could have sent these?' She paused and bit her lip. 'Maybe it's Paul? Maybe he's trying for a reunion?'

Ruby shook her head. 'Paul would never send flowers like these.' Then she smiled. 'Paul would never send flowers full-stop. Which is why we're not together any more. That, and a whole lot of other things.'

Paul could never live up to the memory of Alex. Sometimes it felt like a figment of her imagination. Something so special that only she could remember. The only person she ever spoke to about it was Polly.

She'd tried to forget about him—she really had. She'd even lived with a lovely guy called Luke for a couple of years. But things just hadn't worked out between them, and in her heart she knew why. No matter how hard she tried, she just couldn't forget about her mysterious prince.

Rena smiled and touched Ruby's arm. 'Well, you've obviously got a devoted, secret admirer. It's romantic. It's mysterious. I could probably work it into a book somewhere.'

Ruby laughed. 'Rena, you write about murder and mayhem. I'm not sure I want to end up in one of your books!'

She cast her eyes over the flowers again. Stunning. Really stunning. Beautiful tropical colours. Red, pinks, yellows and oranges. Like a burst of sunshine on a rainy day.

She swallowed. The flowers had stopped for a few years. Right around the time when it had been all over the news that Prince Alex had married Princess Sophia of Leruna. A perfect fairytale princess. Dainty and blonde—nothing like Ruby. A baby had followed quickly afterwards. Followed by her tragic death due to breast cancer.

All that crammed into the space of two years. And not a single bunch of flowers over that time.

The coincidence played on her mind. The deliveries had started again around eighteen months ago. Could the flowers have been from Alex all along?

Something coiled deep inside her.

She walked over to the window and stared outside at the pouring rain of London. Another wasted five minutes thinking about her prince.

Her prince. What a joke. She'd never used those words out loud and never would. It was bad enough that they circulated around her brain.

Alex might have had tragedy, but he'd also had a life. Promotion for Ruby had come at a price. She'd been working so hard these last few years. Trying to change the lives of children who had been born with speech difficulties. It had left no time for her, no time for relationships, and no time to think about having a family.

The responsibilities of being in charge of a department in one of the best hospitals in London were relentless.

Sometimes she felt like a hamster, running in a wheel that she could never get off.

A porter brushed past, sending the scent of the beautiful flowers to meet her. It brought her back to reality quickly.

There was no point dreaming. She was nobody's princess.

And it was time to get back to work.

She was dashing around like a mad woman. Everyone in this hospital was the same. It had taken five different attempts for him to finally get some directions.

He stopped for a second to breathe. Ten years. Ten years since that night in Paris.

How different his life might have been. If his father hadn't been taken ill he would have met Ruby a few hours later in Paris and taken her sightseeing. That thought still made his stomach tighten.

She looked almost the same. Her dark curls were a little shorter. Her figure was just as curvy. But the expression on her face was more serious. Tired, even. And there were little lines around her eyes.

He didn't even want to look in the mirror lately. Although only ten years had passed since they'd last seen each other he was sure he'd aged about twenty.

The flowers he'd sent were sitting on the desk behind her. She wasn't even looking at them. Everyone else was oohing and aahing over them. But Ruby was too busy. Ruby was focused.

He watched her hurry around; she had a pile of cards in her hands.

'Seventeen new referrals,' she said to a nearby colleague, 'and Caroline is stuck in a traffic jam in the middle of London. How on earth are we going to get all these children assessed?'

He sucked in a breath. He'd never doubted for a second that Ruby would be dedicated to her work. But would it stand in the way of what he wanted her to do?

She tucked a curl behind her ear. It made his fingers tingle. *He'd* done that once.

'Can I help you?' someone asked him.

He shook his head. It was now or never.

He stepped forward. 'One of those referral cards will be from me.'

Ruby spun around to face him. The professional mask fell as quickly as the cards from her hand. His accent was unmistakable; she couldn't fail to recognise it.

'Alex,' she said. Nothing else. Her eyes locked on to his.

'Ruby.'

She tilted her head to the side, as if she were contemplating a million different questions, before sucking in a deep breath and giving a visible little shake of her head.

Ten years. Ten years since he'd run his fingers through those soft dark curls and looked into those chocolate-brown eyes. Ten years since he'd felt the silky softness of her skin, tasted the sweetness of her lips.

Every sensation, every touch, every taste flashed in front of him in an instant.

But Ruby wasn't caught in the same spell that he was.

She bent down to retrieve the cards and he knelt to help her. It was inevitable that their hands touched as they reached out towards the same card.

She pulled her hand away as if she'd been stung. 'Why, Alex? Why are you here?'

It was as if someone had reached into his chest and twisted his heart. There it was. In a few simple words a whole multitude of hurt. No one else would hear it. No one else would understand. But Ruby's deep brown eyes were fixed on his and he could see everything there. She looked wounded. Ten years on and her hurt was still easily visible.

But what did she see when she looked at him? He wasn't Alex the twenty-four-year-old any more—the bachelor Crown Prince with the world at his feet. He was a father. He was a widower. He was Prince Regent. The Prince continually in waiting.

And he was desperate.

In his head this had all been so easy. *Find someone you would trust with your daughter. Find Annabelle the expert help she needs.*

It had even seemed sensible to the palace advisors. If they'd questioned his choice of therapist at first, once they'd researched Ruby's qualifications and seen her recent publications all queries had vanished.

But now he was here in the flesh it was so much harder. Now he could see her. Now he could hear her. Now he could smell her. Her light floral scent was drifting around him.

He'd had no idea of the effect seeing Ruby again would have on him. Ten years… Ten years lost. Ten years of what might have been.

'Alex?'

The word jolted him and he smiled. No one called him Alex any more. No one had ever really called him just Alex.

He straightened up and handed her the final cards.

'I'm here because I need your help, Ruby.'

Any minute now a bunch of unicorns would come cantering along the hospital corridor, with exploding rainbows all around them.

She'd dreamt about Alex before. But never like this. Never in her workplace. All those dreams had been set back in Paris. Or in the Euronian palace that she'd looked at online.

But Alex standing in front of her at work, asking for her help…? She was obviously losing her mind.

He reached out and touched her bare arm. Short sleeves were essential in a hospital environment, to stop the spread of infection. This time she didn't pull away. This time she let the feel of the pads of his fingers spread warmth through her chilled arm.

He was really here.

This wasn't a strange hallucination due to overwork or lack of chocolate.

Ten years she'd waited to talk to this man again. Ten years waiting to ask him what the hell had happened back in Paris and why he'd never contacted her.

Alex—her Alex. *Her prince* was finally standing right in front of her.

He was every bit as handsome as she remembered. Better, even.

Tanned skin, dark hair and bright blue eyes. She'd sometimes wondered if she'd imagined how blue they were. But she hadn't. If anything she'd underestimated their effects. But, then again, she'd never seen Alex in daylight.

She wasn't imagining any of this. All six foot four of him was standing right in front of her.

Her eyes lowered to where his hand was touching her. Tiny electric pulses were shooting up her arm. She didn't know whether to cry or be sick.

Every part of her imagination had just turned into reality.

In a way, it was a relief. She *had* met Alex. He *did* remember her. So why was that making her so darn angry right now?

He pulled his hand back from her arm and she lifted her head, pulling her shoulders back. *He'd taken his hand away.* And it had left her feeling bereft. Now she was feeling angry with herself. She didn't have a sensible thought in her head right now.

She swallowed and looked him in the eye. 'How can I help you, Alex?' The words were automatic. It was all she could manage right now.

He looked around. 'Is there somewhere we can talk?'

She nodded and gestured with her arm for him to walk down the corridor, stopped at a door, pulled a key from her pocket and unlocked the door.

Her office. It even had her name on the door: 'Ruby Wetherspoon, Head of Speech and Language'. She'd done well. Most days she was proud. Today she had no idea how she felt.

The office was small, but neat and tidy. She pointed to a chair and invited him to sit. It was almost a relief to sit at the other side of the desk and have the heavy wooden structure between them.

'How exactly do you think I can be of assistance to you, Alex?'

Her words were formal, her professional façade slipping back into place. The juggling of the cards on the table-top was the only sign of her nerves. She hoped he wouldn't notice.

'It's not me. It's my daughter Annabelle. She's three years old now and she isn't speaking.'

Ruby nodded automatically. His daughter. Of course. Why else would be come to her?

She had this sort of conversation every day. This one wouldn't be much different.

'Three years old is still an acceptable age for speech development. All children develop at a different rate. Some children have a delay in their speech and language development. Have you had her hearing checked?'

He sighed. She was going back to basics—which was the correct thing for a health professional. But she could tell from his expression he'd heard it all before.

'I've had ten different professional opinions on Annabelle. The latest of which is selective mutism. Her hearing is fine. Her comprehension is fine. She doesn't seem to *want* to speak.'

She could feel herself bristle. Ten assessments on a child? Talk about overkill. Why not just let her develop at her own pace? She tried to be pragmatic.

'How does she communicate with those around her?'

'She signs.'

Ruby was surprised. 'Proper signing?'

He nodded. 'We have a member of staff who's deaf. She's been able to sign since she was young.'

It wasn't particularly unusual in children who were deaf, or in children who had deaf siblings. But it *was* unusual in a child who could apparently hear and speak.

She lifted her hands. 'Then maybe she thinks that's normal?'

He shook his head.

It was time to ask some more questions.

'Has Annabelle ever spoken? Ever said a few words?'

'Only on a few select occasions.'

Strange… Ruby couldn't help but be a little curious. Selective mutism was certainly unusual but she'd dealt with a few cases before. She'd even published some professional papers on it.

Ruby lowered her voice. 'Does she speak to you, Alex?'

The question was straight to the heart of the matter. It was a natural question for any health professional, but she saw him recoil. She'd seen this before. He felt this was his fault. She'd dealt with lots of parents who felt guilty about whatever issue their child had. Most of the time it was just hard luck. Genetics. A developmental delay. A head injury or similar accident.

She asked the most practical question. 'Does Annabelle have anything significant in her medical history?'

'No. Nothing.'

They sat in silence for a few seconds. She couldn't take it. She couldn't take it a second longer. Her professional façade was slipping. After all this time—just to turn up like this and expect her to help him—just because he asked? Did she have *mug* stamped across her forehead?

She couldn't even acknowledge the flutters in her stomach. She couldn't even explain her feeling when she'd heard his voice and turned to see him again after all this time. It had been like a sucker punch.

It was time to stop being so polite.

Ruby leaned back in her chair. 'I don't get it, Alex. After all this time, why come to me? Why come here? You must have plenty of people in Euronia willing to help with your daughter.'

His brow was lined with deep furrows that marred his handsome face. It made her feel self-conscious. She only had the lightest dusting of make-up on, to emphasise her brown eyes and pink lips. How much had she changed in the last ten years? Would he be disappointed by what he saw?

Why was he here? Why, after all this time, had he been convinced that this was the right thing to do?

'I want to feel as if I've tried everything possible for Annabelle. I haven't had faith in any of the people who have seen her and assessed her. And, whilst the latest diagnosis seems reasonable, I'm not happy at the treatment plan for Annabelle.'

Maybe that's because you should have left her alone to be a normal toddler. Ruby was still imagining what ten assessments had done to that poor child. But she couldn't say those words out loud.

It was difficult. This was Alex, her mysterious Frenchman—who wasn't a Frenchman after all. She'd never thought she'd come into contact with him for *work*. She never thought she'd come into contact with him again.

'What *is* the treatment plan for Annabelle?'

He pushed a folder he'd been carrying across the desk towards her. She opened it and scanned it quickly. Whilst the assessment might have been thorough, she didn't agree at all with what was in the plan, or with the conclusions it had already surmised.

Ever the professional, she raised her head and selected her words carefully. 'Every professional will have a different idea of the correct plan for your daughter. It's not really my place to disagree.'

He pointed to the file. 'What would *you* do?'

She opened her mouth automatically to speak, then closed it again. 'What does it matter?'

'Because I'd like you to come to Euronia and assess Annabelle for yourself. I'd like you to be the one to plan her care and treat her.'

He might as well have dumped a bucket of ice-cold water over her head. She was stunned. 'That's impossible.'

'No. It's not. I know you have a job here, and patients, but I've offered your Director of Services a generous annual bequest if you'll agree to come and work for me—for Annabelle,' he added quickly.

'What?' She stood up, the chair behind her flying backwards. 'You've done *what*?'

She couldn't believe her ears. The tiny glimmer of hope that he'd searched her out for any reason other than his daughter died in an instant. He might be a prince in another country, but he didn't seem much like a prince to her now.

'And you did that without speaking to me first?' She walked around the desk, reached down, and grabbed hold of his jacket, pulling him to his feet. 'How dare you, Alex? How *dare* you? Ten years later you think you can just walk into my life and *buy* me?'

Anger and the untold resentment that had festered for ten years came spilling out. This wasn't her. She never acted like this. But she just couldn't help it.

She shook her head fiercely, blazing with fury. 'You can't buy me, Alex. I'm not for sale.' She held out one hand. 'I have a job. Responsibilities. I have staff to take care of—patients to take care of.'

She stared at her other hand, still gripping tightly to the lapel of his jacket. What on earth was she doing? Her knuckles were white and she quickly loosened her grip and took a step backwards. Her heart was thudding in her chest. Her head was thumping.

'And you could do it better if you had two more permanent members of staff.' He cut her off before she had more time to think about it.

Her mouth fell open. 'What?'

'That's what I promised your director. Permanent funding for two more members of staff if they'll release you to work with Annabelle. Plus filling your post while you're gone.'

Her brain was whizzing. Two more members of staff could make a world of difference to this place. Time. It would give her staff time. The one thing she couldn't conjure up for them.

She hated rushing assessments. She hated not having enough time to allocate to the children who needed her. She hated having to turn children away because there just wasn't enough space for any more patients. Two more members of staff was a luxury she couldn't afford to ignore.

'Why on earth would you do this?'

He sat back down in his seat and put his head in his hands.

She'd read about everything that had happened to him in the last ten years. Now here he was, right in front of her, and she actually felt sorry for him.

She started shaking her head. 'It feels like blackmail, Alex. I haven't seen you in ten years. *Ten years!* Not a word from you—nothing. And now this.' She started pacing around the small office. 'I know what happened to your father. The whole world knows. But you never contacted me. You never said anything. I was left sitting in that hotel for two days, wondering if I'd imagined everything. Thank goodness Polly dragged me out and about.'

His head shot up. 'I did contact you. I sent a message.'

'I never got any message!' She was still angry.

'But I sent one. My head of security—he took it to the hotel. Gave it to the reception clerk. You *must* have got it.'

She shook her head and lowered her voice. 'There was no message, Alex. None. I waited and waited.'

She hated the way the words made her feel. She hated the way she wanted to reach out and grab them. Grab the fact that Alex *had* tried to reach her—no matter what else had happened in his life. But it was the expression on his face that was worse. He looked hurt. He looked injured.

But, most importantly, he looked tired.

She knelt down in front of him. His father had been sick for ten years. He had a country to run. His wife had died from cancer—she was assuming he'd nursed her through that—and he had a daughter whom he clearly loved but needed help with.

She reached up and touched his hand. Her skin coming into contact with his almost made her smile. Her pale skin against his tanned skin. A world of difference.

The sensation she felt touching his skin was still there.

Still electrifying. But she had to put a reality check on things.

She spoke quietly. 'Why now, Alex? Why me?'

It was only a few words but they meant so much more than she was actually saying. He knew that. He must.

He reached up and touched her cheek. *Zing.*

'Because there is no one else. No one else I could trust with the thing that is most precious to me.'

She blinked, trying to stop the tears forming in her eyes.

Nothing about wanting to see her again. Nothing about wanting to know how she was.

But he had just told her he trusted her with the thing most precious in the world to him. His daughter.

She didn't know whether to be happy or sad.

He pulled a picture from his wallet. A sad-looking blonde-haired toddler. She was beautiful. Just like her mother had been. But she wasn't laughing. She wasn't playing. She didn't look happy.

'Oh, Alex…' she breathed.

'Will you come?' His voice sounded as if it was breaking.

She stood up, her mind whirling. 'I'll need to think about it. You'll need to give me some time.'

How ironic. Ten years later she was asking him for time.

How on earth could she not do this? The picture of the little girl had broken her heart. She had no idea if she could help or not—but she could try.

Outside her office she could see figures rushing past. The hospital was always busy—never enough time to do everything. It was wearing her down. She loved her job, but the truth was she'd spent the last few months searching the vacancy bulletins.

One thing. If she did this one thing she could help this department and these kids for ever. Was it really such a hard task?

A chair scraped along the floor behind her. Alex had

stood up, a resigned look on his face. He nodded at the desk, 'I'll leave those things for you to look at. My contact details are there. Let me know when you make up your mind.'

He thought she was going to say no. And right now that was the way she was leaning. What would she do with her flat—her cat—if she left to go abroad?

The file and the photo of Annabelle sat on her desk. He had his hand on the door handle.

'Alex? How did you know where I was?'

It had bothered her since he'd first arrived.

His bright blue eyes fixed on hers. It was the first time she'd seen anything resembling the eyes she'd looked into ten years ago.

'I've always known where you were, Ruby,' he said quietly as he opened the door and walked down the corridor.

CHAPTER TWO

THE PLANE JOURNEY was smooth. The private jet immaculate. Any other person might have taken the opportunity
to relax, but Ruby's stomach had been jittery ever since
they'd left London.

She stared out of the window as the plane came into
land. Her first sight of Euronia. A stunning, winding coastline overlooking the Mediterranean Sea. A population of
two hundred thousand people over an area of only seventy
kilometres. The rich and famous flocked here because of
the tax benefits. The press loved Euronia because it seemed
to host every celebrity wedding that had ever existed.

The plane landed quickly and glided to a halt on the
Tarmac. She hadn't spoken to Alex since she'd seen him
at the hospital. The number he'd given her had been for his
secretary—a chirpy little man who'd been delighted when
she'd said she would come to Euronia and had spoken with
great fondness about Annabelle. He'd arranged everything.
Even advising on what kind of clothing to bring and asking
her for her dress and shoe size so he could provide some
extra items if required.

The pilot and the stewardess had both been polite but
formal. She wondered if they were used to fading into the
background.

A black limousine was waiting for her.

'Welcome to Euronia, Ms Wetherspoon. It will only

take ten minutes to reach the palace. Please make yourself comfortable and help yourself to refreshments.'

Another man in black. She hid her smile. Any minute now she would hear the theme tune to that movie in her head. It was the same garb that the men in Paris had been wearing all those years ago. Those men had made her uncomfortable. This man was a little different. His eyes were scanning the horizon constantly. Was he a chauffeur or security?

She settled into the comfortable leather seats. The 're-freshments' in front of her were wine, champagne and beer. It was ten-thirty in the morning. What she'd actually like was a cup of tea.

She watched the scenery speed past.

Polly's words echoed in her ears. *'This isn't a movie. He's using you, Ruby. Don't get any ideas about this at all.'*

Her disdain had been apparent as soon as she'd heard what had happened. Polly had long since abandoned any romantic notions of her prince. She'd been the one to see exactly how devastated Ruby had been. But it was all right for Polly. She'd got her happy-ever-after—a doting husband and a baby in her arms.

'How long will you be gone?' she'd asked Ruby moodily.

'I have no idea.' And she really didn't. She couldn't plan anything until she'd assessed Annabelle.

The car swept through some regal gates, past armed guards and down a long pale yellow sweeping drive. The view over the Mediterranean was breathtaking.

No turning back. She was here now. She tugged at her pale green dress. It was a little more formal than what she normally wore, but at least it didn't crumple.

The palace came into view. Nicknamed the Pink Palace, the Palace Principale was built from pink and red sandstone. She'd seen pictures on the internet, but seeing it in reality was entirely different.

Ruby took a deep breath. There must be a million little

girls' birthday cakes all over the world based on this palace. Four square turrets and it seemed like hundreds of slim windows looked down on her. The palace doors were enormous, with wide sweeping steps leading up to them.

Intimidating. Definitely intimidating.

She would be lying if she claimed she'd never thought about this. Of course she had. Every girl had.

But every girl hadn't kissed a prince.

Oh, boy. She squeezed her eyes shut for a second. This was harder than she'd thought.

Actually being here in Euronia was much harder than she'd imagined it to be.

In her head this was a job. This was professional. So why was her heart fluttering so much? And why did she want to run back along that yellow driveway?

A man was standing at the top of the steps to greet her. It wasn't Alex. Of course it wasn't Alex. He hadn't even spoken to her on the phone.

She climbed the steps and looked out over the Mediterranean Sea. Lots of little white boats bobbed up and down on the beautiful blue water. *Little* boats? They probably cost more than she would earn in her lifetime. This was a whole other world.

But she was here to do a job, not to admire the scenery—no matter how beautiful it was.

The sooner she got started the better.

He watched her step from the car. She was picture-perfect. Her elegant legs were the first hint of what was to come as her slim figure emerged in a pale green dress that fluttered around her in the strong sea winds. It was an occupational hazard of having a palace on the sea.

His mother had always joked that one day a press photographer would get a picture of something they shouldn't. She'd been born before her time, and had been taken much too soon. She would have known exactly what to do with Annabelle.

He watched as Rufus, his private secretary, bustled around about Ruby. He would probably give her a headache in the first five minutes, but his heart was in the right place.

Rufus had organised everything once he'd known Ruby would be coming. From her favourite foods and TV shows to her clothes—everything would be taken care of. The only thing he'd asked for some input with was where to put her in the palace.

Alex hadn't been quite sure, but had finally decided she should be in the West Wing, overlooking the sea. The rooms there had always been his mother's favourites.

It only took a few moments before his phone rang.

'Your Majesty? I'm afraid there's a problem with our guest. Her accommodation is unsuitable. She's requesting rooms next to Princess Annabelle.' Rufus was so over-wrought he was practically squeaking.

'Take her to the library. I'll be along directly.'

Five minutes. That was all it had taken for Ruby to cause turmoil in his life. He just hoped this wasn't a decision he'd live to regret.

He strode down the stairs and along the corridor towards the library. Rufus was flapping around the doorway. He wasn't used to people not going along with his plans.

'Where is she?' Alex looked around the empty room.

'She went upstairs to Princess Annabelle's quarters. She knows Annabelle isn't there but she said she wanted to make herself familiar with the place.'

Rufus cringed. The whole thing was probably giving him palpitations. It didn't take much these days.

Alex waved his hand. 'Leave this to me.'

He didn't need Rufus getting over-excited. What on earth was Ruby *doing*? She'd barely put her feet across the front door.

He bit his lip as he climbed the stairs at a rapid pace. She wasn't used to things like this. Maybe he should try and exercise a little patience. Ruby wasn't used to royal palaces and protocols. She was here because he'd asked her to be. She might have a job to do, but she was also his guest.

He reached Annabelle's rooms quickly. The door was open wide, giving a clear view of the palace gardens and the sea. Ruby was sitting on one of the window seats, but she wasn't admiring the view. One of Annabelle's stuffed toys was in her hands. It was a koala left by the Australian ambassador after his last visit. Ruby was looking around the room carefully.

He stood behind her, looking at her outline, seeing every curve of her body. It sent a rush of blood around his own body.

He hadn't quite imagined how this would feel. Ruby, sitting in his palace, with the backdrop he'd looked at every day for years behind her. It almost seemed unreal.

'Ruby, what are you doing in here?'

She sighed and turned to face him. The first thing that struck him was her big brown eyes. So dark, so deep, so inviting... He really needed to get hold of himself.

'There are rooms right next door to Annabelle's. It would be best if I stayed there.'

'Why?' The rooms he'd chosen for her in the West Wing were brighter, more spacious. The ones next to Annabelle were smaller, usually reserved for staff. 'The other rooms are nicer. They have more space.'

She waved her hand. She didn't look happy. Was she already regretting coming here?

'I need to be next to her, Alex. You forget—I live in London. These rooms will be a penthouse compared to my flat. I need to see her, Alex. I need to see her in her own environment. I need to see how she functions. I need to see how she communicates with those around her. She's three. I need to watch her in the place where she's most comfortable. I'm not just here to assess whether she can

actually speak or not. I need to assess her ability to understand—her cognitive abilities. I need to see how she inter-
acts with those around her.'

She held out her arm across the immaculately kept
room.

'Is this Annabelle's world?'

There was tinge of sadness to her words. As if to her
the beautiful rooms were clearly lacking.

'Where is she now?'

Professional Ruby. The one he'd never really experienced before. She wasn't having wishful thoughts about
him. She was concentrating on the job she was here to do.

He glanced at his watch. 'She's with her nanny. She
goes to the local nursery for a few hours twice a week. Her
nanny thought mixing with other children might be good
for her. She's due back any minute.'

Ruby nodded and smiled.

Alex continued. 'This isn't a big country. Annabelle will
go to the local school with the other children, just like I
did. My father always believed that to lead the people you
had to be part of the people.'

'He sounds like a very wise man.' She turned and looked
out over the sea. 'Where is your father? Is he here?'

He hesitated. They kept details about King Leopold
closely guarded. But this was Ruby. He trusted her with
the details of his daughter—why not his father?

'He's not here. He's in Switzerland.'

'Switzerland?'

'His stroke was severe. We have a hospital in Euronia,
but we don't have ICU facilities.'

She walked towards him, concern lacing her brow.
Clearly no one had told her about the protocol of remaining ten steps away from the Prince. He was glad. He could
see a tiny smattering of freckles across the bridge of her
nose. Had they been there before?

If asked, he would have said that every part of her face

had been etched on his brain. But these were new. It was disconcerting. A part of Ruby he hadn't kept in his head.

She put her hand on his chest. He could practically hear the alarms going off around the building.

'Ten years on your father still needs ICU facilities?'

He was trying not to concentrate on her warm skin penetrating through his shirt. 'Yes—and no. He did at first. His recovery was limited and slow. He was moved to a specialist rehab unit. But now he has frequent bouts of pneumonia and he needs assistance with breathing. He has to be kept near an ICU. Euronia doesn't have those facilities.'

'You could get them.'

Her voice was quiet. She knew exactly what she was saying. It was enough. The rest of the words didn't have to be said out loud. No one else around him would do this.

'I could,' he said gently. 'But my father wouldn't want people to see him the way he is now. It would break his heart.' His voice was strained. Even he could hear it.

It was so strange to have Ruby standing right here in front of him, in his daughter's room. He'd imagined her in many different scenarios over the years, but this had never been one of them.

In his darkest moments, when everything had seemed insurmountable, he'd always been able to close his eyes and go back to Paris, the fireworks and Ruby.

A perfect night. With a disastrous end.

She'd suited her red coat and hat that cold night. And for the last ten years that was the way he'd remembered her.

Ruby—with the sparkle in her eyes, the flirtatious laugh and the easy chatter. Every time he thought of her there were fireworks in the background. Fireworks that matched her personality and her vitality.

But today, in the sun, the pale green chiffon complemented her dark brown curls and brown eyes. The dress covered every part of her it should, but he hadn't expected her to look quite so elegant.

It was just the two of them. No palace staff. No interruptions.

'I've met so many different people, Ruby. I see masks, façades, the whole time. I've never seen any of that with you. Ten years ago I saw someone who was devastated at not getting her dream job—someone who wasn't afraid to say that to a stranger. All the people who have assessed Annabelle...'

He shook his head.

'None of them have felt genuine to me. Oh, they might be professionals in their field. They might have letters after their names. But most of them only tell me what they think I want to hear. Others try and blind me with science. I don't think any of them have ever wanted to find out who the real Annabelle is. They might be interested in the theory or psychology of why a three-year-old won't talk...'

He put his hand on his chest, directly over hers. One set of fingers intertwined with another.

'But none of them have cared in *here* about why she isn't speaking.'

He could lean forward right now. He could lean forward and capture her lips the way he did ten years ago.

Ruby's eyes were fixed on his. 'Well, no wonder.'

'No wonder what?'

'No wonder you came looking for me.'

CHAPTER THREE

IT TOOK ANNABELLE four long days to acknowledge Ruby's existence. At first she completely ignored her, preferring to communicate in her own way with her nanny.

The nanny, Brigette, was thankfully a dedicated and sensible woman. She'd spent all her life in Euronia and had been with the family since Annabelle's arrival. The little girl trusted her completely, but once Brigette realised Ruby was here to stay and help with Annabelle it was clear she was glad of the assistance. She loved the little girl but felt frustrated that she wasn't able to help more.

Ruby was patient. But Alex was hovering around her constantly, asking her questions, destroying her concentration and patience. Any time he appeared her senses went into overdrive. The timbre of his voice, the accent, could make her legs turn to mush.

She had to drive a little bit of her anger back into her head. Her anger that she was here for Annabelle—not for Alex. It didn't matter that it might be irrational. It was the only thing currently keeping her sane.

He appeared at her shoulder, his scent drifting around her. She didn't even turn around.

'Alex, you need to leave me to get on with the job. That's what I'm here to do.'

Annabelle was playing quietly in her room. Flitting between colouring at the table and drawing chalk pictures on her board. There was a television in her room, which she rarely watched, and a tablet on the chair next to her.

She was definitely an interesting study. She was a creative little girl. The drawers at her desk were filled with cardboard, paint, ribbon, glitter and glue. She was never happier than when she was covered in the stuff. But the life of a royal princess meant that she was continually being cleaned, tidied and paraded elsewhere.

The only time she showed interest in the tablet—which she could use easily—was when she watched clips of singing and dancing from films. *Annie*, *The Sound of Music* and *Seven Brides for Seven Brothers* seemed to be the favourites.

There was a mixture of melancholy and frustration that emanated from Alex when he watched Annabelle.

'But I'm her *parent*. Aren't you supposed to talk to me and give me a report?'

Ruby nodded and gave a little sigh. 'I suppose… But I haven't finished my full assessment of Annabelle yet. I can only give you my first impressions.'

She turned around to face him, conscious of the fact that she'd be subjected to his killer blue eyes.

'This will take longer than I thought. I have to wait until Annabelle is ready to communicate with me—to work with me. I'm not going to force myself on her. She's not that type of kid.'

The smile that spread across his face was one of complete relief. He put his warm hands on her shoulders. '*That's* why you're here, Ruby. You're the first person who's assessed Annabelle that has said that to me. You don't care about the time span. You care about the child.'

Because you're paying me to.

It was an uncomfortable thought racing around in her brain. She was used to working for the health service. She'd never seen private patients before. Every child she'd assessed had been given the best possible assessment. But the health services were pushed for time and it sometimes frustrated her. Here she didn't have those worries.

Everything about this was a whole new experience. Staying in a palace. Knowing that after ten years she might bump into Alex at any second. The *you're paying me to* thought had a tiny bit of self-preservation about it. It kept things in perspective. It kept her grounded. It reminded her why she was actually here.

Alex was still touching her shoulders. She was wearing a sundress and his fingers were in direct contact with her skin. The sensations that were currently running like little pulses down her arms were conflicting with all her previous thoughts.

'Why don't we do this somewhere else?

'What?'

Do what somewhere else? She felt panic rush through her. How exactly had she been looking at him?

He lifted his hand from her shoulder and waved it towards the window. 'I've not been a very good host. Let me show you a little of Euronia.' He looked down at her sandals. 'How do you feel about a walk?'

Her sandals were pretty, but flat and comfortable. Her curiosity had definitely flared. 'I feel fine about a walk.'

'Then let's go.'

'Don't you need to let your security team know first, Alex?'

He smiled again and shook his head. 'You know, you're the only person that actually calls me that.'

'What?'

'Alex. No one else calls me that.'

She shook her head in disbelief. 'What on earth *do* they call you?'

He shrugged. 'Prince Regent or Your Majesty. If it's someone I've known a long time they might call me Alexander.'

A different world.

She stepped right up to him, her nose only inches away from his. 'But I know you as Alex. Always have. Always will.'

He smiled and gestured for her to follow him, and led her down a huge array of corridors and out through one of the back doors of the castle.

The gardens were beautiful—colourful and perfectly groomed. She recognised the marble fountain from an old black and white picture she had seen of Alex and his future wife as children.

They walked across the immaculate expanse of green lawn towards the city. It was officially the smallest city in the world—not much bigger than an average town. But it had grown exponentially as the economy of Euronia had grown.

'Did you play in these gardens when you were a child?'

He nodded. 'Yes. There's a secret maze in the forest over there. And my father ordered a tree house to be built and it took the carpenter nearly a whole year.' He gave a little sigh. 'Annabelle is still a little young to play in it. I don't even think she'll like it.'

'Haven't you ever shown it to her?'

He shook his head. 'I've been too focused on other things when it comes to Annabelle. We haven't got around to anything like that.'

Ruby nodded and bit her tongue. It was important that she find out about the relationship between Alex and his daughter. It wouldn't do well for her to criticise, but she could already imagine the kind of recommendations she might make.

'Well, if you show it to me some time maybe I can give you some suggestions on how to make it more appealing to a little girl.'

He gave a little nod as they approached a gate in the high walls. Alex keyed in a code and the door swung open.

'Won't that set off alarms everywhere?'

'No. It's my code. They'll know it's me that's opened the door.'

The back entrance opened directly on to the sea cliffs. The breeze was startlingly stiff and she shivered. She should have brought a cardigan, but the light summer breezes on the castle balcony had been pleasing.

Her bright pink dress whipped around in the wind and Alex pulled off his jacket and put it over her shoulders. The first thing she noticed was the smell of his aftershave as she slid her arms into the jacket and pulled it around her.

'Do you do this often?'

'Of course.' He raised his eyebrows. 'Do you think I spend all my time holed up in the castle?'

'I have no idea, Alex. I have no idea what you do at all.'

She heard him suck in a breath. She wasn't trying to bring up the past, but if she wanted to help Annabelle she had to have a good idea about the environment in which she lived.

The walk into the centre of the city was pleasant. It was less than a mile and they browsed at the shop windows, with several of the shopkeepers coming out to speak to them. One gave Alex some cheese, another some ham wrapped in paper.

'Your favourite,' he said with a smile.

The clothing and jewellery shops were spectacular. No prices in any window. Ruby could only imagine how much things actually cost around here.

She was surprised at how relaxed everything was. The palace was much more formal. People nodded to Alex in the street, but no one seemed in awe of him.

They'd reached the casino in the middle of the city. 'Would you like to sample some of the best cake in Euronia?' he asked.

'Is it better than the cake in Paris?'

Their eyes met. It was a moment. A second for them both to remember that night ten years ago in Paris. Both of them were smiling, as if it were an automatic reaction to the memory.

He leaned forward a little, the heat from his body emanating towards her. 'The cake in Paris won't even come close to the cake in Euronia.'

She lifted her head. They were so close. 'Is that a promise?'

He slid his hand around her back and pulled out a chair for her. 'Absolutely.'

The café Alex had chosen was opposite the casino. She'd seen pictures of the place on the internet. Just about every visitor who came to Euronia visited this café and watched the coming and goings at the casino.

'Aren't you worried you'll get harassed here?'

He shook his head. 'It's Sunday. No cruise ships moor at Euronia on a Sunday and no bus tours run. Today's the best day for me to take a walk around.'

The owner of the café appeared and nodded at Alex. 'The usual coffee and cake, Your Highness?' Alex nodded. 'And for the beautiful lady?'

'You should go and look in the glass cabinet. The cakes are amazing.'

Ruby stood up and walked over to the cabinet, spending a few minutes talking to the café owner before finally settling on a strawberry and cream sponge.

It was surreal. Sitting in the warm sunshine of Euronia with Alex.

These were the kind of things that had drifted into her imagination in the early days. Fanciful thoughts of what might have been.

Alex seemed happy here—more relaxed than he was in the palace, which was strange, as that was his home.

He drank his steaming coffee and devoured a piece of chocolate cake as soon as it appeared. He held out his fork towards her. 'Try some.'

She hesitated, then leaned forward, opening her mouth.

'Mmm, it's delicious. You're right. The cakes here *are* nicer than in Paris.'

He licked some chocolate from his lips and nodded towards her strawberry and cream sponge. 'What? All of them?'

She raised her eyebrows at him and waved her fork. 'I'm warning you—Prince or no Prince. Touch my cake and I'll spear you with my fork.'

He threw back his head and laughed. 'I'm sure you offered me a piece of your cake in Paris.'

She winked at him as she took another bite. 'I might have. But I was trying to impress you then.' She smiled and shrugged. 'Those days are gone.'

'You're not trying to impress me now?'

'No,' she said solemnly. She reached one hand over to his. Her other one was poised carefully. 'I'm just trying to distract you so I can steal some more of your chocolate cake.'

Her fork swooped in and she grabbed another piece.

He held the hand resting over his. 'That's what I like about you, Ruby. What I remember. A girl who likes to eat cake.'

She licked her fork. 'It's my best talent. It's taken years and years of practice.'

She liked this. He was relaxed here. He was much more like the Alex she remembered. Around the palace he seemed so much more uptight.

'How long has the casino been open?' She watched the stream of people entering and leaving.

'Almost three hours.'

She glanced at her watch. 'But it's only one o'clock in the day. I thought gambling would be a night-time kind of thing.'

'Have you ever been to Las Vegas or Atlantic City?'

She shook her head. 'So people gamble here all day?'

He nodded.

'And is that good or bad?'

He fixed his blue eyes on hers. 'You mean for the people, or for the place?'

She shrugged, 'Both, I guess. I don't really know that much about gambling.'

'Neither do I. But tourism is one of the ways to bring money into Euronia. The new port means that cruise ships can easily moor here. We open up part of the castle for tours at different times of the year. We've spent money building five-star hotels that keep the rich and famous happy. And we have some of the most beautiful venues for weddings in the world. That, and the tax benefits, mean that Euronia thrives.'

She listened to his words carefully, hearing the underlying pride as he said them. Ten years ago there had been financial predictions that Euronia would have to be taken over by another country to remain viable. None of those predictions had come true.

'Is that why you went to Harvard and studied business—to find a way to help Euronia?'

He gave a rueful smile. 'If I'd had my way I would have gone to Harvard to study chemistry or physics.'

She sat back in her chair. 'Really? You like that kind of thing?'

He nodded. 'Of course I do. Doesn't every little boy want to be an astronaut? I still want to. Science, maths or engineering—that's what you need a degree in.'

She couldn't help but smile. This was the Alex she'd met back in Paris. This was the guy who'd kissed her until her toes tingled. This was the guy she'd lost a tiny little piece of her heart to.

'You really looked into this?'

'Of course I did.'

She finished the last piece of her cake and licked the fork. It had been delicious. Now she knew this place existed she would try to take a daily trip.

He glanced towards her and it sent a tingle right down to her toes. A cheeky look, a flirtatious look, a maybe-none-of-those-things look, but there was no denying its effect.

It made her feel exposed. It made her feel as if all those fleeting thoughts, all those ridiculous daydreams about being here in Euronia, were being instantly read in her mind.

'Now I'm sold on the cake here I want to come back.'

'I'll bring you any time you like.'

'Good. Because I want you to bring us tomorrow.'

'Us?'

'Yes. You, me and Annabelle. I've watched her in the palace. Later on I'm going to watch her at nursery. But I also need to see how the two of you interact together.'

'But you've seen her with me in the last few days.'

'That was in the palace. This is different.' She held out her hands. 'This is normal.'

He raised his eyebrows at her. 'My life isn't normal?'

She sighed. 'No, Alex. Your life isn't normal. But Annabelle's should be. She's just a little girl. I want to see her come and eat cake or ice cream with her dad.'

If it was possible his tanned face paled. He took a few moments, and she could almost see the thoughts flickering across his face.

Alex had been so relaxed around her for the last hour. She was just praying that the palace portcullis wasn't about to come down, slamming into place.

He gave a slow nod and lifted his bright blue eyes to meet hers. He didn't get it. When he looked at her like that it was magnetising. She couldn't pull herself away if she tried.

She hated it that after ten years he could still do that to her. Still make her feel as if she was the only person around. Make all the noise and people around them just fade into the background.

Her mouth was instantly dry. She wanted to lick her lips,

but was afraid of what that might suggest. It might let him know exactly what she was thinking. And none of her current thoughts could ever be acknowledged between them.

There was one way to break this spell.

'Tell me about your wife, Alex. Tell me about Annabelle's mother.'

There. He looked as if she'd just sucker-punched him. Truth be told, she really didn't want to talk to Alex about his wife. She didn't need to hear how beautiful or wonderful she'd been—the press had already let the world know that. She especially didn't want her stomach to clench so hard she might be sick.

But this was it. This was the way to stop her thinking about her prince. *Her prince*. She was still doing it. It was natural.

And this was a natural question to ask Alex. If she wanted to assess Annabelle properly she had to know the family circumstances.

'What do you want to know?' His voice was hoarse.

She signalled to the waiter. 'Can we have some water, please?' She needed to do something with her own scratchy throat.

The sun was shining down on them, warming her arms and legs. This should be perfect. She was sitting in the most gorgeous setting. From this café she could look across the square at the port and see million-dollar boats bobbing on the sea in front of her. Across from her was the guy she'd thought about for the last ten years.

But she'd just managed to ruin the mood completely. It was time to stop things being personal—it was time to be professional.

'What happened with Sophia? I've seen pictures of the two of you sitting on the fountain at the castle as children. You obviously knew her for a long time?'

He ran his fingers through his dark hair. She was conscious of the furrows in his brow, the lines around his eyes.

He took a deep breath. 'Sophia was my oldest friend. Even though she lived in a neighbouring country our fathers were constantly doing state business together. She was always here.'

Ruby sipped the water the waiter had brought. Nothing would get rid of the dryness in her throat. 'And…?'

He looked at her, then quickly looked away again—almost as if he was embarrassed to speak about Sophia in front of her.

She licked her lips. She wanted to tell him that she only needed to know about Annabelle. But her insides were churning. This was the moment when she'd hear the things she'd always known.

His voice had the slightest tremor. It was only because she was listening so intently that she noticed.

'Sophia came to me after everything had happened. After my father had had the stroke and I'd been made Prince Regent.' His hands went back to his hair. 'Things were a mess. I was totally consumed by finances, by looking for new opportunities for Euronia. But Sophia was sick. I knew it as soon as saw her.'

He sat back in his chair. His body was rigid. One hand clenched in a fist.

'I was furious. She hadn't told me anything.' He fixed his eyes on a point over her shoulder. 'The speculation was right. She had breast cancer. It was terminal. Sophia came and told me after she'd tried a number of treatments. She'd already made her mind up that she didn't want to do that any more.'

There was a sheen across his eyes and it made Ruby's heart ache for him. But down in the pit of her stomach there was something else. A tiny smattering of jealousy that he'd felt so much for this woman.

'So you got married?'

She tried to make it sound casual. But her voice was tight and she knew it. She just hoped he wouldn't notice.

Alex gave the slightest nod of his head.

'Sophia came to me. She told me her diagnosis. She told me the one thing she wanted in the world was to have a baby before it was too late. I couldn't say no to her. I just couldn't. I loved her. People had speculated for years that we would marry—but it never entered our heads. Sophia had plans—she had big plans. She was so creative…she loved art and design. But she also had a really inquisitive nature. She was torn between design and journalism. She loved to write. She had sketches and sketches of dress designs.'

He sighed,

'And then…' he lifted his hand '…the cancer.' He shook his head. 'It was as if all her dreams just evaporated. She'd already made up her mind before she came to see me. If we had a child together it would seal the fate of our two kingdoms. Sophia was an only child. When she died her whole dynasty would die with her. She didn't want that to happen.' His voice steadied. 'Neither of us wanted that to happen.'

He pressed his lips together.

'You probably already know this, but when Sophia's father dies Annabelle will be Queen of Leruna. If he dies before Annabelle comes of age I'll be Regent to the two principalities.'

His lifted his eyes and met her gaze full-on. The implications were huge. He was telling her he'd made a pact with his childhood friend. They'd married. They'd had a child together. They'd cemented their relationship and safe-guarded the future of two countries. How noble.

She was trying hard not to be bitter. And there was still a tiny flicker of hope. He hadn't said Sophia was the love of his life. He'd said he loved her. That was different.

Ruby felt her voice wobble. 'She was really young to have breast cancer, Alex.'

'I know.' He paused. 'She had the gene.' It came out in a whisper.

Her breath caught in her throat. 'Sophia had the gene?' Everyone had heard about 'the gene' by now—the mutation linked with breast and ovarian cancer. 'What about Annabelle?'

He shook his head. 'I had her tested. She's not affected.'

Her breath left her in a whoosh. 'Oh, wow. You must be so relieved.' She toyed with the glass of water in her hands. 'I know it's a silly question, but was there nothing else they could do? It's just that…wouldn't the pregnancy have made a difference to her cancer? I thought they recommend that you don't get pregnant if you have that type of cancer?'

His face was serious. 'Sophia was very single-minded. She knew that she would die eventually. Having a child was the most important thing to her in the world. She could have had some type of chemotherapy while she was pregnant—but she refused. She did have some immediately following delivery. But she was so weak. So tired. She only took the treatment to prolong her time with Annabelle. Once she realised how sick it was making her, and how it really didn't make any difference to the outcome, she decided to stop everything. She wanted some time with Annabelle.'

'And did she have time with Annabelle?'

Ruby was trying to work out the impact on the child. Annabelle couldn't have been much more than a baby. Was there any chance that what had happened then might have had an impact on her future? It seemed unlikely. There was lots of debate as to when a child formed its first memories. Most researchers thought it happened around the age of three. But Ruby had seen a lot of things in her work that had made her question that.

'She had a few months. She spent every possible second with Annabelle. By the end she was just too tired, too sick. Annabelle was in her arms when she died. She was only eleven months old.'

'It must have been devastating for you.'

'She was my childhood friend—the person I grew up with. If my father hadn't had the stroke, if Sophia hadn't had breast cancer, lots of things might have been different.'

Something flickered across his eyes. A tiny moment of recognition. An awareness. A regret.

'I'm sorry, Ruby,' he whispered.

Tears filled her eyes. It was an acknowledgement, however brief, of what had happened between them. He was laying everything out on the table for her. It was just the two of them. No one else to interrupt. No one else to interfere.

He reached over and touched her cheek—just as he had all those years ago in Paris. He tucked a piece of hair behind her ear.

Silence. For the longest time. Lots of words unspoken.

His fingers stroked across her cheek. So many things wanted to spill out of her. But her frustration was dissipating. The years had passed. She couldn't be angry with him any more. She'd lived a whole ten years of her life without him. He'd always been in the background of her mind. No matter how hard she'd tried to push him away. But her memories of Alex were memories of one New Year's Eve and a moment in time.

The Alex she saw in front of her now was the one that really existed. A father. A prince with the responsibilities of a country—two countries. Someone who'd set aside his career ambitions to fulfil his duty to his country. Someone who'd just told her that he was sorry. That meant more than anything.

She'd been harbouring an illusion for the last ten years. Trouble was, the reality was better than the dream.

She felt a rush of blood to her cheeks, but Alex had reached across the table and taken her hand.

'Thank you, Ruby. Thank you for doing this for me. Thank you for doing this for my daughter.'

She stood up quickly. *His daughter.*

'It's time to go. I need to get back and plan for the nursery with Annabelle and her nanny.'

He was being kind. He was being sweet. He was thanking her for doing her job.

Her job. The one he was paying her to do.

If Alex was disturbed by her abruptness he didn't show it. He just signalled to the waiter and left some money on the table.

Her cheek was burning from where he'd touched her. It almost felt as if he'd left a mark on her skin.

She needed some distance. She needed some space.

Most of all she needed to remember why she was here—to assess a little girl. Nothing more. Nothing less.

CHAPTER FOUR

FOR A MOMENT earlier today Alex had been sure there was something in the air between him and Ruby.

He'd managed to persuade his security team to stay a comfortable distance away from them. He knew the palace must be suffocating for Ruby. But he'd never considered it might be suffocating to Annabelle.

Ruby was here to do a job. She'd already made an impact on his staff by insisting she stay in the staff quarters next to Annabelle. He'd tried not to smirk when he'd heard Rufus, his private secretary, scold her for calling him Alex.

'You must address him as Your Highness or Prince Regent,' he'd insisted.

But Ruby had laughed and waved her hand. 'Nonsense. He's Alex.'

There was a hum in the air around her. When she remembered, her manners could be impeccable. But most of the time she was just Ruby, and his staff were starting to warm to her.

Her focus on her task was obvious to all. She was unobtrusive, watching Annabelle and listening quietly. None of her assessment had put any demands on the child. After months of people trying to make Annabelle do things she clearly didn't want to, or examining her ears, tongue and throat, it was a refreshing change.

Ruby. She'd been fixed in his mind for the last ten years. Her brown curls, dark eyes, red coat and a carefree attitude had wrapped their way around him like cotton candy around a stick.

But it was other things he remembered too. The laughter in her eyes, the flirtation, the buzz between them. That moment when their lips had touched and the fireworks had started going off in his head as well as in the sky. Ruby had sent a rush of blood around his body. He'd never felt a connection like that. He'd never had a kiss like that again.

He remembered the feel of her warm curves filling the palms of his hand underneath that red coat. The skin on her cheek where he'd stroked it. Every sensation of just *being* around Ruby.

Part of what he remembered was reality, part fantasy. He hadn't wanted that night to end. To Ruby, he'd been just Alex. At that point in his life he'd been able to do that. But it had been the last night of his life to have that opportunity, and spending it with Ruby couldn't have been more perfect. If only it had ended differently.

He looked down and shuffled the ever-growing mound of papers on his desk. All things that needed his signature. Emails were all very well, but some things still required a signature.

He picked up the phone and dialled the number of the clinic in Switzerland. It didn't matter that he knew the doctors would phone him if they had any concerns. Or that he had a multitude of staff members to do it for him. After ten years, he still liked to keep a check of things on his own.

He moved the papers on the desk again, looking to find a letter for a foreign dignitary. Something fluttered to the floor. A photo. He picked it up and smiled. It was ten years old. Ruby, just the way he remembered her, taken by one of his security team on New Year's Eve. He'd only found out about it a few months later, when he'd wanted to track her down. His Head of Security had admitted they had some photographs and had looked into her past—all to check her authenticity.

It was of the two of them, sitting at the table in that café next to the Four Seasons. They were laughing. Ruby had her head thrown back, her dark hair was glossy, and she was smiling from ear to ear. But the thing that had always struck him about that picture was the way they were looking at each other. Even though Ruby was laughing she was still looking at him, and he at her.

A little moment captured in time.

A million different possibilities. A million different futures.

If he'd turned a different corner that night he'd never have met Ruby Wetherspoon, and that thought made his stomach twist almost as much as the thought of what might have been.

Deep down he knew his father would never have accepted his fascination with an English healthcare worker. He'd never fully understood it himself.

But no one could deny the connection between them. This picture was everlasting proof of that.

When he had his darkest moments—when the nights just seemed to last for ever—it was thoughts of Ruby that gave him comfort. Thoughts of being twenty-four again and having the world at his feet.

He sighed and opened a drawer to put the photo inside. Ruby had never been a threat and his security staff had filed their paperwork away.

He just couldn't do the same.

There it was again. That strange noise.

Ruby moved from the window seat, where she'd been watching the sun start to lower in the sky. Evenings could be long in the palace. Annabelle went to bed early and most of the time Ruby spent her time walking in the gardens, reading a book or talking to Polly on the phone.

Polly was still unimpressed.

The noise again. Was it a whimper?

She stood up quickly. Brigette, the nanny, had gone to bed earlier with a migraine. Could it be Annabelle?

Annabelle's door had been left open earlier, so Ruby walked out into the corridor and hesitated, her hand above the door handle. Part of her was worried. Annabelle wasn't that familiar with her yet. Maybe she would be scared if Ruby went into her room.

She took a deep breath as the whimper continued and pushed the door open. There was no way she could leave any child upset—whether they knew her or not.

The room was dark. Even though the sun hadn't set yet there were blackout blinds at the window. It only took her a few seconds to realise the bed was empty.

She sucked in a breath and suppressed her impulse to shout. Instead she flicked on the light switch and had a quick look around. Annabelle might still be in the room.

But she wasn't. Not under the bed. Not in the wardrobe—even though Ruby hadn't really expected her to be. Not in any corner of the room.

Her heart started thudding as she walked back to the door and quickly along the corridor. The missing child would cause mayhem. The implications were tremendous—and terrifying. She had to take a few seconds to be sure before she called the alarm.

There. In front of her. At the top of the stairs.

A tiny staggering figure in pink pyjamas.

Her legs broke into a run.

'Annabelle!'

She reached her seconds.

But Annabelle hadn't responded to her voice. And it was clear why. She was sleepwalking.

Ruby didn't have any experience with sleepwalking kids. She could vaguely remember something about not waking them up. But Annabelle was perilously close to the top of the staircase. She didn't hesitate. She just swept her up into her arms.

Annabelle's eyes were open, and the movement and embrace by Ruby seemed to give her a little start. Her whimpering stopped and she tucked her head into Ruby's neck.

There was no one else about. Not a single person in the corridor.

She hesitated. What next? She walked back along the corridor and paused at Annabelle's door. Her heart was still thudding after that horrible few seconds of thinking something might be wrong.

She couldn't put Annabelle back into her bed and risk it happening again. She'd need to talk to Brigette and Alex in the morning to see if this was normal for Annabelle. No one had mentioned it, and she knew in some kids it was common, but she couldn't risk Annabelle walking near the stairs again.

She walked back into her own room. There was plenty of space in her bed for both of them. At least then she'd know that Annabelle was safe.

Her eyes were still open. Ruby had no idea if it was just an automatic response in sleepwalking, or if on some level Annabelle was actually awake.

The little arms wound around her neck. Thank goodness for automatic reactions. Ruby just started to rock her.

Familiarity. That was what she needed for this little girl.

She kept her in her arms and walked next door, picking up Annabelle's favourite movie and taking it with her.

Background noise. That was all it needed to be. Something familiar so that if Annabelle woke up she'd be comfortable.

Ruby reached her hand out, juggling the weight of Annabelle on the other arm as she opened the case and slid the DVD inside the player.

They settled back on the bed. Annabelle adjusted her position. She seemed comfortable in Ruby's lap and made no attempt to move. Ruby piled the pillows around them.

If they were here for the long haul they might as well be comfortable.

The screen lit up bright blue as the titles for *Finding Nemo* appeared. Her own 'go to' film as well as Annabelle's favourite. She loved it just as much as any child, and had yet to meet a kid who wasn't enthralled by it.

Annabelle seemed to settle back against her and that was when Ruby *really* started to listen. She'd already heard Annabelle whimper. She had no doubt that on a physical basis the little girl could form sounds. The diagnosis of selective mutism seemed the most appropriate. She wondered if Annabelle spoke in *any* situation.

She seemed a little more awake now, but she hadn't made any sign to Ruby. Her head was definitely turned towards the TV screen, and she didn't seem to have any objection to being in Ruby's bed.

A new thought crossed her mind, completely unrelated to the sleepwalking. Company. This little girl wanted company.

And then it started. Little noises. Little sounds. Gasps when Nemo's mother disappeared. Small, slow body movements along with the music, and then—eventually—a little hum. Ruby did nothing. She didn't react at all. Just listened as Annabelle hummed along. A smile danced across the little girl's face. She was enthralled—lost in the story. Perfect. Just perfect.

She was only three. Her speech wasn't really too delayed. Maybe Annabelle needed a little encouragement and coaching instead of assessing and prodding. She would have to choose her words carefully when she explained all this to Alex. There was no magic wand that she could wave here. Annabelle had to be allowed to develop at her own pace.

Ruby settled back against the pillows. Annabelle's eyes were getting heavy. She would fall asleep soon—and then Ruby could think about this a little more…

* * *

'Ruby!'

Her eyes shot open. The first thing that struck her was the crick in her neck. The second thing that struck her was the three people standing in the doorway—all of them staring at her.

She tried to push herself up, but Annabelle was still curled in her lap, sleeping. Ruby couldn't even begin to imagine what she looked like—rumpled clothes, hair sticking up in every direction but the right one, and more than likely pillow creases on her face.

Brigette, Rufus and Alexander were standing in the doorway, three sets of eyes fixed on her. She tried to edge herself out from under Annabelle without disturbing her. The curtains were still drawn and the TV was flickering on the wall.

Alex rushed across the room. 'What on earth is going on? Why is Annabelle in here?' He seemed furious. 'Have you *any* idea what I thought when I saw her bed was empty?'

He was shouting now, unable to contain his anger.

Of course. The same horrible thought *she'd* had for a few seconds last night, when she'd saw Annabelle's empty bed. The horror. The worry.

She couldn't get the words out quickly enough. 'I'm sorry. I found her sleepwalking last night. She was close to the top of the stairs. I just grabbed her. Then I didn't know whether to try and wake her or not, so I brought her in here. I was worried she might do it again.'

Alex reached over and lifted his still sleeping little girl out of the bed. 'Sleepwalking? Why didn't you call me? Why didn't you call Brigette?'

He was angry with her.

'I'm her father. You should have come and got me if there was something wrong with Annabelle.'

Ruby shook her head. She understood his anger. She understood those seconds of panic.

'There was no one around, Alex. I had no idea if sleep-walking was normal for Annabelle or not. And she seemed to settle with me really quickly. She just wanted some comfort. I did plan to talk to you about it today.'

Alex shot her a look that left her in no doubt about his feelings. He didn't even say another word. Just turned and walked out of the room with Annabelle in his arms, still asleep.

She turned to Brigette. The last thing she wanted to do was get Annabelle's nanny in trouble. 'I'm sorry, Brigette. I knew you had a migraine. I didn't want to wake you when I felt as if I could deal with Annabelle on my own.'

Brigette brushed past her too, leaving Rufus the last person to lock his beady eyes on hers.

She sighed. 'I'm going to take a shower and get dressed.'

Rufus tutted at her and then spun on his heels and left.

Great. Just great.

Now she was awake a little more she wanted to shout at them all to come back and tell them to calm down.

Annabelle was fine. They should talk about her sleep-walking and put steps in place to keep her safe.

But common sense told her this wasn't the time.

He hadn't spoken to Ruby in four days.

It was ridiculous. He'd snapped at her when there had been no reason to. But when Rufus had bustled along the corridor to tell him Annabelle was missing he'd panicked. He could have broken speed records with his bolt along the corridor.

The thought of something happening to his daughter… He couldn't even allow his brain to contemplate it.

But seeing Ruby asleep on the bed with Annabelle in her arms had knocked the wind from his heels.

After the instant relief he'd felt a wave of anger.

Their heads resting next to each other, the mish-mash of blonde curls and long brown hair, the way Ruby had been sheltering Annabelle in her arms had consumed him with an unexpected rage he hadn't felt in a long time.

She couldn't know that, against advice, on lots of occasions Sophia had taken Annabelle in to sleep next to her. She could never imagine that the impact of seeing his little girl in someone else's arms would flood him with unspeakable guilt.

He hadn't loved Sophia the way people thought he had. He had loved her like a best friend. A best friend who'd been cheated out of sleeping next to their little girl and seeing her grow up.

If Sophia was here now he was almost sure Annabelle wouldn't have any problems with her speech.

As for the sleepwalking...? Was that his fault too? It was yet another worry. Another failing. Something else to consult a whole array of doctors on.

He couldn't even begin to understand why it annoyed him all the more that it was Ruby who'd found the problem. She was under his skin in more ways than was imaginable.

Guilt was chipping away at him. Guilt for how he was feeling about Ruby. And guilt because he continually felt as if he were failing his daughter.

What would Sophia have thought? His friend would have dealt with things so much better than he could.

But if Sophia were here now he would never have seen Ruby again. And that was what burned away at his insides. That was what filled him with even more hideous guilt.

The last few days of being around Ruby had lit a fire inside him that had long since died. He could feel her presence everywhere. The staff in the palace seemed happier—less formal. It was almost as if her scent drifted in the air into every room. Light, flowery, lifting the mood.

She'd connected with most members of staff in her polite but informal manner. She wasn't afraid to ask questions, and more importantly she wasn't afraid to laugh. In the space of a few days the atmosphere around him seemed to have lightened. The palace had started to feel happy again.

Years of worry about his father's health, the economy of Euronia, and then the terminal diagnosis of Sophia, followed by the concerns about Annabelle, had made being here oppressive. Every tiny part of this place seemed to weigh on his shoulders relentlessly.

Seeing Ruby's connection today with Annabelle had been unexpected. He'd never realistically thought about someone else stepping into Sophia's shoes.

But he should have. It was inevitable.

At some point he would marry again—this time for love—and that woman would become a mother to Annabelle. He'd been so busy these last few years, and so stressed, he hadn't taken time to think of the impact of that.

The impact on the country. The impact on Annabelle. The impact on him.

And then, there she was, with her mussed-up curls parallel with his child's. Making him see something that everyone had probably already surmised.

It was time to move on.

But was he ready?

CHAPTER FIVE

THE CLOTHES WERE lying across her bed. Seventeen dresses of varying styles and colours—all with matching shoes.

'I don't understand. Did something happen to my clothes?'

Rufus shook his head. 'I told you I would arrange for some other clothing to be sent to the palace for you.'

She reached down and touched the nearest designer dress. It was red…beautiful. Like something you would wear to the Queen's garden party back in London. It certainly wasn't like anything she owned.

'But I'm not sure I really need these. I don't know how much longer I'll be here. And I've got clothes of my own.' She opened the wardrobe, revealing her few dresses, jeans, T-shirts and a couple of pairs of sandals and heels.

Rufus gave an almost imperceptible shake of his head. He turned to leave. 'They're here now—enjoy!' he said, and with a wave of his hand he disappeared, leaving her to perch on the edge of the bed, too nervous to touch some of the dresses.

'How very *Pretty Woman*.' She sighed. Her head was swimming. Was this another way for Alex to buy her? Did he want to dress her up like some doll?

Every dress was beautifully styled and there was a rainbow of colour. It was strange, but whilst they were all different none was in a style that she wouldn't wear. It was almost as if they'd given her friend Polly a free budget and the run of all the designer houses.

A silk one slid through her fingers. It was almost the same blue as Alex's eyes. She gave a little shudder.

Alex. He hadn't spoken to her for four days. Falling asleep with his daughter was obviously a no-no. But while it might have been a little unconventional she really thought everyone had overreacted.

The imaginary walls between herself and Annabelle had definitely started to crumble. The little girl wasn't completely ignoring her any more. Yesterday she'd sat next to Ruby as she'd thumbed through a book. After a while Ruby had asked her if she wanted her to read the story and Annabelle had given a little nod and slid closer.

It was a small step, but gaining Annabelle's trust was the most important thing of all.

She picked up another of the dresses. It was yellow—a colour she never usually wore—and it matched the sun outside and the flowers in the garden directly beneath her window.

She slipped off her T-shirt and Capri pants. The dress dropped over her head and fitted her curves as if it had been specially made for her. Everything was covered, from the round neckline to the flouncy skirt that fell to her knees. She reached behind to fasten the zip. It was a little tricky. She managed to pull it up to her bra strap. Then she reached her hands above her shoulders and over her back, trying to pull the material of the dress a little higher and grasp the zipper.

Someone cleared his throat loudly. She spun around.

She hadn't thought to close the door after Rufus had left. No one ever seemed to come down this corridor.

'Alex!' Colour flooded into her cheeks.

He was leaning in the doorway, his hands folded across his chest, with a cheeky smile on his face. She hadn't even heard his footsteps.

'What are you doing here?'

His smile just seemed to get broader. 'Looks like I'm helping a damsel in distress.' He stepped into the room and twirled his finger. 'Go on—spin around and I'll fasten it for you.'

It was amazing how quickly his presence could cause a buzz in the air around her. She sucked in a breath as she turned around.

Fastening a zip should take the briefest of seconds. But Alex waited. She could feel the material of her dress shifting slightly. The zipper must be in his hand. Then he stepped forward, closing the gap between them.

His head was at her shoulder. She could smell his aftershave—it was coiling its way around her. Who was the snake in that childhood film? Kaa, in *The Jungle Book*—with the hypnotic eyes that could make you do anything that he wanted. She was pretty sure Alex's eyes would have the same effect on her.

'I'm sorry I snapped at you,' he said quietly. 'I thought something was wrong with Annabelle.'

'Okay...' That was all she replied. Her breath was still caught somewhere between her chest and her throat. It was all she was capable of saying right now.

There was a drumming noise in her ears. Her heart was thudding against her chest as she waited to see what would happen next.

'I thought today we could go back to the café with Annabelle—like you asked me to.'

She smiled. Did that mean her mistake was being forgotten, or was this part of his apology? He still hadn't moved. He still hadn't fastened her zipper.

She nodded. Not breathing was getting difficult. 'Okay.'

'Do you like the dresses?'

She could feel his breath warm the skin on her shoulder.

'I love them—but I don't need them. Rufus didn't need to do that.'

'He didn't do it.'

She froze. One of his hands moved and rested on her hip.

This was all becoming remarkably familiar. Richard Gere was going to appear any second now. Didn't he buy Vivian a new wardrobe in *Pretty Woman*?

Her profession might not compare with Vivian's, but the thought of Alex purchasing a whole wardrobe for her was both mildly disturbing and somehow exciting. She didn't know whether to be insulted or overjoyed.

'I don't think I like this, Alex. You can't buy me. You can't dress me up as if I'm your little doll.' She could feel her stomach tighten.

But Alex just shook his head. 'I'm not buying you, Ruby. I don't care whether you wear the clothes or not.' He waved his hand. 'If you don't like them give them away—give them to charity. It makes no difference to me.'

He stepped a little closer.

'I guess I'm just not good at this. I'm trying to say sorry. Sorry about how I reacted over Annabelle. For a second I thought she was gone. I thought someone had kidnapped my daughter—I overreacted. And…' He waved his hands again. 'This is how I say sorry. Doesn't every woman like clothes?'

The tightness in her chest dissipated. It was clear he meant every word.

'What are you going to do if it happens again?'

He smiled. 'Silent alarms. Everywhere. If Annabelle opens her door in the middle of the night alarms will go off in my room, Brigette's room and in Security.' He looked over his shoulder and whispered. 'And, don't tell her, but we've actually had tracking devices sewn into all her pyjamas.'

She laughed. He was sorry, and he'd put steps in place to ensure Annabelle's safety. Of course he had. She hadn't doubted that for a second, but it made her mood lighten.

He nudged her, and pointed to the dresses as he slid a hand around her waist.

'Which is your favourite?'

He was so close. His lips were almost touching her ear. If she just moved her head a little…

'The blue one.'

'Why?'

'I like the colour.' The rush of blood was heating her cheeks. Her answer had been automatic.

She was conscious of the lightness of his fingers on her hip. Would he make the connection between the colour of the dress and the colour of his eyes? No. Guys didn't do that kind of thing.

This time his lips did brush against her ear. 'I like the red one. It reminds me of you in Paris. The same colour as your coat.'

A whole host of tiny centipedes were marching along her arms with their hundreds of legs, making every single hair stand on end.

His finger touched the skin of her back. She gasped. It wasn't cold—it was just unexpected. A thousand butterfly wings had just exploded on her back, and all the little nerve-endings were waiting for the next sensation.

He bent a little lower and whispered in her ear again. This time it felt as if his breath was caressing her skin.

'Ten years is a long time, Ruby.'

He pulled the zipper up with his finger inside, then ran it along the upper end of her spine, resting his fingers at the base of her neck.

Her legs were turning to jelly. It was ridiculous. It was nothing. But she felt as if she'd waited ten years for that.

Ten years of dreaming. Ten years of imagining. Ten years of hoping.

She stepped backwards. Against him. Into him. Feeling the full length of his body next to hers. Her eyes were fixed outside, on the gardens. If she turned around and looked at those blue eyes she might do something much more inappropriate than fall asleep next to his daughter.

She rested her head back against his chest. 'Yes, it is.'

Her voice was tinged with sadness.

They both stood there—neither moving. It was almost as if they were happy for this to be the first tiny step. The first real acknowledgment that their time ten years ago hadn't just been a figment of her imagination that she'd played over and over in her head.

She could feel the rise and fall of his chest against her back. The heat from his body through the thin fabric of her dress. It felt natural. It felt as if this was exactly the place she was supposed to stand. As if this was exactly the place she was meant to be.

His hand moved slightly from her hip around to her stomach. His other hand met hers and he threaded their fingers together in front of her.

This might be wrong.

It might be inappropriate.

But why did it feel so good?

'Your Highness?'

The voice came echoing down the hall and they sprang apart. Alex disappeared out of her door in flash to meet Rufus, who was muttering again.

Ruby's feet were stuck to the floor.

Had that really just happened?

Her body was telling her yes. Every sense seemed to be on fire.

But her brain was turning to mush. Sensible, rational thoughts seemed to have flown from the building.

Ruby was logical. Ruby was always sensible.

The one time in her life she hadn't been entirely sensible had been ten years ago in Paris. Ten years ago she'd acted on impulse. And look where that had got her.

But ten years ago she'd felt the same tiny flicker of

warmth and excitement that was burning inside her right now.

This was the first time she hadn't felt like the hired help.

This was the first time she'd felt as if she wasn't here just for Annabelle.

Question was: what was she getting herself into?

CHAPTER SIX

ALEX'S HANDS WERE still shaking. That had been it. The situation that—in his head—he'd dreamed about being in.

Him and Ruby alone.

Getting private time in the palace was harder than it seemed.

Ruby's questions a few days ago had started to play on his mind. How much time *did* he actually get to spend with Annabelle?

He tried to be there most mornings when she had breakfast. He always tried to see her before bedtime. But in a world where visits to other countries were inevitable and midnight conference calls were normal it wasn't always possible.

Annabelle was the spitting image of her mother. He'd already been friends with Sophia at her age. And, although he loved his daughter with all his heart, sometimes she was a painful reminder of the friend he had lost.

Perhaps he'd overreacted when the nanny had mentioned Annabelle's speech seemed a little behind?

Alex had no experience with children. And the internet seemed like a dangerous tool sometimes. He'd paid for expert upon expert to assess her—all the while terrified that there was something wrong with his child.

When Ruby had said that as part of the assessment she wanted to see how Annabelle and Alex interacted with each other he'd felt a wave of panic. Was it a criticism? She hadn't made it sound like that. Maybe he was just feeling under pressure.

He'd planned carefully. He'd had someone pack a picnic to take to the palace grounds, then they would walk into the centre and have some ice cream—just as Ruby had suggested.

Then he gone to find Ruby and she'd been surrounded by the dresses he'd ordered and been half dressed.

Maybe not strictly true. But that glimpse of the skin on her back had been enough to send his blood pressure rising. When he'd offered to zip her up it had taken all his strength not to pull the zip down.

Alex was always in control. That night in Paris years ago had been the first time he'd shaken off his security team in years. Bumping into Ruby had made the whole night perfect. Having her in the palace again was bringing a whole host of sensations he hadn't acknowledged in years.

Rufus had mumbled in his ear all the way along the corridor. The look of surprise on his face to see Alex exiting Ruby's bedroom had spoken volumes without a single word being said.

Neither of them had acknowledged it. Alex had immediately started talking business and given Rufus a list of instructions for the rest of the afternoon.

Annabelle and her nanny were waiting at the main entrance for him. After a few minutes Ruby came down the main staircase carrying a bright pink ball in her arms. Her face was slightly flushed. A sure sign they'd been doing something they shouldn't.

Brigette gave a nod and left while Alex offered his hand to Annabelle and put the picnic basket over his arm.

'A picnic? You never said we were having a picnic,' said Ruby.

'Didn't I?'

He glanced at the ball, then at her feet. She was wearing a pair of white trainers with a yellow dress. It brought a smile to his face. Ruby didn't really worry about who might take her picture and claim she'd made a fashion *faux pas*.

'I didn't take you as a footballer.'

Ruby pulled at the skirt of her dress and smiled. 'I have lots of hidden talents. But maybe I should have worn something different—trousers, perhaps?'

He shook his head. 'I think your dress will be perfect. Now, let's go.'

There was a further little flush of colour in her cheeks. Both of them were remembering exactly why he liked the fact she was wearing a dress.

But Ruby wasn't giving anything away. She bent down in front of Annabelle. 'A picnic—wow. It's been years since I've been on a picnic. Why don't you take us to your favourite place in the palace grounds and we'll eat there?'

She gave Alex a little smile and walked out through the door, waiting for them to join her.

He could sense the general unease in the air. There were a few members of staff staring at them. Was it really so unusual that he spent time with his child—or had word spread even more quickly than he'd thought that he'd been seen leaving Ruby's bedroom?

He gave Annabelle's hand a squeeze and they walked out into the beautiful sunshine. Ruby's idea was good. He'd been trying to decide between going near where the horses were stabled, to the ornamental gardens, the duck pond or the palace maze. But Annabelle had other ideas. She was leading them around the side of the palace, her little footsteps assured.

It only took a few minutes, then she plunked herself down on the grass directly behind the ornamental fountain.

Alex blinked. This was the place where he'd had that picture taken with Sophia. They'd both been about Annabelle's page and the photo had been zoomed around the world with the press headline *'Future King and Queen?'*

Had Annabelle ever seen that picture? He wasn't sure,

but he could tell from a fleeting glance at Ruby's face that *she* certainly had.

Whatever her thoughts on the matter, she sat down next to Annabelle on the grass, not even waiting for him to lay out the picnic blanket he'd brought along.

The little girl started to fumble with her shoes. Ruby gave her a smile and knelt down next to her, taking off her white leather sandals and frilly socks.

She held out her hand to Annabelle and the two of them walked over to the fountain. Annabelle hadn't said a word and he was confused. How did Ruby know what she wanted?

He moved closer as Annabelle stood up on the wall surrounding the fountain and dipped her toes in the water. She let out a little laugh and he took a deep breath.

His little girl's laughter. How beautiful it was—and how rarely he'd heard it.

Annabelle was walking around the fountain now, holding Ruby's hand to keep her balance. She had the biggest smile on her face.

He walked in pace with Ruby. 'How did you know that's what she wanted to do?'

He couldn't take his eyes off his little girl. Couldn't believe how much she looked like her mother. It alarmed him how much he noticed.

Ruby shrugged. 'It's exactly what I would do if I were Annabelle's age.'

They reached the point where they'd started and Ruby put her arms around Annabelle's waist and swung her in the air.

'Whee!'

Annabelle laughed again as Ruby swooped her through the air and landed her on the blanket that he'd spread out. She picked up a corner of the blanket and started drying Annabelle's toes.

Alex opened the basket and started unpacking the food.

The palace chef had outdone himself, as usual, but the most curious thing was a small tub full of steamed-up food.

Annabelle gave a little shriek of excitement and grabbed it, pulling open the lid and searching for a spoon.

Ruby wrinkled her nose and leaned closer. 'Macaroni cheese? Is this one of Annabelle's favourites?'

Alex nodded. 'Apparently.' He peered in the basket. 'I'm not quite sure how it managed to find its way into the picnic basket, though.'

Ruby grabbed an apple, bit into it, then leaned back on her hands, staring up at the palace. 'I can't say I've ever had a picnic in front of a palace before.'

He stared up at the hundreds of windows. There might be a whole host of palace staff looking down on them at any moment. It might look like a private picnic, with no one visibly around them, but the truth was it was anything but.

He pulled a bottle of water out of the basket and popped the tab for Annabelle. 'Would you like to go and see the horses? Or the maze?'

She shook her head and continued to eat the macaroni. He reached into the basket for some more food, and squinted when his hand came into contact with something strange. A leg. A plastic doll's leg. And another doll. And another.

He pulled them out. One was in a princess dress, one in a swimsuit and one in a semi-naked state with her arms partway into a spacesuit.

He winked at Ruby. 'Ruby, I see you brought your dolls to play with.'

She laughed and grabbed the blonde astronaut, pushing her arms and legs into the silver and white suit and fastening it appropriately. 'Of course I did, Alex. I like playing with dolls.'

Annabelle's head shot up and she gave a little smile, abandoning the macaroni and walking over to the dolls.

Her comprehension was perfect. She understood everything that was going on around her. So why didn't she talk?

Ruby held up the princess doll and the swimsuit doll. 'Which one do you like best? The pink one or the purple one?'

He wondered what she was doing. Annabelle screwed up her face and shook her head. There were no pink or purple clothes.

Ruby just smiled, as if this was something she did every day—which she did. She held each doll higher. 'Oh, I *see*. Silly me. Blue or red, then?'

Annabelle came over and picked the doll wearing the pale blue dress and pointed towards her own.

Ruby nodded. 'You like blue, then?'

She gave Alex a secret smile. Every little thing she did was part of Annabelle's assessment. Every other person who had come to see her had been much more rigid in their processes, wanting Annabelle to do certain things at certain times. Being three was difficult enough. But Alex had been made to feel as if Annabelle was being difficult or uncooperative. She didn't seem that way with Ruby.

Annabelle took her dolls and walked over to the ornamental fountain with all three.

'I think they're all about to go for a swim—costumes or not,' murmured Ruby.

She seemed perfectly relaxed out here. She picked up a ham sandwich and started to eat. He reached in and pulled out his favourite. Tuna. Hardly royal. Probably not the thing that most Prince Regents would eat. But this had been Alex's favourite since he was a child.

The tension between them wasn't as high as it had been in the room when they were alone. But then again, they hadn't been on display there. He kept wondering if there *were* any unseen eyes watching what should be a private affair.

'She knows her colours. For a three-year-old that's good.' Ruby was watching Annabelle again.

'You can tell just from that?'

She shook her head. 'Oh, no. I've done a few other exercises as well.' She leaned forward and pulled her knees up, wrapping her dress around them. 'Listen...' she whispered.

Alex sat a little straighter, straining to hear what Ruby had heard above the constant trickle of water from the fountain.

There it was—floating across the air.

Ruby touched his arm. 'She's humming. She did that the other night with me.' She gave a tiny shake of her head. 'I know that one of the reports about Annabelle questioned whether she could even make sounds. But she can. You've heard her laugh. You've heard her squeal. And she can communicate with sign language. She's *choosing* not to speak.' A frown marred her complexion. 'I've just got to figure out why.'

Her eyes were fixed on Annabelle playing with her dolls. This was all so easy for Ruby. Annabelle was just a patient. She didn't have the same investment, the same emotional connection that he did. She didn't have the same frustrated feeling that there must be something else he could do. She was a professional with a puzzle to solve.

'You make it sound so easy.' He couldn't help the way the words sounded. He'd forced them out through gritted teeth.

But Ruby didn't react. She just kept looking at Annabelle. 'I don't think it's easy, Alex. I just think that you—and I—are going to have to be patient. That's the only way this can work.'

Her eyes met his. For a second he wasn't quite sure what she was talking about. They were talking about Annabelle, right? Because those words might sound as if she were talking about them instead.

'What's your first memory, Alex?'

'What?' He was surprised by her question.

She smiled at him. 'I can honestly say the first thing I remember is from around age seven. I was on holiday with my mum and dad in Boulogne in France. I can remember walking about with cases because we couldn't find our hotel. Then my father thought it would be interesting to go and watch the fishermen.' She gave a shudder. 'Watching fishermen gut their fish was not something I wanted to see as a seven-year-old.' She turned and smiled at him. 'That's my first real memory.'

He sat back a little, unsure where this was going. 'I can remember having to sit very still for a long, *long* time. It was at some awards ceremony and my father glared at me every time I moved. I hated the shirt and tie I was wearing because it felt too tight.'

She nodded. 'What age do you think you were?'

He shrugged. 'Around five, I think.'

She lifted her hand towards Annabelle. 'Here's the thing. Science tells us that the first three years are the most important for a child's brain development. It's the first time we're supposed to form memories—but I can't remember anything from back then. The experts tell us that young children's memories change over time, replacing old memories with new ones. So I'm looking at Annabelle and wondering what she remembers.'

'What do you mean?' This was starting to make him uncomfortable.

She interlinked her fingers. 'The brain has connections—hard wiring. Children's brains are like a sponge—they take in everything all around them. Children are born to learn. By their first year seventy-five per cent of the hard wiring is in place.' She pointed at Annabelle again. 'By age three ninety per cent of the hard wiring is there.'

She ran her fingers through her hair.

'Under the age of two, lots of their development depends

on attachment. I wonder if Annabelle's speech issues could actually be down to the loss of her mother.'

'What?' Alex shook his head. It was something he hadn't even considered. 'But she was only eleven months old when Sophia died.'

Ruby nodded slowly, 'Exactly. A baby recognises its mother's voice in the womb. Once it's born it puts the face and voice together. It responds to those. You said that Sophia was a good mother and spent most of her time with Annabelle?'

He nodded. 'Yes, she did.'

'Then for eleven months Annabelle's hard wiring was formed all around her mother.'

Ruby sat back, letting what she'd said sink around him. She seemed to know when she'd said enough.

She wasn't apportioning any blame. She wasn't being confrontational. She was being logical. She was giving him information and letting him think for himself what it might mean.

He sat quietly. Ruby was relaxed and Annabelle seemed happy. She was busy trying to drown all her plastic dolls in the ornamental fountain and probably block the pumps from here to eternity.

No matter what Ruby had just told him it was comfortable. It was relaxed.

The sandwiches disappeared quickly, followed by some little cakes at the bottom of the picnic basket. Ruby didn't feel the need to chatter and fill the silence. She was entirely happy to lie back on the blanket and watch Annabelle.

This was something he never got time to do any more.

There was always something to be signed, someone who needed to talk to him urgently. An email or a letter to write. A dignitary to entertain. A celebrity to pander to in order to bring extra publicity and business to Euronia.

Where was the time for Annabelle in all that?

Where was the time for him?

He never got time to be just a father. He never got time to be just Alex. Did anyone in the palace even think of him as just Alex?

He watched as Ruby moved, crawling on all fours, ignoring her dress and bare knees, creeping across the red stones to meet Annabelle and start splashing her with water from the fountain.

Annabelle shrieked in delight and ran around the fountain. It was the finest sound he'd ever heard.

Two minutes later Ruby had the pink plastic ball and was throwing it over the top of the fountain to Annabelle at the other side. But that was soon too safe—too ordinary. Within a few seconds they'd both climbed on the wall at each side of the fountain and were throwing the ball to each other while balancing precariously on the low wall.

He should intervene. He should tell them to stop being so silly. Last time they'd had to replace the blue tiles in the wall of the fountain it had taken for ever. He couldn't even remember the cost.

But both of them were laughing out loud. He couldn't remember the last time he'd seen Annabelle so happy. And it was Ruby who was responsible for that.

Something twisted inside him. Part of it was pride, part of it a little inkling of jealousy. Deep down he knew that *he* should be the one making his little girl laugh like that. But if it couldn't be him he was so glad that it was Ruby.

Ruby was genuine. Ruby related to his daughter in a way that none of the other professionals had.

He had been so right to bring her here.

Even when the palace officials had voiced their obvious concerns about his latest plans to get Annabelle assessed he'd known that this was the right thing to do.

He'd been right to remember the passion in her eyes when she'd spoken about missing out on the job she would have loved. He'd followed her for years…sent her unsigned flowers. He remembered his surge of pride when he'd found out she'd got her dream job, when she'd been promoted, when she'd published professional papers. All those things had made him happy for her.

Now, in a few short days, she'd started to connect with his daughter.

With him.

There was a scream, followed by a huge splash. A flash of moving yellow rushed before his eyes. He was on his feet instantly.

Annabelle's eyes were wide. She jumped down from her side of the fountain and ran around it towards the splash, meeting her father as they both peered down into the few feet of clear water.

Ruby was completely under the water, tiny bubbles snaking out from her mouth, her yellow dress billowing around her. Alex leaned over to put his hand in and pull her up—then gasped as she opened her eyes.

The expression on her face was priceless. Annabelle dissolved into fits of laughter as Ruby burst up through the surface of the water, shrieking with laughter.

Alex's eyes shot up towards the hundreds of windows of the palace. He could only imagine what anyone on his staff might say if they'd witnessed this.

But the laughter was infectious. And Ruby wasn't at all worried about the fact that her hair was sodden and she was soaked to the skin.

She reached towards his outstretched arm, smiled, and tugged sharply—pulling him straight in next to her.

Even though the sun was shining the water in the fountain was freezing.

His landing was partly cushioned by the soft body of Ruby. Water was dripping from the end of her nose, her hair was flattened to her head and her clothes hugged every part of her body.

'Who are you laughing at?' She winked.

He couldn't do anything other than laugh. Annabelle was still jumping up and down at the side of the fountain.

Ruby reached down and picked up a submerged princess doll. 'I came in to rescue the doll—what's your excuse?'

He smiled, their faces only inches apart. He lifted his eyebrows, 'Oh, I definitely came in to rescue Ruby.'

His arms were on either side of her, his chin just above her head. Every part of him was soaked.

'Who says I needed rescuing?' she quipped.

She didn't care. She didn't care about her wet clothes or how she looked. She wasn't constantly looking over her shoulder for a camera. Ruby was just Ruby.

And it was at that moment that he realised. Realised this was bigger than he ever could have imagined.

Every thought, every memory of this fountain had been imprinted on his brain for thirty-four years. That famous photo had been shared firstly in the newspapers, and later around the world on the internet.

Every single time he'd looked at this fountain it had brought back memories of Sophia and their childhood. He could clearly remember sitting on the edge of the fountain with her, banging his heels on the stonework.

But now, and for ever, every time he looked at this fountain this was what he'd remember. *This.* A water-soaked, laughing Ruby with a twinkle in her eyes and a bright-eyed little girl watching at the side.

Some memories were worth changing.

CHAPTER SEVEN

THERE WAS DEFINITELY something wrong with her. She was getting used to these clothes. She was getting used to opening the closet and seeing the rainbow colours of the beautiful garments hanging up and just waiting to be worn.

Her blue jeans had been stuffed in the back of the cupboard, along with her baseball boots. It had only been two weeks and she didn't even want to pull them out any more.

Even the pale green dress that she'd worn when she'd arrived—the best thing she had—looked like a poor cousin hanging beside all the designer clothes.

It made her skin prickle. She'd never been like this before. Every girl liked nice things. But she hadn't expected to get used to it so suddenly.

What would happen in a few weeks, when she was back in London, in her flat, wearing her healthcare uniform again? She'd always worn that uniform with pride. What on earth was happening to her?

Alex had been keeping to his side of the bargain and spending a certain amount of time with Annabelle. She'd been trying not to interfere—no matter how much she wanted to.

It was important that there was time for just father and daughter. But the rest of the palace staff didn't seem to understand that. She'd had no idea how busy Alex really was. It seemed that a country/principality didn't run itself.

After watching the constant interruptions of their father/daughter time she'd appointed herself guardian of that little part of the day. She'd started to stand guard outside the door.

By the time Annabelle was settled into her bed and he'd read a few stories to her there was usually a queue of people standing outside the bedroom, waiting to see Alex. Not one of them ever got past her.

The hard wiring talk seemed to have done the trick. It had given him the gentle kick up the backside he needed to say no to people who weren't his daughter. It was sad, but clear, that Alex hadn't been able to spend as much time with Annabelle as he would have liked.

Now he made it his priority. And Ruby's role was to make sure that father and daughter got that protected time together.

'Knock-knock.'

The voice made her jump. She was sitting in the palace library, looking out over the gardens.

This had quickly become her favourite room. The beautiful wood and paper smell crept along the corridor towards her and drew her in like a magnet. The dark wooden bookcases filled with beautiful hardback books seemed to suck her in every time she walked past. The set of steps that moved on a rail to reach the books at the top almost made her jump up and down with excitement. Every time she entered the room she climbed a few steps and moved them on just a little.

She'd even taken to bringing her computer down here and answering any emails she received from work in her favourite environment. She needed to stay in touch with her colleagues to make sure things were running smoothly back home. There were only a few emails each day— mainly about patients, asking for a second opinion or a referral route for a patient with unusual conditions. Nothing she couldn't handle from thousands of miles away.

She spun around in her chair, 'Alex? Is something wrong?'

He smiled. 'Do I only come and look for you if something is wrong?'

She leaned her elbow on the desk and rested her head on the heel of her hand. 'Let's see—maybe?'

She was teasing him. Sometimes he made it so easy. But most things were easy around Alex—except for the times when he was surrounded by palace staff. She could almost swear that Rufus stalked him from one end of the palace to the other.

'Well, let's change that. You've been here for a few weeks now, and apart from the palace grounds and a few walks into the city centre you've hardly seen anything of Euronia. How about we remedy that?'

He held his hand out towards her. She hesitated. Since the dress incident and the day at the fountain something had changed between them. It was happening slowly. Almost without her even noticing. But the way Alex looked at her was different.

Sometimes she caught him staring with the blue eyes of a man ten years younger, without the responsibilities of today on his shoulders. Those were her favourite moments.

Ten years of thinking about 'what ifs'… It was easy to pretend that she hadn't. That she'd been busy with work and life and relationships. But underneath all that there had always been something simmering beneath the surface.

Her first sight of him in her hospital department had knocked the breath from her lungs—not that she'd ever admit that. She had a hard time even admitting it to herself.

In her mind, Ruby Wetherspoon had never been that kind of girl. Dreaming of princes and happy-ever-afters. But her brain kept trying to interfere with her rational thoughts. It kept giving her secret flashes of holding hands, or more kisses. It kept making her imagine what might have happened on the rest of that night on New Year's Eve.

But there was no point dreaming of the past. Today was about looking to the future.

She was beginning to feel a glimmer of hope that there could *be* a future. Her confidence around Alex was starting to grow.

She stood up. The only 'what ifs' were for the here and now.

She reached out and took his hand, his warm skin enveloping hers. 'Where do you plan on taking me?' She looked down, 'And am I suitably dressed?'

He grinned. 'You might need alternative clothes.'

'Really? Why?'

He winked. 'You'll see.'

If the crew were surprised to see him accompanied by a lady they did their best to hide it. It had been a few months since he'd been out on the yacht, and in the past he'd always gone alone.

He hadn't even mentioned the yacht to Ruby, and her face had been a picture as they'd walked onto the dock.

She'd blinked at the gleaming white yacht. It was made of steel and over three hundred feet long.

He waved his arm, 'Ruby, I'd like you to meet the other woman in my life—the *Augusta*.'

'She's huge.' She could see all the staff on board. This wasn't a one-man sailing boat.

He nodded and headed over to the gangway. 'Five bedrooms and an owner's stateroom with living room, bedroom, bathroom and veranda. She's pretty much a guy's dream come true.'

Her foot hesitated at the gangway. His heart gave a little twist. He hadn't even asked her if she was afraid of water. *Please don't let this be a disaster.* He'd already arranged for some swimming and snorkelling gear to be dropped off at the yacht.

But her hesitation was momentary and she steadied

her balance on the swaying gangway by holding on to the rail.

'Shouldn't a boat have sails?' she whispered as they walked over the gangway.

'It's a yacht. And it doesn't need sails—it's got four diesel engines. It can probably go faster than some cars.'

She grinned and stopped mid-step, 'Well, aren't *we* a bit snippy about our boat?' She was clearly amused by his automatic response.

He wrinkled his nose. 'Snippy? What does that mean?'

She stepped a little closer. She'd changed into a pale blue dress and flat sandals. He could see the tiny freckles across the bridge of her nose and feel her scent invade his senses. It didn't matter that the smell of the Mediterranean Sea was all around them. The only thing he could concentrate on right now was the smell of some kind of flowers, winding its way around him.

'It means you don't like anyone calling your yacht a boat.' She waved her hand. 'Boat, ship, yacht—it's all the same to me.'

He laughed and shook his head. 'What's that word you use in the UK? Landlubber?'

She nodded as he guided her up on to the deck. 'I'll wear that badge with pride. I know absolutely nothing about sailing. The only boats I've ever sailed were the ones in my bath tub.'

There it was—that little twinkle in her eye. It happened whenever they joked together, whenever Ruby was relaxed and there was no one else around but them. He didn't see it often enough.

She settled into one of the white chairs as the yacht moved smoothly out from the port. The sea could be choppy around Euronia, but today it was calm.

His steward appeared. 'What would you like for lunch, Ms. Wetherspoon? The chef will make whatever you desire.'

He saw her visibly blanch. There were so many things he took for granted. At any time in the palace he could ask for whatever he wanted to eat. There was always staff available to cater to his tastes. Ruby looked almost embarrassed by the question.

'I guess since I'm on the sea it should be some kind of fish.' She shot the steward a beaming smile. 'What would you suggest?'

If the steward was surprised by her question he didn't show it. 'We have crayfish, mussels, clams and oysters. Or, if you prefer we have sardines—or bouillabaisse. It's a fish stew, practically our national dish.'

'That sounds lovely. I'll have that, thank you.'

The yacht was working its way along the coastline. Within a few minutes the pink palace came into view.

Ruby stood up. 'Wow! It looks so different, seeing it from the sea. It really does look like something from a little girl's toybox. It's gorgeous.'

Alex rolled his eyes. 'You can imagine how I felt as a teenager, living in a pink palace.'

She smiled. Her eyes were still sparkling. 'I *can* imagine. But look at it. It's impressive enough when you see it on land—but from here...? It's like something from a fairytale.'

'What's your favourite room?'

'In the palace?'

He nodded.

The steward had brought some champagne and an ice bucket and Alex popped the cork and started pouring the champagne into glasses.

She took a sip from the glass he handed her. 'It has to be the library. It's the smell. I love it. I could sit in there all day.'

'That was my mother's favourite room too. She was always in the library.'

Ruby turned to face him. 'You don't really talk about

your mother. What was she like? I've seen some photographs. She was beautiful.'

He nodded. 'Yes, she was. Most people talk about the clothes she wore and her sense of style. Marguerite de Castellane was known the world over for her beautiful wardrobe. But I remember my mother as having a really wicked sense of humour. And she was clever. She spoke four languages and brought me up speaking both English and French. She died from a clot in her lung—a pulmonary embolism. She'd had the flu and been off her feet for a few weeks. Her legs were swollen and sore—but she didn't tell anyone until it was too late.'

He couldn't help but feel a wave of sadness as he spoke about his mother. To everyone else she had been the Queen. But to an only child with an almost absent father his mother had been his whole world.

She'd kept him grounded. She'd made sure he attended the local school and the local nursery. She'd sent him shopping for bread at the bakers and meat at the delicatessen. Everything he'd learned about being a 'normal' person he'd learned from his mother.

His father had aged twenty years after she'd died. Still working, still ruling his country, but his heart hadn't been in it.

The relationship between father and son had always been strained. And it hadn't improved with age or with his father's ill health.

Ruby had little lines across her forehead now. Even when she frowned she still looked good. He felt a surge of emotion towards her.

He didn't talk to *anyone* about his mother. In years gone by he had spoken to Sophia, but that had been like talking to a friend. Ruby hadn't known his mother. She would only have whatever had been posted on the internet to refer to.

It felt good to share. She made it so easy to talk.

With her legs stretched out in front of her, sipping champagne from the glass, she looked right at home. But he knew she wasn't.

She might be comfortable around him, but she wasn't comfortable around the palace. The formalities of palace life were difficult for her.

She didn't ask or expect anyone to do things for her. Rufus had already mentioned how she'd ruffled some feathers by trying to do her own laundry or make her own toast.

'What about your family?'

She smiled. 'My mum and dad are both just about to retire. They've already told me they plan to move to the South of France. They bought a house there last month. They've holidayed there for the last ten years and have really got into the way of life.'

'Have they ever been to Euronia?'

She rolled her eyes and took another sip of champagne, holding the glass up towards him. 'Only billionaires come to Euronia, Alex.'

He was instantly defensive. 'That's not true. There are cruise ships moored every day in port, and we have bus tours that come across the border from France—'

'Alex.'

She leaned over and touched his arm. The palm of her hand was cool from holding the champagne glass.

'I was teasing.'

The smile reached right up into her eyes and he wrapped his hand over hers.

'Sometimes I'm just not sure.' He stayed exactly where he was. His eyes fixed on hers.

She wasn't shy. She didn't tear her gaze away. Her lips were turned upwards, but as he looked at her more closely her smile seemed a little sad.

'What do you think would have happened between us, Ruby?'

He didn't need to fill in the blanks. She knew exactly what he was talking about. He saw her take a careful breath in.

'I have no idea, Alex,' she whispered. 'Sometimes I've thought about it—thought about what might have happened if things had been different. But neither of us know. Neither of us can really imagine. Ten years changes a person. I'm not the girl I was in Paris, and you're not the boy.'

He nodded his head and grinned at her. 'You thought I was a *boy*?'

Now he was teasing. But she was right. They could spend hours talking about what might have been but it wouldn't do either of them any good. He'd spent too long thinking that Ruby had slipped through his fingers.

But she was right here. Right now.

He ran his palm along her arm. 'I thought about you, Ruby. I thought about you a lot. When you didn't reply to the message I left you I just assumed you'd changed your mind.' He met her gaze again, 'Or that you'd seen the news and didn't want any part of it.'

'Oh, Alex...' She lifted her hand and stroked her fingers through her hair. Her head shook slowly. 'I never got your message, Alex. And once I realised who you were I assumed you didn't want to know me—plain old Ruby Wetherspoon. You were a *prince*, for goodness' sake— with a whole country to look after. I didn't think you'd even remember me.'

He reached up and touched her cheek. 'You have no idea at all. And you've never been plain old Ruby to me.'

'The flowers... They were from you—weren't they?'

He nodded. 'I didn't want to interfere in your life. But then there came a time when it wasn't appropriate to send them any more.' His chest tightened as he said the words.

He didn't need to go into detail.

He'd always harboured hopes about Ruby. But once he'd known he had to make a commitment to Sophia it had become inappropriate to keep sending flowers to another woman. Alex would never have done something like that.

'I guess now I'm free to send you flowers again,' he said quietly.

'I guess you are.'

She gave him a little smile and set down her glass. The yacht was moving around the coastline, dancing along in the waves—just as they were dancing around each other.

'Why did you ask me to come, Alex? Why did you want me here?'

There it was again. That tiny tremble in her voice. He loved the fact that she was fearless. That she was courageous enough to ask the question out loud.

Ruby wasn't bound by a country. Ruby wasn't bound by two whole nations hoping she'd be able to keep them financially stable. Ruby didn't have to bite her tongue to prevent international incidents with foreign diplomats. Ruby had her own life—her own responsibilities. Could he really be honest? Was he willing to expose her to the world he lived in?

It was time to take a risk.

'I didn't just ask you here for Annabelle, Ruby. I need your help with my daughter. That much is clear.' He reached over and took her hand. 'But I asked you here for me too.'

She bit her lip. He could tell she was trying not to interrupt, but she just couldn't help it.

'But what does that *mean*, Alex? I need you to say it out loud.'

She was drawing a line in the sand. And she was right. He knew she was right.

He met her gaze and touched her cheek. 'I want us to have a chance, Ruby Wetherspoon. I'm not your everyday guy, and what I have isn't your everyday job. I'd like to see where this can take us, but I understand the pressure of being here and being with me. I don't want to expose you to anything before you're ready.'

She shook her head. 'Not enough. Who *am* I, Alex? Am I Ruby Wetherspoon, speech and language therapist for your daughter? Am I Ruby Wetherspoon the hired help who might catch your eye? Or am I Ruby Wetherspoon the girl you might decide to date?'

She stood up and walked across the deck, held on to the railing, looking out over the sea.

'You touch me, Alex. You kiss me. You bring me out on day trips that make my brain spin. What are you doing, Alex? What are *we* doing?'

He stood up to join her, and then slowed his movements as he neared. He didn't want to stand next to her. So he did what was the most natural thing in the world. He stood behind her, his full body against hers, with his arms wrapped around her waist, sheltering her from the sea winds.

He lifted his hand and caught her hair that was blowing in the breeze. 'Ruby, you can be whatever you want to be. But be warned: being around Alex de Castellane isn't easy. If you want to be the woman I date, that's fine. If you want to do that in public or private, that's fine with me too.'

He moved closer to her, whispering in her ear, nuzzling her.

'I lost you once, Ruby. I don't intend to lose you again. But I'll take your lead on this.'

He held his hands out towards the cliffs and the view of Euronia.

'The world out there can be hard. I want to give this a chance. I want to see where this will take us. I'd love to be able to walk down the street with you without everyone whispering—but that will never happen. I'm public property, Ruby. The world owns me. I don't want it to own you too. At least not until we're both sure about what we want.'

She turned herself towards him, tears glistening in her eyes.

He lowered his hands and wrapped them around her waist. 'What do you say, Ruby? Are you willing to give us a try?'

She wrapped her arms around his neck and stood on her tiptoes, whispering in his ear. 'I think I might need a little extra persuasion.'

'What kind of persuasion?' He liked the thought of where this might go.

'I might have questions. Conditions.'

He was surprised. 'Okay...' he said slowly. 'Like what?'

This time the expression on her face was a little bit cheeky, a little bit naughty. 'If we start dating do I get to look in all the palace rooms that are currently out of bounds to me?'

'*That's* what you want to know?' He couldn't help but smile.

'I also want to check for secret passages and dungeons.'

He nodded solemnly. 'That might be difficult. I'll have to see what I can do.'

'Can I slide down the banister?'

'That might be taking things a bit far.'

She shrugged. 'It'll save the staff from polishing.'

He nodded. 'True.' And then he sighed. 'I wish I'd thought of that explanation twenty years ago. You could have got me out of a whole heap of trouble.'

She stood up and whispered in his ear again. 'How about painting the palace a brighter shade of pink? Doesn't every girl want to live in a pink palace?'

He laughed. 'You don't think it's pink enough already? It might be every girl's dream but guess what? It's not every teenage boy's. I told you—I hated living in a pink palace.'

She shook her head. 'Silly boy. You just don't know what you had.'

He stopped smiling and touched her cheek. 'But I do now.'

She bit her lower lip again. He couldn't help but fixate

on it. They weren't entirely alone on this boat. But right now he didn't care. It seemed as if he'd been waiting for this moment for ever.

He bent forward and captured her lips against his. She met him hungrily, pushing herself against him and letting her fingers gently stroke the back of his neck. The sensation shot directly down his spine and into his groin.

He pulled back. There was a whole host of things running through his mind right now. But none was as important as being here with Ruby.

He grabbed her hand and pulled her inside.

'There are seven staff on this boat. They would never disturb us, but things aren't exactly private here. If we're going to see where this takes us we have to agree what you're comfortable with.'

She looked a little unsure. But her face was flushed and her hands were touching his waist—almost as if she didn't want to let go.

He glanced down at them and gave a laugh. 'Careful, Ruby. You've no idea where my *brain's* currently taking us.'

He opened the door and pulled her along a narrow corridor,

'I've made plans for us today. Let's cool off. There are some swimsuits inside this room along here. We'll anchor the boat, do a little swimming, and then have some dinner.' He stopped outside the door of one of the rooms and hesitated. 'It'll give you time to think.'

He was aware that she hadn't said anything—was terrified that he might have frightened her off. Ruby probably hadn't considered the real consequences of being involved with a prince and he'd just laid them all bare to her.

He'd lived with press intrusion all his life. But in his world it was slightly easier for men than women. When the heir to the throne in the United Kingdom had got married his new wife had been constantly under the glare of the spotlight. Even now every outfit she wore, every friend she spoke to, even the appointments in her diary were scrutinised continuously.

Euronia might not be the UK, but it was a hotspot for the rich and famous. The press were always lurking somewhere in the background. He was surprised no one had commented on Ruby's presence before now. She must have slipped under the radar as a member of staff. But that wouldn't last much longer.

Her smile faltered. 'Alex, what if we're making a mistake? What if we're both caught in the memory of ten years ago and what we've imagined and reality is totally different?' She looked up through heavy eyelids. 'We might not even *like* each other.'

His stomach twisted. It was true. It was a fair comment. But it went against his gut. It went against how he truly felt.

He didn't know Ruby that well. Someone, somewhere in the palace would have a report on her—they had one on every staff member. And his security staff would have the report from ten years ago on the woman he'd been with when they'd found him at the café in Paris. Someone would know which schools she'd attended in England, what the occupations of her mum and dad were, if she had any political affiliations.

But he didn't want to find out from a bit of paper. He wanted to find out in real time—with Ruby.

So he did what his gut told him to do. He leaned forward and brushed a kiss against her cheek. 'Then let's find out.'

She stepped inside and closed the door behind her, instantly feeling the coolness of the air-conditioned room. Her cheek burned from where he'd kissed her.

Kissed her—and left her. Walking down the corridor, leaving her to fixate on his backside and broad shoulders. She felt like someone from a bad movie.

Her stomach was turning over and over. *'Let's find out.'*

She'd waited ten years to find out. Ten years of secret thoughts and wild imagination. Did this mean anything between them was destined to fail?

She picked up her mobile and pressed the quick call button. She'd never needed to talk to someone so badly.

'Polly? Are you free? Can you talk?'

'Ruby? Where on earth have you been? I tried to call you three times yesterday. Are you coming home?'

'No. Not yet. And maybe…'

'Maybe what?' Polly got straight to the point. 'What's happening with you and Prince Perfect?'

Ruby sighed and leaned against the wall. 'He just kissed me, Polly. He kissed me and I didn't want him to stop.'

'Oh, no. Don't start all this dreamy kissing stuff again. Does this guy have stars and rainbows in his lips? One kiss and you go all squishy.'

She smiled. It was true. Trust Polly just to come out with it. 'I'm worried, Pol. He's told me he wants to give us a chance. He's asked me if I'm willing.'

'Willing to what? Flounce off into the sunset on matching unicorns? What exactly does he need you to be willing *for*?'

'To give us a go. To see where this takes us.' She started to slide down the wall. 'But I can't think straight, Pol. I'm just Ruby. I'm not a princess. I'm not a supermodel. How can I possibly live up to the expectations he has? I don't even know what fork to pick up at dinner.'

'Ruby Wetherspoon, you listen to me. This isn't about his expectations. This is about yours. You don't *need* to be a princess or a supermodel. You're better than both. He is lucky to have met you. He's lucky you agreed to go and help with his daughter. This isn't about you being good enough for him. The question is: is Prince Perfect good enough for *you*?'

Trust Polly. She could always boost her confidence and make her feel better. It was like having her own professional cheerleader and piranha all in one. But whilst she loved what Polly was saying, she just wasn't sure she believed it.

Polly hadn't finished talking. 'And as for the forks— just start on the outside and work your way in. Never fails.'

Ruby was shaking her head. 'I like him, Polly. I really like him. But this is a whole other country. There's so many people watching me. So many people watching *him*.'

'He's a prince, Ruby. What do you want?'

She sighed. 'I want to do normal things. I want to get to know him better. I want the chance to go out and have a glass of wine with him. I want to go to the cinema and fight about who is the best action hero or the best *Star Trek* captain—'

'Picard.' Polly cut her off quickly. 'It's always Picard.'

Ruby heard the squeak of furniture as Polly obviously sat down.

'I hate to break it to you, honey, but going for a glass of wine and heading to the multiplex is probably a no-no. Anyway—doesn't Alex have a whole cinema in the palace?'

'Probably. I don't know. I just can't think straight around him, Pol. He walks in a room and my whole body—it just *tingles*.' She gave a little shake as she said the words.

'Oh, no. No tingling. Definitely no tingling.'

'People here—they're different. The way they treat Alex. The way they treat me when I'm with Alex…'

Her voice drifted off as her train of thought started to take her down the railway line to mild panic.

'His mother spoke four languages. I can't do that. I know nothing about politics. Or history. Or modern studies. I only got a passing grade in geography because I memorised stuff about eroding coastlines.'

'What exactly do you think you're auditioning for here, Rubes? You're a speech and language therapist—an expert in your field. You've published professional papers. You work at one of the finest hospitals in London. Why do you think you're not good enough for him?'

She started shaking her head. 'It's not that I think I'm not good enough. I'm just worried. Alex wants to give us a chance—*I* want to give us a chance—but what about the rest of the world?'

'Hang the rest of the world, Ruby. This is *your* life. Not theirs.' Polly groaned. 'You know I want you back here with me. But *ten years*, Ruby. Ten years you waited for this guy to come back into your life. You can't let what anyone else thinks matter.'

Ruby straightened up. Polly was right. Alex was right. He was just trying to prepare her. Trying to let her understand that things might be difficult.

But Alex de Castellane wanted *her*—Ruby Wetherspoon. It had to mean something.

She walked over to the other side of the cabin. 'Oh, Pol. He's bought me clothes.'

'Again? What is he—a personal shopper or a prince?'

She lifted up a scrap of material from the bed and squinted at it—trying to imagine what it covered. 'Well, they're not clothes, exactly. More like tiny bits of cloth. I think they're supposed to be for swimming.' She started to laugh and shake her head as she moved her phone to snap a picture and send it to Polly. 'What on earth is *that* supposed to cover?'

There were five different styles of swimming costume on the bed, along with a whole host of scraps doing their best impression of itsy-bitsy teeny-weeny bikinis. She picked up the first and checked the label. At least they were her size—but there was no way she was wearing one in front of Alex. Not right now anyway.

There was a screech at the other end of the phone as Polly got the photo. She started howling with laughter. 'Gotta go, honey—the baby's crying. But, please—if you wear that you've got to send me a photo!'

Ruby smiled as the call was disconnected. She always felt better after talking to Polly. But Polly's life had moved on. They were still best friends. But Polly had a husband and a baby. She'd found her happy-ever-after. What about Ruby's?

She picked up a red swimsuit, slightly padded with a ruched front. Perfect. Something that actually covered the parts it should. It only took two minutes to put it on, and she grabbed a sheer black sarong to knot around her waist.

It was time to get out there.

Let's find out.

Alex was doing his best impression of a male model in white trunks. She gulped. She was going to have to avert her eyes. Either that or put a sign on her head saying that if she looked at that area it would make her knees go weak.

He was waiting for her out on deck and he led her around to the back of the yacht this time. Again there were some seats, but Alex had also laid down towels on a flat area overhanging the edge. There was no ladder down the side. This flat part seemed to have been designed purely for getting in and out of the sea.

She sat down on a white towel and blushed as she noticed his appreciative gaze. 'What do you normally use this for?'

'Diving. I used to do a lot of diving with friends. Nothing too spectacular. Just for fun. So when I commissioned the yacht I knew I wanted a diving platform attached.'

'You *commissioned* the yacht? You didn't just buy it from a catalogue? Just how rich are you, Alex?'

She was laughing as she said the words and turned to dip her toes in the water. Even though the sun was blistering hot the sea was cold.

'Youch!'

She pulled her feet back in as Alex laughed. 'Here.' He

tossed her some sunscreen. 'Put some of this on or you'll burn your nose.'

It was easy to forget how hot the sun was with the sea breezes around them. She smeared some sunscreen on her face, arms and legs, then stood behind him, poised to put some cream on his back.

But he grabbed her arm and pulled her into his lap. 'I've already got some. You, however, need some on *your* back. Give me that.'

He squirted some cream on his hands and started to rub it over her back. She was almost scared to move. Her position was precarious. They were right at the edge of the moored boat and she was balancing on his knees. Right now there were only two very thin pieces of fabric separating them. Her right arm was pressing against his bare chest, the dark curling hairs tickling her skin.

His hand movements slowed, going from initially brisk and efficient to sensual, circling her back, slipping under the straps on her shoulders and smearing cream across every part of her skin. She breathed in sharply and his hand circled lower, fingertips sweeping below her swimsuit.

His voice was husky, his accent thicker. 'You didn't like the bikinis?'

'I didn't like *me* in the bikinis.'

'Why ever not?' His fingers slowed and stopped, staying just underneath the back of her costume. 'You're a beautiful woman, Ruby.'

She felt her cheeks flush, instantly embarrassed by his words—which was ironic, really, since she was sitting half clothed in his lap. Could anyone see them, sitting here on the back of his yacht? In front of her all she could see was the Mediterranean Sea. There wasn't even another boat in sight.

His hand moved gently around her waist, touching the fabric of her costume and resting next to the knot of her sarong. 'This is definitely your colour. You suit red, Ruby. It seems as though your mother named you well.'

'My mother named me after the ruby slippers in *The Wizard of Oz*. But I'll tell her you appreciate her choice,' she teased.

This was too much. She was sitting here, feeling the rise and fall of his chest next to her arm, the warmth between his skin and hers. Their faces were inches apart. Not touching him properly was torture.

She moved that little inch, putting her hand at the back of his head and tugging him closer until their lips touched. His fingers started tugging at the knot on her sarong. It fell apart easily.

The kiss quickly intensified. She could easily tell the effect their close contact was having on his body—just as it was having an effect on hers. Kissing him was too easy.

They weren't in Paris any more. It wasn't New Year's Eve. But she could almost hear the fireworks going off in her head.

The sun wasn't heating her skin any more—Alex was. Every nibble, every tiny touch of his tongue electrified her. She let out a little moan as their kiss deepened, his hands running up and down the bare skin on her back.

'Ruby...' he muttered.

'What?' She didn't want him to stop. She didn't want this moment to end.

'We're out in the open. I know it doesn't feel like it, but...' His voice tailed off.

She was still kissing him, never wanting it to end.

A few minutes ago the sea had seemed deserted. But other boats had passed them on their journey around the coastline. And the crew might not come down here, but if she didn't stop this now...she might live to regret it.

She broke the kiss. 'Alex?'

'What?' He looked up, those gorgeous blue eyes connecting with hers.

She smiled. 'You're right. It's time to cool off.'

Her arms were still wrapped around him and she just leaned backwards, pulling them both into the cold blue sea.

The plunge was a little further than she'd expected, and the shock of the cold water on her skin pushed the air from her lungs as it closed around her. It only took a few seconds to push to the surface and break out into the warm sun. She was laughing and coughing and spluttering all at once.

She slicked her wet hair back from her face as Alex surfaced next to her, shaking his head and showering her with droplets of water.

'This is getting to be a habit,' he said as he swam next to her and put his hands around her waist underwater.

The cold water was doing nothing to dampen their desire and she wound her hands around his neck again as they trod water.

'It is, isn't it? Maybe you and I shouldn't be around water.' She laughed.

'What should we be around?' he asked as the waves buoyed them up.

'I don't know. Pink palaces, Eiffel Towers, fireworks and yellow dresses.' She could see the twinkle in his eye as she said those last words.

'Come on,' he gestured towards her. 'Let's swim around the boat. It might be best if we have some water between us.'

Her hand touched his arm as they separated in the water.

They laughed and swam around the boat, occasionally stopping next to each other as Alex told her a little more about his country.

'The caves down there were traditionally used by pirates.'

There were two dark caves carved into the bottom of the cliffs on the rocky shoreline. Her body had grown accustomed to the temperature of the water but she still gave a shudder.

'No way. Fairytales. Made-up stories.'

He lifted his hand out of the water. 'You forget—this is a land with a pink palace. You think we didn't have pirates?'

'When you put it like that it doesn't seem quite so crazy.'

'I'll show you some of the things in the castle vaults. I think my ancestors might have been in league with the pirates. Either that or they just kept everything once they'd captured the pirates.'

'Are you allowed to do that?'

He shrugged his shoulders as they continued to swim around the boat. 'We have some old doubloons, some jewellery and some weapons. The assumption is that they are Spanish, but the Spaniards didn't want them back when they were offered a few hundred years ago. There isn't enough to be of any real value—we've kept them safe because of the historical importance.'

She kept swimming. 'I'm going to add that to my list of conditions from earlier—a visit to the pirate caves.' She winked, 'I might even ask you to dress up.'

As they rounded the hull of the yacht another boat came into view. It was not quite as big as Alex's, but equally sleek in white and silver.

Alex sighed. 'Let's get back on board.'

'Do you know who owns that boat?'

He stroked out towards the diving platform. 'It's Randall Merr and his wife. They can be unbearable. I'll tell the crew to head back to port.'

Randall Merr. A billionaire with houses all over the world—including in Euronia.

Part of her stomach twisted. Maybe Alex didn't want to introduce her to his friends? Maybe he was embarrassed by her?

She put her head in the water and struck out towards the platform. Alex reached it first and turned round to help her out of the water, offering her a towel and her sarong.

The electricity between them seemed to have dissipated.

All of a sudden she felt very exposed—and it wasn't because she was wearing only swimwear. The magic bubble that she'd felt earlier around her and Alex had vanished in the blink of an eye.

'Ruby, what's wrong?'

He was picking up the other towels and the sunscreen from around them.

She started up the steps. 'Nothing's wrong. I'm going to put some clothes on.' She hated that tiny waver in her voice.

He caught her arm. 'Ruby, tell me what's wrong. Are you angry with me?'

The words that were spinning around in her brain tumbled out of her mouth unchecked. Nothing she would ever really want him to hear.

'Why would I be angry with you, Alex? You tell me it's up to *me* to decide how this goes—then as soon as we see someone you know you try and bundle me away. As if I'm some kind of employee you can't be seen with. Which, when you think about it, I really am—aren't I?'

His brow crumpled and confusion swept over his face. He shook his head and tightened his grip on her arm, pulling her hard against him. She was above him, on the first step of the stairs. Their faces were perfectly level.

'You think I want to hide you? After everything I've said?'

His nose was almost touching hers and his eyes were blazing. She'd angered him.

But instead of being intimidated she just felt another fire spark within her. 'Well, that's what it looks like.'

His lips connected with hers. His hands jerked her hipbones against his. This was no delicate kiss. This was no teasing, no playing with her. This was pure and utter passion.

His hands moved from her hips and his fingers tangled in her hair, tugging her head one way then another. His teeth clashed with hers and his tongue drove its way into her mouth. She could hardly breathe. He was devouring her.

He finally released her just as the white boat passed directly behind the yacht. It was so close the yacht bobbed wildly in its wake.

'There,' he growled, without even turning around. 'Randall Merr and his wife got a prime-time view. If you didn't want anyone to know about us it's too late. That woman practically has a satellite connection to the world's press.'

She gulped. Was that really what she wanted?

Truth was, she hadn't answered Alex because she was unsure.

She wasn't unsure about him. Not for a second. But she was definitely unsure about his world.

How could she possibly ever fit in to his lifestyle? She was already sure that some of the staff didn't like her and suspected something might be in the air between them.

She wanted the Alex she'd met ten years ago in Paris. The gorgeous, slightly mysterious man with a bit of an accent.

But that wasn't Alex at all. *This* was Alex. The acting ruler of one country and potentially the temporary head of another. The father of a young daughter. The son of a sick man. A businessman with the financial responsibility for all the inhabitants of his country.

Her Alex had only really ever existed in her head.

And whilst the living, breathing Alex in front of her was sexier than she could ever have dreamed of, she was still wondering if this was all a figment of her imagination.

After ten years he'd come looking for her.

After ten years he'd told her he'd let her decide the pace.

She was finding it hard to believe it. These were the kind of dreams she'd had ten years ago and never told anyone about.

Alex de Castellane had spent his life surrounded by supermodels and movie stars. They all flocked to his country—a tax haven. They all wanted to be seen with him, to be photographed with him.

And Alex, Prince Regent, was charming. He knew how to show interest and talk to people as if they were the only ones in the room. There was something enigmatic about him. And for most people it would be easy to get lost in his world.

But Ruby was different. Ruby wasn't looking for a fairytale.

Maybe the Alex she'd always imagined was just a figment of her imagination. Maybe he'd never really existed.

The man she'd spent a few hours with that night had been excited about life. Had had plans for the future. He'd offered to show her around Paris and she had gladly accepted.

Accepted the chance to spend a few more hours in his company. Accepted the chance to be the focus of his attention for a few more hours.

Would she have accepted any of it if she'd known his real identity?

Most of the world would have screamed *yes*. Most of the world would have claimed it was every girl's dream to be a princess. But most of the world wasn't Ruby Wetherspoon.

Her hand was still on his arm. Droplets of sea water were running down his skin, running from his hair down his chest. Physically, she wanted Alex. Emotionally, she wanted Alex. Mentally, she wanted Alex. But all wrapped up together?

It was terrifying. And she couldn't put it into words. She didn't know how to explain the feeling of wanting to reach out and grab him, yet feeling totally overwhelmed.

Right now she wanted to be back in her room at the palace. The room next to Annabelle's. She wanted to be curled up with Annabelle, watching a movie and observing her. In an environment of peace and calm. In a place where she felt safe.

A place where she didn't feel so exposed.

'Get changed. Ruby. Put some clothes on. I'll meet you back on deck and we'll have some food, then go back to the palace.'

The Alex of earlier was lost. The man who'd looked at her almost adoringly and whispered in her ear had vanished from her grasp.

The warm sea breeze had turned distinctly chilly. It swept around her, making every little hair on her arms stand to attention. She wrapped the towel around her shoulders.

Her feet slipped and squelched along the wooden-floored corridor until she finally reached the room with her clothes and she sagged down, wet and cold, onto the bed.

All of a sudden the designer bathing suits didn't seem quite so attractive any more.

She lay down on the bed—just for a second—and closed her eyes.

CHAPTER EIGHT

ALEX WAS HAVING trouble keeping his emotions in check.

Today, all he'd been able to think about was Ruby. He hadn't worried about share prices. About price indexes. About gas, electricity and oil prices.

Today he'd just thought about the beautiful, bright-eyed woman in front of him. For a time it had seemed perfect.

Their familiarity and warmth had developed over the last few weeks and he'd finally managed to put into words the things that had been circulating in his brain.

Then—*bam!* It felt as if everything was ruined.

He was pacing up and down the deck. The crew all seemed to have vanished into the mists—as if they knew he was brooding. Cold diet colas had appeared magically in a silver cooler. His steward had obviously realised that this wasn't the time for more champagne.

He couldn't even face eating right now. So much was circulating in his head that his stomach was churning over and over.

How had he managed to mess this up? He'd planned it in his head. *Give her time to think about this. Don't rush her.* He was sure he'd seen a flicker of doubt in her eyes and that had almost killed him. He was treading so carefully around her.

Then the Merrs and their darn boat. Mrs Merr had probably buzzed them deliberately. Anything to see what the Prince Regent was up to.

He'd thought he was giving Ruby time. He'd thought he was giving her space. Wasn't that what she wanted?

But a few moments ago she'd seemed angry—annoyed that he'd tried to hide her from prying eyes. He'd only been trying to protect her. But her words had practically sent a flare up.

He wanted to be seen with Ruby. He wanted to tell the world that he was willing to take a chance on where this might go.

But he was also terrified that harsh treatment by the world's press would send her running for the hills.

How on earth was he supposed to know what was right and what was wrong?

Would he ever be able to fathom the way Ruby's brain worked?

Right now it seemed unlikely.

He glanced at his watch. She hadn't appeared. He went into his cabin, pulled out his laptop and sat at the table.

Time. That was what he needed to give her.

In the meantime, he still had work to do.

Ruby hovered at the glass doors. He was concentrating fiercely on the laptop screen in front of him.

She'd sat down on the bed for just a minute and ended up sleeping for an hour. When she'd woken she'd been embarrassed. But it had been too late for that, so she'd showered and changed before coming out.

She'd half expected to find the boat moored back in the harbour, and was pleasantly surprised to find they were still out at sea.

Here, there was nowhere to run and hide. Here, she would need to talk to Alex.

She'd changed into a turquoise-blue maxi-dress and flat jewelled sandals and pulled her hair up into a ponytail. She wasn't trying to seduce Alex. She wasn't trying to entice him away from anything else.

She was here to have one of the hardest conversations of her life.

This had all crept up on her. She'd known it was always there—hovering in the background. But things had become crystal-clear to her.

It was so easy to think that this was about her. About whether she could stand the press attention or not. But it wasn't really. It was about him. She just had to be brave enough to say the words.

Her stomach growled loudly and he turned sharply in his chair.

'Ruby.'

It was more like a grunt than a greeting—not a good start. But it gave her the kick she needed. She took the few steps across the cabin and pulled out the chair opposite him.

'Sorry. I sat down for five minutes and fell asleep.'

'You obviously don't find my company riveting enough.'

It was a barb. And she could take it or she could react.

She leaned over and snapped the laptop shut on his fingers. 'Got your attention now?'

He snatched his fingers back and glared at her. 'I was working.'

'You're always working.'

It was as if all the barriers around them had come crashing down. Right now she wasn't afraid to say anything—and from the looks of it neither was he.

'Make up your mind what you want, Ruby.'

'I can't. There's too many variables.'

No nice words. No beating about the bush. Two people with everything at stake.

'Well, let's start with the things that can't change. The non-variables.'

She leaned over and grabbed a can from the silver bucket, popping the tab and taking a sip. This could take a while.

'Is this like a quiz show, Alex? Do I win something if I get the questions right?'

Their eyes locked. They both knew exactly what was at stake here. They both knew what the prize was.

He sucked in a deep breath and held his hand out for the can of cola. It was the first sign that this really was going to be a discussion.

His voice was low. 'I'm always going to be the King of Euronia. I'm always going to be father to Annabelle.'

She nodded. 'I've never questioned those things.'

He held her gaze. 'But I've never really told you that those are things that I *wanted*. Not just things that were forced upon me or inherited by birth. When I was young I thought being King would be a whole lot of pressure on my shoulders—with no say in it for me. As I've grown older I've accepted that not only is this my destiny, it's something I actually want.'

She ran her tongue along her lips. Deep down she'd always known this. Even though Alex hadn't told her who he was when they'd met. This wasn't just his inherited future. This was a future he was willing to embrace.

It was a first step. It was the first time he'd actually admitted to her what he wanted in life.

He leaned back in his chair a little. 'I went to the US to study and learn business. It was my idea, not my father's, but he fully supported it. The world is changing constantly—it's getting smaller—and Euronia needed to move into the twenty-first century.'

'And now?'

'Now I need to use everything that I've learned to help my country prosper.'

'So where does that leave us?'

So many things were sparking in her brain. Did Alex suspect what she was about to say to him?

'How do you feel about me, Ruby?'

The question blind-sided her. She knew they were having a frank discussion, but she hadn't expected him just to ask her outright.

'I…' Her voice tailed off as her brain tried frantically to find the right words.

He shook his head.

She hadn't even answered yet and she'd disappointed him. But how could she tell him how she really felt when they still hadn't dealt with the heart of the problem? She had to say the words.

'What if Sophia had lived?'

'What?' He looked confused. Blind-siding worked both ways.

'What if her cancer had been cured and she'd lived—what then?'

He shook his head. 'That would never have happened. Sophia's cancer was already terminal. Nothing was going to change that.'

'But what if it had? Would you still have married her? Still have had Annabelle? Would you have come looking for me at all?'

Her voice started to shake a little and she took a deep breath. She needed to be calm. She needed to be rational and not blinded by her emotions.

'I need you to be honest with me, Alex. I need you to be honest with yourself.' This was hurting more than she could ever have imagined. 'If Sophia was alive today, where would she feature in your life?'

'Don't paint her as the villain in this piece. You're angry with me because I married another woman. Just say it.' He blurted it out straight away.

'You're right. I *was* angry. More than that, I was bitterly disappointed—even though I'd no right to be. But I don't understand. If you'd really wanted to find me you could have. In fact, you did. You sent me those flowers. Why didn't you just come and see me? Why didn't you ever jump in your million-pound jet and come and find me?'

She was sounding desperate and she hated herself for

being like that. But if it was going to be all out there—
then so be it.

'You didn't answer my message, Ruby. I left you a message—I got no reply. What was I supposed to do? Search
for a woman who didn't want me to find her? Embarrass
myself and put you in vulnerable position?'

She bit her lip. It was a reasonable reply. But it didn't
make her like it any better.

He kept going.

'I thought my father was about to die. The things I'd
been working towards were being thrust on me from a great
height. I didn't have time to think about it any more—I
had to just do it. No wonder my father had agreed for me
to study business. The country's finances were in a mess.
We were teetering on the brink of disaster. For the best
part of three years I juggled finances, moved money, in-
vested money, watched stock markets and persuaded people to come to Euronia—persuaded people to invest in
Euronia. Most nights I got around four hours' sleep. I was
a mess, Ruby. I didn't have time to sleep, let alone think.
How would you have felt if you'd been around a man who
was too busy to spend time with you? Too busy to talk?
Too busy to sleep? What kind of a relationship would that
have been?'

'But you found time for Sophia.'

She said it so quietly the words were barely a whisper
above the hum of the yacht's engines.

Alex's eyes widened and his response was immediate.
'Sophia appeared just as things were starting to look up.
She was desperate, Ruby. She was dying and she was my
friend. Sophia's illness brought me back to reality. What's
the point of taking care of a country if you can't take care
of those around you?'

She could hear the emotion in his voice. It was starting
to break. This was it. This was the whole crux of the mat-

ter. This was the enormous big grey elephant in the room and it was time to smash it to smithereens.

'So what happened with Annabelle, then?'

The words echoed around them. She hadn't really meant to say them out loud. They'd come into her brain and out of her mouth almost instantly. It was cruel. It was uncalled for.

It was unintentional.

He sat back sharply—almost as if she'd thrust a knife into his chest.

'You think it's my fault, don't you?'

She looked him straight in the eye. Everyone had danced around Alex. Everyone had chosen their words carefully. But this was it. This was the only way to give them a fighting chance.

'I think that when Sophia died Annabelle didn't just lose her mother, she lost her father too.'

She took a deep breath and continued.

'You keep claiming Sophia was only your friend. And you can tell me that as often as you like. But your little girl is the spitting image of her mother. Do you think I've not noticed that there's no photograph of her mother in her room? Do you think I don't see that little fleeting gaze of something when you look at her? Don't ask me what it is, Alex, but it's there. I've seen it. Children pick up on these things. And I think Annabelle has picked up on it. You don't want to be around her. She reminds you too much of what you've lost.'

She could almost see the shock registering on his face, but she couldn't stop.

She pointed her finger at him. 'I know you've been busy, but I don't think you've been as busy as you claim to be. When I laid it out for you that you *had* to spend time with her you managed to do it.'

She was hurting him. She could tell. And she really didn't want to. But it had to be said. She had to try and move them both forward.

'She's improving, Alex. She is. I know that when she's around you, and around me, she exists in her own little bubble. But it's our job to expand your daughter's world in a way that makes her feel safe.'

'This isn't about Annabelle. Today isn't about Annabelle. This is supposed to be about you and me.'

He looked stunned. Stunned that someone had challenged him on his feelings about Sophia. Stunned that someone was suggesting the reason his daughter might not be speaking was his fault.

It was only natural for him to try and deflect the conversation.

'But it can't be, Alex. It can't be until you deal with this first.' She kept her voice steady. 'Tomorrow I'm going to find the nicest photo I can of Sophia and put it in a frame next to Annabelle's bed. She needs to be able to look at her mother every day. She needs to know that there was someone in this world who loved and adored her.'

'You mean I don't?'

He was furious. His eyes were blazing. But no matter how much it made her stomach ache this was exactly what she had to do.

'Don't you get it, Alex? There can't be an "us". There can't be the start of anything between us until you face up to your past. Annabelle wasn't created in a dish. She wasn't a test tube baby. You slept with your wife. You created a child together. Part of you loved her.'

She waved her hand.

'Stop trying to tell me otherwise. I've accepted it, Alex, and so must you. If you want us to be seen together—if you want to kiss me like that again—then it has to be on the condition that you've grieved for your wife. It has to be on the condition that you can look at your daughter and love her the way you should.'

Tears started to roll down her cheeks.

'This isn't about me trying to decide if I want to be seen

in public with you or not. I can't even answer that yet—
because we're not there yet. It's easy for you to put all the
responsibility for this relationship on my shoulders. Because then you don't need to think about Sophia or Annabelle at all.'

The tears wouldn't stop. Her heart was breaking.

Alex's face had crumpled. She didn't have a single doubt
that she loved this man sitting across from her. This proud,
passionate, potential king.

It would be so easy to get swept along with the wonder of the pink palace, Euronia, and a prince who'd come
looking for her after ten years.

She wanted him for herself. She really did.

She almost wished she could take back everything she'd
just said and walk through that door again and wrap her
arms around his neck and kiss him.

But this would always have been there.

This would eventually have festered between them.

She wanted to be free to love Alex. And she wanted
him to be free to love her. Things just didn't feel like that
right now.

'This is killing me, Alex,' she whispered.

He stood up sharply, his chair screeching along the
floor. He ran his fingers through his hair. 'I need to think.
I need to think about all this.'

His eyes were vacant. As if he couldn't look at her,
couldn't focus.

The tables had turned completely.

He'd been telling *her* to take her time.

But the reality was after ten years it was Alex who
needed to take his time.

She stood up and walked back towards the glass doors.

This time it was her turn to say the words. 'Take all the
time you need.'

CHAPTER NINE

For two days he avoided Ruby.

There was too much to think about—too much to absorb.

Any time he was around Ruby he was drawn to her and wanted to touch her.

But horrible little parts of what she'd said were keeping him awake at night.

The photograph part was easy. He knew exactly which picture to frame for Annabelle. It was embarrassing to think he hadn't even considered it before.

He—and the advisors around him—had just assumed that Annabelle wouldn't remember anything about her mother.

He hadn't deliberately kept her pictures away from Annabelle—he just hadn't thought to talk to Annabelle about her mother.

She was playing in her room now. One blonde doll seemed to be driving a racing car around the furniture and over most of the other toys. She was making noises again—a *brrrrmm* for the racing car and a gasp as the doll plummeted over the bedcovers.

His heart twisted in his chest. If Sophia had lived would their little girl have been like this? It was a horrible thing to consider. It meant facing up to facts—facing up to a responsibility that he'd thought he had fulfilled.

Ruby thought differently.

He couldn't hesitate any longer. He walked into the room, keeping his voice bright. 'Hi, Annabelle. I've brought a picture for you.'

He put the silver frame on Annabelle's bedside table.

There was an audible gasp. It almost ripped him in two.

The picture was almost exactly at Annabelle's head height. She tilted her head to one side, her eyes wide.

He could have picked from a million pictures of Sophia. Once Annabelle was old enough to use the internet she would find another million pictures of her mother online.

But this was his favourite. This had always been his favourite. It was the picture he still had of Sophia in his mind—not the frail, emaciated pale woman she'd become.

This picture had Sophia on a swing, her blonde hair streaming behind her, her face wide with laughter and her pink dress billowing around her. She was around eighteen in this picture and it captured her perfectly. It captured the fun-loving human being she'd been before illness had struck her down.

He had other pictures. Pictures of her holding Annabelle not long after the birth and in the following months. There were lots of those.

But all of those pictures were touched with inherent sadness. The inevitability of a life lost. He'd put some into a little album for Annabelle. Those were for another day.

She reached out and touched the photo, obviously captivated by the joy in the picture. That was the word it conjured in his brain. *Joy.*

He knelt beside her. 'That's your mama, Annabelle. She was a very beautiful woman and you look just like her. I thought it was time for you to have a photograph of your own.'

Her little brow furrowed for a moment. He could almost see her brain trying to assimilate the information. Her lips moved, making the M movement—but no sound came out.

He rested her hand at her back. 'Look—your dress is the same colour as hers.'

He could see the recognition on his little girl's face. His whole body ached. Why hadn't he done this sooner?

A wave of shame washed over him. He should have known to do this. He should have known that his daughter needed this. But Alex had no experience around children. He had no relatives with youngsters, and as an only child he didn't have much experience to draw on.

He'd had friends—peers—during his life. Sophia had been among them, as had his schoolmates and university friends. But he hadn't been exposed to a life of looking after other people's children.

His sole experience of children before the birth of Annabelle had been on royal tours, where he was expected to talk to kids and hold babies. That was all fine, but it only lasted minutes. It didn't give him a taste of real life.

He looked down at the little girl in front of him. She'd gone back to her dolls and was racing them around the room again. Just like any three-year-old should.

His eyes glanced between his daughter and the photo. The wave of grief was overwhelming. Ruby was right. Sophia *hadn't* just been his friend.

Would he have married her if she hadn't been sick? Probably not. Their relationship hadn't been destined to go that way. Sophia had had wanderlust. She would likely have travelled and married someone from a distant country.

But the genetics of life had changed all that.

He took a deep breath. He hadn't felt the surge of emotion around Sophia that he felt around Ruby. There hadn't been that instant connection. More like a slow-growing respect. But other than Ruby she was the only woman on this planet he'd actually felt anything for.

In his head it had all been about duty and loyalty. He hadn't wanted to let his heart get involved. But if he wanted to move on with Ruby he had to acknowledge that she'd been more than just a friend.

He held his hand out to Annabelle. 'Annabelle, honey. Come with Daddy. We're going to go and put some flowers on your mama's grave.'

Another tiny step. Another massive milestone.

When was the last time he'd visited Sophia's grave?

He knew for sure he'd never taken his daughter there.

That was all about to change.

The changes were subtle at first.

The first thing she noticed was the picture in the silver frame next to Annabelle's bed. It made her heart squeeze in her chest. One, because he'd done it himself, and two, because Annabelle's mother had indeed been beautiful.

She wasn't jealous. She couldn't bring herself to be jealous of a dead woman. Those initial little pangs of frustration had disappeared. On dark nights—for some horrible moments—she'd wanted this woman never to have existed. Irrational and unreasonable thoughts had filled her head momentarily: Sophia had stolen those ten years she could have had with Alex.

All nonsense.

Life was life.

There was a gorgeous little girl running about around her legs and that was what she should focus on.

Her brain could be logical. It could tell her that she was there to do a job. It could tell her that she was the best person possible for Annabelle.

And there were discernible changes in Annabelle. Small ones—as if the little girl's walls were being finally worn down.

She wasn't quite so reserved. Her play and interaction at the nursery had changed. Humming was rapidly becoming normal now. Little noises, little sounds would be made with excitement—or sometimes fright if they were watching *Finding Nemo* again.

A small flick-through book of photographs of Annabelle and her mother had appeared. The picture on the front was amazing. One half in black and white, one half in colour. Annabelle and her mother, both sitting on the fountain, at around the same age. Two captured moments in time.

Anyone who didn't know Annabelle would think it was the same little girl.

Ruby could already predict that in her teenage years Annabelle would blow up that picture for her bedroom wall.

The first time she'd flicked through the book with Annabelle talking her through the pictures had been hard. A weight had pressed down on her chest and it had been all she could do to stop the tears rolling down her cheeks. But it became easier, and soon part of their routine every day involved five minutes of flicking through the photos.

It had also become part of Alex's bedtime routine with Annabelle. The staff had finally got the message and stopped queuing outside the door at night. Alex was adamant that this time was Annabelle's.

And it had done them both good. Alex was more relaxed around his child. He knew what her favourite foods were. He knew who her best friends were at nursery. He could sing along to all the songs in *Finding Nemo*. And gradually the sad tone in his voice was replaced as he told stories of happy memories while they flicked through the photo album.

Ruby stayed in the background although she was working tirelessly with Annabelle. There were no more romantic interludes with Alex, no matter how much she hoped for them. No other heated moments when the air was so thick a wrecking ball couldn't pound its way through.

He still watched her. Sometimes when she lifted her head she would meet his bright blue gaze. The sparks were still there. They were both just treading more warily.

If they brushed hands as they played with Annabelle, or if he moved closer for any reason, the buzz thrummed through her body. Every part of her still wanted to be with him. But she was more confident around him.

She didn't feel the need to look like a supermodel. She didn't feel outclassed by visiting royalty. Alex wanted her. She knew it. He knew it.

Getting there was a slow process. But she could live with that.

Every day she learned something new about Euronia. About its history—the subterfuge, the pirates and the Kings. The history was chequered with colourful characters. Alex's father was probably the quietest ruler of them all.

He was still in Switzerland. Once Alex had flown there, when his father had suffered another bout of pneumonia and had to be ventilated. She'd offered to go but he'd asked her to stay with Annabelle. They both knew the little girl needed stability and she'd been happy to oblige.

The long summer came to a close around the end of September, when Ruby finally had to pull her cardigans out of her cupboard to cover her arms.

And before the leaves on the trees started to change colour Alex started to appear around her again.

At first it was simple. Coffee. Cake. Days sitting in the late summer sunshine in the café in the square. Their visits became so frequent that the café owner stopped asking her what she wanted. After she fawned over a new apricot sponge the café owner started to bake it for her every other day.

Then there was the lunches, and their time spent together that included Annabelle. Sometimes it was in the palace grounds. Sometimes it was in and around Euronia. Once he even took them to Monaco for the day.

This time it felt as if she was the one with the barriers in place and it was Alex who was chipping away at her walls. But it felt right. The momentum was building at a pace that felt comfortable for both of them, for Annabelle, and for the people around them.

Clothes kept mysteriously appearing in her wardrobe— all of them beautiful, all of them fitting perfectly. The palace staff had stopped being prickly around her. Her devotion to Annabelle was clear, but Alex's respect for her was even clearer. Even Rufus had started to come round, and had given her a key to the palace library so she could work undisturbed.

'Ruby?'

Her head shot up. It was late at night and she was sitting on one of the ancient chaise longues, with her feet tucked up underneath her, reading on her electronic tablet.

There were no fancy clothes tonight. Tonight she was wearing a sloppy white top, grey jogging trousers, and her hair was tied in a knot on top of her head.

'Is something wrong with Annabelle?'

It was the first thought that came into her head.

Alex crossed into the room, holding up his hand as he walked. 'No. She's fine. I was looking for you. I should have known I'd find you in here.'

There was a warmth in his eyes as he said the words, a flicker of a memory, and she remembered he'd told her this had been his mother's favourite room.

He pointed at the tablet. 'Isn't it sacrilege to read that in here?'

She shrugged. 'I couldn't work the ancient light switches. Every time I pressed one it seemed to light up the wrong part of the library. Plus, I like being in the dark.'

She pointed to the gardens outside, where some light from the fountain and its walls was spilling up to meet them.

'There's something nice about looking out over the world.'

She turned to face him.

'What have you got?'

He was holding something wrapped in brown paper in his hand, along with two large cups. The smell of something wonderful was winding its way through the air towards her.

'Midnight snacks.' He grinned as he sat down next to her. 'I was starving and went for a rummage around the kitchen to see what I could find.'

She lifted her eyebrows. 'I'm surprised Rufus's inbuilt internal alarm didn't go off at you stepping into the palace kitchens unattended.'

He shrugged. 'I was too. Here,' he handed one of the cups to her and she lifted it to her nose, inhaling.

'Soup?' She glanced at her watch. 'At one in the morning?'

He smiled. That goofy smile he sometimes gave when it was just the two of them. 'I'm hungry. Leena's soup is the best there is.' He held up the brown paper package. 'I even managed to find some freshly baked rolls.'

She opened it up and looked in. Fresh crusty bread in the middle of the night did have a certain appeal.

'Come on,' he said. 'It's no fun eating on your own.'

There was a twinkle in his eye. It was the most relaxed she'd seen him for a while. Spending time with his daughter was doing him the world of good. This wasn't the uptight guy who'd visited her months ago in her hospital department. This wasn't the guy who'd looked as if a permanent grey cloud was resting on his shoulders.

She moved over to the table and he joined her, breaking open his bread roll and dipping it into the soup.

'I've got something else to show you.'

He pushed a file across the table towards her. It was pale beige and looked official.

She flipped it open and gasped. A picture of her and Alex from ten years ago in Paris.

He shrugged. 'It always bothered me that you never

got my message. I trust my Head of Security. If he said he
sent it I know he did. I had to work out what went wrong.'

'After all this time?'

It had always bothered her too. She'd assumed an absent-
minded clerk just hadn't bothered passing the message on.

She looked at the file again. Read the notes. All of them
were about her. It was more than a little unnerving. Then
she let out a gasp. 'Oh, no!'

His hands closed over hers. 'What is it?'

She smiled at him. 'Hotel du Chat. That's not where I
was staying. It says in the notes that your Head of Security left a message at Reception there.'

Alex's brow furrowed. 'He did. But that's what you told
me.'

She squeezed his hand. 'Hotel du Champ, Alex. Not
Hotel du Chat.' She shook her head. 'After all these years
I don't know if that makes me feel better or worse.'

Alex put his head in his hands. 'I was so sure. So sure
you said Hotel du Chat.'

'It was noisy, Alex. It was New Year's. You'd just had an
urgent message about your father.' She took a deep breath.
'Mistakes happen.'

His finger reached up and touched her cheek. 'I hate
mistakes,' he whispered.

'So do I.'

They sat in silence for a few seconds. Both of them letting the revelation wash over them. For Ruby, it felt like a
relief. It didn't matter that Alex had assured her he'd tried
to contact her. There had always been a tiny sliver of doubt.

But he had. And, strangely, it made her feel good.
Maybe life would have been different. Who could possibly know? What she did know was that they couldn't
change the past.

'What did the message say?' She couldn't help but ask.
It had always played on her mind.

He gave a little nod and held her gaze. 'It was simple.'

He shrugged. 'We'd just met and barely had a chance to get to know each other. It said that I was sorry I couldn't meet you, that I really wanted to see you again but had been called away to a family emergency—something I really wanted to explain to you. I left my number and asked you to call as soon as you got my note.'

She gave a sad kind of smile. 'And that—as they say—was that.'

They sat in silence again for a few seconds, thinking of what-might-have-been.

There was no point second-guessing now. Time had passed. They'd found each other again. What happened next was up to them.

Alex pointed back to her soup. 'Better eat that before it gets cold.'

She nodded and picked up her spoon. 'This makes me feel as if I'm in one of those boarding schools that Enid Blyton wrote about and we're having a midnight feast.'

His brow wrinkled. 'She was a kids' author, wasn't she? I must have missed those books.' He gave her a wink. 'Boarding school wasn't so bad.'

'You went to boarding school?' She was fascinated.

'Not until I was twelve. I went to primary school here in Euronia. The same one that I'm planning on sending Annabelle to.'

Her bread was poised over the cup. 'Do you plan on sending her to boarding school when she's older?'

It was almost as if a little breeze had chilled her skin. It was all right joking about these things, but the thought of Annabelle going to boarding school in a few years made her blood run cold.

'I don't know that much about girls' boarding schools. Maybe... I'd need to see how she was doing first.'

It was a touch of relief, but not enough. She had no business saying anything. But she didn't care.

'I don't think you should.' The words were out before she'd thought about them.

'You don't?'

He seemed surprised. But the atmosphere between them was still relaxed. She felt able to continue.

'I just wonder if that will be the right environment for Annabelle.' She leaned across the table and touched his arm. 'I've something to tell you about today.'

'What is it?'

She gave him a smile. 'Today, when I was at the nursery watching Annabelle, I'm almost sure she spoke to another child.'

'What?'

She nodded. 'She was with a little boy. They were playing together. I was at the other side of the nursery but I saw her look up and her lips moved. The little boy's head snapped up, so she must have said something. But at that point she resorted to signing again. It was almost as if his reaction reminded her that she didn't talk.'

Alex looked as if he could hardly believe her. His face was a mixture of surprise and relief. 'But you didn't actually hear her?'

'No. I was too far away—and, believe me, it's bedlam in the nursery. The noise levels are incredible.'

'So, this is good. Isn't it?'

'I hope so. It's one of the concepts of selective mutism that in some situations children will talk and in others they won't.'

'What do you think?'

'I think that I can see changes all the time, Alex. They're slow, but steady. In my head, Annabelle is a little flower with all its petals tightly closed. It's only now that she's starting to bloom. We need to nurture her. We need to keep letting her develop at her own pace, her own speed.'

He nodded. 'I think so too. I didn't want to say anything, but when we were flicking through the pictures the other day it was almost as if the "mmm" sound was hovering around her lips. It wasn't quite there, it wasn't quite formed, but I could almost hear it in the air around us.'

'You think she was going to say Mum?'

He gave a rueful smile. His fingers moved. She was still touching his hand and this time he interlinked his fingers with hers.

'You think I'm just being silly? Is it just a father's wishful thinking?'

She shook her head. He was so sincere.

'I think you're being the same as any parent, Alex. You're putting the welfare of your child first.'

'And so are you.'

He said the words so quietly they took a few seconds to sink into her brain.

His bright blue eyes were fixed on her. The implication was clear. Alex was acknowledging something that she hadn't yet acknowledged herself.

Her other hand was still poised over the soup, with the already sodden piece of bread threatening to fall into the cup. Her hand was trembling. She couldn't pull her eyes away from his.

She dropped the bread in the soup and pushed it away. The library was mainly dark, the gardens outside giving only a glimmer of deep gold light. But it didn't matter how dim the light was—the only thing she could fixate on right now was him.

His other hand stretched over and tangled in her hair. She sucked in a breath as he stroked the back of her neck. Every part of her skin was tingling.

He moved. It was only one step but he was kissing her, pulling her up into his arms. She wrapped her hands around his neck. Last time he'd kissed her they'd been on the yacht. Tension had been in the air all around them. This time it was different.

This felt like the most natural thing in the world. Every

touch of his fingers sent shivers down her spine, building expectation.

This didn't feel as if a man with a kingdom was kissing her. This felt as though *Alex* was kissing her. Alex whom she'd met in Paris all those years ago.

The man she'd watched change over the last few weeks and months. The man who'd taken on board what she'd told him about his child and tried to make changes. He respected her opinion. He'd taken her seriously.

She didn't feel as if she were there as a paid employee any more. It felt like so much more. This felt natural. This felt right. This felt as if it were the place she was supposed to be.

He pulled away and looked down at her. He was smiling. The twinkle in his eyes was back.

'Ruby Wetherspoon...?'

She blinked, not quite sure where this was going. His voice was serious, but the smile hadn't moved from his face. It was almost as if he knew the answer before he asked the question.

'Yes?'

All she could concentrate on right now was the heat of his body against hers. She didn't care that she was wearing ratty clothes. She didn't care that her hair was a mess. All she cared about was the fact she was in Alex's arms.

'Would you do me the honour of coming to Euronia's Annual Charity Ball with me?'

Her throat instantly dried and she wanted to lick her lips. But she couldn't because Alex was kissing her again.

It was almost as if he knew that for a fraction of a second she'd be filled with doubts and he was determined to kiss them away.

This was the first official function he'd invited her to. They'd spent lots of time together—lots of time alone and with Annabelle—but this would be the first time Alex sent a message to the world.

He'd told her he would give her time. And she'd known that he needed time too.

But that time had passed. It felt as if they were both on an even footing. Both in a place where things could develop in the way they wanted.

So she said the thing that felt the most natural to her in the world.

'Yes, Alex. I'd love to.'

CHAPTER TEN

THE DRESS WAS BEAUTIFUL. More stunning than anything she could have imagined.

Red satin, with a ruched sweetheart bodice encrusted with silver crystals. It hung from the wardrobe door, the crystals glittering and sending sparkles around the room. There were matching silver sandals.

Her stomach was fluttering over and over. Her food tray lay on the table untouched. She couldn't even think about eating.

One of the palace staff had come and set her hair in rollers—a silent girl who'd been ruthlessly efficient: tugging the rollers into place within a few minutes, with strict instructions not to remove them until five minutes before she was ready to leave.

It felt so unreal. Even her face in the mirror looked unreal. The black kohl she occasionally put around her eyes had been smudged uselessly across one cheek. It had taken her two attempts before it looked anything like it should. And the red lipstick seemed too severe. It was a perfect match for her dress—together they would look magnificent—but next to her white skin and dark hair in the bathroom mirror she felt she looked more like the Wicked Queen in *Snow White*.

Doubts were creeping into every corner of her mind. Alex had asked her to come. His reasons seemed valid. But she was just an ordinary girl who knew nothing of visiting dignitaries or the traditions of other countries. At first this had seemed exciting, flattering and little fairytale-ish. Now it seemed terrifying. Every handshake, every nod of her head, every word she said could be wrong.

The last thing she wanted to do was embarrass him.

Maybe things would be better if she stayed in her room?

The door handle creaked and the door edged open. Ruby gasped, her hands automatically going to her bra-covered breasts and her bare abdomen.

But it was Annabelle, dressed in pink pyjamas and with sleepy eyes. She didn't seem the slightest bit concerned to see Ruby half dressed.

'Is something wrong Annabelle?' She knelt on the floor next to the little girl.

But Annabelle's eyes were wide as she looked at the sparkles on the red dress. She let out a little squeak of excitement and pulled her thumb from her mouth, reaching over to touch the dress.

It swung on its hanger, making the sparkles move like little stars in the sky.

The thumb had left a smudge on the delicate fabric, but Ruby didn't care. 'Do you like it, Annabelle?'

The little girl nodded. So Ruby let it swing some more, sending the sparkles further. She lifted Annabelle into her arms and swung her around, then picked up an abandoned book from the floor.

'Let me take you back to bed,' she said, slipping her arms into her satin dressing gown and padding next door.

She read the caterpillar book until Annabelle fell asleep. She almost wanted to stay there. It would be so much easier falling asleep next to Annabelle than putting on that dress and going out to meet the world.

Alex had asked her to accompany him. What exactly did that mean?

She was Ruby Wetherspoon from Lewisham. She couldn't speak any other languages. She didn't know how to address dignitaries. There was every chance she would seriously offend someone by not shaking their hand the correct way. Her stomach was turning over and over.

Annabelle looked so peaceful. Her attachment to Ruby was growing. It was Ruby she'd seek out now when she was looking for company. It was Ruby she wanted to draw pictures and play games with.

And these last few weeks had brought changes in her demeanour. She wasn't quite so shy. She was gaining confidence. She was interacting better with the children at nursery. She might not be talking, but every day Ruby heard more sounds and expressions. It was almost as if a tiny little valve had been released and she was becoming more comfortable.

Last night Ruby had been convinced that the humming along to *Finding Nemo* was becoming a murmur. She'd been careful not to react. She'd stayed exactly where she was, letting Annabelle lie in her arms until she'd fallen asleep and then gently sliding her arms out from underneath her.

The thought of going away and leaving this little girl was starting to play on her mind. The hospital in the UK had started to ask her for the date of her return. It seemed reasonable. She hadn't expected to be here this long. But the days had quickly turned into weeks, and the weeks into months. Euronia was starting to feel like home—no matter how many times Polly phoned her and told her it was time to return to London.

She wasn't sure she wanted to leave Annabelle.

She wasn't sure she wanted to leave Alex.

Where had *that* come from?

Her face flushed and she walked back into her own room, shedding her dressing gown and pulling the red dress from the hanger and stepping into it.

She sucked in her breath and slid the zip up at the back. It fitted perfectly—just like everything the palace had provided. The silver sandals were elegant, but comfortable. The only thing missing was jewellery.

Nothing really suited. Her plain gold earrings and chain looked paltry next to the designer gown. Maybe it would be better with nothing at all?

She smiled at her reflection in the mirror. With the rollers removed her dark hair was hanging in curls, covering her shoulders. The boning and the crystals on the dress gave her a more curvaceous shape than normal. And now, with the dress in place, her skin didn't look quite so pale or her lips so red.

Her hands trembled as she took off her gold earrings.

Tonight she was going to a ball in the palace.

Tonight she was going to a ball with her own prince.

Just for tonight she might actually be a princess.

Just for tonight she might actually look as if she was worthy of Alex.

And tonight, for the first time, she might actually feel as if she was part of a couple—even if it was only in her head.

Alex had been pacing for the last thirty minutes, wondering when Ruby would appear.

The palace was buzzing. It had been over a year since there had been a ball at the palace. When his mother and father had ruled there had been several balls every year, all raising money for various charities.

Alex had given some instructions on which charities he wanted to support, and the various people he wanted to invite. But all the details had been dealt with by his staff.

In less than a few minutes over a thousand people would be in the palace. He had guards in all corridors, letting the guests know which areas were open to the public and which were not. The corridor that held Ruby and Annabelle certainly wasn't.

He walked along its length, cursing himself for not saying goodnight to Annabelle earlier. He opened her door just a crack—she was already sleeping, her book and a stuffed caterpillar beside her on the bed.

He walked across the room and dropped a kiss on her forehead before quietly closing the door behind him. His fingers tightened around the black velvet box in his hands. He was still unsure. This felt right—he just didn't know how Ruby would react.

He knocked on her door before he could change his mind.

She opened the door and met him with a smile. 'Hi, Alex. What do you think?'

There was a tremor in her voice. An uncertainty.

He couldn't speak. He must have the dopiest smile on his face right now. What did he *think*? She'd just blown him away!

Ruby was always gorgeous—usually understated, but gorgeous nonetheless. But he'd never seen Ruby the grown-up.

The scarlet dress was stunning. Elegant without giving anything way. Hugging her curves but sweeping the floor and keeping everything covered. The beads along her bodice sparkled in the dim evening light snaking through the windows. Her hair had been styled into large curls, covering her bare shoulders. She was wearing more make-up than usual, but it was perfect. Highlighting her flawless skin, dark brown eyes and red lips.

He held out the black box towards her. 'You look *almost* perfect, Ruby.'

'Almost?'

It was obvious she knew he was teasing her. She stepped forward, reaching out for the box.

He could tell she was nervous—her hands were trembling slightly. Would she know he was nervous too?

She lifted the lid and let out a little gasp. The diamonds were dazzling. The jewels on her dress paled in comparison to these. He knew instantly he'd done the right thing.

'Alex…' Her eyes were wide. 'Where did these come from?' She held up one of the earrings, its thirty hanging diamonds bright and clear.

'They were my mother's. I knew you were nervous about tonight. I thought it might be nice if you had something of hers to wear.'

'You want me to wear *these*?' She looked almost terrified. 'But they must be worth a fortune.' Her fingers went automatically to her earlobe. 'What if I lose one?'

He shook his head and smiled. 'You won't. Don't worry.'

'But—'

'But nothing.' He spun her around to face the full-length mirror in the room and held up one of the earrings next to her ear. 'Can't you see how perfect it looks?'

She could hardly argue. Her face said exactly how she was feeling.

She put her hand up over her heart. 'They're beautiful. They set off the dress perfectly.' She turned around towards him. 'How did you know?'

'Because my mother had impeccable taste, Ruby. It wouldn't have mattered what you wore tonight—these earrings were always going to be a perfect match.' He bent a little lower and whispered in her ear. 'You have a lot in common with her.'

'What does that mean?'

'It means that you look beautiful.' He pressed the earrings into her hand. 'Here—put them on and let's go.'

She stood in front of the mirror, putting the earrings in place, then stopped for a second to study her reflection. She was trying to calm herself. Trying to steady herself for the night ahead.

He put his arms on her shoulders. 'You're going to be the most beautiful woman in the room, Ruby Wetherspoon.'

He was standing by her shoulder, looking at their reflection in the glass. He knew she was nervous. He was nervous himself. Although this was meant to be a private function, nothing could ever really be private when a thousand people were involved.

This would be the first time since Sophia had died that he'd officially invited someone to be his partner. He was well aware of how some of his guests might react. But the charity ball had always been an informal occasion. In a way, it might give Ruby a taste of what could lie ahead.

He hadn't even broached that question with her on the yacht. There had been too much more to deal with. But now the time was right.

He slid his hand into hers. 'Are you ready? Because you look beautiful.'

She nodded slowly and touched the glittering diamonds in her ears. 'I'm ready now.' She sounded more confident. More sure.

He didn't have a shadow of a doubt. His mother would have loved Ruby Wetherspoon.

The first disaster was tripping over her dress. Even though it was gorgeous, and made-to-measure, she wasn't standing quite as straight as she should be. As a result the bottom seam of the dress kept catching on her toes.

A strong hand at her elbow stopped her face-planting on the floor. At first she thought it was Alex, but he was on her other side. A quick glance proved it to be one of the waiters, with a whole silver tray of canapés in his other hand.

He gave her a little conspiratorial nod. 'Mind your step, m'lady.'

She gathered up part of the dress in her hand. Her stomach was turning over and over. Another waiter proffered a tray with champagne flutes but she shook her head—champagne was the last thing she needed right now.

Alex turned and smiled at her. It was the first time she'd really seen him in formal dress. He'd been pressed up behind her next to the mirror, and she'd been so dazzled by the diamonds that she hadn't noticed how handsome he looked. The black dress uniform suited him perfectly, with its sweeping red sash across his chest and adorned with several gold medals.

It hadn't even occurred to her that the sash was the exact same red as her dress. Had Alex done that deliberately?

They walked through the ballroom doors side by side. It wasn't so bad. There was no audible hush when they appeared, just a few quiet gestures and murmurs.

Alex immediately went into charm mode—working the room and talking to lots of the guests, his arm behind her, gently guiding her from person to person. Sometimes he spoke in French, sometimes in German. After the first few words she was mainly lost, and just nodded and smiled along, shaking a proffered hand when appropriate.

The diamonds had felt dazzling in her ears upstairs—if a little ostentatious—but in this room it was clear that Ruby was the least adorned woman there. Everywhere she turned there were rings the size of rocks and twinkling tiaras.

She'd recognised a few faces from royal families across Europe, all in dazzling jewels. And even the movie stars and supermodels were adorned with diamond necklaces and bracelets.

A blonde actress—one of her favourites—was right in front of her. She was immaculate, as usual, in a figure-hugging black dress high at the neck but with virtually no back. How she kept the dress in place was a mystery to Ruby.

She spun on her heels and tilted her head, unashamedly studying Ruby. Waves of discomfort washed over her, along with a distinct flow of blood to the cheeks. She was determined not to be intimidated.

She held out her hand. 'Maria Cochette? It's a pleasure to meet you. I'm Ruby Wetherspoon.'

Her hand stayed in the air for the longest time.

'I know who you are.'

The Italian accent that sounded so cute on screen was harsh in real life. Maria's eyes swept up and down Ruby

with obvious distaste. The dress that had felt so perfect upstairs suddenly felt old-fashioned and overdone.

This was a woman who had charmed in every interview Ruby had ever watched. She exuded elegance and
grace. But the look she was giving Ruby now held none
of those things.

She moved closer, still ignoring Ruby's outstretched
hand. Her voice lowered. 'So how did you do it? How did
little Plain Jane manage to catch the Prince's eye?' She
sneered. 'Or was it just too easy for him to do the hired
help?' The vulgar words were spat out. 'Lydia Merr told
me about you. She said you weren't even eye candy—and
she was right.'

Ruby had never been a girl for conflict. But if she'd been
any other place, at any other time, she would have punched
the perfect Maria clean in the face. Alex had warned her
that Mrs Merr was a renowned gossip, and it seemed their
kiss hadn't gone unnoticed.

For the first time that night she drew herself up to her
full height. She almost felt her dress lift from the floor. Up
close, Maria wasn't so perfect. Botox had made her eyebrows arch unevenly. Her suntanned skin couldn't hide the
wrinkles around her eyes.

Ruby lifted her hand up to her ears and smiled sweetly,
though she knew her eyes would be shooting daggers. She'd
dealt with too many difficult patients and members of staff
over the years to simper around a woman like this.

'I guess some of us have hidden talents, Maria. Or
maybe our core values and ethics are just apparent.' She
let her fingers run over the sparkling drop diamonds. 'Do
you like the earrings Alex gave me to wear? They were
his mother's.'

The diamonds were elegant, in contrast; the bling from
Maria was almost blinding her.

She met the cold grey eyes with another smile. 'I always
think that less is more, don't you?'

She didn't wait for an answer—just turned and walked away, ignoring the stifled noise of indignation behind her.

Ruby never behaved like that. But something had burned inside her. Was it the way Maria had looked at Alex? Or her total disrespect for Ruby?

Her stomach flipped over. Would this be something she would need to get used to?

She almost stumbled over her feet. Where had *that* thought come from? This was their first official outing together. It might lead to nothing.

But all of a sudden, even after all their talks and all this time, Ruby felt woefully unprepared. Alex had said nothing to her, but this almost felt like a test to see how she would do. A test she was about to fail spectacularly if her exchange with Maria was anything to go on.

She looked around the room. She didn't have a single friend here.

It was a sobering thought.

And all of a sudden she felt very alone. When was the last time she'd spoken to Polly?

She was planning on spending Christmas with her parents in France—that was only a few weeks away—but for the first time since she'd got here she missed her colleagues, she missed her friends, she missed her flat.

It was this. It was here—standing in this room with hundreds of people and the only person who had her back was Alex.

It was as if he felt the vibe across the room. He looked up and his gaze met hers, and he gave her a quizzical are-you-all-right? look. It was impossible, but she felt as if she could see the bright blue of his eyes even from this distance.

He started to walk towards her and her feet automatically moved in response. All she could do was smile. It didn't matter who else was in the room. The only person who mattered was Alex. And he was looking at her as if he felt exactly the same way.

The voices, the jewels, the chatter all around her just faded to background noise. Her smile was getting broader by the second. It was the strongest urge, the greatest pull she'd ever felt. Like metal being drawn towards a magnet from a million miles away.

Several people tried to talk to him as he made his way towards her, but Alex didn't even blink—he just kept his eyes focused entirely on her.

Seconds later he filled her entire view. For another second both of them hesitated. Then his arms were around her waist, her hands were resting on his shoulders.

'Are you okay?'

'I am now.'

She'd never felt more sure of anything. This time there *was* a hush in the room. Their actions had attracted everyone's attention.

But Alex's bright blue eyes were still fixed on hers. 'You're the most beautiful woman in the room, Ruby.'

His voice was low, for her ears only.

'That's the way I always feel around you,' she murmured.

'Good.'

His lips met hers. She could hear the audible gasps around her but she didn't care. Alex was kissing in her in front of everyone. Alex was making his intentions clear.

It was as if she could soar. Soar above the shocked faces in the ballroom and soar above the pink palace. The kiss in Paris had been special—had been electric—but this kiss was everything. He spun her around as he kissed her and they both started to laugh. Knowing entirely how it looked.

He pulled his lips back, their noses still touching. 'You're mine, Ruby Wetherspoon. And the whole world knows it.'

'And you're mine right back.'

She'd never thought she'd say those words. She'd never thought she'd believe them. But this moment was hers. Hers and Alex's.

'I don't really want to look around,' she said. 'I don't want anyone to spoil what's happening between us.'

His eyes were still fixed on her face. He was smiling. 'Who could do that?'

It was almost as if a gong had sounded. Some ancient clanging noise reverberating around the room. But it was actually the opposite.

Silence. Pure and utter silence.

No one was talking. No one was murmuring. All she could hear was her and Alex breathing. Every tiny hair on her arms stood on end. It was as if someone were walking over her grave.

'Alex?'

He looked up and his hands dropped from her waist. There was an elderly couple standing in the doorway. Immaculately regal. Both were staring at Alex.

It took her a few seconds. She'd never met or seen pictures of Sophia's parents. But for a reaction like this it had to be them.

She glanced nervously at Alex. How much had they seen? Had they seen him kiss her, or just hold her?

Those few seconds whilst he gathered himself seemed to stretch into hours. She saw everything. The fleeting moment of panic followed by the worry of what to do next.

Her heart plummeted. He'd been carried away. He hadn't thought of the consequences of kissing her in front of everyone. This was a disaster.

Every eye in the room flicked between them and Sophia's parents.

She heard Alex suck in a deep breath, then his hand moved over and took hers.

The feeling of skin against skin was unexpected. Her gaze fixed on their hands as he intertwined their fingers. He moved forward in long strides and she struggled to keep up, having to gather her dress in her hand to stop it from tangling around her feet again.

He gave a courteous bow to the King and Queen. 'Ruby Wetherspoon, I'd like you to meet Annabelle's grandparents—King Henry and Queen Isabelle of Leruna.'

Her brain was racing. What on earth would they think of her?

There were a few expanding seconds of silence. Then their immaculate breeding kicked into place.

The King gave a nod of his head, 'Ms Wetherspoon.'

The Queen took a little longer. But her wide-eyed look had disappeared. Ruby could almost tell that to this woman composure was everything.

She held out a hand towards her. Ruby felt a second of panic—was she supposed to shake it or kiss it?

Alex made the tiniest movement and she reached out and shook the Queen's hand. Something from fairytales long ago made her curtsy. 'It's a pleasure to meet you, Queen Isabelle.'

As she stood up it was clear the Queen was regarding her carefully. Her heart was fluttering madly in her chest. If she didn't calm down soon she'd end up in a crumpled heap on the floor. She felt as if the whole room was watching her. Anything she did right now would be crucial. Her actions and demeanour would temper what everyone in the room thought of her.

It was as if a lightbulb had gone off in her head. All of a sudden she realised just how much of a chance Alex had taken on her.

She sucked in a breath. She was worthy. She was worthy of his faith in her. She just had to show it.

She was still holding the Queen's hand, and Isabelle's eyes were starting to smart with disapproval.

Despite her glittering tiara and her sumptuous silver gown, Ruby knew a clear way to connect with this woman. In her job she'd managed to charm the most difficult family members over the last ten years, and she could do it again now.

'It's been a pleasure to work with Annabelle these last few months. She's such a wonderful little girl and she's making real progress.'

Isabelle looked a little startled at the familiarity. People probably didn't speak to her like this. But as soon as Annabelle's name was mentioned it was clear she was interested.

'You're the speech therapist.' There was just the slightest hint of distaste—as if she were trying to put Ruby in her place.

'She's my friend.' Alex's words were quiet, but firm. Shooting a crystal-clear message across the tension-laden air. It was like a subtle counter-attack.

But this woman with decades of experience didn't even blink. Her eyebrows rose a little. 'Progress? Is she starting to talk?'

She was clearly surprised.

Ruby nodded and moved closer to her, away from the prying ears that were straining all around the room to hear their conversation.

Alex shot her a look that was a cross between pure relief and pleading, and with an almost imperceptible nod engaged the King in conversation, leading him over towards a drinks tray.

Ruby held out her hand to let the Queen lead the direction of their steps, and was unsurprised to find her leading them towards the entrance to another room filled with antique mahogany chairs. The door was closed quickly behind them by one of the palace attendants.

The Queen settled herself in one of the chairs and arranged her skirts around her before gesturing to Ruby to sit down too.

'Tell me about Annabelle.'

Ruby smiled. 'I've seen definite progress in the last few months. It's slow. But steady. I don't dispute the diagnosis of selective mutism. But do you know that in some cases children will speak in some circumstances but not others?'

The Queen gave the smallest of nods, so Ruby continued. 'Annabelle was silent when I got here. Over the last
weeks and month we've noticed noises.'

'Noises?'

'Yes. Gasps of excitement. Whoops of pleasure. Whim-
pers when we're watching scary movies.'

'My granddaughter *whoops*?' There was an amused
edge to her voice.

'Yes, she does. But that's not all—she often hums along
to some of the songs in her favourite films. She seems to
do it quite unconsciously—usually when she's most relaxed or when she's tired.'

'And she's that way around *you*?' The timbre of the
Queen's voice had changed slightly.

'It's taken her a while to get to know me,' said Ruby
quickly. 'But she's been spending more time with her father.'

Part of her wondered if she should be saying this. She
didn't want to make it sound as if Alex had neglected Annabelle in any way at all.

'We've made sure that all the palace staff knows that
his time with Annabelle is to be uninterrupted. It's time
they spend alone—together.'

She was starting to get nervous and her mouth was running away from her. She wanted to be clear that she wasn't
trying to push herself between Alex and his daughter. The
last thing she wanted was for the Queen to think she was
trying to take Sophia's place.

'And is this working?' There was a tone of slight disbelief. As if she didn't quite understand the significance.

'It's definitely working. Annabelle is changing. Her confidence has increased in leaps and bounds. She's a different little girl than the one I met when I arrived.'

For the smallest of seconds—almost instinctively—the
Queen's eyes narrowed. She straightened herself in her
chair, pulling herself up to her full height. 'Why do you
think my granddaughter doesn't talk, Ms Wetherspoon?'

There was a whole host of things she could say here. But experience had taught her to go with her instinct.

'I think she misses her mother,' she said simply.

There was the tiniest sound. A little gasp from the Queen. Then the woman's eyes clouded, as if they were fogged by impending tears.

It was the clearest and most confident Ruby had felt all evening. Isabelle might be a distinguished queen—something that was way out of Ruby's realm of expertise—but she was also a concerned grandmother—something Ruby *could* understand.

Ruby leaned over and squeezed her hand, and then changed position, gathering her dress and kneeling in front of the Queen.

'Science tells us that even babies can form memories. Annabelle heard and recognised her mother's voice for nine months in the womb, and then for another eleven months after she was born.' She let go of the skirts in her hand and pressed her other hand over her heart. 'She remembers her mother in *here*.'

Her voice was becoming huskier. She wasn't trying to upset the Queen, but she felt it was important to be honest with her.

'Alex has put a picture of Sophia next to Annabelle's bed. He has made a picture album with photos of the two of them—as children they almost look like twins. It has pictures of Sophia alone, and pictures of her with Annabelle.' She squeezed the Queen's hand again. 'He talks about her every night with Annabelle.'

If the Queen disapproved of Ruby using the familiar form of Alex's name she didn't show it. A slow tear trickled down her cheek. 'He does?'

Ruby nodded. 'It's not sad. It's not morbid. He just tells her a little story—something about her mother—and they move on to something else. They play a game. Watch some TV together.'

The older woman's lips were trembling. 'And who has helped him to do that?'

Isabelle's pale grey eyes were fixed on hers. Ruby took a deep breath. 'I have. Everything about their relationship has changed. I think Alex had a lot of grief locked up inside. Talking and spending time with his daughter has helped them both.'

The Queen's gaze was fixed on Ruby. 'You did this? You did this for them?'

A flash of recognition crossed her eyes, along with a whole host of fleeting emotions.

Ruby could step back at this point. She could fall into professional mode. It would keep her safe. It would keep her guarded. But the Queen had already seen Alex's arms around her. Maybe she had seen more. It was time for honesty.

'I care about them. I care about them both very much.'

The Queen licked her lips. 'Do you think my grand-daughter will ever talk?'

'I can't say for sure—but I do think so. I think she spoke the other day at nursery. I think she might have said something to one of the other children. But I didn't want to make a scene. I didn't want to draw her attention to the fact. We all have to be patient.'

'And are *you* patient, Ruby Wetherspoon?'

The question shocked her. It might sound simple, but the Queen clearly wasn't talking about Annabelle's speech any more. She meant something else entirely.

Was she brave enough to be honest?

I've waited ten years were the words on her lips.

'I am.'

There were another few moments' silence. It was almost as if the Queen were taking time to digest all she'd told her. She shifted a little closer to the edge of the chair—a little closer to Ruby.

'Alexander was Sophia's safe place.'

Her voice was shaky, but controlled. Her silver-grey eyes were fixed on Ruby's.

'He was the one person she trusted to give her the ultimate gift.'

Ruby's stomach squeezed. It would always hurt. It would always reach little parts of her that she couldn't share.

Her voice was shaking too. 'Annabelle is a beautiful gift. Of that there is no doubt.'

Their eyes met again and she felt the common understanding between them. This woman had lost her precious daughter. Her life would never be the same again.

If she wanted to she could hate Ruby. She could make life difficult for Alex. She could make their relationship impossible.

But it seemed she had no wish to do that.

'I'm glad my granddaughter has someone who has her best interests at heart. I'm glad that Alexander is looking to build a life for himself and his daughter again.'

She pushed herself up from the chair and gave a little nod to Ruby with the hint of a smile.

'And I would very much like to hear my granddaughter speak.'

Ruby straightened up and her knees gave an unexpected crack. She let out a nervous laugh—it certainly displaced any anxiety in the room.

Queen Isabelle gave her a serene smile. 'I'm tired. But if I retired for the evening now people would talk. We should return to the ballroom together. I'll be able to leave after a while.'

Ruby nodded. Of course. People had seen them leave the ballroom together and their tongues would wag if they didn't return together.

Then the Queen did something she didn't expect. She held out her elbow towards Ruby. An invitation to take it. Before it had been polite and because they were in company. In the confines of this room, when it was just the two of them, it was something she didn't have to do.

Ruby didn't hesitate. She slid her arm next to the Queen's and joined her in walking towards the door.

Isabelle's smile had stayed on her face. 'Beautiful earrings, Ms Wetherspoon. They seem familiar. Queen Marguerite had exquisite taste, didn't she?'

Ruby's heart squeezed inside her chest. *She knew.* She knew Alex had given them to her to wear this evening.

They walked through the door arm in arm.

The glass doors from the ballroom leading out to the gardens were open, letting the cool fresh air sweep in. Ten years ago New Year's Eve in Paris had been cold, but winter in Euronia was much warmer. People drifted in and out of the ballroom and the gardens as the music played.

People were curious about her now. Alex appeared by her side every ten minutes or so, introducing her to diplomats and other royals. They shook her hand and gave her guarded smiles. The celebrity guests were much more up-front. Apart from her earlier encounter with Maria Cochette, everyone else seemed to want to be her new best friend. It was odd. Perhaps it was the fact that Alex had kissed her in front of everyone. His message had been clear.

The scene that everyone had expected in front of Sophia's parents hadn't materialised. When she'd re-entered the ballroom on the arm of Queen Isabelle some mouths had dropped open. Even Alex had looked a bit shocked, but he'd covered it well.

His hands had appeared at her waist a little later and his mouth at her ear. 'What did you do?' he whispered.

'I told the truth,' she said simply, and he'd twirled her around in the next dance.

The evening passed by in a flash. She didn't even notice when the King and Queen of Leruna slipped away—she was too busy focusing on Alex.

He was more attentive than ever, leaving her in no doubt

of his attentions. Every tiny brush of his fingertips on her skin ignited the fire within her. Every time he caught her eye, or gave her a smile from across the room, she felt as if she were the only person there.

When finally the last person left her feet were throbbing and her jaw was aching from smiling so much.

Alex appeared at her side and took the champagne glass from her hand. 'Are you tired?'

She shook her head. 'No. I don't want this night to end.'

He took her hand in his and led her up the huge curved staircase and along the corridor towards his rooms. Their footsteps quickened as they walked, their anticipation building.

He swung the door of his apartment wide. She'd never been in here before. Alex had always been around her and Annabelle in their rooms, or in the main parts of the palace. She'd had no reason to visit his rooms.

The room was stark. Different from the other very ornate rooms in the palace.

No antique furniture. No sumptuous furnishings. It was white and black—like a modern apartment in the middle of New York—certainly not what she expected to find in a pink palace.

'Alex?'

She turned to face him and her heart squeezed at the expression on his face. These were the rooms he'd shared with his wife. He didn't need to say anything. Everything in this room had been stripped bare—just like his heart. She understood in a heartbeat.

She closed the door quietly behind her and stepped over to him. 'Oh, Alex...'

She ran her fingers through his hair as he closed his eyes.

Everything—all their conversations—had been about *her* being ready. But the truth was it was about *him* being ready too.

Part of this was painful. Because after tonight she'd

never been more sure about what she wanted. It was Alex.
It had always been Alex. It would always be Alex.

But did he really want her? Or was she just someone to
plug the gap his wife had left?

It should unsettle her that these were the rooms he'd
shared with his wife. It should make her feel uncomfortable. But she had a feeling that there wasn't a single part
of Sophia left in here.

Her fingers were still running through his hair—his
hands were planted firmly on her hips. She stepped closer
to him and placed a gentle kiss on the soft skin at the side
of his neck.

'Are you ready for this, Alex? Are you ready for us?'

Every knot inside him was beginning to unravel. He'd held
himself in check all night. From the first second he'd seen
Ruby in her red dress he'd wanted to have her in this position. She was everything to him. And now he was finally
free to say it—finally free to let the world know.

The arrival of Sophia's parents had been more than unexpected. They were always invited to formal occasions at
the palace. But since Sophia's death they'd never attended.

They saw Annabelle on regular occasions, but they were
always private times.

He'd been horrified when they'd arrived—horrified that
their first view of Ruby was in his arms with his mouth
on hers.

With a few hours' hindsight he realised that Queen Isabelle must have heard through the grapevine about Ruby.
They'd attended with the sole reason of meeting the woman
who might replace their daughter in his affections.

Isabelle had always known the truth of their relationship
and their marriage. But she'd supported them both every step
of the way. She'd once told Alex that there were lots of forms
of love. Some with fireworks, some with steady steps, and
some with bonds of loyalty that would forsake all others.

The King had mentioned nothing of Ruby at all. He'd spoken to Alex at length about business worries and difficult negotiations.

When Alex had watched Ruby and Queen Isabelle leave the room together he'd felt sick. *Should he intervene?* But he'd been almost sure that Ruby wouldn't want that.

And when they'd returned some time later Queen Isabelle had been serenely graceful, as always, when she'd told Alex that Ruby seemed like 'a nice girl'.

His sense of relief had been enormous.

And now here they were. In the one place he'd wanted to bring her all night.

'I've been ready for ten years, Ruby,' he whispered in her ear. 'I've waited a long time for this.'

'Me too.'

Her brown eyes were fixed on his. Just like that night in Paris. The only thing missing was the reflection of the fireworks.

Ruby… Every bit as beautiful as she'd been ten years ago. Those brown eyes seemed to pull him right in, touching his heart and his soul. For the first time in ten years he was free to love exactly who he wanted to love. He had the strength and the power of his convictions and he knew what was right for him and what was right for his child. *Who* was right for him and who was right for Annabelle.

Ruby might not be Annabelle's mother, but her patience and affection for his little girl was clear. Their relationship had changed exponentially. Ruby spent hours playing with her, not just assessing the little girl. Trust had built between them. When Annabelle smiled at Ruby and looked at her in that way she had, it made his heart melt.

His little girl was every bit as much in love with Ruby as he was.

He ran his fingers along her velvet skin, from her fingertips to her shoulders. She gave a little shudder of pleasure as she smiled at him. When his fingers reached her shoulders he swept one hand along the back of her neck and traced the other gently across her décolletage. His fingers stopped mid-point as she closed her eyes and swayed a little. The curve of her breasts was highlighted in the figure-hugging dress. If Ruby knew who'd actually designed it for her, and how much it had cost, she would probably be horrified.

His hands joined at the back of the dress, where he caught the zipper in his fingers and started to release it slowly. She was holding her breath as he inched it lower. The shimmering red fabric slid from her frame and puddled on the floor at her feet as he tangled his fingers in her hair and pulled her against him.

Kissing Ruby before had been tantalising. Magical. Full of expectations and promise.

Kissing Ruby in his room as he shucked off his jacket and trousers was more than he could ever have imagined. He walked backwards, pulling her with him as they sank down on to the white bed.

The eiderdown enveloped them both. He'd dreamed about this for the last ten years. But the reality was far more incredible than his imagination could ever have envisaged. And he could envisage quite a bit.

He pulled his lips back for a second as his fingers brushed against her underwear. 'Are you sure about this, Ruby? Because there's no going back. This has to be right for both of us.'

She was holding her breath again, fixing him with her chocolate eyes. His fingers danced along her silky-smooth skin.

Her perfect red lips broke into a smile as she pressed against him. 'This is right, Alex. This has *always* been right.'

And then she kissed him again and he forgot about everything else.

CHAPTER ELEVEN

P_EOPLE WERE LOOKING at her. People were fixing their eyes on her and muttering under their breath. She'd been in the shops in the city centre on lots of occasions recently but she'd never noticed this.

Even Pierre in the baker's shop wasn't his usual friendly self. He hardly even made eye contact before he handed her a brown paper bag of baked goods and waved his hand at her attempt at payment.

It made her feel uneasy. She might not speak fluent French, but she'd always muddled through and felt welcome in Euronia before.

This morning had been so strange.

The thing that she'd secretly dreamed about for such a long time had finally come true. Waking up in Alex's arms had been fantastic.

Stealing along the corridor with her dress clutched around her hadn't been quite so fantastic. But she hadn't been sure if any of the staff—in particular Rufus—might routinely go into Alex's room to wake him.

There was still so much about the palace protocols she had to learn. And last night she hadn't thought to ask Alex about any of these things—there had been far too many other sensations occupying her mind.

It had seemed so much easier to duck out and get back to her room to shower and dress. But once she'd got ready her stomach had begun churning again.

On one hand she'd wanted to go back to Alex's room. On the other she'd wanted to give him a little space. And yet they had to talk about what would happen next. About Annabelle. About Sophia's parents. All the things they hadn't really focused on last night when they'd been in each other's arms.

She loved him. She was sure of it. She just hadn't told him yet.

Maybe tonight they would be able to re-enact the whole thing. Maybe she could tell him then. But the truth was as soon as Alex had started kissing her everything else had gone out of the window except the feel of his body pressed against hers. The touch of his fingers on her skin. The sensation of his lips on her neck…

The newspapers outside one of the nearby shops fluttered in the wind. Something caught her attention. It was the colour on the front page. The exact colour of one of the dresses in her wardrobe back at the palace.

Her feet were drawn automatically. Her hand was pushing back the fluttering pages.

Princess Ruby?

The words leapt out at her and she jumped backwards on the pavement. *No. It couldn't say that.* Her heart was pounding in her chest. What on earth…?

She stepped forward again. Pushing the front page back and scanning the page. It was totally in French. She couldn't understand what was written at all.

But she really didn't need to understand. The picture said it all.

It must have been taken a few months before—just after she'd arrived. She and Alex were sitting at the café and her bright pink dress was fluttering around her—just as the newspaper pages were doing today.

But it was the moment that the picture had captured.

That second when Alex had leaned forward and cradled her cheek. He was looking at her as though she was the only person in the world and she was looking at him exactly the same way.

That moment had literally been the blink of an eye. A tiny, private fragment of two lives captured for eternity for the world.

And it had changed everything.

It was printed alongside a picture from the ball. Ruby in her long red dress with diamonds glittering in her ears.

Some eagle-eyed journalist had found and printed a picture of Alex's mother wearing the same earrings years earlier.

She couldn't understand any of the words that were written. But she could understand the panic clamouring in her chest.

No. Just when things between her and Alex seemed to be heading in a perfect direction.

What was happening between them was private. It wasn't for the world's consumption. She felt indignant. She felt angry. She felt stupid.

Alex was a prince—at some point would be King.

This would always be the life of whoever he showed interest in. She was a fool to think otherwise. And this was exactly what he'd tried to warn her about.

She leaned back against the newspaper rack, breathing heavily. She was seeing tiny stars in her peripheral vision. People were staring at her and whispering. Her phone started to ring and she grappled with her bag to pull it out.

It was a number she didn't recognise. 'Hello?'

'Ruby Wetherspoon? This is Frank Barnes from *Celebrity News*. We'd like to interview you.'

'How did you get this number? This is a private number.'

'We'd like to know about your relationship with the Prince Regent and the recent photos that have been taken of the two of you together. We understand that you're working together. But it looks a whole lot more personal than that. Would you like to do an exclusive with us?'

Every word sent a chill down her body. For a few seconds she couldn't even speak. Then, 'No. Don't phone again.'

She disconnected the call and looked around her. Alex. She had to talk to Alex.

Her phone started to ring again. Another unknown number. She pressed the button at the top, switching the whole thing off.

She put her head down and her legs on automatic pilot, walking back to the palace. She resisted the temptation to break into a run.

The warm sun was usually pleasant, but her face felt flushed and she could feel the sweat running down her back. The usually enticing smells from the delicatessen, the baker and chocolatier made her stomach flip over.

All she wanted to do was talk to someone—talk to Alex. Talk to Polly. Talk to anyone—anyone but a journalist.

Her legs were burning. The warm air didn't seem to be fully filling her lungs. There it was in the distance—the pink palace. She reached the gates and crossed the gardens quickly. The driveway had never seemed so long.

When she finally reached the palace entrance the doorman barely glanced at her. Was that a sign of something?

As she stepped into the hallway she was aware of the absolute silence. Usually there was always noise from somewhere—talking servants, discussions between visitors, footsteps from people going about their daily business.

Today the whole palace seemed silent.

She turned on her heel and headed for the library. If she'd had an ounce of common sense about her she would have purchased one of those newspapers. Instead she was reduced to doing an internet search.

The amount of hits made her cringe. *How many?*

Her eyes widened as she read, and tears formed in her eyes as a horrible feeling of dread crept over her skin.

Pictures really did speak a thousand words.

If Alex had any doubt about how she felt about him, once he'd glanced at these pictures he—and the world— would know for sure.

If she was an ordinary girl, in an ordinary world, this might seem quite nice. The looks and glances in the pictures were reciprocal. She wasn't just fawning over him. Their gazes were locked together—as if, for that second, they were the only two people on the planet.

Little moments, captured in time.

Tears started to roll down her cheeks. She'd tried to be so careful. She'd tried to be guarded. She didn't want the whole world to know that she'd loved Alex de Castellane for the last ten years. It had taken her long enough to admit that to herself.

Things were good between them right now. Things were great. Annabelle was showing real signs of improvement. And Alex...

He was showing real signs of moving on. *Really* moving on.

Last night had been wonderful.

She clicked on another link. This time it was a red-top newspaper from England. It carried the same photographs as the others. But the text took her breath away.

Vitriol. Libel.

Ruby Wetherspoon had been plotting to get her hands on Alex de Castellane for years. She'd come to Euronia purely with the purpose of trapping the world's most eligible bachelor into marriage. She was a devious woman with money on her mind.

No mention of Annabelle. No mention of her job.

She clicked on the next link. An exclusive from Maria Cochette, telling of how Ruby Wetherspoon had laughed at the way she'd tricked Alex into giving her his mother's

diamond earrings and said it was only a matter of time before she got a whole lot more. Apparently Maria had known
right from the start what kind of woman she was—and
Alex was still heartbroken after the death of his wife...
he was vulnerable.

Ruby retched. Any minute now she was going to be sick.

This was all her own fault. She should never have
crossed Maria Cochette last night. Of *course* someone like
her would have newspaper contacts. The truth was Ruby
had no idea how to handle people like that. She was unprepared for what she was up against—and it showed. She
just wasn't equipped to be part of this world.

The tiny little bit of backbone she'd shown last night
had backfired spectacularly.

How many times had she picked up a newspaper or
a glossy magazine and devoured all the headline news?
She'd read about affairs, arguments, secret children, kidnapping, celebrity diets and drunken parties. Although
she was sure it was sometimes blown out of proportion,
she'd never really given much thought as to how much of
it was actually lies.

She'd never given *any* thought to the fact that some of
those people might be hurt by what was being written about
them. She'd never considered it at all.

Not until now.

It seemed some of the papers had gone to extremes.
One had tracked down an ex-boyfriend for a whole range
of quotes about her that had been blown out of proportion.

She cringed. Luke wasn't that kind of guy. He wasn't
malicious and she knew that. He'd just been blind-sided.
But the words *'I always knew she wouldn't stay with me'*
still hurt.

The truth was Luke had never really stood a chance
against the memory of a guy he knew nothing about. None
of her exes ever had.

She was feeling swamped. Overwhelmed. No one men-

SCARLET WILSON   173

tioned the kiss. No one mentioned the fact that Alex had
kissed her in front of everyone and made it clear how he
felt about her.

Maria Cochette claimed she'd hung over Alex all
night—apparently her conduct had been 'desperate and
embarrassing'.

Other reports said the King and Queen of Leruna had
been 'horrified' by her presence and had seemingly reacted with shock at the thought of Princess Ruby replacing their daughter.

Was this true? Had she maybe misread the whole situation?

Right now she didn't know what was right and what
was wrong.

Her eyes swam with tears. Reaction was overwhelming her, swamping her with emotions she didn't know how
to control.

Today should be a happy day. Today should be the start
of a new kind of relationship with Alex.

Instead it was turning into the worst day of her life, with
the world thinking she was some kind of sad, desperate
woman who wanted to trap a prince.

Not a girl whose heart was filled with joy because she'd
finally connected with the man she'd loved for ten years.

There was a noise behind her. Alex. His face was almost
grey and the warm eyes she'd expected to see were clouded
with worry. Rufus and another advisor were at his back.

'There you are, Ruby.' He walked across the library in
long strides. 'We need to talk.'

Today wasn't supposed to be like this. He was supposed
to be smiling. Taking her in his arms and telling her that
he loved her.

But Alex looked distant.

She could almost see all her hopes and dreams disinte-
grating in front of her.

This was all her nightmares come true.

* * *

For a few seconds that morning everything had been perfect—right up until he'd woken up and found his bed empty.

Ruby was gone. He'd expected her still to be in his arms, expected to touch her soft hair and stroke her silky skin. Instead there had been a little dip in the bed where she'd lain.

He hadn't had much time to think after that, because Rufus and the other advisors had arrived, their faces grim.

It had been more than bad news. Ruby had been painted as a villain across the world's media. He guessed that jealous Maria Cochette had phoned most of her contacts to give the most skewed and inaccurate view of the evening.

His worst fears. People had painted his marriage to Sophia as a fairytale. No woman could live up to the aftermath of that. It was what he'd always feared and tried to protect Ruby from.

In his head, he knew exactly what he should have done. He should have introduced Ruby gradually to the world's press. He should have made it clear she was no longer an employee. She was a friend. A family friend.

But his heart hadn't been able to keep the slow pace required. He'd already waited ten years for Ruby. He didn't want to wait for the media to catch up with him. He didn't want to waste a tiny second. But his impatience had probably cost him everything.

This was all his fault. Totally his fault.

He should have spoken to Ruby about this. He should have spoken to his advisors. He should have prepared her, taken his time, treated her with the respect and love that she was due.

He was unworthy of Ruby. He'd failed her completely.

And from the look on her face she thought that too.

'I went to the shops...I went to buy us breakfast,' her words faltered. 'I know that they have everything in the kitchen, but I wanted to get something special—for us.'

Her voice was shaky and her eyes were strangely blank, as if she was disengaged. As if she couldn't really comprehend what was happening in the world around her. His heart twisted in his chest. She'd walked into the city. She'd found out about this on her own.

There were tear trails down her cheeks, glinting in the morning sun. He ignored the advisors in his ears and knelt next to her chair, staring at the computer screen in front of her.

'I'm sorry, Ruby. I should have prepared you for this.'

Her eyes widened in clear disbelief. 'You can prepare people for *this*? For these lies? This complete invasion of privacy?' She shook her head. 'They phoned me. Someone phoned me this morning, wanting an interview—'

'What did you say?' butted in Rufus.

Alex held up his hand to silence him.

She was still shaking her head. 'I hung up. How did they get my number?'

Alex took a deep breath. 'It's not hard, Ruby. They do things like this all the time. You get used to it.'

'You get used to *this*? How?'

He reached out and took her hand. It was icy cold and that shot a little fear into his heart. He could see the hopes and dreams for the way all this should go begin to crumble all around him.

It was her face. The expression on her face. She was devastated. Beyond devastated. And he was the one who'd exposed her to this.

She pulled her hand backwards. 'What about Annabelle, Alex? How will you keep Annabelle from this? Is this the kind of life she'll have? Every teenage kiss, every hand-hold, every party plastered across the press?' She was shaking her head and tears were flowing freely now. 'How on earth will you keep her safe from all this?'

Safe. The word struck fear inside. Ruby didn't feel safe. But something else had resonated with him. Even now she

was thinking about Annabelle in the future. She was raising the issue of trying to protect his daughter.

'We have rules in Euronia, Ruby. Photographers are not
allowed to take unofficial pictures of any members of the
royal family. We're strict about these things. They know
they have to respect our privacy.'

'Really?' She spun the laptop around to face him again.
'So what happened here, then?'

It was one of the photos from the newspapers. A picture
from months ago, when he'd first taken her to the café in
front of the casino.

'What happened to respecting your privacy? What happened to respecting *my* privacy. This was when I first got
here—how many more private pictures do they have of
me, Alex?'

Her breaths were ragged, the pain on her face sending
shards through his heart. This was exactly what he hadn't
wanted to happen. But these last few days his feelings for
Ruby had just started to overwhelm him.

She'd been in his mind and his thoughts for ten years.
Having her under his palace roof had taken every single
element of his self-control. She'd opened his world again—
asked him the right questions, made him question his own
thoughts and feelings. She'd influenced his relationship
with his daughter. It had improved beyond all recognition.

It was almost as if she'd taught him how to be a parent.
How to love every part of Annabelle and, more importantly, how to communicate with a little girl who wouldn't
talk to him. Before he'd been confused and felt guilty. Now
he took each day as it came. His time devoted to Annabelle
was never compromised.

Ruby was still crying, the tears slowly trickling down
her cheeks. He reached out and touched her cheek but she
flinched.

'I'm not the person they say I am,' she whispered. 'I
don't want people to write things like that about me.'

His heart was breaking for her. 'Ruby, I'm sorry. I should never have invited you to the ball. I should have waited. *We* should have waited. If we'd introduced you slowly the press would have been easier. My advisors could have told you how to act, what to say. This is my fault.' He shook his head, 'I just didn't want to wait any longer, Ruby. I wanted you to be part of my world—part of Annabelle's world.'

Right now he couldn't care who else was in the room. Right now he was only interested in Ruby. The pain on her face was tearing him apart. More than anything he wanted her to look at him and tell him that was what she wanted too. To be part of his world. But even though she was looking at him it was as if she'd switched off.

She shook her head. 'But that's just it, Alex. I don't *want* someone to tell me how to act and what to say.' She pressed her hand against her chest. 'What's wrong with just me—Ruby Wetherspoon?'

He took both her hands in his. 'Nothing—nothing at all. We can make this better, Ruby. I promise. *I* can make this better. We can work together. We can find a way to deal with the press. I'll find the photographer who took those pictures of us and he or she will never be allowed in Euronia again. This isn't as bad as you think.'

There was a noise behind him. The tiniest clearing of a throat...the squeak of a shoe. Ruby's eyes darted to the advisors behind him. He winced. He didn't need to turn around to know what the expressions on their faces must look like. He'd heard them talk incessantly since they'd knocked on his bedroom door this morning.

Their solution was simple: Ruby must go. The good name of Euronia must be protected and if the Prince Regent wanted to date then it must be handled by the press team.

He hated this. He hated all of this. For the first time in his life he wished he was free of all this. Free of the responsibility. Free of the ties. He wanted to be free to love the woman he'd loved for the last ten years. He wanted to be free to tell the world that. He didn't need to ask their permission.

'Ruby, talk to me. Tell me what you're thinking. Whatever it is you're worried about—we can fix it. We can make this work. You and I can be together. I love you, Ruby. I'm not going to lose you twice.'

She sucked in a deep breath. It was the first time he'd told her how he really felt about her. But this wasn't the way he'd wanted to do that. Telling someone you loved them should be for sunsets and fireworks—not bright libraries, with three other people listening to every word.

Ruby pushed herself up from the chair and walked over to the window, looking out over the gardens. It was almost as if she hadn't heard his words.

'I need to go, Alex. I need to get away from all this. I can't think straight.' She reached out and touched one of the ornate curtains at the window. 'I need to get away from here. This isn't my place. This isn't my home.' She spun around to face him. 'I need to get away from *you*, Alex.'

It was like a wave of cold water washing over him. She hadn't reacted to his words. She hadn't even acknowledged that he'd said he loved her.

Doubts flooded through him. Maybe he'd been wrong all along. Maybe she didn't feel the same way as he did. Maybe this was her way of letting him down gently.

He felt his professional face fall into place—his Prince Regent face—the one he'd never had to use around Ruby.

'Where will you go?' He couldn't help it, his words were stumbling.

This time her eyes seemed more focused. 'I'd always planned on visiting my mum and dad at Christmas. I'll go now. They're in France. I can get there in a few hours.'

Her shoulders straightened. He watched her suck in another deep breath and look his advisors square in the eyes.

She was determined. It was almost as if now she'd made a decision nothing would get in her way. She started to walk forward.

He tried to be rational. He tried to think logically. 'I'll arrange for the jet to take you.'

She gave him the briefest nod and walked straight out of the door. Not a single hesitation or backward glance.

His advisors all started talking at once. But Alex couldn't hear them. All he could focus on was the stillness of Ruby's skirts as she walked along the corridor. The spark and joy he'd felt around her last night had vanished. Even the sway in her steps had been curtailed.

His Princess Ruby was vanishing before his eyes.

She couldn't breathe. An elephant was currently sitting on her chest, squeezing every single breath from her lungs.

Her legs burned as she climbed the stairs and strode along the corridor to her room.

Alex had told her that he loved her.

Alex had told her that he loved her.

Her heart should be singing. Instead it felt as if it had been broken in two.

All those conversations. All those questions about whether she was sure, whether she was ready.

The cold, hard truth was that she wasn't. Right now she doubted she ever would be. Waking up to see people she didn't know telling lies about her, people the world over reading and believing those lies, was like being dunked in an icy-cold bath.

Was this what her life would become?

She opened the cupboard and pulled out her suitcase, leaving it open on the bed. She started yanking clothes from their hangers, not bothering to fold anything.

Then she stopped, her fingers coming into contact with some of the more delicate fabrics. Some of the more beautiful designs.

Were these clothes even hers?

Should she even take them?

Confused, she walked into the bathroom and emptied the area around the sink with one sweep of her hand into her toiletries bag.

There was a movement to the side of her eye. She sighed. Alex. She needed some space.

Except it wasn't Alex. It was Annabelle, her eyes wide as she looked at the disarray in the room.

Ruby was shocked. She dropped to her knees and put her hands on Annabelle's shoulders. The little girl's bottom lip was trembling.

'Oh, honey,' she said. 'I'm sorry. But I need to go away for a little while. I need to leave.'

Annabelle shook her head. Her mouth opened and she scowled fiercely.

'No.'

It was one word. It was a tiny word—fuelled by emotion. But it was the biggest step in the world.

She flung her arms around the little girl. She hadn't thought it was possible for her heart to break any more. But she hadn't counted on this.

She cradled the blonde curls in her fingers and whispered in Annabelle's ear. 'I love you, honey. And I'm so proud of you for saying that word. You are such a clever little girl.' She pulled back and held Annabelle's face in her hands. 'That's the best word I've ever heard.'

'No.'

Annabelle said it again, and pointed to the case. There was another movement to the side. This time it *was* Alex. His face was pale.

'Ruby?'

She nodded. 'Yes. She spoke to me.'

She kissed Annabelle on the forehead, then lifted her and handed her to Alex as she continued to pack her case.

Alex was the parent here—not her. It was his job to be

by his daughter's side. She doubted she could ever fulfil her professional role again. Loving both Alex and Annabelle had wrecked her perspective. Becoming emotionally attached would make leaving harder for them all. She had to draw a line in the sand.

Alex's face was racked with confusion. 'And you're still going to go?'

She nodded. She had to.

Everything was too much right now. She didn't just love Alex. She loved his little girl too. If she didn't leave now she didn't know how her heart could ever recover.

She jammed the last thing into the case and closed it. Picking it up, she turned to face him.

He was clutching his daughter and shaking his head. 'How can you? How can you go now?'

'Because I have to. Because this is the right thing to do.' She stepped up close to him. 'Because if I stay this will only get worse. You think I didn't see the panic on your advisors' faces? You think I don't know that every single action you take could affect the people in this country— your trade agreements, your business? I'm not so stupid as to want to destroy the country that you've built. I'm not that stupid and I'm not that selfish.'

'But what about us?' He glanced down towards Annabelle, who had cuddled into his chest. 'How can you leave us now?' He was getting angry. He was getting frustrated. 'Don't you have a heart?'

She flinched. But it was exactly what she'd needed to hear. It made it so much easier.

'I left my heart in Paris ten years ago, Alex. You should know.'

And she held up her head and walked out of the room before her shaking legs could stop her.

CHAPTER TWELVE

IT WAS STRANGE, spending Christmas in France. The weather was unseasonably warm. Ruby was used to Christmases in England, with freezing temperatures and snow.

Her mother appeared at the door. She had a pale cream envelope in her hand. 'This came for you. I had to sign for it.' She turned it over and over in her hands.

Ruby sighed. 'Is it from Alex?'

She stared at her desk. It was already littered with A4 envelopes—some from Alex, and some from his advisors. All full of details on how to deal with 'the situation'. Pages and pages of plans for dealing with the press.

A plan for how often she could be seen. A plan for how much time they could spend together. A plan for when Alex could eventually put an arm around her. Followed by detailed protocols and information on the history of Euronia and Leruna. It was like studying for a university degree all over again. But this wasn't a qualification. This was a plan for a life. *Her* life.

And she just didn't know if she was strong enough.

In amongst the plans were little handwritten cards from Alex. He'd sent one every day, his pleading words increasing in intensity with each card.

'You'll have to speak to him sooner or later,' her mother said. 'He phones three times a day. I'm beginning to feel like he's part of the family already.'

The words twisted inside her. 'I can't speak to him, Mum, you know that. I need some time.'

Her mother sighed and sat down next to her. 'Why do you need time away from the man and the little girl that you obviously love?'

Ruby was shocked. She'd never used those words to her mother. She hadn't said those words out loud to anyone.

'What? You think I didn't know?' Her mother waved her hand. 'It's been written all over your face from the second you got here. I've never seen you so miserable. It was a few lousy newspaper articles. You know what your dad says—today's news, tomorrow's chip paper.' She gave a half-shrug. 'You only made two lines today in the British press.'

Ruby gave a half-smile. Her father had been surprisingly good-natured.

She stared at the letter. 'I don't think I can read anything else from Alex.'

Her mother shook her head. 'It's not from Alex. It's from Leruna. Who would be writing to you from there?'

Her skin prickled. She couldn't have—could she?

She took the heavy envelope in her hand and opened it, sliding the paper out. There was no doubt. The royal mark was in the top corner. Queen Isabelle.

She blinked. 'Give me a minute, Mum, will you please?'

Her mother nodded and disappeared out through the door. Ruby unfolded the letter on her desk. No typing. This letter was full of beautifully crafted handwriting.

Dear Ruby

I hope this letter finds you well. It was a pleasure to meet you at the Ball and I was delighted to see your obvious affection for Annabelle and your commitment to her.

I understand that you are upset over the recent media coverage. Please be assured that this is a cross

*we all have to bear. I only hope that a little time will
give you the strength and courage of your convictions to fight for the love and family that you deserve.*

*Alex and Annabelle have blossomed in these last
few months. I have no doubt who is responsible for
the transformation of their relationship. The press
can be cruel to us all, but I hope that you won't allow
others to impact on the life you could have.*

*My granddaughter misses you terribly. The spar-
kle that had returned to her eyes has gone again.*

*My beloved Sophia is gone. She was a kind-
hearted girl with a much wilder spirit than she was
credited for. I believe that she would have wanted
both Alex and Annabelle to be loved with the passion that they deserve.*

*I want you to know that you will always be wel-
come as my guest in Leruna. You have our full support.*

Good grace and wishes,

*Her Majesty Isabella DeGrundall, Queen of
Leruna*

Ruby's head was swimming. She could never have expected this. It wasn't even the words that Queen Isabella
had used. It was all the unwritten things in between. She
was giving Ruby her blessing. She was acknowledging
her presence in Alex and Annabelle's life. The invitation
was clear.

'Ruby?'

Her mother was hovering around the door again.

'The car that brought the letter…it's still there. It's waiting for you.'

'Waiting for me?' She glanced outside.

Her mother smiled. 'It seems there's a celebration for
New Year's Eve tonight in Euronia.' There was a rustle

and she held up a clothes hanger and a shimmering dress.
'Apparently your attendance is non-negotiable.'

The flight took less than an hour. The stewardess helped
Ruby into the dress and escorted her down to the waiting car.

Her eyes were squeezed shut for most of the drive as
her stomach turned over and over.

So many thoughts and questions spun around in her
brain. Although having some space had served her well,
reading over the plans for her gradual romance had been
mind-boggling.

She didn't want to live her life to a plan. But rational
thoughts were starting to creep in. She loved Alex. She
loved Annabelle. They weren't your average family. And if
Ruby wanted this life she was going to have to work for it.

Was it really so unreasonable for her to learn how to
handle the press? Would learning about a new country and
its customs really be so different from gaining the professional degree and qualifications she already had?

She knew she had the ability to learn. She knew she
had the ability to adapt to different situations—she'd been
doing it for years in the health service.

She was thinking with her heart instead of her head. If
she thought with her head this all seemed rational—practical. It seemed like something she could actually do.

The car turned down the driveway towards the palace
and she gasped. The pink palace was outlined in dozens of
white lights. It was spectacular. People from the city were
within the grounds. It seemed the party had already started.

The car pulled up in front of the palace doors and a
guard opened the door and held out a hand to help her out.

She glanced at her watch. Eleven o'clock on New Year's
Eve. Eleven years ago she'd been in Paris. Eleven years ago
she'd met Alex for the first time. Eleven years ago they'd
shared their first kiss.

Alex. He was standing at the top of the steps waiting for her.

She'd thought she'd hesitate when she saw him again—she'd thought she'd waver.

But she didn't. She moved away from the car and took her first step towards him.

Her dress was shimmering silver, crying out to be touched, but he kept his hands firmly at his sides as she climbed the steps towards him.

The designer who'd made it had assured him it would look perfect on her. But 'perfect' wasn't close enough to how it actually looked.

The silver beads sparkled in the white lights around the palace. If Annabelle were watching she'd think that Ruby was some kind of fairy. It was almost as if a movie spotlight were shining on her.

She stopped just a few steps away, her hair curled around one shoulder, brown eyes fixed on his and her red lips inviting his kiss.

He held out his hand towards her. 'I'm so glad you came, Ruby. I was worried you would never come back to Euronia.'

'I wasn't sure if I wanted to.'

He could see the uncertainty on her face. She still hadn't decided what she wanted to do. This was it. This was his final chance to convince her to stay.

'I don't want to be part of someone's plan, Alex. I appreciate the work that your staff has done. But I don't think I can live my life like that.' She gave a sorry smile and a little shake of her head. 'I can't wait to love you, Alex. I can't wait to love Annabelle. But I don't have royal blood. I haven't been brought up in the same circumstances as you.' She held out her hands. 'I think we both need to face facts. I just don't fit in around here.'

Her dress shimmered some more, reflecting light back

up onto her face. She'd never looked so beautiful. She'd never looked so radiant. And he couldn't bear not to touch her for a second longer. His heart was filling with joy and breaking at the same time. She'd told him that she couldn't wait to love him. She couldn't wait to love Annabelle. But it was too hard. There were a million obstacles in their way.

But all that mattered to Alex was the fact that Ruby loved him and his daughter just as much as they loved her.

At the end of the day, what more did he need?

He would do anything to make this work.

He wrapped his arms around her waist and pulled her close.

'Eleven years ago in Paris I met the woman of my dreams. Eleven years ago I met the woman I was destined to be with for ever. Fate tried to get in the way. Life tried to get in the way. But from the first time I met you—from the first time I kissed you—I knew, Ruby. I just *knew*. I think that you did too.'

The palms of her hands were resting against his chest. Her bottom lip was trembling.

He smiled at her. 'Ruby, I don't ever want to let you go. You are the only woman I want by my side. But more than anything I want you to be happy. You are the best woman I've ever known. I love you, Ruby. Annabelle loves you too. I'd love to tell you I don't care what the media says—but that wouldn't be true.'

She flinched and he pressed on, moving one hand from her waist and pressing it above her heart.

'I care because *you* care. I don't want anyone to hurt you. I don't want anyone to upset you. I want you to be happy. I want you to be safe. I want to love you, cherish you and keep you for ever. I want you by my side whatever I do.'

'But what about me, Alex? What about my work? I'm not a stay-at-home kind of girl.'

Even as she said the words she wondered how true they were. She'd already been thinking of changing her role at work and trying to find a less stressful kind of job. She loved her patients. She just didn't love the bureaucracy.

He smiled. 'I want what you want. I want to support you in any work you want to do. What is it you want to do, Ruby? Can you do it Euronia?'

She nodded slowly. 'I want to work with people, Alex.'

'Then you can. We have a hospital here. You can be the people's Princess Ruby. If you want to work there—you can.'

'Really?' Things were starting to seem more real. More possible. More within her grasp.

'I want you to be the person I turn to when I need guidance. I want you to be the person Annabelle comes to when she cuts her knee, quarrels with her friends and...' he grimaced '...needs boyfriend advice. I want you to be the person holding my hand and squeezing it when Annabelle says her first sentence. When she starts school. When she's crowned Queen of Leruna.'

Her voice trembled. 'That's a whole lot of wants, Alex. Some parts even sounded like wedding vows.'

He nodded slowly. 'They did—didn't they?' He reached up and tangled his fingers in her hair. 'Here's another one, then. I *want* to make this work. I want to make this work for you and me.'

Tears were forming in her eyes. 'I want this to work too, Alex. I've missed you, and I've missed Annabelle these last few days. I felt as if I'd left part of me behind. But I still want to be normal too, Alex. I'll let you down. I'm not cut out for this kind of life. I'm just Ruby Wetherspoon from Lewisham.' She gave the slightest shake of her head. 'I can't be Princess Ruby.'

One tear slid down her cheek. He pulled her closer and whispered in her ear. 'I think you can. I think you and I can figure this out together. There's no one else for me, Ruby. It's just you. Tonight is our anniversary. Tonight, eleven years ago, someone was smiling down from up above and telling me to reach into the crowd and pull the girl in the red coat up next to me. And that was it.'

He pulled back and pressed his hand over his heart.

'That was it for me, Ruby. Our defining moment. Everything in between has been just smoke and mirrors. Everything that's happened has brought us to here and now.' He held out his hand over the palace grounds. 'This is where we're supposed to be right now. This is what we're supposed to be doing.'

'Paris was a fairytale, Alex. Every girl knows that fairytales don't come true.'

He smiled and slipped an arm around her shoulders, turning her to look out over the crowds. 'But fairytales are magic, Ruby—don't you know that? Every girl doesn't get a prince. Just like every guy doesn't get a princess. But I'm hoping that tonight my fairytale comes true.'

The fireworks started immediately.

The crowd in the gardens all turned towards them. They were spectacular. White and gold Catherine wheels streaking across the black sky. Flashes of blue and red confetti cannons. Roman candles and rockets firing into the sky and exploding in a cascade of brilliant lights. The effects were dazzling.

Multi-coloured waterfall fireworks came at the end of the display, mirroring the fireworks in Paris eleven years ago. They'd been put there at Alex's special request. Would Ruby remember them?

Of course she did. She turned and smiled at him.

'It's almost identical.' Her voice was low and hoarse. 'I haven't watched a firework display since then, Alex. I didn't want anything to spoil the memories I had of Paris.'

His heart lifted. She felt the same as he did. 'Ruby, I love you. I want you to stay with me in Euronia. I don't want you to be Annabelle's speech therapist. I don't want you to be an employee. I don't want you to be waiting in the wings. I'm ready, Ruby. I'm ready to tell the world that I love you and I want you by my side.'

He held his hand up to the fireworks.

'This is for us, Ruby, and I'll recreate these fireworks every year for us. Eleven years ago was the start. I wish we'd had a chance to continue from there. And while I wish my friend Sophia hadn't died I couldn't ever wish my daughter Annabelle wasn't here. Maybe it was always destined that our two countries would be united. But what I know in my heart is that I was always destined for you.'

He knelt down on one knee and pulled the ring he'd had made out of his pocket.

'I love you, Ruby Wetherspoon. Will you do me the honour of agreeing to become my wife? I promise to love and cherish you for ever. I promise to be by your side no matter what happens. Whatever you want to do, you will have my full support. And I hope I will have yours. What do you think, Ruby? Can we create our own fairytale here, in Euronia?'

The fireworks continued to explode behind her. The shimmering silver dress reflected every one of them in the dark night. The colours lit up Ruby's face and there it was—the sparkle in her eyes again. The thing he'd longed for and hoped to see for the last two weeks.

She reached down and pulled him up. She was smiling. 'Don't kneel for me, Alex. That's not where I want you.' She slipped the custom-made ruby and diamond ring on to her finger. 'I want you right by my side.'

He slipped his arms around her. 'Is that a yes?'

She slid her arms around his neck and tipped her lips towards his. 'That's definitely a yes.'

And he kissed her as the fireworks lit up the sky behind them.

Princess Ruby was here to stay.

EPILOGUE

RUBY ADJUSTED HER veil nervously while Polly fussed around her.

'How long *is* this train?'

They were currently all enveloped in the back of the car by mounds and mounds of jewelled pale cream satin. She practically couldn't even see her father at this point.

'Twenty-five feet.' She smiled, even though she was afraid to move. 'Apparently it's a tradition.'

'It's a tradition, all right. Can you even walk with this thing?'

Ruby nodded. 'I've been practising.'

Polly's eyes widened. 'You have? When?'

She smiled again. 'At night. Rufus—Alex's private secretary—has helped me for the last few nights. We've practised up and down the main staircase and out through the main doors.'

'Wow.' Polly handed Ruby her red flowers and lifted her hands to straighten the ruby and diamond tiara on Ruby's head. 'Seems like someone has introduced a few traditions of their own.'

'Ooby—look!' Annabelle was practically standing on one of the other seats, waving at the crowds as they passed, her short red bridesmaid dress bouncing around her.

Ruby stretched over. 'Come here.' She gave Annabelle a hug. 'You look beautiful, Annabelle. You're going to be the most gorgeous girl anyone has ever seen.'

The little girl couldn't stop smiling. Her speech was improving every day. Simple words…

The car pulled up outside the church and Ruby couldn't wipe the smile from her face. *This was it*.

It seemed to take for ever for Polly and her father to unwind her dress and the train from the car. Then there was a nod as Polly took Annabelle's hand and led her ahead.

She waved to the crowds and headed to the church door, the heavy train hampering her steps. If she had her way she'd be running down the aisle to meet Alex.

The crowd in the church was hushed. Queen Isabelle turned from the front pew and gave her the tiniest nod of her head. But Ruby's eyes were fixed on Alex.

There was no tradition here. Her groom would never stand facing the front, waiting for her to appear.

Alex had turned around to face her, his bright blue eyes fixed firmly on hers, smiling from ear to ear. He'd never looked more handsome. She'd never been so sure.

Ruby's father took her arm. 'Ready?'

She nodded. 'Always,' she said, and took the first steps that would start her new life.

* * * * *

AMNESIAC EX, UNFORGETTABLE VOWS

ROBYN GRADY

*This book is for my fellow Romance
Writers of Australia and Romantic
Book of the Year finalists.*

Couldn't have wished for better company!

*With thanks to my fabulous editor, Shana Smith,
and super agent, Jennifer Schober.*

Robyn Grady left a fifteen-year career in
television production knowing that the time was
right to pursue her dream of writing romance. She
adores cats, clever movies and spending time with
her wonderful husband and their three precious
daughters. Living on Australia's glorious Sunshine
Coast, she says her perfect day includes a beach, a
book and no laundry when she gets home.

Robyn loves to hear from readers.

You can contact her at www.robyngrady.com.

One

A muffled conversation, barely audible, filtered in through the closed hospital room door. Laura Bishop raised her bandaged head off the pillows and, concentrating, pricked her ears. One voice was female, the other distinctly male—her fiery sister and equally passionate husband. Laura rolled her teeth over her bottom lip and strained to make out the words. No luck.

But neither Grace nor Bishop sounded pleased.

When Laura had taken a tumble at her home this morning, Grace, who was visiting, had insisted they have the bump on her head checked out. Waiting to see a doctor in a cell phone-free waiting room, Laura had asked Grace to contact Bishop at his Sydney office. She hated to bother him but stints at Casualty could wind on forever, and she didn't want her husband coming home to an empty house and worrying.

Besides, Bishop would want to be informed. He was a protective man…at times, overly so. With her congenital heart condition—and his own family history—Laura supposed he had good reason to be.

The door clicked. When it cracked open an inch, Laura propped up on her elbows.

"I won't have her upset," Laura heard Grace hiss from the corridor.

Laura's husband growled back. "I haven't the least intention of upsetting her."

Wincing, Laura eased back down. How she wished the two people she cared about most could get along, but Grace seemed to be the one woman on earth who was immune to Samuel Bishop's compelling brand of charm. Laura, on the other hand, had been smitten by his sizzling charisma and smoldering good looks from the moment they'd met. Even so...

Lately she'd begun to wonder.

She loved Bishop so very much. She was certain he loved her, too, but given what she'd rediscovered about herself this past week...was it possible they'd jumped the gun and had married too soon?

The door fanned wider. As that familiar athletic frame entered the room, their eyes connected, locked, and suddenly Laura felt dizzier than she had all day. After six months together, Bishop still stirred in her this breathtaking, toe-curling effect, the kind of reaction that flooded her core with want and left her quivering like a half-set jelly.

He looked as magnificent in that dark, custom-made suit as he had that first night, decked out in an impeccable tuxedo, a wicked gleam igniting his entrancing blue eyes when he'd affected a bow and had asked her to dance. Today his eyes were hooded in that same heart-pumping way, but his gaze didn't glow with anything close to desire. In fact, his eyes seemed to reflect no emotion at all.

A shiver crept over Laura's skin.

He was always so caring and attentive. Was he annoyed that she'd slipped? That she'd pulled him away from his work? Shaking herself, Laura broke the spell and touched the square bandage that sat above her left temple. She gave a sheepish smile.

"Apparently I fell."

His dark brows swooped together then his head slowly cocked. "Apparently?"

She hesitated at his single word reply and cast her mind back. "I…I can't remember it now. The doctor said that's not unusual. A person has a fall, knocks their head and they can't recall the incident."

He was unbuttoning his suit jacket, running a deliberate palm down his crimson silk tie. His fingers were long and lean. His hands, large and skilled. She loved his hands. Loved the way they knew precisely where, and precisely how, to please.

"So what *do* you recall?"

Her gaze bounced back to his questioning expression and she examined the sterile but comfortable private room.

"I remember arriving at the hospital. Meeting the doctor. Having a scan…and other tests."

Bishop's mirror blue eyes narrowed.

He wasn't fond of tests, as she'd found out two months into their relationship—the night he'd proposed. He'd presented a dazzling white diamond ring and, overwhelmed with surprise and new love, she'd instantly agreed. Later that evening, curled up in his strong arms in his penthouse's sumptuous bed, she'd told her fiancé about her heart condition—hypertrophic cardiomyopathy. Never one for attention or pity, she normally kept that information to herself. But if they were to be married, of course Bishop needed to know.

"Grace said she saw you when she was driving up the path to the house," Bishop said now, flicking back his jacket to slide his hands into his trouser pockets. "She saw you tumbling from the garden's footbridge."

Laura nodded. A drop of around six feet. "That's what she told me, too." Like she'd said. She couldn't remember.

A pulse pumped once along the dark shadow of his jaw.

"Grace also said you're feeling fuzzy. That you seem... uncertain about some other things, too."

"I'm clear on everything else." She pulled herself higher on the bank of pillows at her back. "In fact, I feel clearer today than I have in a long while."

His eyes flashed. She knew he'd heard the backbone in her tone, but he didn't probe. More tellingly, he didn't come near, gather her up and comfort her, the way he had that evening after he'd proposed.

That night, when she'd confided in him about her illness, he'd drawn her extra close, had brushed his lips tenderly over her brow then had asked about the odds of any offspring inheriting her disorder. She'd done lots of research. Statistics attested to the fact that a baby could inherit the condition as she had done, however, screening precautions were available. An early termination, due to medical considerations, could be performed. Thankfully, from the hard set of his jaw, she'd gleaned he was as uncomfortable with that scenario as she was. But neither was he convinced that they should take a gamble and simply hope for the best.

In the quiet of the hospital room now, Bishop's head angled and he continued to study her as if he wasn't certain who she was. As if she were some new and curious anomaly. Laura's nerves frayed more and she thrust her hand out, beckoning. She couldn't stand the distance a moment more.

"Bishop, please come over here. We need to talk."

The ledge of his shoulders went back and, as an almost suspicious expression darkened his face, her stomach knotted more. When his eyes skimmed her brow, her cheek, her lips, her skin heated, and not in a pleasant way. The vibes he gave off...

If she hadn't known better, she'd think he disliked her.

Finally he came forward, but his gait was guarded, as though he expected to be ambushed at any moment. Had the doctor spoken to him about more than her fall? If not, she'd better tell him now, herself, before someone else could. How would he react when she told him that, no more than an hour ago, she'd taken a pregnancy test?

Pulling herself up, she swung her feet onto the floor so that they could sit side by side. Bishop cut the remaining distance separating them in three purposeful strides. Her stomach jumped when, in a commanding gesture, he cast the covers back more. Avoiding her gaze, he tipped his head at the sheets and a lock of his immaculately groomed hair fell over his brow.

"Get back in bed."

She contained the inappropriate urge to laugh. This was absurd.

"Bishop, I'm fine."

His gaze slid to hers and his brows lifted. "You are?"

"Perfectly."

"Do you know where you are?"

She suppressed a sigh. What was it with a knock on the head and endless questions? She'd been barraged by them half the day.

"I've been through this already with the doctor." As well as Grace and a handful of nurses. But when his implacable look held, she exhaled and supplied the name of the hospital and added, "Which is west of Sydney and east of the Blue Mountains." Where they lived.

"What's my name?"

She tacked on a smug smile and crossed her legs prettily.

"Winston Churchill."

Familiar warmth rose up in his eyes—a comfortable, sensual glow that left her aching to reach for him. But then that serious line cut between his brows again and he cleared his throat like he did whenever he was uneasy.

"No games."

She almost rolled her eyes. But anyone who knew Bishop knew his stubborn streak. The sooner this was over and he was assured, the sooner she could get her change of heart out in the open, the sooner they could work this issue through, and the sooner they could get on with their life together.

God willing.

"Your name is Samuel Coal Bishop," she stated. "You enjoy reading the Financial Review cover to cover, long distance running and the occasional good bottle of wine. Furthermore, tonight you're celebrating an anniversary." She smiled… soft, inviting. "Three months ago today, you and I were married."

Her words hit Bishop squarely in the chest, knocking him completely off balance. It was all he could manage not to cough up his lungs and reel back from the blow. Instead he ran a rather unsteady hand through his hair.

Good God in Heaven. She'd lost her mind.

Grace, the nurse…they'd said Laura had hit her head and was a little hazy. No one told him that she'd lost two years of her life! That she thought they were still *married.* As for falling off that same footbridge…

Bishop hid a cringe. Was this some kind of sick joke? Would the host of a lame candid-camera show jump out, sock him on the arm and point out a hidden lens?

But looking into Laura's unsuspecting emerald eyes now, Bishop knew she was deadly serious. Gazing up at him, with such unabashed innocence and adoration, was the face of the fair-haired angel he'd married. He hadn't been able to figure out why he'd been asked to come here today. Now Laura's request for her sister to call him made sense. So did Grace's inability to look him in the eye when he'd hammered her for details a few minutes ago.

Bishop resisted the urge to drop his head into his hands and groan out loud. He should have insisted on seeing a doctor. He'd been set up. He knew by whom and he could sure as hell guess why.

Laura's sister set the blame for their marriage's breakdown solely upon his shoulders. Chances were that Grace had hoped when Laura laid eyes upon the fiend who'd deserted her, a deluge of sordid memories would come flooding back. Laura's memory would be restored. Once again, *Belligerent Bishop* would be the bad guy and control freak Grace would be number one in her little sister's life. If he'd had a low opinion of Grace before, this took the cake. He'd deserved to know the facts.

Laura had deserved that courtesy, too.

After so long of a silence, worry began to cloud Laura's eyes. His brow damp, Bishop adjusted the crimson knot at his throat and scanned through the maze in his mind. But the harder and longer he searched, the more dead-ends hit him in the face.

Only two things were certain. He couldn't throw up his hands, walk out and leave her here, wondering. Neither could he callously dump the truth of recent events on her. He and Laura might have said goodbye under less than amicable terms—downright hostile, actually—but now she was ill.

And, dammit, he'd loved her once. Deeply. She may or may not thank him for it later, but he had to make an effort to ease her though this...reunion.

He found a small, amiable smile. "Laura, you're not well. You need to stay overnight. I'll speak with the doctor and—" He stopped. Blinked.

And *what*?

He cleared his throat. "And we'll go from there."

She uncrossed her legs only to ravel hers arms over her waist and ease up her chin.

"No."

He frowned. "What do you mean, no?"

Her arms unwound and, her expression imploring now, she reached for him.

Bishop froze. He should pull back. Crush any possibility of

physical contact. He'd never been able to resist her whenever they'd touched.

But the last time they'd been anything close to intimate was well over a year ago. Perhaps that part of him—that primal, perpetually hungry part—was largely buried, along with the love they'd once known.

And so, to curb her suspicions—to keep her calm—he reached out, too, and allowed her delicate fingers to lace through his. Instantly his blood began to stir, and when her sparkling eyes looked into his, the awareness he saw there delivered a pleasure-pain jolt that pierced his ribs and stole his breath.

"Darling," she murmured, "I've spent enough of my life in hospital rooms. I know you mean well, but I don't need to be wrapped in cotton wool. I'm not a child. I have my own mind and I know I'm okay."

Swallowing the dry brick lodged in his throat, Bishop eased his hand from hers, slid a foot back and, determined, injected a take-no-prisoners tone into his voice.

"I'm afraid you're not in a position to object."

Her eyes darkened and her lovely mouth turned slowly down. "I didn't give up my rights when I married you—"

Stopping mid-sentence, her head went back and she flinched, as if someone had slapped her. Gradually her dazed expression faded and her face filled with all shades of remorse.

"Bishop...oh, God. I'm sorry." Confusion swam in her glistening eyes. "I didn't mean that. Not a word."

Bishop let go of the breath he'd been holding. Apparently, a lack of memory couldn't suppress her true, less than charitable feelings toward him. The person who'd challenged him a second ago had sounded like the Laura who'd glared at him when she'd told him to get out. The Laura who had mailed divorce papers a year to the day after that.

Laura was the one who'd ended their marriage. Of course

he'd been upset. Hell, he'd been wounded to his core. But he'd never hated her. He didn't hate her now. Nor did her love her. Which should make this situation easier than it was.

He nodded to the bed. "You need to lie down."

"I need to *talk* to you."

He held the cover back again. "Lie down."

When she stood up, refusing, he fought the urge to force her to act in her own best interests and do as she was told. But that was out of the question, for more reasons than one. She was still a beautiful woman…more beautiful than he even remembered. As much as his brain knew they couldn't live together, his physiology understood only that she was uniquely, tormentingly desirable.

How easy it would be even now to sweep her up, whisk her away and take shameful advantage of this situation. So easy… And more destructive than any act that had ever come before.

He loosened the knot at his throat. He'd try to reason with her one more time.

"You might think you're all right, but—"

"I thought we were pregnant."

The back of his knees caved in. Tipping sideways, Bishop propped his shoulder against the wall then, mind spinning, slid to sit on the bed. His ears were ringing. He felt as if a bomb had exploded inches from his face. Holding his brow, he waited for the stars to fade then finally found the wherewithal to question his ex-wife.

His voice was a croak.

"You thought…*what?*"

She folded down beside him and held his hand as she beseeched him with her eyes. "I was so happy. And worried. Worried about what you would say."

His chest squeezed around a deep ache at the same time a horrible emptiness welled up inside of him. He felt ransacked. As if his insides had been ripped out and thrown on the floor.

He couldn't go through this again, not for anything. Not even that trusting, desperate look on Laura's face.

He turned more toward her, willed the truth to show in his eyes. "Listen to me…you *couldn't* be."

"I know we use protection," she countered, "but nothing's a hundred percent."

The breath Bishop held burned in his chest. This was worse than he'd thought. Was now the time to serve it to her cold? If he were in her shoes, he'd prefer it that way. He wouldn't want to feel like a fool later on. Laura wouldn't, either. They weren't married anymore, much less pregnant.

Her green eyes glistened over at him and as her fingers kneaded his, unbidden brush fires began to heat and lick familiar pathways through his veins. Closing his eyes, he worked to kill the desire to take her in his arms and comfort her as a devoted husband would. So vivid, so hauntingly clear…it all might have happened yesterday. Their meeting, the wedding, the honeymoon, that fall from the northern footbridge, then the slow agonizing death of "them."

"You are *not* pregnant." His words were strained, controlled. *Or, if you are, I'm not the father.*

Her slim nostrils flared with quiet courage and she nodded. "The doctor told me. I was mistaken." That hope-filled light came back up in her eyes. "But when I thought I had a baby growing inside of me, a tiny new life that *we'd* created, it made me realize…"

Her gaze grew strangely distant and yet somehow stronger. Then her shoulders rolled back and a fire lit her cheeks.

"My illness won't make a difference to how I feel," she told him. "I know there's a risk, but I want a baby, Bishop. *Our* baby." She held his hand tighter, angled her head and brought his fingers to her hot cheek. "We just need to have faith."

Bishop closed his eyes as a scolding, prickling sensation crawled up his spine. They'd already had this conversation.

Going on two years ago. It had been the beginning of the end…a long, drawn out, bitter affair.

Laura's broken voice cut through the haze.

"I'm sorry. I shouldn't have blurted it out like that."

Again Bishop tugged the Windsor knot at his throat and, finding it increasingly difficult to breathe, lengthened his neck. Other than Laura's light floral scent, the air in here seemed stale. He needed some space to try and work out how to diffuse this crazy situation before it got any worse.

Winding his hand out of hers, he found his feet and an impassive voice.

"Is there anything I can get you? Anything you need?"

Three fingers of scotch sat at the top of *his* wish list.

"There is one thing." She stood, too, leaned closer and placed a warm palm on his chest. Unbidden flames ignited in his sternum as her slightly parted mouth came near. "I need for you to kiss me."

Two

In her eyes—in his heart—Bishop understood that today Laura loved him. He also understood she was far from her true state of mind. Fighting the raw ache in his throat, he found his ex-wife's arms and urged her gently away.

Refusing her affection was one of the most difficult things he'd ever had to do; toward the end of their marriage he'd have given anything to have had her show him love again. But while his hardening body whispered for him to accept what she offered now, his conscience said a resounding no. Laura was far from well, and no man for any reason needed to take advantage of that.

But he had to be careful how he handled this problem. He didn't want to tip her over whatever mental precipice she so obviously teetered on.

He put a calming note into his voice. "Laura, this isn't the time."

"Not the time?" Her face pinched. Then she blinked several times. "I don't understand. We're husband and wife. We always kiss."

His heart lurched but he wouldn't let that twist of emotion show. How in God's name would he ever navigate through this mess? He felt as if he'd been thrown into the mouth of an active volcano. Everywhere he stepped he got burned. A lot like their marriage, really.

But information was power. He'd get the facts, a professional's opinion and see what was what.

Laura was still looking at him, confusion and hurt brimming in her eyes. In the first three months of their marriage, he hadn't been able to keep his hands off her, and vice versa.

Even now...

Needing to reassure her, he relented and let one palm slide down her arm. Immediately, that minimal contact sent up a flare and a throb that echoed like a warning bell through his blood. Setting his jaw, he put up both his hands and took a resolute step back.

"I'll go speak to a doctor."

"About the pregnancy test."

His gut knotted and jaw tightened more.

"Yes. About that."

He left her standing in a white hospital gown, uncertain, beside the bed. In the corridor, he took a moment to orient himself and order his blood pressure to drop. Laura might be the one who'd had a fall and lost her memory but he was the one feeling off balance. Still, there must be a rational, safe way to maneuver through this hopscotch of emotional landmines. And damned if he wouldn't find it, and find it fast.

At the nurses' station, Bishop made an inquiry and a man in a white coat studying a file down the hall was pointed out. He sped off.

"Doctor—" Bishop glanced at the name tag as he came to a stop "—Stokes, I'm Samuel Bishop. I was told you examined Laura Bishop earlier."

The middle-aged doctor peered over his bifocals and set aside the folder. "You're Mrs. Bishop's husband?"

"In a manner of speaking."

The doctor gave a knowing grin and they crossed the room, away from others' earshot.

"Head trauma," Doctor Stokes summed up. "Retrograde memory loss."

Bishop nodded. "How long will it last?"

"Usually in these cases, memory returns gradually over the following days. It can take longer. In some rare instances it never returns."

Bishop's head began to tingle. He needed to clarify. "In *rare* instances?"

"Initial tests were free of fractures or contusions. She could stay overnight but, as long as she takes it easy and you keep an eye on her, there's no reason she can't go home. When she sleeps, wake her every three to four hours and ask those same simple questions—name, address—to be sure she's stable. You can see your own GP for a follow-up."

Take her *home*…?

Bishop scratched his temple. "Thing is, Doc, we're not married anymore."

One of the doctor's eyebrows lifted. "Your sister-in-law hinted as much."

"Ex-sister-in-law."

The older man's eyes conveyed his sympathies for the situation before he slotted his hands into his coat pockets. "Subtle jogging of the memory. Perhaps photos when you think she's ready. When she's in familiar surroundings, I'm sure more recent events will resurface soon enough." Doctor Stokes seemed about to say more but then he merely tipped his head. "Good luck, Mr. Bishop."

As the doctor moved off, Bishop fell back into a nearby chair. He'd need a whole lot more than luck.

His cell phone vibrated against his hip and he scanned the text from his second-in-charge, Willis McKee.

Where are you? A buyer's on the line. Wants to speak with you ASAP.

Bishop's jaw shifted. Already?

He'd listed Bishop Scaffolds and Building Equipment, the

business he'd built to a multimillion dollar entity, only last week. At the price he'd set, he'd never expected such a quick response, and he wasn't certain how he felt about it.

Over these past few months, since the finality of the separation had sunk in, he'd felt a certain restlessness. One chapter of his personal life had closed and he'd begun to wonder whether he needed a new challenge in his professional life, as well. But he hadn't given a lot of thought as to which direction he should take.

Still, he was pleased he'd taken the initiative to move forward. He'd been seeing a nice woman for just over a month, too. Nothing serious; he wasn't certain he'd ever do serious again. But he enjoyed Annabelle's company. She wasn't high maintenance. Didn't ask the impossible.

Bishop snapped the cell shut.

And now Laura was back in his life, and given the doc's opinion, who knew for how long? What the hell was he going to do? He couldn't simply walk away. Then again, how could he stay? He was stuck like a bug under a shoe.

A tap on the shoulder brought him back and his head snapped up. When he saw Grace poised beside him, he groaned. At this moment, she was his least favorite person. What was new?

Grace made herself comfortable in a seat alongside him and laced her peach-tipped nails on her crisp linen lap.

"So now you know."

He slid her a bland look. "Thanks for the heads-up."

"She didn't remember?"

"Laura thinks today is our three-month anniversary."

"How are you celebrating?"

He pushed to his feet. "Don't be smart, Grace." He set off toward Laura's room. He'd have to speak with this woman again and soon, but right now he didn't trust himself to keep his hands from circling her throat. He didn't care how much she disapproved of him; he should have been warned.

The only good thing to come from his and Laura's bust up was getting rid of one very toxic influence in his life. Always sticking her nose in, stirring up trouble. Laura had defended her sister, but he wondered if deep down she wondered if she'd picked the short straw in the sister pool of life. Grace was one hell of a control freak.

Of course, he'd heard people say the same about him, but that was different. He had a business to run. People who relied on him to get things done right, and that meant the first time.

"I still think you could have saved the marriage."

Grace's silky words hit his back and, temper spiking, Bishop edged around. He set his hands on his hips to keep from making fists.

"First, redundant observation, Grace. There isn't a marriage anymore. Second—" steam rising from his collar, he strode back "—are you trying to have me think you want Laura and me to get back together? Because I'd sooner believe in the Easter Bunny."

Fingers unlacing, Grace found her feet, too. She always came across as so damn perfect—hair, nails, prissy platinum blond French roll. He'd love to rattle her cage, but this wasn't the place. Already, interested people were staring.

"You're wrong," Grace said, "if you think I want to see Laura unhappy."

Grace wasn't interested in anything but being right. "You never wanted us married."

"I didn't want you to marry so soon. You both needed time to think things through. You didn't give yourselves a decent chance."

"And you've been gloating about that ever since."

Her head tilted as her gaze searched his. "Have you considered using this time in a positive way? This might be an opportunity to do things differently. To listen to her this time. Try to understand."

Bishop only glared. Even now she was trying to manipulate. Grace knew nothing. She hadn't lived in their home during that turbulent time. He'd done his best. From the start, when Laura had said she'd changed her mind and wanted to have a baby of their own rather than adopt, he'd tried to understand. Their downfall wasn't due to his behavior but to Laura's conscience; she'd made the wrong decision and had never gotten over it.

Her hopeful look dissolving, Grace sighed.

"I've said goodbye to Laura." She collected her handbag and headed toward the wing's exit. "Take good care of her."

He almost called out; where the hell did she think she was going? Grace had always been so ready to ingratiate her presence into Laura's life before. Now, when Laura really needed her, she was walking out? But the question marks on their curious audience's faces roped back any choice words. As uncomfortable as this would be with his ex, having Grace around would only make the situation ten times more difficult. If Laura's parents were alive, he was certain they would step up, but both her mother and father had died long before Laura met him.

Like it or not, this was his problem, as well as Laura's, to work through.

Resigned, Bishop returned to the private hospital room. When he entered, Laura was standing by the window, her arms wrapped around her middle. She rotated back. Her delicate face was pale. Clearly she wanted to go to him, but after his earlier reticence, she hesitated.

"I spoke with the doctor," he said.

"And?"

Bishop considered his reply. He thought about Grace's opinion—a second chance—then the doctor's remark regarding *rare instances*. Might Laura never regain her memory? Could this accident give them another shot at their relationship? After all the anguish, a full year apart, was there any piece of him that even wanted that? He didn't love her. Not anymore. Too much water under that bridge. For now, however, he could only take one step at a time.

Willing the bite of tension away from between his shoulders, he came to her, offered his hand, and innocent hope flickered bright in her eyes.

"Get dressed," he said with a small but encouraging smile. "The doctor says we can go home."

An hour later, as Bishop steered up that familiar spiraling mountain road, Laura gazed out the window, a warm smile tugging her lips. She wanted to roll down the window and enjoy a good long lungful of that fresh, clean air. The glorious cloud-wisped sky, those endless forests of eucalypt and pine, so many colorful birds swooping between branches... Everything looked somehow brighter.

She'd loved this part of the Blue Mountains countryside from the moment Bishop had first driven her to his estate two weeks after they'd met. Now, almost six months on, she couldn't imagine living anywhere else. Or being with, and loving, anyone else. Although...

Laura stole a curious look at the driver.

Bishop looked somehow different this afternoon. Tired from a busy week at the office most likely. Worried about her, of course. But she hadn't noticed those fine lines branching from his eyes before. And he'd seemed so distant all the drive here. She didn't need to be Einstein to know he was avoiding the subject she'd brought up in the hospital. He didn't want to discuss the possibility of renegotiating what they'd decided upon before taking their vows.

That night four months ago, when he'd suggested adoption as their safest bet, a rush of emotion had stung her eyes and hurt-filled tears had brimmed. But he'd assured her that he was only being practical. Sensible. Yes, he understood that her own condition was easily managed, but there was no guarantee that a child might not inherit a more severe form of cardio impairment. Surely the most important thing, he'd said, was to be together and raise a healthy baby. An adopted child.

She'd respected his concerns—still did—but she'd come to realize that he needed to respect her feelings, too. Feelings that weren't about to go away. From as far back as she could recall, she'd wanted her own family, particularly in her late teens after her parents had passed away. She had her Arts History and Literature degree—her parents had been big on education—but her dream was to be a homemaker, a good wife and great mother. She wasn't career-minded in the twenty-first century sense, and she didn't care who knew it. She wanted to bestow upon her children the same kind of love and support she'd known and valued growing up. Never had she considered the possibility of raising another woman's child.

But she *did* want a healthy baby, and she most certainly wanted to marry Bishop, so she'd agreed to his suggestion. Over these past months, however, the weight of that decision had pressed on her heart like a stone. More and more she'd begun to believe there must be a thing as being *too* cautious. It was far from certain that any child they conceived would inherit her disorder. And there was always medication and a simple operation to implant a defibrillator to regulate the heartbeat if need be. Of course, if a child were severely affected, more involved surgery might be needed. A pacemaker. Even a transplant.

But in this age of high technology and information, parents-to-be were aware of so many frightening things that could go wrong in vitro. Then there were the concerns surrounding keeping a child safe later on, from disease and accidents and predators. But most people didn't let those fears beat them. A husband and wife hoped for the best, knowing they'd be there for one another, no matter what.

As long as she was fertile—and there was no reason to believe that she wasn't—she wanted to try. The reward would be well worth the risk. Was she wrong to want what so many women longed for?

A child of her blood. A child of her own.

Deep in thought, Laura absently ran a hand over the car's armrest, and then something odd struck her. She'd been so caught up in memories and today's events, she hadn't noticed until now.

"You didn't mention you were getting a new car."

Bishop's eyes, beneath their aviator sunglasses, didn't leave the road. "Willis negotiated a good lease on the Land Rover."

Her mind wound back but didn't hook onto anything. She shrugged. "Willis who? I don't remember you mentioning that name before."

"Haven't I? He's my assistant. New assistant."

"What happened to Cecil Clark? I thought you said he did a good job. He seemed nice enough at that charity dinner we went to last month."

"He...got another offer."

"You should have matched it."

His voice dropped. "Sometimes you just have to let people go."

Four-wheel drive tires crunched as he braked at the top of their lengthy gravel drive. Rather than one of the four garages, he'd parked in front of the house, a sprawling ranch-style dwelling cut into the hillside. Both inside and out, the house combined tasteful luxury with a homey rural feel—enormous individually crafted open fireplaces, large yet cozy bedrooms, two massive home offices, a fully equipped gym with sauna and indoor pool for laps.

On Sundays, Laura served eggs Benedict on the eastern porch and together they would watch the southern hemisphere sun climb higher toward the far-stretching haze of mountains to the west. Even more she loved what came after coffee... returning to bed to savor her delectable, insatiable husband.

Touching the small bandage above her temple, Laura frowned and thought back. Had they enjoyed their ritual this Sunday past? She couldn't remember.

Bishop swung out of the driver's side and performed his usual courtesy of opening her door. Together they moved up the slate-paved steps that led to the lofty teak and glass paneled entry door. Halfway up, he paused to clear his throat and rattle the keys awkwardly in his palm.

"My, uh, house key must be on my other set."

"I have mine." She didn't recall grabbing her bag before leaving for the hospital—silly, but she couldn't even remember this bag. Still she dug in, rummaged around, fished out a set of keys...but then her eyes rounded and she froze.

Horror slow-dripping through her veins, she rotated her left hand one way, then the other as panic fisted tight and fierce inside of her.

"My rings," she got out. "The nurse must have taken them off before the scan."

Common sense said her diamond-studded wedding band and magnificent princess-cut engagement ring must be filed away at the hospital somewhere safe. Clearly it was an oversight that they hadn't been returned before they'd left. But the staff would have records. There was no reason to believe she wouldn't get them back. Still she couldn't loosen the suffocating knot in her chest. She felt naked without them. Somehow so vulnerable.

Standing on the expansive veranda, with the sun arcing toward the towering eucalypt trees behind, Bishop took a step closer. "Don't worry. I'll take care of it. You need to rest."

He'd said it kindly enough but it was on the tip of her tongue to tell him that she'd been resting all day. Still, the truth was that suddenly she did feel tired, and a few degrees off balance. Maybe she should swallow her pride and do as he asked. Lie down.

But not alone.

She twined their fingers and tugged until the back of his hand pressed against her heart. She hoped her teasing grin was persuasive.

"You look like you could use a rest, too."

Emotion flared in his eyes, hot and cold at the same time. "I didn't have a fall today," he reminded her. "You did."

Her heart dropped. He sounded so...detached. But unlike earlier in hospital, this time she knew why. Of course he wanted to be with her. Of course he wanted to caress and kiss her. But safety-first Bishop was determined not to go against professional advice. During the drive home, he'd made a point of repeating the doctor's instructions that she ought to take things easy for a day or two. Still...

"You know something?" She moved closer until their hands lay flat between them like pressed flowers. "I can't think of a better way to relax than making love with my husband."

As if infused by a sudden rush of blood, a cord rose and pulsed down one side of his throat. His chest expanded on a giant breath and that odd emotion in his eyes flared again.

"We'll go inside." His free hand opened the door. "I'll fix you something to drink."

"Champagne?" she asked, trying hard not to sound hurt by his flat tone as he herded her in. "It's our anniversary, after all."

"Tea, iced or hot." He shut the door and walked past. "In a couple of days we'll see if you still want champagne."

Three

When Laura relented and took herself off to bed, Bishop sent up a silent prayer of thanks.

She'd tried to corner him into joining her in the bedroom, but he'd dodged another bullet, albeit with a minimum of skill. He only hoped his ex-wife's memory returned before either of them had to endure that kind of farce again.

In her mind, they were married. Married couples enjoyed conjugal intimacies, and he and Laura had been intimate often. What bothered Bishop most now was how strongly his body responded to the possibility of holding Laura close. Naked. Loving. His again.

As she disappeared down the wide hardwood hall, gait slow, head down, Bishop shoveled a hand through his hair and threw a glance around. Same furniture, same stunning yet homey fireplace. How many times had they made love before the flames he'd stoked there?

After several moments remembering back…wishing something, somewhere, had turned out differently…he bit down and wheeled toward the door.

His hands bunched at his sides. The urge to walk out was overwhelming; he could only see this ending badly. But he couldn't leave. At least not yet. If Laura's inability to remember lasted beyond Sunday, however, he'd fabricate a business trip and organize assistance…a nurse perhaps. Or Grace would need to make arrangements. Until then, he was stuck.

But he wouldn't sit around twiddling his thumbs. He might be away from the office, his apartment, but he could still get some work done.

He brought his laptop in from the car and without much thought, moved into his former home office. He let his eye linger over the heavy rosewood furniture, the maroon couch, his Rubik's Cube and the framed photograph of Laura that, remarkably, still sat on the polished desk. He moved forward and let a fingertip trail the cool silver frame.

Hell, he thought she'd have demolished this room and every reminder in it the first chance she'd got. Which led him to thoughts of her "lost" wedding rings.

They weren't at the hospital. She'd probably flushed them or tossed them in the fireplace, as he'd done with his band a raging moment before he'd slammed the door shut on this place forever. Or believed that he had. But his stay here this time would be short-term. After the long drawn-out business that had led to their separation, the shorter the better.

Settling into his chair, he connected with Bishop Scaffolds' server and brought up some recent specs. New dies were under discussion but he wouldn't commit until he was certain the designs were exactly right.

With a background in engineering, he'd always enjoyed a natural affinity with machinery. Routinely he checked presses, calibrations and product tolerances. It wasn't unusual to find the boss manning equipment should a worker be called away or need a few minutes off. This past week, after listing the company, he'd spent more time than usual in the factory where equipment was manufactured, stored and dispatched. He considered himself as much a part of the working machine, a cog in the wheel, as his employees, every one handpicked and valued.

But maintaining a manufacturing presence in Australia was a tricky ball to juggle. The uncertain slope of the Aussie dollar against other currencies, the force of reduced labor prices in neighboring countries, plus the quality versus cheaper options argument kept Bishop on his toes. The threat of any company folding to the sum of those pressures was real.

When he'd lost a couple of key contracts not long after his and Laura's split, an unsettling sense of doubt had clung to him. He'd never failed at anything of real consequence, but if he could fail at something as important as his marriage, might he not fail in business, too? If he began second guessing himself, losing his edge, maybe it was time to get out and hand over the business to someone who had the mind-set to keep it strong. He wanted to be that man, but then he'd also wanted to keep his marriage solid.

He went into a few emails but found he couldn't focus. Visions of Laura's toned form, tucked under a light cover in the bed they'd once shared, had seeped into his mind and now he couldn't shift them. Images of her chest softly rising and falling and the way her hair splayed over her pillow while she slept were glued in his mind. He thought of how perfectly her mouth had fit under his—how everything had seemed to fit—and for one frightening moment, he battled a tidal wave urge to stride down the hall and join her.

Growling, he pushed back his laptop and glared at the ceiling. Dammit, he'd never wanted his marriage to end. He'd fought to save it. But no matter what Grace thought about second chances, he'd be an idiot to entertain such a crazy idea. He was here because he had no choice. Laura would get her memory back and then they could each forget this episode and get on with their individual lives.

Laura woke with her heart hammering in her chest. The room was quiet, the walls stenciled with soft-edged shadows. The green numerals on the side table read 2:04.

Shivering and feeling inexplicably alone, she tugged the covers higher. Then she remembered Bishop and her smile warmed her right through. Carefully, she rolled over, reached out in the darkness...and that warmth dropped away.

The space beside her was cold and empty. Why hadn't Bishop joined her? Because he worried about her bandaged head? Didn't he know that his embrace was the only medicine she needed?

Well, if he didn't know, she'd simply have to go and tell him.

After wrapping up in a long, soft robe, she padded out into the hall. Outside Bishop's office, a wedge of light shone on the timber floor. Frowning, she huddled into the robe's warmth more. He was working at two in the morning?

She headed off but stopped in the doorway, her heart melting at the sight. Bishop was sprawled out on his Chesterfield couch, an ankle hung over the far armrest, one foot on the floor, his left forearm draped over his eyes. He'd taken off his shoes and trousers, and his white business shirt was undone to his navel. The steady rise and fall of his beautiful big chest told her he was sleeping soundly. Familiar heat sizzled through her. God, how she loved him. How dearly she wanted him. And there was another feeling swirling through her blood... one that was strangely difficult to pinpoint or analyze.

She *missed* him. Missed him like she hadn't seen him in years. The knowledge left her with a hollow ache in her chest. A chunk cut out of her heart. But she surrendered to a self-deprecating smile. He'd been away from their bed half a night. How would she cope if he left her for a week? A month?

She wriggled her toes on the cool floor. She wanted to go to him, wrap him up under her robe, rub her leg over the hard length and rouse him. Despite doctor's orders not to overdo it, if her hands were to knead his body and she poured words of love in his ear, surely he'd relent and make love.

Or would he be unhappy with her? He worried so much about her health.

She was still making up her mind when the ridges of his six-pack suddenly crunched and Bishop woke with a start. Driving back a breath, he sat bolt upright as if a monster had chased him out of a dream. His gaze shot to the doorway, to where she stood. His dark hair was mussed and his bronzed legs beneath the white shirt looked as strong as steel pylons. The tips of Laura's breasts hardened against the gentle fabric of her robe. How she longed to trail her fingers up over that steel, every blessed inch of it.

His blue eyes focused then narrowed slightly as they raked the lines of her body. A pulse began to beat in his jaw at the same time his eyes grew lidded and she knew he was visualizing the curves and valleys he loved to touch and taste.

Then he scrubbed a hand over his face and, shaking himself, sat straighter. His voice was thick from sleep.

"It's late. Go back to bed."

"If you come with me."

He held her gaze then looked to his desk. "In a few minutes. I have some things to wrap up."

She crossed the room, sat down beside him and gave him a level look.

"We can't avoid it, you know."

He leaned back the barest amount. "Avoid…what?"

"We need to talk."

She put her hand on his thigh. He promptly removed it.

"Not in the middle of the night." He pushed to his feet and, grabbing his hand, she pulled him back. He had the strength to resist, but a yielding expression touched his mouth, his eyes, and slowly he lowered back down.

"When I was old enough to understand about my condition," she began, "that I would need to be careful about overexertion and such—I felt…different. My parents made sure every teacher knew which activities I could or could not do. Once, when we were short on numbers, Mrs. Carols insisted I moved off the sideline and team up for the 500m relay. When he found out, my dad hit the roof. He threatened the principal's job and demanded an apology from Mrs. Carols as well as from the school."

Bishop's brows had knitted. "Why are you telling me this now?"

"Because I want you to understand that I know better than anyone what I'm asking of you, of myself and of any children we have."

As if he were considering her words, his gaze lowered. He saw his buttons undone and, deep in thought, he began to rebutton. "Laura, it must be close to three o'clock—"

"Junior school was lonely sometimes," she plowed on. She didn't care about the time. She needed to say this and he needed to hear it. "I couldn't do cross-country or horse riding at camp. Kids can be cruel and some laughed behind my back. A couple even called me a cripple."

Redoing the final button, his hands fisted in his shirt. "I wish I'd been there."

"I had good friends too, though. We ignored the girls who needed to make themselves feel taller by bringing someone else down. Then university happened and the entire world didn't need to know anymore. I was just like everyone else. A year after graduation, I met you."

A small smile hooked one side of his mouth. "That night I kept you up talking till dawn."

Smiling, too, she turned more toward him. "Eight weeks and one day later, you proposed. When you still wanted to marry me after you learned about my secret, I didn't think anyone could be more lucky...or more in love..." Her gaze dipped before finding his again. "Even if you didn't quite understand how deeply I felt about conceiving and having our own child. After I agreed we would adopt, I tried to deny it to myself."

He broke their intense gaze and cleared his throat. "We'll talk about it in the morning."

She touched the square bandage on her head. Feeling a faint throb coming on, she surrendered with a nod. It was enough for now that she'd opened that door a little wider. Tomorrow they would talk more, and when he realized how much carrying and giving life to her own child meant to her—when he accepted that history didn't need to repeat itself, hers or his—he'd come around. He loved her, and love could surmount any obstacle.

She found her feet and put out her hand. "Coming?" His gaze slid to her bandage and she grinned. If he thought he'd get away with another excuse, he was mistaken. "Or we can stay up and finish this conversation now?"

He stood. "You win. But remember, you're taking it easy."

She looped her arm through his and guided him toward the door, toward their bedroom.

Beside the bed, she slipped out of her robe while he unbuttoned his shirt again, which seemed to take an inordinately long time. When she slid between the covers, feeling sexy in the lacy negligee she'd donned when she'd first lain down, she watched as his gaze filtered over her in the golden glow of lamplight. Snuggling into the pillows, she slipped back his side of the covers.

"On my honor," she said, half-serious, "I promise not to ravage you."

A moment later, the mattress dipped as he moved in beside her. Lying on his side, resting on an elbow, he searched her eyes. Then he brushed a curl from her brow and said, "I promise the same."

The next morning, a world of birds' calls dragged Bishop from a deep sleep. Groaning, he rubbed his eyes, but before he could piece together the previous day's events, he recognized the room, the unmistakable crisp smell of mountain air. He also recognized the angelic form asleep beside him.

Laura lay on her back, her silky hair splayed around her head like a halo. One thin black strap had fallen off her shoulder. Beneath the lace bodice, he saw the rosy tips of her breasts.

Desire—thick, fierce and hot—plunged through his system, from the soles of his feet to the hair on his head and most definitely everywhere in between. On reflex, he reached to cup her flawless cheek but thankfully in time he set his jaw and forced his hand away. It was bad enough that they'd slept in the same bed last night. When he'd promised not to take her, Laura had no idea how serious he'd been. But when she'd curled into him, how could he stop her? Or the acute physical arousal that had kicked in.

Clamping his eyes shut, he'd forced himself to think of anything other than her faint jasmine scent and the satin feel of her negligee...of her skin. He had no idea how long he'd lain awake, forcing himself not to stroke her back or brush his lips over hers.

Now he was fighting the same merciless war. The urgent pulsing in his groin said to forget honor and let his palm slide over all those gorgeous contours. The arousal fueling his erection demanded that his mouth glide down and taste her breasts, her hips, the honey between her legs. He imagined her dreamy sigh as she woke slowly, then her fingers winding through his hair as her hips arced and the trapped pounding in his blood found its release. He thought of her climaxing once, twice, and the possibility of them spending all day in bed.

Hardening more, Bishop swallowed a tortured groan. He'd better get out of this room before he convinced himself what he wanted was not only natural and necessary, but appropriate.

Quietly, he eased up and pushed to his feet. He slipped

his arms into the sleeves of his shirt, which brought another problem to mind. What would he wear over the weekend? Perhaps a quick trip into Burniedale, the nearest township, was in order.

He glanced at his watch.

The shops were two hours from opening yet.

Behind him, Laura stirred but when he turned to study her, she didn't look uncomfortable. In fact, the corners of her too-kissable mouth were curved into a heavenly smile. The doctor had suggested he wake her every few hours and ask routine questions, but she'd been fine four hours ago. She looked so peaceful now, perfectly healthy but for that small bandage above her temple. He wouldn't disturb her. Besides, when she was asleep he wasn't walking on eggshells, wondering when and how the memory pennies would begin to fall.

A few minutes later, he stood in his office, collecting his BlackBerry off the desk. He checked his messages and found another from Willis.

Where the hell are you?

Bishop headed outside. Where was he? Living in a time warp where the woman he'd once loved—who had once loved him—couldn't remember that she didn't want him in this house, let alone in her bed. The bigger, far more dangerous issue was, as difficult as it was proving to be, he needed to remember that, too.

Moving out onto the eastern porch, he siphoned in a lungful of the fresh morning air. The birds were deafening. Living in the city heart this past year he'd forgotten how loud they could be. But it was a relaxing and at the same time invigorating noise. Another thing he'd missed. Something else he'd tried to forget.

He thumbed in Willis's quick dial and, phone to ear, waited for the call to connect. He'd swung a hip over the wood railing, was watching a hand-size echidna and its porcupine quills trudge into the brush, when Willis picked up.

"Are you in the office already?"

Bishop's gaze skimmed the dense forest of gum trees. "I'm nowhere near the office."

"Did you take care of whatever it was that dragged you away early yesterday?"

"It'll be sorted by Monday."

"Good, because I promised these potential buyers you'd speak with them then. I'll get a confidentiality agreement then talk to Saed about putting together the documents they'll want to see."

Bishop listened to Willis's plans while he examined the weathered stump he'd once used to chop logs for the fire. When Willis finished, Bishop absently agreed. "Sounds good."

Two beats of silence echoed down the line. "You don't sound as pumped as I thought you'd be."

"I'm pumped," Bishop argued. "I just didn't think we'd get any nibbles this soon."

"This isn't a nibble, Sam. It's a walloping great bite. The agent said the interested party is none other than Clancy Enterprises."

Bishop let out a long low whistle. "They own half the companies on the east coast." Manufacturing as well as retail.

"We're talking serious money and, if we can go by their track record, we don't have a whole lot of lead time. These guys move fast."

A family of wild ducks, two adults, four chicks, waddled out from behind a boulder. Bishop shifted his position on the rail. "How fast?"

"Just sign the on the dotted line fast."

A touch on his shoulder sent Bishop's heart lurching to his throat. Jumping off the railing, he spun around. Laura stood before him, wrapped up in that fluffy pink robe, the tip of her nose already red from the morning air's cool kiss.

Her gaze homed in on his phone and she stepped back, whispering, "Sorry, I didn't realize."

As if calling from another world, Bishop heard Willis's voice coming down the line. "Sam? You there?"

"That's okay," he said to Laura, thinking how young and fresh she looked, the same age she'd looked when they'd married. The bitterness he'd seen a year ago seemed to have left her face completely. "I was finishing up." He set the phone back to his ear. "We'll talk later."

Willis didn't ask questions, which was part of the reason he was paid so well. Willis knew when to push. He also knew when to back off.

Laura hunched and hugged herself, snuggling into her robe. It might be spring but up here the mornings still got mighty chilly.

"Must have been something urgent to be calling at this time?" she asked.

"Nothing for you to worry about."

But a line had formed between her brows and her gaze had gone from his face to his chest and lower. She shook her head slowly and Bishop braced himself. Something had clicked. Perhaps the fact she hadn't seen him on this porch in over a year. Or something he'd said, or his tone, had set off a memory. If it all came flooding back, he could be gone in two minutes. He'd simply find his shoes and be on his way. He had no desire to hang around and argue, which seemed to be all he and Laura had done those last few months.

Her head slanted to one side. "Why are you wearing yesterday's shirt?" Her frown eased into a reproving grin. "Anyone would think you don't have a change of clothes."

What could he say? He didn't live here anymore. He wouldn't find any clothes in what had once been his wardrobe. If he'd gotten to the shops in time and had bought a couple of shirts...

But this kind of thing was bound to happen. He wouldn't

try to explain. He'd simply show her his empty wardrobe and let her memory take it from there.

So they walked back inside the house, down the hall, back into the bedroom, and while she pulled up the sheets to make the bed, he stood before his former wardrobe doors. Holding himself firm, he eased out a long breath.

Do it. Just do it.

His fingers curled around the knob. And pulled.

What he found inside left his legs feeling like rubber. His jaw dropped, and he stepped closer.

Clothes hung from the rails. But not just anyone's clothes. *His* clothes. Suits and shirts, trousers and jeans. He held his brow. This didn't make sense. Yes, he'd left everything behind. He'd had clothes enough back at the Darling Harbor apartment. He didn't need anything here. Didn't need anything to remind him.

But he'd assumed that once he'd gone Laura would have bundled up his clothes and shipped them off to charity. Or burned them. Why hadn't she gotten rid of all this like she'd gotten rid of him?

"Need some help?"

Her voice, coming from directly behind, found a way through the fog. A moment later, her palms were sculpting over his shoulders and arms. As the contact lit fires all through his body, instinctively he leaned back into her touch. She pressed a kiss between his shoulder blades and as her grip hardened on his upper arms, he closed his eyes and tried to stay lucid.

"Of course, we don't have to wear anything at all," she purred, and her hands filed down his arms, arrowing over his hips, finally finding and wrapping around the weight confined beneath his trousers.

A whirlwind of darkest desire spiraled through him. His hand covered hers and pressed in as his mind went deliciously blank but for the need to have her again. To drown in her kisses and fill her with his—

Coming to with a jolt, Bishop pried her hand away. Clamping down on the frenzied heat racing through his veins, he turned to her and forced his mouth to curve into a breezy smile.

"You're certainly persuasive."

"And you are dying to say yes." Her gaze heavy with want, she reached up on tiptoe and tugged his bottom lip with her teeth.

A fireball shot to the top of his inner thighs and ignited a very short fuse. When she drew a line around his unshaven jaw and her mouth opened over his, Bishop shuddered and leaned into her kiss. With lava flooding his veins, every cell in his body cried out for more. Then her mouth opened wider, inviting him in deeper. Wanting to possess her, his hands found her shoulders and drew them in.

She tasted the same. Felt the same. And now he knew he was the same hungry man who craved to be with his wife.

She hummed in her throat and the vibration released bright-tipped sparks in his belly that unleashed an inferno a few inches below that. Instinctively, one hand left her shoulder and searched out her breast. As his touch grazed the soft, pert mound, his tongue dipped deeper, running over hers, and any sense of right or wrong vanished beneath the blistering force of mutual need.

Her hands were fanning beneath his shirt, but when he rolled her nipple between finger and thumb, she found his other hand and set it low on her belly. His fingers speared down. She wore no panties. He felt her damp and ready beneath the satin of her negligee. Pushed to his limits, he groaned against her lips.

"This always felt so right."

"Make love to me, Bishop," she murmured back.

"You don't know how much I want to."

"Oh, but I do."

He felt her grin against his lips as her palm slid down his side and the pressure built to flashpoint.

He was ready to forget that this wasn't real…was ready to drop her back onto the bed and enjoy what she offered in a very real way. And yet…

Still holding her, he sucked down a breath and, struggling, got his thoughts together.

"I…think we should stop."

Her tongue ran along his bottom lip. "Don't think."

Good God, but someone had to.

Gritting his teeth, he pried her a little away. "The doctor said—"

"I don't care what the doctor said."

"Listen to me," he growled. "We aren't doing this."

Her head came back and she probed his eyes for a long searching moment. "Is it because you think I'll ask you not to use protection? That I want us to make a baby now?"

Well, that was as good an excuse as any. Rolling back his shoulders, he lifted his chin. "Let's cool down, have a shower—"

Her eyes flashed. "Fabulous idea!"

"—*alone*. We'll have something to eat. You must be hungry. And later…" Later? He promised, "We'll discuss it."

And they would. If any conversation could bring her around—bring them *both* around—it'd be one highlighting the risks associated with her falling pregnant.

Four

Thirty minutes later, Laura's high-pitched cry, coming from the bedroom, sent the hairs on Bishop's scalp standing on end and his feet hurling him out of his chair. His heart belting against his ribs, he tore through the open glass sliders, slammed through the main sitting room and bolted down the hall.

What the hell had happened?

When Bishop had stepped out of the shower earlier, he'd heard the main bedroom pipes still running. Laura loved her baths; she'd be a little longer yet. He'd thought about jumping back on his laptop and sorting out a few budget discrepancies but had opted for checking around the house instead, seeing if the outdoor pool and gutters were free for starters.

After finding the net in the pool house, he'd skimmed the outside pool assured in knowing that Laura would have someone coming out once a fortnight or so to keep an eye on its upkeep. Money wasn't a problem. After their parents' deaths, both Laura and Grace had received a good inheritance, and after the split he'd also passed on a generous monthly allowance. Lawyers had advised him to wait until after the divorce when a settlement could be drawn up, but he wanted to contribute. Last month, however, the divorce became final and the settlement was, well, settled. He'd given her this house and land. Knowing that he'd see ghosts in every corner, he would only have sold it anyway no matter how much he loved the area. Neither of them had been overly concerned about snakes or spiders, poisonous though many of them might be. After hearing Laura's cry now, Bishop wondered if he needed to reconsider.

Had a deadly Brown crowded her into a corner? Had she fallen somehow again? Of course there was also the chance she'd gotten her memory back and, realizing she wanted to kill him for letting her make a fool of herself yesterday, had screamed out in blind rage.

Outside his home office, they collided. Her face was flushed, her legs temptingly long and tanned in a pair of white tennis shorts. She waved her hand in front of his face and squealed again. Not scared, not angry but rather...*excited.*

"They're here!" She bounced on her toes. "They were here all along."

He held her arms to steady her. "Hey, slow down. What's here?"

"These."

She wiggled a set of fingers. The gold and diamonds he'd slid onto her third finger two years ago sparkled in ribbons of morning light that streamed through the floor-to-ceiling eastern arch window.

"I must have taken them off before going to the hospital," she told him. "I'm not sure why. I can't remember any of it."

He eased out the breath he'd been holding. No falls. No bites. Thank God. If she couldn't remember taking her wedding rings off...

"It doesn't matter now," he muttered.

But, of course, it *did*. The doctor had said that with gentle prodding her memory should return. To his mind, bringing her back here to the scene of the crime ought to have been prodding enough. After a final argument, they'd barely exchanged a word for over a week until they'd run into each other on this very spot. After an awkward moment, he'd said he had work to do and pushed by. She'd told him he might as well *live* in the office—his office in town. Then she'd hic- cupped back a sob and said that she meant it. That he could pack his things and leave. Leave *now*. She couldn't take this anymore and neither could he.

"Now it's the weekend you can wear yours, too," she was saying.

He came back to the present and his frown deepened. She was talking about *his* wedding ring?

"I understand you can't wear it during the week," she went on. "I know how you like to keep your hand in at the factory and accidents can happen. Rings can get caught. But on the weekends…" She bounced up and snatched a kiss from his cheek. "It's only you and me."

Over a year ago, he'd left his wedding band here. Actually, he'd thrown it in the fireplace before he'd stomped off. He'd always imagined that she'd built a roaring fire and had happily watched the gold circle melt into a shapeless blob. So how was he supposed to assure her that he'd wear it now?

But then her other hand came out, fist closed, palm up. When her fingers peeled back, the gold band he'd tossed into the fireplace a year ago gleamed up.

His heart lurched up the back of his throat. Dumbfounded, he shook his head. It couldn't be.

Carefully, he collected the ring and inspected the inscription inside. *Always and Forever.*

His voice sounded as if it'd been dragged through molasses. "Where did you find them?"

"Where I always put them," she said, studying both her rings and the gold band lying in the centre of her palm. "In my jewelry box."

His stunned gaze went from the ring to his wife's—his *ex*-wife's face. Her jewelry box? Had she dug the ring out of the fireplace after he'd gone? There was no other explanation. And yet whenever he thought about the hurt and frustration, how he'd believed every loaded word that she'd said—

"Aren't you going to put it on?" she asked.

Bishop opened his mouth, ready to say no way. The divorce was done and dusted, no matter what she might think. But for the life of him, he couldn't come up with a way out. He could hedge but what would that accomplish? Only suspicion on her part. Agitation on his.

She'd remember soon enough. Until then…

He gave a stilted nod, lifted his left hand and Laura held the band over his fingertip, ready to push it on. For a moment his thoughts wavered. *What does it matter?* Then, *This has gone far enough.* But then the ring pushed up over his knuckle and Laura's eyes were sparkling all the more.

Grace had implied this might be a second chance. The idea had seemed absurd yesterday, particularly coming from his arch nemesis. And yet this morning, being back in this house, spending the night in that bed, having this ring on his finger…

Bishop shook himself.

No. It was crazy. Not possible.

Not happening.

"What would you like to do today?"

His gaze jumped from his finger to her beautiful animated face. The lilac-colored top she wore was cut tastefully but, to his current way of thinking, provocatively low.

He swallowed deeply. "What did you have in mind?"

"Want to teach me to play chess? You said you would."

He'd already taught her and she'd proven a quick study. He'd thought about letting her win a couple of times, but she was too clever to fool that way. She'd vowed that she'd beat him fair and square one day. If they sat down at that chessboard now, would she remember the moves he'd taught her, or had that part of her memory been wiped clean, too?

He ushered her into his office, to the chess set he'd left behind. "What do you know about the game?"

"There are bishops."

He gave a soft laugh. "Right."

"White moves first."

"Right again."

Maybe she did subconsciously remember their lessons, which, most likely, meant she would remember more. And that was good, right?

He twirled that band around his finger—still a perfect fit—and sat behind the black. She took the chair behind the white.

He tapped the piece sitting directly in front of the black king. "This is a pawn."

"They move one space at a time."

"Only forward."

"Except when taking a piece, then they move diagonally."

"Perhaps we should do away with the lesson and start a game."

She laughed and the sound tinkled through him. "Oh, Bishop, everyone knows that."

"What else do you know?"

"I know the castle—"

"Rook."

"—gets to move across and up and down. That the horse is the prettiest piece and the queen is the most powerful."

He relaxed back in his seat. That was more like it. "That doesn't sound very technical."

"Tell me...is it as difficult to play as everyone says?"

"Only if you can't guess the other person's move before they make it."

He knew what came next in *their* game...every step, every misfire, after she'd let him know she'd changed her mind and wanted to conceive their own child, irrespective of any health concerns.

No matter the challenge he'd met it head-on, strategized, worked out the kinks and had always stayed one step ahead. Except where their marriage had been concerned. And that black mark had always stung. Always would.

Unless...

Puzzled, Laura was looking over the board. "Know the person's move before they make it? How are you supposed to do that?"

He shaped two fingers down the sides of the black queen. "By skill," he said, "and luck. And sometimes even by accident."

When Bishop had to take a phone call midway through their first chess lesson, Laura decided to stretch her legs. She headed off to the kitchen, poured a drink and told herself that getting a handle on the basics of the game shouldn't be too difficult. And once she was up to speed, no doubt Bishop would enjoy the competition.

She'd spent time playing cards whenever she'd been in the hospital in the cardio ward—sometimes with the nurses if she couldn't sleep, more often with the other kids. But, before yesterday's incident, she hadn't spent time in a hospital bed in years. She'd had a defibrillator fitted and was on a low dosage medication, which kept her well.

The condition had been passed on through her mother's side. An aunt had died unexpectedly in her teens and that's when the family had been tested and the condition diagnosed. But Laura suspected that Bishop's own family history had as much, if not more, to do with his pro-adoption stand.

He'd been the twin who'd survived and she didn't need to ask if he felt guilty about it. Bishop had told her briefly about the story surrounding his birth and the subsequent death of his baby brother. When she'd tried to delve deeper, he'd withdrawn, other than to say he'd heard enough about it from his parents growing up. Laura had envisaged a boy fighting not to be overshadowed by his mother's and father's ongoing grief. But Arlene and George Bishop had seemed pleasant enough, even welcoming, at their wedding. They'd said how proud they were of their only son and that they wished they lived closer; they'd moved clear across the country to Perth five years ago. But they intended to keep in touch and had asked that the newlyweds do the same. Laura got the impression there wasn't so much of a rift between parents and son as a gradual drifting apart that had, over time, come to be accepted.

Conversely, she and Grace had been so very close, to each other and to their parents. The sisters were devastated when first their father had died in a vehicle accident then cancer had taken their mum—a melanoma discovered too late. But as much as the sisters still figured in each other's lives, it was no secret that Bishop thought Grace wielded too big of an influence over Laura.

But what was too much? They were close, always had been. Grace had her own family—a four-year-old boy and a three-year-old girl—but she'd always let Laura know she was welcome in her home at any time for any reason. If Grace had been a little outspoken about her concerns before the wedding, it was because she believed no one loved and cared for her sister more than she did.

If Bishop's twin had lived, perhaps Bishop would better understand the sisters' situation. They said twins shared a special connection. Maybe Bishop was somehow aware of that connection and missed it more than he knew.

When she'd finished her ice water and Bishop was still on the phone, talking about the sale of something or other, Laura decided to take in some fresh air. She'd had enough of chess for one day.

Outside, the sun spread a warm golden hue over the spires of the eucalypts and pines. She peeled off her cardigan and, marveling at their balance, studied a koala and her baby dozing high up in the fork of a tree. Beyond that clump of gray-green trees lay the rock bricks and planks that made up the northern footbridge.

Her stomach gave a mighty kick. She winced and slid her foot back.

The fall—before and after—she couldn't recall, but it'd be a long while before she crossed that bridge again. Had she been trying to see something over the edge? Had a lizard scuttled up and scared her from behind? Had she slipped on the dew—

A flash—a fuzzy freeze frame—flicked on in her mind. The image… She couldn't hold on to it long enough, but the residue of the pain hit her first in the lungs and then lower. Holding her belly, she flinched. When she opened her eyes, her brow was damp with perspiration. She eyed the bridge, shuddered to her toes, and promptly set off in the other direction.

She was headed toward the gazebo when Bishop caught up. The planes of his face were hard in their naturally attractive way, but his blue eyes shone with relief. His hands caught her bare shoulders and urged her near. The heat of his touch, the sincerity in his eyes, left her feeling warm and loved all over.

"I couldn't find you," he said in a low, graveled voice. "I was worried."

"It looked so beautiful out here and I didn't know how long you'd be on that call. It sounded important."

His hands slid down her arms then dropped away altogether. A muscle ticked in his jaw before he answered. "I'm thinking of selling the company."

Laura's breath caught. She couldn't believe what she'd heard. He was so proud of what he'd built from scratch. He had plans to expand even more.

"When did this happen?"

"I've been mulling over it for a while."

But selling his company was *unthinkable*. He was so capable and responsible…still she had to ask the obvious question. "Are you in financial trouble?"

He began walking down a slate path lined with gold and lavender wild flowers. "Just thinking I might want to try something new."

"Do you think you'd be away from home more often? Not that it would matter," she added quickly. "I'd be okay. It's just if you were…well, I've been thinking about getting a dog. Someone to keep me company through the day."

He nodded slowly, considering. "I think a dog is a good idea."

"Really?"

He smiled. His eyes were so bright in the spring sunshine, they glittered like a pair of cut jewels. "We'll do some research."

The urge overtook her. She threw her arms around him and kissed his bristled cheek. She loved his weekend shadow, the sexy roughness against her lips, the graze when he gifted her one of his delectable morning kisses.

"For some reason I thought you'd say no."

"What will you call him?" he asked, slipping his hands into his trouser pockets as they continued down the sweet-smelling path that led to the gazebo. The white lattice was patterned with a riot of cardinal creeper blooms, deep vibrant scarlet in color. Beautifully fragrant, too.

"I'd have to see him, or her, first," she told him. "I've never thought you could name a member of the family until it arrived."

On their way up to the gazebo platform, his step faltered and Laura gnawed her lip. As lead-ins went, it'd been a clumsy one, but they had to talk about it sometime.

When he sat down on the surrounding bench, she positioned

herself close beside him and folded a fallen lock away from his brow.

"I don't want us to be afraid of what might go wrong," she said, "when it has to be better to think about everything that can go right."

When he only looked away, Laura chewed her bottom lip again. After considering her next words, she delivered them as carefully as she could.

"I know it must have been hard when your brother died."

"We were newborns," he said, his brow creasing as he found her gaze. "And that has nothing to do with us."

"I was only trying to talk—" But the line of his jaw was drawn so tight, his eyes suddenly looked so shuttered. Knowing when to back off, she ordered her locked muscles to relax. "I know you don't like talking about it. I shouldn't have brought it up."

Bishop drove a hand through his hair and groaned. She was dead-on. He didn't like discussing his twin. It dredged up feelings he'd rather not entertain. Feelings of guilt and helplessness and, the real kicker, loss.

But looking at Laura and her bowed head now, Bishop felt something inside of him shift. They'd never really talked about it during their marriage. If she wanted to discuss it now, hell, maybe he ought to. Perhaps something would tip off her memory and he would be on his way—out of the damnable bittersweet mess.

"We were identical," he began, letting his threaded hands fall between his open thighs. "I got most of the nourishment before we were born. The other twin—"

"Your brother."

"—died four days later."

"And you feel bad about that."

He felt an urge to explain that it wasn't his fault. That was life and his parents had never held it against him. But they had been the half truths he'd told her the first time.

Hell, his parents had made him live through that time every birthday, every Christmas, first day of school, on Easter egg hunts, at graduation. *If only your brother were here. How sad your twin isn't at your side today.*

Okay. He got it. He respected their regrets and dedication to the son they'd lost. But just for once in his life he'd have liked to achieve and be noticed without mention of that incident.

He blew out a breath and admitted, "Yeah. If ever I think about it, I feel...bad."

Laura was nodding. "My mother felt bad about passing on her heart condition. Until I told her I was so grateful she had me and if the price was having a metal bit in my chest and taking some medication, that wasn't too high."

"But when you were conceived your mother didn't know the risk." He and Laura had been aware. Therefore they'd had a duty to act responsibly.

"I'm glad my mother didn't know about her condition," Laura said. "And she admitted she was glad she didn't, either. She always said her children were her life."

A smile tugged at his mouth. What mother wouldn't be proud to have such a beautiful daughter? And Grace? Well, Grace might be a witch but, after her comment yesterday about second chances, the vote was out. Even if it was too little too late. He wished they'd had her support when it mattered.

"And all this," he said, getting to the heart of the matter, "is leading up to the fact that you want to have a family the old-fashioned way."

Her eyes glistened with innocent hope. "I really do."

The last time they'd had this conversation almost two years ago, he'd agreed. Laura had been thrilled and within weeks had confirmed her pregnancy. It should have been all rainbows and happy families from there on in.

Far from it.

He didn't know which had been worse. Watching his mother trying to hide her pain for years after his brother had died, or going through Laura's pain after her miscarriage. If he'd stuck to his guns and had said it was adoption or nothing, would she have told him to go? Or would they be happy now with a healthy baby, a healthy past, present and, hopefully, future?

"So…what do you think?" she asked.

He opened his mouth to shut down the conversation once and for all, but then he saw the hope swimming in her eyes and the steam went out of his argument. He held his breath, considered the options.

There weren't any.

"I think…"

Her lips curved up. "Yes?"

"I think we need to think about it more," he ended.

Her smile wavered and her eyes dulled over, but then the disappointment faded from her expression, replaced by the inherent optimism he'd always loved.

She pointed her white-sandaled toes out and flipped them prettily in the air.

"*The Nutcracker*'s playing in town," she said, changing the subject. "Tonight would be sold out but I wonder if we could get tickets for tomorrow."

The *ballet?*

The last time they'd gone they'd had an argument. One of his more notable clients and his wife had witnessed the scene. Bishop wasn't a fan of tutus and tights at the best of times. After that night he'd sworn never to sit through another *Fouetté en tournant* as long as he lived.

Sensing his reluctance, Laura let her toes drift down. "I know ballet's not your thing…"

"No, it's not. But it is yours," he added.

Going to Sydney tomorrow evening would leave them with another twenty-four hours in this environment. If a few lightbulbs went off…if he were lucky… Hell, they might not get to the ballet at all.

Five

Before Bishop drove off to the nearest shops to get a few provisions, Laura had sussed out whether he needed condoms. She'd already checked the bedside drawer where he always kept them, and he didn't need to stock up. There was plenty of contraception on hand.

That was okay. She'd only broached the subject of them falling pregnant yesterday. Getting her husband to come around to her way of thinking—the way that put faith ahead of doom and gloom—might take a little doing. She could wait. She and Bishop had too much going for them to let this difference get in the way.

She baked some pastries and had sat down at her laptop in her office when Bishop returned. She swung around in her high-backed chair as he moved up and lifted her face to him, waiting for a kiss hello. He searched her eyes for a long, heartfelt moment, then lowered his head and dropped a chaste kiss on her cheek.

A band around her chest pulled tight. He'd avoided kissing yesterday, last night. But for that peck, he hadn't kissed her at all today, and she wasn't happy about it. Rather than sounding testy or upset, however, she thought she'd go for teasing.

"Hey, I didn't hurt my lips when I fell."

Before he could see it coming, she caught him around the neck and brought him back down. Her mouth zeroed in on his with the precision of a ballistic missile. His lips were slightly parted, and she made certain to take advantage of that, too.

She aimed to kiss him swiftly but thoroughly, and as her mouth moved over his, her fingers kneaded the back of his strong, hot neck. There was a second of resistance on his part when she thought he might jerk away. But then a growl rumbled from his chest up his throat. The vibration tingled over his lips, ran over her tongue, then he was kissing her back.

The connection didn't last long enough. Just when she was thinking a trip to the bedroom might be in order, his hands found her shoulders and he pushed himself away. Before he could prattle on about doctor's orders again, she spoke up.

"I had it wrong," she told him.

An emotion she couldn't name darkened his eyes as he slowly straightened and those broad shoulders rotated back. "What have you got wrong?"

"*The Nutcracker*'s not playing. It's *Swan Lake*."

That emotion flickered again and then his brow furrowed and his voice deepened more. "*Swan Lake.*"

Understanding his tone, she tilted her head. "We don't have to go." Frankly, after that kiss she'd be more than content to stay in. But he surprised her.

"No, we'll go," he said, his gaze shifting from hers to the computer screen. "I'll never forget the last time we went."

Laura cast her mind back. "We've only been together once. Just before we were married."

"I could've sworn we'd gone again after that."

He looked so earnest, she coughed out a laugh. "Was it that bad? Sounds like you had nightmares about men coming after you in tights."

His gaze dipped to her lips and he smiled softly. "Yeah.

Maybe that's it." He thrust his chin at her chair. "Shift and I'll book."

"What? My Amex card isn't as good as yours?"

"Just trying to do the gentlemanly thing and pick up the tab."

As if he ever let her pay for a thing.

Lifting out of the chair, she thought about kissing him again. But she'd let him book and then they could get back to…business.

"In that case, guess I'll go occupy myself in the kitchen."

Deciding on which outfit to wear to the ballet—her Lisa Ho cream wraparound or that new season black sequined jacket with a classic little black dress—Laura hummed as she made her way down the wide central hall and into the well-equipped kitchen.

She liked to cook—roasts, Thai, experimental appetizers, mouth-watering desserts. Her mother had always said the way to a man's heart was through his stomach. Laura could vouch that her husband certainly enjoyed his home-cooked meals—almost as much as he enjoyed making love.

And after dinner she would remove the bandage from her head and persuade her husband that tonight the doctor didn't know best. She'd rested long enough.

Entering the kitchen, she was a little taken aback at how many grocery bags lay on the counters. Seemed Bishop had stocked up. He usually left the major shopping to her. She stacked the fridge and the pantry then flicked on the oven to warm half a dozen bakery scones. Tomorrow she'd whip up a fresh batch herself.

She slid open the cake tin drawer, dug in to select a tray but, as she reached down, her mind went strangely blank. After a moment, she remembered what she was after and shuffled again through the pans. But where was her favorite heating tray? Straightening, she stuck her hands on her hips and glanced around the timber cupboard doors. Where on earth had she put it?

Of course it was no big deal. Definitely no need to worry Bishop with the fact that her memory was foggier than she'd first realized. Just little things, like wondering at the unfamiliar brand of toothpaste in the attached bath, or pondering over leftovers in the fridge that she had no recollection of cooking.

A rational explanation existed for it all, Laura surmised, wiggling out a different tray for the scones from under the hot plates. Things were a little jumbled, but they'd sort themselves out soon enough.

When she arrived back at her office, brandishing two cups of steaming coffee—one black, one white—Bishop had a different webpage open. She caught a glimpse of the images—bundles of fur with cute black noses and gorgeous take-me-home eyes. She gave a little excited jump and coffee splashed onto the tray.

"Puppies!" Eyes glued to the screen, she set down the tray on a corner of the desk and dragged in a chair. "I was thinking maybe a cocker spaniel."

Elbow on the desk, he held his jaw while scanning a page displaying a selection of breeds. He grunted. "Aren't they dopey?"

"They're soft and gentle and a thousand times cuddly."

"Maybe something bigger."

"You mean tougher."

He collected his mug and blew off the steam. "You haven't got too many neighbors around here," he said and then sipped.

"*We* haven't got too many neighbors," she corrected. What was with this *you* business?

He set down the mug, turned back to the screen and clicked a few more searches. "Maybe a Doberman."

"I'm sure they're lovely, but I can't imagine snuggling up

into a powerhouse of muscle and aggression." She ran a hand down his arm. "Present company excluded."

"They're supposed to be very loyal," he said, as if he hadn't noticed her compliment, and pictures of dogs with gleaming black coats, pointed ears and superkeen eyes blinked onto the screen. Laura's mouth pulled to one side. Sorry. Just not her.

"Did you have a dog growing up?"

He clicked on a link and a list of breeders flashed up. "A golden retriever."

"Guide dogs."

"One of the breeds used, yes."

"Can you tap that in?"

A few seconds later, images of the cutest, most playful puppies on the planet graced the screen and childlike delight rippled over her. Her hand landed over his on the mouse and she scrolled down for more information. Nothing she read or saw turned her off.

"They're so adorable," she said as Bishop slipped his hand from beneath hers and covered his mouth as he cleared his throat. "They look like they're smiling, don't you think? I can definitely see us with one of those."

"Good family dog," he read from the blurb. "Gentle temper-ament. Prone to overeating, shedding and joint problems." Obviously uneasy, he shifted in his seat. "One of my foremen spent over two grand getting his cat's broken leg fixed. Bad joints mean huge vet bills." He clicked the previous page back. "Let's look at Rottweilers."

She grinned. It wasn't about money. "I don't want a guard dog. I want a companion. A personality that will become part of our family." And would eagerly welcome new members in. "Just tell me…do you still like retrievers?"

"Of course."

"Then if we both want a retriever and somewhere down the track he needs some medical attention, wouldn't you rather have what we really want than settle on something which may or may not have other problems? There are risks everywhere, Bishop. Risks in everything."

His jaw jutted, but the dark slashes of his eyebrow quirked. While he considered, Laura folded her hands in her lap. She'd made her point. She was talking about far more than which dog to buy.

"But we don't have to make a decision today," she ended in a placating tone. "There's no hurry."

"You're right." He clicked on the top right-hand X and the puppies disappeared. "No hurry at all."

The phone rang. Not his cell phone this time. Which meant there was a good chance the call wasn't about business. Maybe Kathy from the library. They'd been talking about starting a literacy program for over-fifties.

Trying to recall what their last discussion had outlined, Laura pushed back her chair but Bishop was already up.

The *bbbbrrr*-ring of the phone ripped through to his bones, as unsettling as a bank alarm. Moving quick, his hand landed on the extension.

During his drive to the shops earlier, he'd considered the phone and the problems surprise calls could cause. If one of Laura's friends contacted her, it wouldn't take long for inconsistencies to rise and questions to flare in both parties' minds. Laura didn't need to be backed into a corner, faced with a reality that seemed Hitchcock-esque given what she could and could not remember. Prodding was far different to someone knocking you for a complete loop during a phone call.

Driving back, he'd decided to intercept calls, not to keep Laura from her friends and others who cared, but to forewarn of the situation and ask that they tread lightly for now. Eventually, Laura would check emails. Oddities like *Swan Lake* playing rather than *The Nutcracker* would become more obvious. Dates wouldn't mesh, like the dates he worried she might see on the web when trying to book those tickets. Soon there'd be questions. Ultimately, as she needed to know and was ready to hear, there'd be answers.

But for now...

His hand still on the receiver, he said, "I'm expecting a call." Then to divert her, "Is that scones I smell warming?"

Leaping up, she cursed and sprinted out. "I forgot."

Waiting until her padding down the hall quieted, he answered the call. He should've known who it would be.

"How are things going?"

He exhaled and a measure of his tension dissolved. *Grace.*

He ran a finger over a tiny crystal clock. "Not as bad as I thought."

"She hasn't remembered?"

"Not a thing that I can tell."

"I should probably come up and see her."

Or not.

"That's up to you."

"But you'd rather I stay away."

Smirking, he pushed the clock back. "You can read me like a book." He liked as much distance between himself and Grace as possible.

"But she's happy?"

He imagined Laura in the kitchen she loved, drawing the scones from the oven then finding those special little spoons she saved for serving jam. She made the best jam.

He surrendered to a smile. "Very happy."

There was a long pause. Bishop could imagine Grace smoothing her French roll. "I hope she'll understand when this is all over."

"Depends on who ends up sticking around. This Laura or the one who couldn't wait to see the back of me."

"Did I hear my name mentioned?"

Bishop's heart squeezed to his throat and he spun around.

Laura held a tray with scones, whipped butter, jam and those tiny silver spoons. From the open look on her face, she hadn't heard too much.

He hoped his smile didn't look manufactured. "Your sister."

Her eyes rounded playfully and she stage whispered, "You're having a conversation with *Grace?*"

"About your condition."

"My fall?" He nodded. "If it gets you two talking at last, it was worth it." Setting the tray down, she accepted the phone. "Hey, Grace. How're you doing? Oh, I'm fine." She gave Bishop a wink and angled toward the window view. "Better than fine."

Unable to pass, he dabbed some homemade jam on a scone and bit into the doughy sweetness. Grace would keep Laura on the phone for a while. He didn't need to listen in.

He wandered out from her office, his gaze skimming the same surrealist paintings that had frequented the hallway walls when he'd left. Further on, he took stock of the kitchen, its polished granite benches and gleaming utensils that Laura had taken such pride in when making those superb dinners she whipped up seemingly out of thin air.

He stopped beneath the ornate arch that led to the main living room. Same chintz couches, crafted timber furniture and grand fireplace, which they'd spent so many evenings cuddled up in front of, she reading a bestseller, he browsing over papers from work. In the beginning they'd felt so relaxed together and yet the steady thrum of excitement had always been there, too. A buzz that not only connected them, but drew them irreversibly, magnetically near.

Those were the best days of his life.

His gaze inched along the knickknacks on the marble mantelpiece...silver candlesticks, some ballerina figurines, a cup she must have accidentally left there. His eye line drifted higher. Then his heart stopped beating.

Their wedding photo was gone.

And why wouldn't it be? This was her house. They'd lived separate lives for over a year. His bet was she'd used the photograph as fuel for the fire. But then she'd kept his clothes and wedding ring. Maybe the photo was stored away, too.

More immediately, what would *this* Laura say when she realized the picture she adored was missing?

He swung an urgent glance around. Should he hunt in some cupboards, try to find and hang it back up before she noticed? Or would seeing the photo missing press a necessary button to jump-start her memory?

Although what had just happened between them should have sent up some flags.

The inevitable had happened. He'd kissed her. Or rather she'd kissed him. And he hadn't stopped her. But for a brief moment of "what the hell?" he hadn't even tried.

He'd mulled over how it would feel should he relent. Strange? Pleasant? Knock-your-socks-off fantastic? Check box three. And now, God help him, he couldn't help thinking about later, because Laura was going to want far more than lip service tonight.

"I was thinking I might come up and see you tomorrow," Grace said down the line while Laura made herself comfortable in one of the winged armchairs positioned beside a window view in her office.

"I'd like that, Grace, but Bishop and I are going into Sydney. The ballet's on."

"You're going out? Do you think that's wise?"

"Oh, Gracie, not you, too!" How many times did she need to tell people she was fine? A bit of a foggy memory didn't count.

"Learn to live with it," Grace returned. "I care about you."

Laura laughed softly. "I got that."

"Will Bishop be staying in town?"

"Tomorrow night? Why do you ask?"

"He's a busy man. I thought he might want to stay down rather than drive out again Monday morning to the office."

"I don't think so." Laura concentrated on the chess piece, thinking back. No, she was certain. "He didn't say he would."

"How is Bishop?"

Laura put on a suspicious tone. "Why this interest in Bishop all of a sudden?"

"Just making sure he's treating my little sister right."

"Always and always."

"Really?"

A prickle of annoyance rolled up Laura's spine and she held the receiver tighter. "Grace, I know you thought we married too soon. And maybe you were right," she admitted, knowing she'd thought the same herself yesterday in the hospital. "Maybe we should have waited a little longer to iron things out. But we love each other. That's what gets a couple through."

"I take it you're going to tell him you don't want to adopt?"

"I brought it up yesterday." And again today. "We're going to work it out, Grace."

Her sister sighed down the line. "Oh, sweetheart, I hope you're right."

Six

Laura cooked a roast dinner with all the trimmings and rosemary cream gravy. When Bishop took himself off to his office after dessert, Laura steeled herself against disappointment. He was avoiding her. Or, rather, avoiding that touchy subject.

But as she finished packing the dishwasher and headed off for a shower before bed, she put herself in her husband's shoes. Analytical. Methodical. He was divorcing himself from her until he thought she was completely well, as well as settle in his own mind the conundrum of adoption versus conception. If he thought she needed rest and he needed to be left alone, she would accommodate his wishes.

Up to a point.

As she'd told Grace, they were going to work this problem out. And if he didn't want to talk… Well, she'd simply have to grab and hold his attention some other way.

Before her shower, Laura removed the bandage from her head. She fingered the raise and shadow of a bruise in the gilt-framed vanity mirror. Barely a scratch. No sign of a headache. Quite honestly, she thought she ought to have done more damage given the six-foot distance off the bridge to the river rocks she must have landed on.

After a long, hot shower, she took care drying off, dabbing Bishop's favorite talc powder in all the right places, then slipping into the negligee she'd worn on their honeymoon in Greece. She mustn't have worn it since then. She'd found the mauve silk pushed to the back of her drawer behind other negligees.

Moving into the bedroom, she glanced at the clock: 8:43. She filled her lungs and, confident, sashayed down the hall.

But a few moments later she discovered that Bishop wasn't in his office. She found him out on the eastern porch, leaning against a column, seemingly counting the stars, and given tonight's luminous night sky, there must be more than a trillion.

Crossing to stand behind him, she filed her hands around his waist and set her cheek against the broad expanse of his back. His unique scent filled her lungs, burrowed under her skin. Her eyes drifting shut, she circled her nose over his shirt between his shoulder blades and imprinted the smell…the moment…onto her memory forever.

He must have heard her coming. He didn't move when she embraced him. Now, however, as her fingers trailed up his shirtfront and her palms ironed over his ribs, his hands covered hers and tightened around them.

"It's chilly out here," he said in that rich, smooth voice she loved.

She grinned against his back. "I hadn't noticed." Then she twined around and stood between her husband and the view of slumbering mountains. He opened his mouth, but she cut him off by placing a finger to his lips. "I don't want to hear about doctor's orders. I'm not cold." She threaded her arms around his middle. "Not while you're near."

As a breeze rustled through the leaves, in the shadows he focused on her brow. "You've taken your bandage off."

"I'm hoping to take off more than that." She found his hand and shaped his palm over her shoulder until the strap of her negligee slipped down. Then she angled her head to press a lingering kiss on the underside of his wrist. "I love you so much, Bishop," she whispered as her lips brushed his flesh. "So much…sometimes it hurts." She dropped tender kisses on his palm then on each fingertip in turn. "How long has it been since we made love?"

He exhaled. "Too long," he said.

Arching her neck back, still holding his hand, she skimmed his fingers down her throat. "I feel as if you haven't held me in an age."

Without her help, his hand continued over her shoulder then down the line of her back until it reached the rise of her behind. Laura sighed as the million sparks zapping through her blood caught light. Humming out a smile she grazed her lips over the hot hollow at the base of his throat and placed his other hand on her breast.

"Bishop, take me to bed."

As she pressed softly into him, familiar, simmering heat condensed high in his thighs.

Bishop grit his teeth but, although he knew what he ought to do, he didn't release her. His hold—on her breasts, on her behind—only increased while in his gut he felt an almighty battle raging, a war so fierce, the pull of yes-no threatened to tear him apart. If he did as she asked…if he took her to bed…they would each win and both lose. They wanted this, they'd always been electric together in the bedroom, but this time there'd be a heavy price to pay.

Unless her memories of that time before were lost forever.

His heartbeat pounding in his ears, Bishop searched her eyes and challenged himself again to do what Laura would want him to if she could only remember. But all he could see was pure clean love glistening in her eyes, pouring from her face. At this moment, she truly loved and believed in him. If he made an excuse this time it would only hurt her. And yet, if he complied…

Breaking, Bishop groaned and brought her closer.

What the hell. If she got her memory back during the night, she could hang him in the morning.

His head dropped lower and as his mouth claimed hers, he swept her up in his arms and headed inside. When he reached the foot of their bed, he released her lips and set her gently on her feet. While his pulse hammered through his veins, his gaze drank in the heavenly sight of her standing in the moonlight flooding in through the bedroom's ten-foot-high windows.

She raised her arms and, understanding, he folded the light fabric up in his hands and eased the negligee over her head. Before the silk and lace hit the floor, his head had lowered over hers again. He felt her dissolve in his arms as she happily, completely surrendered.

Laura trembled inside and out as her hands wandered over the granite of his chest and muscled sides. Then, only half aware, lost in the kiss, she was helping him tug the shirttails from his belt, unbuttoning the front, winding the fabric off his shoulders, down his arms. His kiss was so skillful, thoughtful, and at the same time, demanding. An avalanche of stirring sensations…of memories…rained down and filtered through her. When his mouth left hers to feather a tingling path over the sensitive curve that joined shoulder to neck, the energy, already so strong, multiplied. Intensified.

Laura's head rocked back.

She reveled in the feel of him. Her senses reeled at his clean male scent. As her palms sculpted over his shoulders and biceps, her mind visualized those hot mounds of steely flesh—how she loved to cling to them when he thrust above her—and she smiled.

His thumbs rubbed mesmerizing deep circles high on her arms as his mouth trailed her collarbone then dipped lower until the warm wet sweep of his tongue twirled and teased one nipple. Every atom of oxygen in her lungs evaporated. Gasping back air, she drove her fingers through his hair while tiny brush fires flashed and ignited through her veins. And the slow burn only grew, second by second, with every heartbeat and breathtaking loop of his tongue.

Light-headed, she tugged at his belt and murmured into the shadows, "We don't do this enough." His teeth nipped and tugged the bead at the tip of her breast and she sighed. "In the beginning we'd spend entire weekends in bed."

"I remember," he groaned, then drew her deeply into his mouth.

He'd heeled off his shoes. Now he tugged and stepped out of his trousers. When he hooked her under each arm and laid her upon the bed, she moaned with barely contained anticipation and delight. Like a big cat on the prowl, on all fours he edged up until he hovered over her. His head slowly dipped to kiss her mouth, her brow, the shell of her ear, as her back arched higher and his erection throbbed and grew.

"Should we flick back the quilt?" she asked between breathless kisses and running her leg over his. "Get beneath the covers?"

His palm, large and slightly rough, scooped under her hip. In a slow, languid movement, his muscular body grazed up against hers, drawing an urgent gasp of want from her lips. His knees nudged between hers. When his tip found her moist...silky, swollen and ready...he grinned against her parted lips.

"I'm good," he said, and eased in more. "How about you?"

In answer, her pelvis tilted up at the same time his came down and he drove three parts in. The thrust hit a hot spot so bright she gasped for air. Her nails dragged up over rippling tendons as she swallowed loving words from his mouth.

Making love with Bishop had always been wonderful, but this time…

This time was something *beyond* incredible. With the iron ruts of his abdomen grinding against her, his mouth sipping from her throat and strong fingers curling through her hair she felt consumed by a blanket of heat. The burn lifted her to a place no woman had ever flown to before. He felt so deliciously heavy on top her…so delectably, alarmingly male.

Smiling into the shadows, Laura held tight to the feeling.

He still wanted her. Of course he did. The same insatiable way she wanted him.

The slow, steady friction soon turned to leaping flame. As the energy—the raw imploding power—built and pulsed, she clung to his arms as her muscles contracted around him and every particle shivered, focusing on the indescribable magic awaiting her only a heartbeat away.

Perspiration slicked his skin; he slid and ground against her, making her burn wherever they touched. A rumbling groan sounded in his chest and in the shadows she saw him set his jaw. And then, without warning, he rolled away.

Working for breath, it took a few seconds for her to realize he wasn't coming back. She pushed up onto her elbows, worried.

"What's wrong?"

Stretched out on his back, out of breath, he laced his fingers over his brow. "We need protection."

Protection?

Laura fell back. She wanted to say just this once, couldn't they forget it? But there wasn't a chance he'd listen to that. Unprotected sex could result in an unwanted pregnancy. Unwanted on his part, anyway.

So she waited for Bishop's side drawer to open, for her husband to reach in and fish out a foiled packet from the place he always kept them. But he didn't move. Not an inch. And as the stillness eked out, the cool in the room compressed and settled upon her.

He'd been so insistent. After being concerned about her welfare last night and today, finally he hadn't wanted to stop long enough to pull back the covers. And yet now...

She pushed higher. "Bishop, what's the matter? They're in the drawer, right there beside you."

Another few seconds ticked by before he rolled onto his side away from her. Laura watched the long powerful line of his silhouette moving, heard the drawer slide open then his grunt.

She sat up a little. "What's wrong?"

"Condoms. They're there. A whole pack."

Grinning, she brushed her lips against his shoulder. "We don't have to use them all in one night."

"I just..." He shrugged and exhaled. "Never mind." She heard him remove one before he turned back. Once again his mouth slanted over hers and instantly any chill was gone, replaced by the heat he so effortlessly brought out in her. The embrace intensified, the kiss deepened and the need to join in the most fundamental way grew again. When her palm filed down the hard trunk of his thigh, his own hand mimicked her move, curving down her spine then sliding between her legs. He began to stroke her, tease her, and as he kissed her thoroughly she knew this night wouldn't end without that ticking bomb deep inside of her exploding at least once.

Teetering on the edge, she murmured against his lips, "I love when you kiss me. Anywhere. Everywhere."

As if she'd given the golden command, he began moving down, his mouth roaming, suctioning here and there, over her ribs, her belly, around the ticklish dip of her navel. And every kiss took her that much higher, drew her that much nearer. Had her falling that much more in love.

* * *

In the dark recesses of his mind, Bishop knew he'd lost the plot. When he'd found a box of sealed condoms in the drawer where he'd always kept them, he'd sent up a prayer of thanks then had plowed on. He'd expected Laura to have ditched the contraceptives long ago, but like the wedding photo and rings, she'd left them alone. Because she couldn't bear to touch them? Because she'd secretly wished for her husband back?

Hell, at this precise moment in time, he was way too pumped to wonder.

He'd succumbed to Laura's wiles and, God help him, he couldn't regret it. Particularly now as his mouth trailed an unerring course over her flat stomach and lower. When he reached those soft, moist curls, his brain stopped working altogether.

While her hips slowly rotated, he nuzzled down. After dropping a few barely there kisses on her inner thighs, he got more comfortable and, using his fingers and his tongue, exposed more of her. Her sigh of pure pleasure heightened his own, and as he made love to her with his mouth—with everything he was or had ever been—he understood that this time was beyond compare. Because it was forbidden? Or because they'd denied each other for too long? He only knew she'd never tasted sweeter and his desire for her had never been stronger.

It seemed like he'd only begun when he sensed the intensity building inside of her. Wanting to give her an experience without equal, he held her hips while his mouth covered her and he did what he knew she liked best. Her spine pushed down and she trembled, barely noticeably at first. But as the rolls of energy grew, she began to shudder and moan.

He stayed with her, adoring her fingers bunched in his hair and the series of contractions that urged him not to stop. When she was still floating down, he moved away just enough to open that foil wrapper and rolled down their protection.

When he joined her again, her eyes were closed, her head was slanted to one side and a fan of fair hair was flung over her face. Sighing, she clung to him as he eased in.

With one arm curled over her head, he gazed down at her face, more beautiful than any woman's alive. As he moved above her, found just the right rhythm, he wanted to tell himself to go slow. Make this last. Tomorrow he might not be welcome in Laura's life much less her bed.

As the heat of the inferno licking through his veins intensified, so too did his pace. Still, as his lips traced down her cheek and he stole another penetrating kiss, he was certain he could hold out. This was simply too good to let go yet. But then she quieted and a heartbeat later bucked beneath him, peaking again and riding another orgasmic curl. The push was too much.

Murmuring her name, concentrating on the delicious burn and how glorious she felt surrounding him, he drove in again and jumped off into the firestorm that consumed him inside and out. As white-hot flames swirled though him, Bishop held on tighter and for the first time hoped she didn't remember too soon.

The next morning Bishop sat on the eastern porch, gazing blindly out over the hills, listening to the early morning laughter of kookaburras and wondering what the hell had possessed him last night.

What had he been thinking? Sleeping with Laura once had been a bad idea. Sleeping with her again, and again, had to be moronic. Sure, it'd felt great. Unbelievably fantastic! But that wouldn't save him when her memory returned and she demanded to know why he'd taken advantage of the situation like he had. Never mind that she'd as good as drugged him with her words and her touches and her smiles. When the real Laura returned she wouldn't listen to a word of it. *That* Laura wasn't in love.

No more than he was.

Nothing could obliterate the words they'd exchanged during their roughest patch. The things they'd said to each other would crush the worthiest of loves. It had certainly killed his.

But love aside, clearly he still had feelings for her. He was still smitten by her scent, her voice, the cute sway of her hips whenever she walked. Laura affected him at his most basic primal level. Even when he'd sworn he never wanted to clap eyes on her again, he'd been on the verge of forcing her to hush by kissing her senseless. There'd been a time after they'd split when he thought he never wanted to sleep with another woman, the tough times had affected him that much. Truth was, until last night, he hadn't broken the drought. Although, he'd been heading that way with Annabelle.

His elbow on the outside chair armrest, he held his brow and rubbed his temple.

What was he going to do about that? He and Annabelle weren't in a relationship, as such. They'd seen each other a few times. They seemed to like the same things, got each other's humor and respected each other's space. But after what had happened between him and Laura last night…

His hand dropping from his brow, he blew out a breath.

Clearly, he wasn't anywhere near ready to even think about getting involved with Annabelle or any other woman.

Shifting his hip, he dug the cell out of his back pocket. A moment later the recipient's soft voice drifted down the line.

He straightened in his chair. "Annabelle. It's Samuel."

"Sam? I was hoping you'd phone this weekend. You've been busy?"

"You could say that."

As usual, she was understanding. "There's still most of Sunday left."

He cursed himself. He'd never felt more like a heel, but there was no way around it.

"Look, this is probably not a conversation we should have over the phone. But…" His gaze wandered over the bush, the gazebo, the setting that used to be so much a part of his life and seemed to be again for however long. "I'm afraid this can't wait."

"Something's wrong?"

"I told you I'd been married."

"Yes…you said it ended badly."

"Thing is, Laura, my ex, had an accident Friday."

He imagined Annabelle's long dark lashes batting as she took that in and then her eyes widening as she made a likely assumption. "You're with her now?"

"I took her home from the hospital."

"You're…patching things up?"

"It's complicated." He rubbed his brow. *Really, really complicated.*

"But you're together?" Her tone was less fragile now.

He answered as honestly as he could. In a sense… "Yes."

He waited as Annabelle no doubt composed herself. But she sounded calm when she spoke. Understanding, even. She'd make someone a great wife someday.

"Then I guess there's nothing more to say."

"Except, I'm sorry."

"Can I ask you not to lose my number, you know, in case things don't work out?"

"Sure. I'll do that."

But as he hung up, Bishop knew he wouldn't contact Annabelle again. Not because things would work out between him and Laura; he was damn close to certain it wouldn't. But because if they saw each other again, Annabelle would always wonder whether he was thinking about his ex. If he were in her position he might do the same.

Besides, Annabelle deserved someone who could offer

her a future and Bishop hadn't been after commitment even
before Friday's incident.

And so another short chapter in his life was closed, while
the case of the amnesiac ex was still wide-open.

As he slotted the phone away, his nose picked up on an
aroma that came from the kitchen. Butter melting in a pan.

It was Sunday. Tradition decreed they have brunch on this
porch. Hash browns and bacon, pancakes and maple syrup,
or their old favorite, eggs Benedict? No matter which, from
experience he knew the meal would be mouth-watering.

Bishop moved inside, thinking how easy it'd be to slip back
into this lifestyle...*if* Laura remained this Laura and they
could work their issues out. But it was dangerous to think
that way. Yes, he'd had the best sex *ever* last night with his ex.
He knew no complaints would be coming from her quarter.
But relationships were about a whole lot more than physical
attraction and sexual gratification. If he'd understood that
over two years ago, he'd have held off asking Laura to marry
him.

He hated to admit it, but snooty Grace was right. He'd
fallen in love so hard and so fast he hadn't spared the time to
think things through. Amazing, given his stellar track record
regarding decision making.

He moved down the hall and as that delicious hot butter
smell grew, so did his concern.

In sleeping with Laura last night he'd set a precedent. This
afternoon they were off to Sydney, and she would expect
them to make love again tonight. And he couldn't deny that
he wanted to do just that. More to the point, if she didn't get
her memory back between now and then, he knew that he
would.

Seven

"Sam Bishop? Is that you?"

In response to the male voice at their backs, Laura pulled up at the same time Bishop swung around. A smile breaking on his face, Bishop offered his hand to the jovial-looking man striding up.

"Robert Harrington." Bishop shook the man's hand. "It's been a while."

Mr. Harrington, a rotund man in an extralarge dinner suit, arched a wry brow. "Enjoying the ballet, son?"

Bishop tugged an ear. "It's…lively."

The man chuckled as if to say he understood. Obviously, Robert Harrington wasn't a *Swan Lake* fan, either.

Earlier, on the heels of their Sunday morning eggs Benedict tradition, she and Bishop had journeyed to Sydney and, after strolling around the Rocks, one of Sydney's most historic harbor-side suburbs, had checked into their Darling Harbor residence, a five-star-hotel three-bedroom penthouse Bishop used if business kept him in the city during the week. Soaking up the sunshine on the balcony and watching the boat activity on the sparkling blue waters below had absorbed the rest of their lazy afternoon. They'd arrived at the Opera House with barely enough time to be seated. Five minutes ago they'd joined the rest of the Opera Theater's glittering crowd to partake of refreshments during intermission.

Their seats could have been better, but Laura wouldn't complain. It was the thrill of the experience she adored. Her mother had introduced her to the theater, in all its guises, at an early age. She'd dreamed of perfecting pointe work and pirouettes and one day starring in the Australian Ballet. But professional ballerinas were superb athletes; heart conditions, even mild ones, weren't the norm. So Laura, along with Grace on occasion, had been content to enjoy a number of magical performances as enthusiastic spectators.

Laura wished Bishop shared her love of the art form, but she was only grateful he hadn't bleated on about coming along; a lot of men might suggest their wives take a friend while they chilled out at a football match or poker game. But Bishop was one of the most supportive people she'd ever known.

That's why she was certain they could work out this difference regarding how to start their family. When he truly understood how important having her own child was to her—when he evaluated the risks from a less, well, paranoid point of view—he would come around. He'd support her, as he always had. This time next year, they might even be singing lullabies to their firstborn.

Boy or girl, she'd be beyond happy with either. Or both.

Laura put those thoughts aside as she smiled a greeting at this middle-aged couple. Wherever they went, it seemed Bishop bumped into someone he knew. Why should a night at the Opera House be any different?

"You haven't met my wife." Robert Harrington turned to a lithe, graceful-looking woman. "Shontelle, this is Samuel Bishop. We had business dealings a year back."

"Pleased to meet you, Samuel." Shontelle's pearl-and-diamond necklace sparkled under the lights as the chattering crowd wove around them. Laura waited. Bishop was usually prompt with introductions but, for once, he missed a beat.

Taking the initiative, she introduced herself. "Pleased to meet you, Robert, Shontelle. I'm Laura."

While Shontelle returned the greeting, Robert scratched his receding hairline. "Laura... Sam, wasn't that your wife's name?"

Her cheeks pinking up, Shontelle delivered her husband's ribs a silencing nudge.

But Laura only laughed. "Not was. *Is.*"

Robert's eyebrows shot up and his smile returned. "Well, that's great." He clapped Bishop's tuxedo-clad shoulder heartily. "Great to see you together."

The two couples bantered on a few minutes more, then went their separate ways. She and Bishop found a relatively quiet corner in the bustling room, away from the heart of the glitter and constant clink of glasses.

Laura spoke over the rim of her champagne flute before she sipped. "That was strange."

"Strange?"

She imitated Robert Harrington's baritone. "*Wasn't that your wife's name?* Didn't you think that was odd?"

Bishop raised his glass in a salute. "Guess we should get out more often."

"You know what else is strange? I've lost weight. I've been the same weight for years but now this dress is big on me."

"It looks beautiful on you. You probably just haven't worn it for a while."

She examined the fall of her red evening dress. The bodice was highlighted by black lace inlays and the back decorated with multiple ribbon crisscross ties, which she'd drawn tightly to compensate for her leaner figure.

"I wore it a month ago to that business dinner in Melbourne, remember?"

His chin lifted the barest amount. She could have sworn his eyes narrowed as his gaze roamed her face.

"What else do you remember?"

He hadn't finished the sentence before that northern foot-bridge flashed to mind. Then she remembered the hospital, thinking that she was pregnant. She remembered the doctor, the test, the tears—

Laura sucked back a quick breath then, blinking into her champagne flute, frowned.

There hadn't been any tears. She'd been disappointed that the pregnancy test was negative, but also grateful she hadn't risked a baby's well-being when she'd taken her tumble. She remembered being so happy to see her husband and wondering at his odd behavior…that Bishop hadn't come and embraced her straight away. It had taken a little while for him to thaw, even when they'd gotten home. But last night, he'd been as loving as ever.

So why this gnawing, niggling feeling at the back of her brain all of a sudden? A wavering sense that something, somewhere, between them was missing? Robert Harrington's curious comment hadn't helped.

Wasn't that your wife's name?

"Laura, are you okay?"

Bishop's deep voice hauled her back. He was looking at her intently, his brows drawn. And the bell was ringing, calling them back to their seats. Feeling off balance, she slid her flute onto a nearby ledge.

Was she okay?

Willing the faint dizziness away, she pinned up her smile. "Absolutely fine. I'm looking forward to seeing the rest of the ballet."

As they moved back through the crowd, the bell ringing low and persistent, Bishop threaded his jacketed arm through hers. She always felt so proud walking beside him. People noticed her husband—not only his movie star looks, but that unconscious quality that radiated off him like crackling heat off a fire…a vibrant warmth that was inviting and yet also potentially dangerous. Instinct told people you didn't want to get on the wrong side of Samuel Bishop. Not that *they* would ever be on opposing sides. Their difference of opinion on how to start a family didn't count. As she'd told Grace, they'd work that out.

"You didn't have much for dinner," he said as they climbed the carpeted stairs behind the slow-shifting throng. "We'll order some supper when we get in."

One part of her wanted to go straight back to the apartment, make love and then order a cheese platter and a fruity wine to savor throughout the night. Another part wanted to eke out as much of this dazzling evening as she could. Bishop was right. They did need to get out more.

"Let's walk back to the apartment," she suggested as they arrived at their gate. "We can stop for a bite on the way."

He flicked a suspect glance at her red high heels. "In those shoes?"

Teasing, she bumped her hip to his. "These shoes deserve to be shown off."

The corners of his eyes crinkled as he smiled, the bell stopped ringing and the theater lights dimmed. "Then shown off they shall be."

Laura didn't want to tell Bishop she hadn't remembered buying the shoes…like that handbag…like forgetting she'd slipped off her rings before Grace had driven her to hospital. In hindsight, she probably shouldn't have mentioned she thought she'd lost weight. But they were trivial bits and pieces that would filter back in time. And when they did, no doubt this annoying niggling—that *there's something missing feeling*—would up and fly away.

After the curtain had dropped and thunderous applause faded, he and Laura left the theater to stroll down the many Opera House steps, then along the boardwalk.

The night was mild and still bubbling with life—buskers strumming, tourists milling, night owls taking advantage of the round-the-clock restaurants. Laura was praising the prima ballerina's performance in the last act when Bishop's step slowed out front of an open-air café. Cozy tables dotted a timber deck that overlooked dark harbor waters awash with milky ribbons of moonlight. The coffee smelled out-of-this-world good.

"How are the heels holding up?" he asked. "Your feet need a rest?"

"I vote chocolate cheesecake."

His gaze flicked from the dessert display window to her knowing eyes, and he laughed softly. She was well aware of his sweet tooth and he was aware of hers.

"With two scoops of ice cream?" he suggested.

Her hand in his, she tugged him toward the tables. "Done."

He pulled out a chair for her by a roped railing, and a waitress took their orders.

"What time do you have to be at work tomorrow?" Laura asked casually as she skimmed the ballet's keepsake program for the tenth time. But despite the casual tone, Bishop knew she was already wishing the morning away. He'd worked long hours when they'd been married. Still did. She'd always dreaded Monday mornings when he left her to travel to his office in the city.

"Actually, I'm having a couple of days off."

Her eyes popped. "You *never* have time off."

"I'm sure I had time off for our honeymoon." A glorious week cruising the Greek islands. Santorini, Mykonos. The days had been brilliant. The nights were even better.

"Honeymoons are compulsory as far as vacations are concerned." Her finger, trailing his left jacket sleeve, ended its journey by circling that shiny gold band. Her voice took on a note of doubt. "Are you sure the company's not in any trouble?"

"If it were, I'd be chained to my desk." He poured two

glasses from the water carafe. "Trust me, Bishop Scaffolds is stronger than ever."

The worry, pinching her brows, eased and she raised her water glass. "Well, then, here's to a good long sleep in."

While she sighed over how romantic the twinkling bridge looked with a full yellow moon crowning its arch, Bishop made a mental note to text Willis; the boss wouldn't be in until at least Tuesday. From there he'd take each day as it came. Willis was more than competent to handle the day-to-day grind. As for the parties who were inquiring about purchasing the company...

Bishop flicked out his napkin as the cake arrived.

If the potential buyers were keen, they'd wait a few days.

They'd each enjoyed a first succulent taste of slow baked heaven when an elderly gentleman sporting an olive green beret presented himself with a flourishing bow at their table. He carried a battered easel. Two pencils sat balanced behind one ear.

"Would your wife care for a portrait?" the gentleman asked with a heavy French accent.

Bishop smiled dismissively. He liked his privacy.

"I don't think—"

"She'd *love* one," Laura piped up, before sucking chocolate sauce off her thumb and sitting straighter. "She'd love one of the both of us."

Out the side of his mouth, Bishop countered, "Do you really feel like posing for half an hour?"

"No posing," Frenchie said, flicking out his squeaky easel and wedging the legs into the planks. "Eat, talk. Reminisce. While I—" he whipped a pencil out with a magician's finesse "—*create*."

"I know what we can reminisce about." Laura's foot under the table curled around his pant leg. Bishop imagined her red painted toes as they slid up his calf. "Those amazing days we spent together sailing the Aegean."

He angled slightly down. Out of sight, his hand caught her foot and he tickled her instep. "How about that unbelievable night on Naxos?"

"Please, please. Sit closer." Frenchie feathered a pencil over the paper then stepped back to inspect his work so far. "This, I know, will be *magnifique*."

Bishop reveled in the sweetness of chocolate and honey vanilla while listening to Laura's recollections of their honeymoon…what they'd eaten and when, the people they'd met, their private dance on their private balcony in the moonlight that last night. Curious that she'd forgotten their divorce yet could remember every sensual detail of the time directly after their wedding as if it were yesterday. While the Mediterranean breeze and their lovemaking had kept them warm, she'd whispered in his ear and made him promise to take her on a cruise every year.

In between mouthfuls of cake, they talked and laughed. Bishop was so engrossed in their memories of Greece that he'd almost forgotten about the portrait until Frenchie set aside his pencil and announced, "It is done!"

Now, in the shadow of the Opera House's enormous shells, he dragged himself back to the present and reached for his inside jacket pocket.

"How much do I owe?"

Frenchie waved a blasé hand. "Your choice." Then, obviously proud, he pivoted the easel around.

Laura's hands went to her mouth as she gasped. "Oh, Bishop, it's *perfect*."

Bishop had to agree. It captured not only their images but the gay atmosphere of the night as well as their obvious affection for each other. It was like looking back in time.

"It was a pleasure to work with a couple so very much in love." Frenchie beamed.

Laura's eyes glittered in the flickering candlelight. "Does it show?"

"Like a comet," Frenchie enthused with a grand sweeping gesture, "illuminating a velvet night sky."

Laura's expression melted and Bishop slid out a large bill. Frenchie might be a bit of a poet, but his description wasn't much of an exaggeration. That's how they must appear to others tonight. Head-over-heels newlyweds in love. While they'd talked and shared desserts it had felt that way, too. He would've liked nothing better to have sat here, like this, all night.

By the time they finished up, it was late, so Bishop hailed a cab and her feet in their gorgeous heels got to rest.

As they crossed beneath the crystal chandelier of their hotel's grand marble foyer, the efficient-looking concierge—a different man from the one earlier today—glanced up from checking something behind his desk. A big grin etched across his face and he fairly clicked his heels.

On their way to the lifts, Laura commented, "Very friendly staff they have here. You should tip that guy for that special welcome home."

His step faltered the barest amount before he slid over a smile. "It's because you look stunning tonight." With the portrait in its cardboard sheath under his arm, Bishop stopped before the bank of lifts and thumbed a key. "You're glowing."

The lift arrived and she moved inside, smiling at his compliment, but deep down holding herself against a faint stab. *Glowing* was a term often bestowed upon pregnant women. Before that doctor at the hospital on Friday had informed her that she was mistaken—that she wasn't pregnant—she'd actually *felt* as if she were glowing, even with that scrape and bump on her head.

But she could well be glowing tonight. They'd had a wonderful evening out, and with Bishop playing hooky from office duties tomorrow, there were many more hours of "wonderful" ahead.

As the car whirred up to the penthouse floor, she leaned on Bishop to balance as she eased off one four-inch heel then the other.

Bishop took note. "You've shown them off enough for one night?"

Performing, she twirled a shoe around her finger. "Oh, this is only the beginning."

His brows hitched and pupils dilated until the crystalline blue of his eyes was near swallowed by black. When the metallic door slid open, she sashayed out ahead, sandals draped provocatively over one shoulder. She heard his footfalls on the marble tiles behind her.

"Guess you're not tired," he said.

"You guessed right."

They entered the suite, a vast cream, black and crimson expanse, furnished with clean lines and minimalist finesse. She cast her shoes aside. Unable to hold back a moment longer, she coiled her arms around his neck and tipped her mouth up to meet his.

The ballet had kept her occupied earlier, but when they'd sat by those sparkling harbor waters tonight, eating their cake and reliving those fantastic few days abroad after their wedding, there were times Laura had needed to bunch her hand in her lap to divert the energy she'd felt pulling her toward him. It was as if she were hooked on an invisible line and desperately wanting to be wound in…to let him kiss her with all the heat of emotion both their hearts could give.

In the cab home, crossing the hotel foyer, riding the lift, she'd wanted to do exactly this…let him know with a touch of her hand, the stroke of her tongue, that she couldn't live without him. With his breathing deepening now, his bristled chin grazing rhythmically against her cheek and his arms locked around her, the hot need inside of her only grew. Like a bulb without spring sunshine, she could survive without Bishop, but she would never know such true warmth.

Such real love.

That would never change. No matter what challenges they faced, they would always have this. An insatiable, natural need to be close.

When he grudgingly released her, her heart was pounding so hard that the vibration hummed through her body all the way to her fingers and toes. Her hand filed up through the back of his hair as she breathed in the glorious scent he left on his pillow each morning.

"Know what I want to do?"

"How many guesses do I get?" His voice was low and husky with desire, his eyes lidded with want.

"How many do you need?"

"I'll take one."

Her palms splayed over the broad ledge of his jacketed shoulders as she pressed in against him. "What if you're wrong?"

A lazy grin hooked one side of his mouth. "I'm not wrong."

"So I don't need to give you a hint?"

That lazy grin widened. "Hints are always welcome."

"Well, then, first we need to take this off."

She dipped beneath his lapels and scooped the jacket off his shoulders. His lidded eyes holding hers, he tossed the coat aside. She assumed a speculative look as her palms ironed up the steamy front of his shirt.

"And that tie needs to go, too," she decided, tugging the black length free from beneath its collar.

Bishop asked, "What about cuff links?"

"Cuff links are definitely out."

He managed the links while she saw to his dress shirt studs. When the last button was released, her touch fanned the steely ruts of his naked abdomen then arced up through the dark, coarse hair on his chest. She let out a sigh as her nails trailed his pecs before catching the shirt and peeling the sleeves slowly down.

Anticipating the moment, she quivered inside as she lightly pressed her lips below the hollow of his throat; the pulse she found there matched the throb tripping a delicious beat at her core. A cord ran down one side of his tanned neck. When the tip of her tongue tasted a trail up the salty ridge, his erection, behind its zipper, grew and pushed against her belly. Growing warmer by the second, she blew a gentle stream of air against the trail her tongue had left.

"Do you remember what we were wearing on the balcony that night on the ship?"

His hands were kneading her behind, rotating her hips to fit against his as he attentively nipped the shell of her ear.

"I remember what we *weren't* wearing." Cooler air brushed her back as he tugged on a ribboned bow and her bodice loosened. "Would you like to slow dance on this balcony tonight?"

Sighing, she ground against him. "I thought you'd never ask."

A knock sounded at the door, then a call. "Room service!"

Laura's stomach jumped while Bishop's chin went down. He searched her eyes.

"We haven't ordered anything, have we?"

"It's a mistake." Slipping back into the mood, she wove a hand up over the hot dome of one shoulder. "Ignore it."

"It might be important."

"Not as important as this."

Falling back into the magic, she drew his head down and kissed him more thoroughly than the first time.

But the call came again. "Mr. Bishop, room service, sir."

Groaning, Bishop unraveled her arms and headed for the

door. "Remind me to hang the sign up as soon as he's gone. *Do. Not. Disturb.*"

A bellboy with a sun-bleached surfer's mop stood behind the door. He didn't raise a brow at Bishop's state of half dress but merely handed over a shiny silver bucket, its sides frosty and the well filled with an impressive-looking bottle as well as two chilling glasses.

"Compliments of the house, sir," the young man said, then spun on his spit-polished heel with a cheerful, "Good night."

As Bishop hung the sign then closed the door, Laura crossed over and read the note, penned on hotel stationery.

"Welcome back, Mrs. Bishop." She shook off a laugh. "I was here just a couple of weeks ago, and a week before that." Staring at the note, she cast her mind back then set the note down on the teak hallstand ledge. "We should send this back. They've made some sort of mistake."

"Have they?"

She shot him a questioning look then shrugged. "There's no other explanation."

"Maybe there is."

As he held her gaze, she sent him a dry grin. "Then I'd like to hear it."

"Would you?"

Her jaw tightened and she crossed her arms. "Don't do that, Bishop."

"Do what?"

"*That.* Answer everything with a question."

As Bishop's eyes hardened—or was that glazed over?—an icy shiver chased up her spine. Feeling bad, *foolish,* she pressed her lips together. Her tone had been brittle. She hadn't meant it to be. It was just that...

Well, first there'd been that Robert Harrington and his odd comment, then the concierge's almost surprised reaction at seeing them, now this offering from the hotel management as if she'd been gone for years.

It didn't make sense.

But she was aware of the look on Bishop's face. Removed? Concerned? He thought she'd overreacted and he was right. Management had sent champagne. He was suggesting there was some good reason. Which was feasible. And unimportant. She was making more of this than she needed to. She was curious—puzzled—that's all.

Pasting on a smile, willing the flush from her cheeks, she nodded at the bottle.

"Either way, it's a nice gesture. We should thank them in the morning."

Bishop moved past and carefully set the bucket on the coffee table. If Laura thought she was confused, he hadn't a *clue* what he was doing or what he planned to do next.

Every step he'd taken since Friday afternoon had led to precisely this moment. Logical steps. Steps that had made sense at the time. Even making love last night. In his defense, he could put up a good argument for that. What man in his right mind could've refused? Particularly when it was this man with that woman.

When she'd waxed on tonight about how unbelievable their honeymoon had been, recreating all those images and feelings while they'd nibbled on cake, she'd accomplished something he would never have dreamed possible. She'd taken him back—*really* back—in time. He'd looked into her eyes, so animated and thirsty for life—for him—and, God help him, he'd only wanted to stay.

And that awareness made this situation—where they stood now—different than it had been last night, or this morning.

He hadn't wanted to force any recollections back too fast, too soon. He'd tread lightly, initially, because he hadn't known how to go about it, then because he'd liked to see her happy. Ultimately he'd liked feeling happy again, too.

He'd been very happy tonight.

Before the champagne had arrived, they'd been on the brink, about to make love again, and yet when she'd looked so frustrated and confused just now, he'd tried to force that memory door open again, and more than a crack. He'd pushed to try to make her remember. And he'd done it for a reason. A selfish reason.

If this happened—if they had sex, made love, came apart in each other's arms—he wanted it to be real. Maybe if she remembered the past, the ugly breakup, while she was feeling the way she did about him now, the anger and pain would pale enough for them to be able to work something out. That's all he'd ever wanted.

To work things out.

He folded down into the circular leather lounge, smoothed back his hair with both hands then found her eyes again.

"Laura, come here. We need to talk."

"About what?" She crossed and sat close to him, her beautiful face wan, her emerald eyes glistening with questions.

"We need to make an appointment."

"An appointment for what?"

"A follow-up. To get you checked out."

She blinked several times then tipped away. Even laughed a little. "I'm fine."

"Are you?" She went to object and he held up his hands. "Okay. No more questions. Except one. And I want you to think about it before you answer."

She searched his eyes and eventually nodded. "All right."

"At the hospital, you said you thought you were pregnant. It is possible you were mixed up? That maybe…"

Not wanting to say it but needing to, he exhaled and reached for her hand. Gripped it tight.

"That maybe you'd been pregnant before?"

Her expression cracked—half amused, half insulted. As if she'd been burned, she pried her hand away.

"That's ridiculous. For God's sake, Bishop, I'd know if I'd been pregnant before."

So adamant. *Too* adamant.

He swallowed against the ache blocking his throat. Out of anything he could have asked her—anything that would have set off a battery of alarm bells—that question had to have been it. And yet the only reaction he got was a disgusted look as if he'd called her a name. If he bit the bullet, went further and tried to explain about their discussions two years ago, how she'd been so happy with his decision to try to conceive, then ultimately so crushed...

Her eyes glistened more. A hint of panic hid behind the sheen. But her voice was hauntingly level when she spoke.

"Why are you looking at me like that?"

His midsection clenched and his gaze dropped away.

He'd had no illusions, but this was way harder than he'd thought. Near impossible.

He believed he'd asked the right question, but there was another. And now that he'd come this far, he had to ask it, for both their sakes.

After finding her gaze again, he lowered his voice. "Laura, how do you think you'd handle losing a child?"

She let out a breath. And smiled. Hell, she looked relieved.

"Is that what all this is about?" She leaned nearer and braced his thigh. "Nothing bad will happen. We have to believe that. I know everything will be all right. Have faith. Have faith in us." She squeezed his leg. "I do."

The emotion clogging his throat drifted higher and stung behind his nose. How could he respond to that? He had nothing. Then a crazy notion hit. So crazy, he wanted to laugh.

Wouldn't it be something if she fell pregnant again and this time everything worked out? If she didn't get her memory back, what man would convict him? She'd be happy. His soul would be redeemed. Or, if she fell pregnant before her memory returned, couldn't they work through to reinvent the happy ending they'd both deserved the first time around? Was that too crazy to hope for? Another chance?

Her hand left his thigh. "You mentioned something about a slow dance on the balcony."

Before he could respond, she stood and held out her hand. He looked at her for a long, tormented moment. There was no right or wrong. No win or lose. No way to predict how this would end. Or *if* it would.

His fingers curling around hers, he found his feet and led her out onto the balcony.

A cool harbor breeze filed through their hair as he cradled her close and she rested her cheek against his fast-beating heart. With the distant hum of traffic for music, he began to rock her gently around. After a few moments she murmured, so softly he barely heard.

"I love you, Bishop."

High in his gut that tight ball contracted more and time wound down to a standstill. The decision was instinctive.

He put aside the man he was now, the man whose heart had been mangled and who had vowed to never marry again. He tamped down the voice that said not to lie. That cried out what he planned was unforgivable. Instead, he assumed the mask of a man just three months married. A man who knew he should let go of the guilt over surviving his brother and forego the fear of "what ifs" in the womb and beyond. A man who wanted their own child as much as Laura did, no matter what.

No matter what.

He brushed the hair from her cheek, whispered her name then, willing himself to believe it, said, "I love you, too."

Eight

The next morning, in their Darling Harbor penthouse, Laura had trouble getting out of bed.

She wasn't sick. She'd never felt healthier. Or happier. After the hours she and Bishop had spent writhing in each other's arms, she only wanted to stay there, close to her incredible husband, soaking up his magnificent heat, reveling in the way he fulfilled her, each and every time. In the broader scheme of things, they hadn't known each other long, but she couldn't imagine these intense emotions ever waning. The texture of his hair, the sound of his rich, smooth voice, the intoxicating scent she inhaled whenever her nose brushed his chest.

She only hoped he never tired of her. She might have been dealt a bad card—her heart condition—but that was little or no problem now. And fate had more than compensated by gifting her the love of an extraordinary man like Samuel Bishop.

At around nine, while Bishop made some calls, she slid into the bathroom to shower. As she lathered her hair, she smiled, remembering how he'd mentioned during the night that he had a surprise for her this morning. It couldn't be jewelry. He'd already given her enough to weigh down a queen. Perhaps after their reminiscing, he was going to book another cruise.

Laura dried off, knowing that whatever he had planned

she would love. She wouldn't let her mind wander so far as to consider he might want to window-shop for baby things. Furniture, pink or blue jumpsuits, high chairs, stencils for a nursery wall. And she wanted to buy one of those faith, hope and love trinkets. She'd adored the idea of those symbols, and their meanings, since knowing a friend in primary school who had worn around her neck on a thin gold chain. If she and Bishop had a girl, the heart, anchor and cross would go onto a bracelet; if a boy, she'd attach them to the cot.

Laura stopped to gaze at her pensive reflection in the fogged up mirror.

With so much to organize, perhaps they *should* start looking now.

But as she slipped the light butter-colored dress over her head, Laura berated herself. They hadn't agreed to fall pregnant. Not yet. It was an important and delicate matter, one they both felt strongly about. Still, perhaps she ought to bring it up again sometime today. Logically, she knew they had oodles of time to start a family; she was young and, at thirty, so was he. But that didn't quell the awareness she felt building every day. More and more she noticed mothers with prams, baby commercials on TV, schools and parks with swings and kids laughing and chasing each other around like mad things.

After applying a lick of mascara and lip gloss, she set a brush to her towel-dried hair. Her thoughts wandered more, to places they'd never traveled before, and the brush strokes petered out.

Frowning at her reflection, she shook her head. No. She would never do it. Even if there were a way. Bishop used protection; his nature was to be cautious, to think before he leaped. Still…

How would he react if she accidentally fell pregnant? Last week she'd honestly believed that she had. She hadn't planned it. Starting a family was a decision both people in a relationship needed to agree upon.

She started brushing again.

Definitely not. She would never intentionally, accidentally fall pregnant. Bishop would come around soon enough and then they could both go into this next important phase of their lives confident and with a clear conscience.

When she emerged from the bedroom, she found Bishop standing by the wall-to-wall windows that overlooked Darling Harbor's sun-kissed sights. But he wasn't interested in the view…traffic on the water, the busy restaurants, the fanfare facade of the Maritime Museum. Bishop being Bishop, he was still on the phone.

He caught sight of her, smiled, then obviously needing to concentrate, angled a little away. After the dinner suit he'd worn last night, those dark blue jeans, zipper at half-mast, were a different but still ultra-sexy look. No doubt he'd team it with a brand-name polo shirt. But for her part, she could gobble up the sight of that magnificently sculpted chest all day long. Every drool-worthy muscle was perfectly defined. The angle of those quarterback shoulders might have been crafted by Michelangelo.

He often stood with his weight favoring one leg. That unconscious pose now, in those heaven-sent jeans, gave him a too-hot-to-handle, rebel's air that left her mouth dry. Still focused on the call, he shoveled a hand through his shower damp black hair and Laura's pelvic floor muscles squeezed around a particularly pleasant pulse. With his fingers lodged in his hair, that bicep on display…

Laura fought not to fan herself. She only wished she had a camera to capture the moment and remember exactly how heart-poundingly handsome he was right now.

He disconnected and swung back to face her. Graceful, fluid… He didn't *walk* so much as *prowl*. And the quiet throb, ticking at every erogenous zone in her body, said she wanted very badly to be caught.

Joining her, he dropped a kiss on the side of her neck and lingered to hum appreciatively against her throat.

"You smell almost too good to eat."

Smiling, she dissolved against him. "*Almost* too good?"

His big hands measured her waist then slid higher. They didn't stop until long lean fingers were splashed over her back and a thumb rested beneath the fall of each breast. His head angled more. She shivered uncontrollably as his teeth nipped the sensitive sweep of her throat. The pads of his thumbs grazed her nipples as he murmured, low and deep, against her skin.

"You heard me."

That syrupy I-can't-get-enough-of-you feeling sizzled like sparking gunpowder through her system. Her knees threatened to buckle and her lungs labored, unable to get enough air. When her hand drove up his arm, over the sinewy rock of one shoulder, her eyes drifting closed, she sighed as he nipped and his morning beard grazed.

"Are you suggesting we stay in today?" she asked, sounding drugged and feeling that way, too.

"I'm saying you can make me lose my mind."

"That can't be a bad thing."

His face tipped up. His eyes were so hooded, she could barely see the blue.

He blinked once then asked, "Promise?"

She laughed. It was meant to be light, but he'd said that word with such earnestness…she wasn't certain how to respond.

For once too overwhelmed by his intensity, she touched a kiss to his cheek and, winding out of his hold, moved to the galley kitchen. There were times she felt completely consumed by him. That wasn't a complaint, but she wondered whether another woman might be able to handle his brute magnetism better. She didn't see his innate power ever diminishing.

She didn't want it to.

"I had blueberry pancakes sent up," he said, reaching for a casual shirt resting on the back of the lounge.

Her gaze darted to the meals area and her previously distracted senses picked up on the smell. Feeling guilty after that slab of cheesecake last night, she held her stomach.

"You're trying to make me fat."

"Fat, thin…" He strolled to the table to remove the silver dome. "I'll take you any way you come."

Inhaling again, eyeing the fluffy discs dotted with berries and dusted with icing sugar, she conceded. She had lost some weight, after all.

Joining him, she collected a fork, cut a portion off the top offering and slid the cake into her mouth. She chewed slowly, savoring the divine butter and fruit textures and flavors. Swallowing, she groaned with appreciation as well as disappointment.

"I wish mine turned out as good as this."

"Have I ever complained about your cooking?"

She gave a coy grin. "Never."

"The benefit with room service is…" He curled over her and stole a kiss from her ice-sugared lips. "More time for us."

More than tempted, she touched her lips where he'd tasted hers as she sliced off a little more cake. "You really do want to stay in, don't you?"

"That's a given. But there's also that surprise I had planned."

Her mouth was full again but, needing to know, she talked almost incoherently around it. "Wha ith it?"

He laughed and pulled out her chair. "Finish your breakfast and you'll find out."

* * *

Ten minutes later, he and Laura were walking through the hotel lobby. He had the ticket out, ready for the concierge to retrieve his car, when he recognized a figure standing in front of the lofty automatic glass doors.

Bishop's step faltered.

What was Willis doing here?

When his second-in-charge recognized him too, he waved and came forward. Bishop slid a sidelong glance at Laura. He and Willis were friends. Willis knew he'd been married and how badly it had ended. But he didn't want to explain this to the younger man here or now.

As Willis joined them, Bishop made succinct introductions. "Willis McKee, this is Laura."

Willis took her hand. "Pleased to meet you."

"Bishop tells me you're his new assistant," Laura inquired.

Willis cocked a brow. "I wouldn't have said *new*."

"Willis and I have known each other a while now," Bishop chipped in. "Laura, can you excuse us for a minute?" Taking Willis's elbow, he led him off to a quiet corner.

When they were alone, Bishop's no-problem exterior cracked. He never had a day off. Now he was being hounded by the man he knew could handle the job, and for more than twenty-four hours. Nothing could be this important.

"What are you doing here?"

"You didn't answer your phone or emails last night," Willis replied, no sign of a tail between his legs. "And these guys are keen, Sam. Dead keen. They've been on the phone yesterday and already this morning. They want to look at the books as soon as possible." Willis's eyes narrowed and he crossed his arms. "You're still interested, right? I mean, I understand—" he flicked a glance Laura's way "—you're busy. But *Laura?* I thought you were seeing an Annabelle."

"Laura's my wife. Ex-wife to be precise."

Willis's jaw hit the ground. "Your *what?* From what you'd told me, I got the impression there was more chance of a blizzard descending on the Simpson than you two getting back together."

Bishop rubbed the back of his neck. "Yeah, well, it's complicated."

"If you don't mind me saying, the vibes I get are more of the plain and simple variety."

"Laura had an accident Friday," he explained. "That's why I left early."

Willis took another longer look. "She seems fine now."

"She's great…except for the fact that two years of her life have been erased."

Willis took a moment. "You mean amnesia? And she thinks you and she…" Groaning, Willis held his brow. "Oh, man."

Bishop nodded. "Complicated."

"What're you going to do?"

"I went along at first because I didn't have much choice. Laura thought we were still married. The doctor said if I kept a close eye on her, she could go home. So we spent some time together, and as the hours and days went on…" He rolled back his shoulders, forming the words carefully in his mind before uttering a one. "I'm wondering whether we might not be able to save what we had."

Bishop respected this man; they were friends, but this was extremely private. Should he have been this open? It wasn't usually his style. Still, now the words were out, he knew he'd needed to say them out loud. Maybe then he'd be able to see how ridiculous this all was.

"Save your marriage?" Willis's hands dug into his pockets. "That would be if she remembers, or if she doesn't?"

"That part's a little up in the air."

"It's none of my business, and you probably don't need me to tell you, but you should tread carefully. If you decide to go that way, the road will be full of potholes, deep and wide."

Bishop grunted. *No kidding.*

"I'm going to book her in to see a neurologist midweek. See what can be done. In the meantime—"

"You have a beautiful bride who's all doe-eyed for you, but deep down hates your guts. Talk about being between a rock and a hard place. What a temptation."

Feeling his gills heat up, Bishop lowered his gaze and shuffled his feet.

Willis did a double take, then swore. "Oh, no...Sam, you *haven't.* She locked you out a year ago and now that she can't remember the bad times, you've *slept* with her?"

Bishop growled, "I don't need anyone beating on my conscience about it." His tone dropped. "I've been doing enough of that myself."

"Look on the bright side. Things couldn't get any worse the second time around."

"At least I know what to expect."

"With a woman?" Willis coughed out a laugh. "You're fooling yourself." He drew up to his full height and got back on track. "What do you want me to do about those buyers?"

"Tell them I'm unavailable. We'll get back to them later in the week." He'd thought he was ready to sell. Move on. Now he wasn't so sure. He did know that he didn't want any reminders of his failed marriage, and every time he walked into that office, talked to his team or went on location, he remembered how he'd buried himself in his work during those hard times. In truth, perhaps those memories had more to do with his desire to sell than feeling stale at work.

Either way, he didn't need to make a snap decision. He'd see how he felt in a day or two—in a week—about everything and decide then.

They returned to Laura, and Willis nodded his farewell. "Good meeting you, Mrs. Bishop."

"You'll have to come up to our place in the mountains for dinner one evening," she said. "Bring your wife, of course."

"I'm sure she'd like that. She loves the mountains."

Laura beamed. "Me, too." She looked to Bishop then back at Willis. "Why don't we make it this weekend?"

"This weekend we're having that get-together for my birthday, remember—" Willis stopped.

Bishop was glaring at him.

She's not ready for big groups yet.

The consummate hostess, Laura patched up the awkward moment. "Oh, well, if you have a party on, we'll make it another time."

Bishop quietly exhaled. Ah, what the hell. It would either be a disaster with everyone asking the wrong questions, or they'd have a great time. If her memory returned before then, it'd be a moot point.

"We're invited, Laura." He shrugged, offered a smile. "It slipped my mind."

Laura's eyes lit up. "That's wonderful." She spoke to Willis. "I suppose I'll see you next week then."

"I know my wife will enjoy meeting you." Turning to the doors, Willis sent Bishop a wink. "We'll talk."

He and Laura headed for the concierge's desk. The fellow from last night, Herb, was still on. After the ticket was handed over and pleasantries exchanged, he asked, "Did you receive the champagne?"

Laura spoke for them both. "That was so thoughtful. And unnecessary. But thank you so much."

"You were always so kind, Mrs. Bishop," the older man said. "It's good to have you back."

Looking touched as well as bemused, Laura patted her hair uncertainly then tacked up her smile. "It's good to be back."

They headed out through the doors and, between two soaring forecourt columns, waited for his car to arrive. Hanging on tenterhooks, Bishop knew Laura would mention Herb's comment. *Good to have you back.* She might think it was weird, but Herb hadn't seen Laura in eighteen months, and yes, she had always been kind. She was kind to everyone. The last months of their marriage, with regard to him, didn't count.

But rather than Herb, Laura brought up that other subject.

"Was Willis here about the sale of the company?"

"Yes, he was."

"So you're going in to the office later today?"

"No."

Her eyes rounded as she turned to him. "You're still taking the day off to be with me?"

She looked so innocent, so radiant, he couldn't help but smile. "Don't sound so amazed."

Clearly self-conscious now, she bowed her head. "I know you love me—" she met his eyes again "—but I never imagined you'd take time off when you have such important business to sort out."

The car rolled up. He opened the passenger-side door, thinking that he would never have imagined it, either. What an eye-opener. He hadn't analyzed the dichotomy before, but it was true. He *had* put business first. When they'd been married, the company was still climbing and he'd had no choice but to put in the hard yards. Or that's what he'd told himself. Truth was when things started to slide between him and Laura, he'd hid behind his job, used it as an excuse not to face his problems at home.

He slid in behind the wheel.

How often had he said to himself, *If I had my time again?* Now it seemed he had.

Thirty minutes later, the car slowed down and Laura brought the dented fingernail out from between her teeth.

"I'm nervous."

Bishop swung the Land Rover to the curb. "If you don't like any of them, we're under no obligation."

"I'm worried I'll like them *all*. What do you think? A girl or a boy?"

The engine shut down. "Your choice."

"A girl, I think. Maybe we could get a friend for her later on."

"I'd better watch out or we'll be taking all four home."

On the drive, Bishop had let the cat—or dog, as it happened—out of the bag. Laura had been beside herself, she was so excited to be actually looking at puppies. Now, as a tall, wiry lady answered the door of a pristine suburban cottage, Laura held Bishop's hand tight. The woman introduced herself as Sandra Knightly then ushered them around the back to where a silky coated retriever lay in a comfortable enclosure, nursing four adorable pups.

"As I told you on the phone earlier, Mr. Bishop," Sandra said, "we have three males, one female."

Besotted already, Laura hunkered down. "Only one girl?"

"Right there." Sandra pointed out the smallest. "She's the quiet one. They're six weeks old. They'll be ready to go to their new homes in a couple of weeks."

"Will their mother miss them when they go?" Laura asked.

"Think of it as your own children leaving for college," Sandra replied.

"I don't know that I'd ever like them to go." Laura reached out a hand then drew it back.

She looked up and Sandra asked, "Would you like to hold her?"

Laura's face lit up. "Can I?"

"Of course. It's good to have human contact at this age."

Sandra scooped up the female puppy and laid her in the cup of Laura's palms. She snuggled the sleepy baby close and brushed her cheek along the pale gold fur. The puppy turned her head and nudged her nose against Laura's.

"Oh, my." Her sigh was heartfelt. "She smells so... puppyish."

Standing again, Sandra laughed. "Would you like me to put her aside for you?"

"Not yet." Bishop stepped forward.

And Laura's head snapped up.

"Why not?" Hearing her own tone, more a bark, she bit her lip.

She'd only meant that she knew this puppy was the one. They could look at a dozen more, but she would always come back to this darling. If they didn't put something down to keep her, she'd be snapped up by someone else. She even had a name picked out.

Looking to Sandra, Bishop rolled back his shoulders. "We'd like to discuss it."

"It's a big decision," Sandra agreed. "All the relevant information is on the website where you found me. But feel free to call if you have any questions."

Hating to leave, Laura kissed her puppy between her floppy ears. "You stay put, little one," she murmured against the downy fur. "I don't want to lose you."

Two minutes later they were back in the car, buckling up. So happy and anxious and excited, Laura felt as if she could burst. She gave her thighs a hyped up little drum. "She's totally perfect, isn't she?"

He put on sunglasses. "She's a cute pup."

"So we can get her?"

"I'd like to be thorough. We want to make sure."

Laura clenched her jaw and held back a groan. Why must everything be put through the Samuel Bishop tenth degree decision sieve? For once, couldn't he say, "Yeah. Let's do it!"

"I don't care if she isn't from a long line of champions or if she'll need a hip replaced when she's twelve," she told him. "I'd want her anyway."

"And you wouldn't be crushed if down the road we found out she had a problem…that we might lose her?"

"Of course I'd be crushed. But I wouldn't love her any less, and I wouldn't blame anyone. I certainly wouldn't blame you."

"You wouldn't, huh?"

"I know you want to protect me, Bishop. You don't want anything bad to ever happen. And I love you all the more for it. We can plan and hope and dream our lives will turn out a certain way. We can care for each other and pray that nothing goes wrong. But no one's immune. If we put ourselves out there, sometimes we're going to get hurt. The alternative is to hide away. Wrap ourselves in cotton wool. I would never hold you back from your dreams. If you want to build Bishop Scaffolds into a multinational corporation, I'm one hundred percent behind you. If you want to sell to pursue another venture, I'll support you there. I know you'll support me in my dreams, too."

She was talking about more than buying a puppy, and he knew it.

He searched her eyes for the longest time. She saw the battle going on inside of him. Bishop was a man who made precise moves. He needed to anticipate, to strategize and arrive at the best possible solution to advance. As a wife, his process could be frustrating; *impulsiveness* didn't feature in Bishop's personal dictionary. But he wasn't indecisive. Quite the opposite. When he made up his mind, that conviction was set in cement. But he had to be sure…as sure as he'd been when he'd asked her to be his partner in life.

A deep line formed between his brows as he frowned and he thought. Behind his sunglasses, he was looking deeply into her eyes, but she knew he was envisaging the future…. Her concern if the puppy developed joint problems, her misery should she be struck by a snake or get lost in the bush. He wanted to shield her from pain. That was noble. But Laura wanted to feel, to *love,* and if that meant a possibility she might lose, then she was prepared to accept that, too.

He flicked a glance back at Sandra's house and, after another long moment, nodded once.

"It'll be two weeks before we can collect her."

A yip of happiness escaped and Laura flung her arms around him. He'd agreed they should get a puppy, *this* puppy, but in her heart she suspected she'd broken down a wall and he was agreeing to more.

At least she prayed that he was.

Nine

Bishop put a deposit down on the pup and Laura gave her furry baby another big cuddle goodbye. She spoke of little else all the way to the Darling Harbor apartment or on the way home to the Blue Mountains. Bishop couldn't decide if he felt relieved or ridden with guilt that he'd agreed to her getting a dog.

This time two years ago they'd had very near the same conversation. He'd stuck to his guns about checking out potential pets yet had agreed a short time later to Laura falling pregnant. He knew why he'd made that call. Laura would be able to abide by the logic behind checking out a dog's pedigree, but despite his own reservations, in his heart he understood, now more than ever, that Laura would never forget about conceiving and having her own child. Clearly, regardless of everything they'd gone through—everything *she'd* gone through—Laura hadn't put aside her deeper feelings.

Had he been wrong to expect such a sacrifice on her part in the first place? Had his insecurities been more important than her desire to be a mother in the truest sense? He'd thought he was merely being cautious, a responsible parent-to-be, but perhaps he'd simply been selfish putting his wishes above hers.

After he swung the Land Rover into the garage, he removed the luggage from the trunk, recalling how he'd rationalized this all the first time, when they'd been three months married. If Laura was willing to take the risk, he'd come to the conclusion that he could do little other than support her choice. It wasn't about courage or recklessness or defeat on his part. Back then it had been about love and, initially, she'd understood that. The here and now was about seeing if there was any chance they might get that love back.

When he'd married Laura he'd believed to his soul that she would be his wife for life. Divorce papers and living apart hadn't changed that ingrained perception, which was only one of the reasons he would never marry again. Beneath all the murk of the breakup, behind the smoke and mirrors of her amnesia, did Laura feel the same way? Reasonably, why else would her mind wind back to this precise point in her life, in their relationship, if not for some deep desire to change the misfortune that had come before? Statistics said her memory would return over time. When it did, she could tell him whether he'd taken advantage of the situation or if this time he'd been the one who'd taken a risk that might pay off.

When Bishop moved inside with their luggage, Laura was standing in front of the fireplace, peering up at their wedding portrait, her head tilted to one side as if something wasn't quite right.

While she'd chatted to Grace Saturday morning, he'd found their wedding photograph stashed at the back of a wardrobe in the adjacent guest room. His heart had thudded the entire time he'd perched atop a stepladder and rehung the print, but he had an excuse handy should she walk in. A spider's web had spread across one corner, he'd decided to say, and he'd taken the print down to see if the culprit was living behind the frame.

But she'd stayed on the phone a half hour and hadn't noticed the portrait either way after that. As he watched her now, inching closer to the fireplace, examining the print as though it were a newly discovered Picasso, he considered the other discrepancies she might wonder about now that they were home again. Things that didn't quite fit.

He'd bat the questions back as they came and tomorrow he'd get her into a general practitioner who could give them a referral to a specialist. Until then he'd wing it and let the pieces fall as they may.

Still engrossed in the photograph, she tapped a finger at the air, obviously finally figuring out what was wrong.

"It's crooked," she announced.

After lowering the luggage, he retrieved the stepladder, which was still handy. As he set it up before the fireplace, ready to straighten the frame, Laura continued to analyze.

"It seems so long ago," she said, "and yet…" She released a breath she must have been holding and a short laugh slipped out. "Can you believe we've been married a whole three months?"

He grinned back. "Seems longer."

He straightened the frame. She took in the angle, then nodded. "Perfect."

On his way down the ladder, he remembered the sketch lying on the car's backseat. "Have you thought where you might hang the other one?"

"Mr. Frenchie's? We'll need to get it framed first. Something modern, slim-lined, fresh!"

She was headed toward the phone extension. As she collected the receiver, Bishop's pulse rate jackknifed and he strode over. When he took the receiver from her, her chin pulled in.

Hoping unease didn't show in his eyes, he found an excuse.

"We've only just come home." He set the receiver back in

its cradle. "Don't you want to unpack, have a coffee, before we let the outside world in?"

"I was expecting Kathy to leave a message about the library. I told you about the literacy program we want to set up. We usually get together Wednesdays if there's anything to discuss."

She waited for him to back down, to say, of course, call your friend. But if he did that, Kathy would likely ask what on earth Laura was rabbiting on about. Laura would expand and not clued in, Kathy would laugh, perhaps a little uneasily, and say that her friend was living in the past. That what Laura was talking about happened two years ago.

Should he protect her from such a harsh jolt or hand the phone over and let friend Kathy help unravel this tangle of yarn? He'd been prepared to field any blow when last night he'd questioned her about losing a baby, so what was different now? Other than the fact that he wouldn't have control over how this conversation wound out. No control at all.

He glanced over the luggage by the door then their wedding portrait, rehung on that wall. Were they home again or should he have kept the engine running?

Resigned, he stepped back.

"I won't be on the phone all day," she said, guessing at his problem. She could talk under water once she got started. "I just promised Kathy I'd call her early in the week to check."

"Take as long as you like."

He moved down the hall, feeling as if he were walking the corridor of a listing ship…as if he were traveling back, deeper and deeper through time. If he walked far enough, fast enough, maybe Kathy wouldn't ask questions and the present, and its regurgitated disappointments, wouldn't catch up…at least not today.

He ended up out on the eastern balcony. For what seemed like a lifetime, he absorbed the warm afternoon sun and soothing noise of the bush...the click of beetles, the far-off cry of a curlew. To his left, a couple of wallabies were perched on a monstrous black rock. They chewed rhythmically and occasionally scratched a soft gray ear. Their manner was lazy, instinctive, as it had been for many thousands of years. Bishop breathed in, and the strong scent of pine and eucalypt filled his lungs. As fervently as he'd wanted to leave here a year ago, he'd missed this place.

Hell, he'd missed this life.

But with Laura talking to that friend inside, he felt the cool edge of an axe resting at the back of his neck. Would it fall now? Tomorrow? Next week? How in God's name would this end?

Laura's footfalls sounded on the Brush Box timber floor behind him and the hairs on Bishop's nape stood up. But he was ready for the attack. Like Willis had said, it couldn't get any worse than the first time.

He angled around. Laura was striding out onto the porch but he couldn't read her expression.

"Kathy was home," she told him.

He folded down into a chair. "Uh-huh."

"But her daughter and grandbabies were over. She said there was no meeting this week."

The sick ache high in his stomach eased slightly and he sat straighter. "She did?"

That was it?

"She said she'd call back, but I said not to worry. We'd just got back from the city and had unpacking to do."

We?

He threaded his hands and, elbows on armrests, steepled two fingers under his chin.

"What did Kathy say to that?"

"The baby started to cry so she had to go."

Even more relieved, he exhaled slowly. One massive pothole avoided. Although, sure bet, there'd be more—and soon.

He'd tried being subtle as a brick with his prodding last night. The questions he'd asked about possible pregnancies hadn't ignited any sparks. Rather than approaching this dilemma at ramming speed, perhaps he ought to take this opportunity to scratch around and sprinkle a few seeds—ask some casual questions—that would grow in her mind day-to-day.

He lowered his hands. "How old is Kathy's grandbaby?"

Laura spotted the wallabies. A brisk mountain breeze combing her hair, she moved toward the railing for a better look. "Oh, three or four months, I suppose."

"Kathy has more than one grandchild?"

"Just the one."

And yet she'd said grandbabies, plural, earlier. An unconscious lapse to the present?

"What's the baby's name?"

Her gaze skated away from the bush and she lifted a wry brow. "I think it might be Twenty Questions." Then her grip on the railing slackened off and she gave a quick laugh. "Since when did you get so interested in the local librarian's grandchildren?"

"I'm interested in *you*."

Thinking how the afternoon light glistened like threads of golden copper through her hair, he found his feet and joined her.

Her smile turned sultry as she traced a fingertip down his arm. "How interested?"

"Interested enough."

"Enough to take another day off?"

He focused on her lips.

"Too easy."

The brightest smile he'd ever seen graced her face. But a heartbeat later the joy slipped away and some other emotion flared in her eyes. A cagey, almost frightened look, and he wondered what he'd said. But she didn't say a word, although he could tell from the questions in her eyes that she wanted to.

His hands found her shoulders. "What is it? What's wrong?"

Tell me what you're thinking.

"I—I'm not sure. I guess I'm not used to you taking time off. Not that I don't want you to. It's just…"

He dug a little more. "What?"

Her gaze darted around his face. The color had drained from her cheeks and some of the trust in her eyes had fallen away.

"Bishop…I have to ask." She stopped. Swallowed. Wet her lips. "Is there something you're not telling me?"

She'd just had the strangest feeling. More than a feeling. That niggling again, which, rather than waning, had grown, and a lot. Still, she couldn't put a precise finger on where, or what or who was behind it. She only knew it had been there in the way his assistant Willis had looked at her when he and Bishop had returned from their talk in the hotel lobby. There again when she'd examined their wedding picture after they'd arrived home and just now…some gesture, some word, had brought that awareness shooting like a cork to the surface of her consciousness. It was like a runaway thought she couldn't quite catch…a dream she couldn't quite remember. A moment ago Bishop had asked some everyday questions about a friend and yet, standing on this spot, with those wallabies on that rock and the sun at precisely this angle…

A hot pin had wedged under her ribs and, try as she might, she couldn't remove it. What had happened—what had been said—to make her feel as if she'd crashed into a ten-foot high brick wall at warp speed?

She focused on his eyes. *What aren't you telling me?*

"There is…something," he said.

The hot pin slid out and, breathing again, she leaned back, letting the railing catch her weight.

So it *hadn't* been her imagination. For a second she'd thought she might be going mad! But whatever it was nagging, there was a reason and Bishop was about to tell her.

"I haven't told you…" he began haltingly "…not enough anyway…how much you meant to me."

Like a well filling, her relief rose higher, but then that niggling pricked again and she frowned. What he'd said didn't quite make sense. The tense was wrong. *I haven't told you how much you* meant *to me?*

"You mean, you haven't told me how much I *mean* to you."

"I want you to know it now."

His tone was so grave and his expression… He looked almost sad.

Her heart melting, she found his hand and pressed it to her cheek as a lump of emotion fisted in her throat. Her husband loved her. *Really* loved her. She was so lucky. So much luckier than most.

"I know, darling," she murmured. "I feel the same way."

He seemed to consider his next words. She could almost see him lining them up in his mind.

"I was taken aback when I saw you lying in that hospital bed."

She thought that through and came to a conclusion.

"You thought something was wrong with my heart?" Oh, no! She wanted to hug him so tight. Reassure him everything was all right. "I would've been in a cardio ward. Besides, that's all under control." She turned her head to kiss his palm. "Easy."

That pin jabbed again, deeper and sharper this time and her heart missed a beat at the same instant her gaze trailed away and she tried to grasp on to and hold that elusive, annoying thought.

"I wasn't sure what to expect," he was saying.

Drifting back, she found his gaze again. "That's why you acted so strangely?"

He nodded. "I'd seen you in hospital before."

She narrowed her eyes, thinking back. She'd been in hospital in her younger years, but...

Certain beyond doubt, she shook her head. "I don't think so."

"No?"

The pin stabbed again, so deep it made her flinch. She held her chest and, a knee-jerk reaction, wound away from him. At the same time, a noise—a crunching kind of rattle—echoed to her left. Her gaze shot over. She expected to see—

She held her brow.

—she couldn't think what.

She concentrated to form a picture in her mind, but she only saw those wallabies bounding off; they must have pushed loose gravel over the side. Now their boomerang tails and strong hind legs were catapulting them away, farther into the brush.

Here one minute. Gone the next.

Gone for good.

Those words looped around in her mind. She shivered and hugged herself tight. Her mind was playing tricks. Tricks that were seriously doing her head in. But she had a remedy.

Shaky inside, she feigned a smile. She hated to sound fragile, but she needed to lie down.

"Bishop, do you mind if I take myself off to bed early? Our late night must be catching up."

"You have another headache."

"No. Just...tired." Taking her elbow, he ushered her inside. "Wake me up when you come to bed?" she asked.

As if to confirm it, he dropped a kiss on her crown. As

they moved down the hall, she felt compelled to ask him to promise. That's what a newly married bride would do, no matter how tired, right?

But the words didn't come. And as that pin pricked again—niggling, enflaming—she only wished she knew why.

Ten

The following day, Bishop accompanied Laura into the office of a local GP.

Colorful children's drawings hung on a corkboard, but Bishop's attention was drawn to the top of a filing cabinet and a Hamlet-type skull, only this skull exposed the complicated mass that made up the mysterious chambers of a human brain. A little creepy but, in this instance, rather fitting.

Dr. Chatwin, a woman in her thirties, gestured to a pair of chairs.

"Please take a seat, Mrs. Bishop. Mr. Bishop." While they made themselves comfortable, the doctor swept aside her long brunette ponytail and pulled in her chair. "Your husband spoke with me briefly this morning, Mrs. Bishop."

Dressed in a pale pink linen dress Bishop had always loved to see her in, Laura crossed her legs and held her knees. "Please, call me, Laura."

Dr. Chatwin returned the smile. "You hit your head last week and are experiencing some difficulties, is that right?"

"I wouldn't say that." Laura's clasped hands moved from her knees to her lap. "Not...*difficulties*."

The doctor's brows lifted and she leaned back in her chair. "Some issues with memory?"

Laura froze before her slender shoulders hitched back. "Some things have seemed...a little foggy."

Swinging back around, the doctor tapped a few words on her keyboard. "Any headaches, dizziness, sleeplessness, nausea?"

"One headache."

"Irritability, confusion?"

"I suppose some."

While Bishop stretched his legs and crossed his ankles, happy to let a professional take charge, the doctor performed the usual tests with her stethoscope then checked for uneven dilation of the pupils. She asked a few simple questions. What suburb they were in. Laura's full name. The date. She gave no outward sign of surprise when Laura announced a year two years past.

After tapping in a few notes, the doctor addressed them both. "You'd like to be referred to a specialist, is that right?"

Bishop replied. "Thank you. Yes."

Without argument, the doctor began writing the referral. "Dr. Stanza is considered the best neuro specialist in Sydney. This isn't an urgent case, however, so expect a wait."

Bishop straightened. "How long of a wait?"

"Call his practice," the doctor said, finishing the note. "They'll book you into his first available slot." After sliding the letter into an envelope, she scribbled the specialist's name on the front. "As you're both no doubt aware, there are instances of memory impairment associated with head trauma due to a fall. The doctor last week would've told you recollections usually return over time, although it's not unusual for the events leading up to the incident, the incident itself and directly after to be lost permanently." The doctor pushed back her chair and stood. "You're not presenting with any physical concerns, Laura." Her warm brown eyes shining, she handed the envelope to Bishop and finished with a sincere smile. "I'm sure you'll be fine, particularly with your husband taking such good care of you."

Five minutes later, Laura slid into the car, feeling tense and knowing that it showed, while Bishop reclined behind the wheel, ignited the engine, then slipped her a curious look.

"Something wrong?"

Laura didn't like to complain. Bishop was simply making certain she was cared for. As she'd told the doctor, she had felt irritable on occasion. Some things were a little confusing... clothes she couldn't remember in the wardrobe, a new potted plant in the kitchen...that truly odd feeling she'd had yesterday on the eastern porch when those wallabies had bounded away. But the doctor hadn't seemed concerned. She'd indicated that the missing bits and pieces would fall into place soon enough.

The broad ledge of Bishop's shoulders angled toward her. "Laura, tell me."

"I don't need to go to a specialist," she blurted out before she could stop herself. "You heard Dr. Chatwin. No physical problems. Nothing urgent. I don't want to waste a specialist's time. It'll probably cost a mortgage payment just to walk through the door."

A corner of his mouth curved up. "We don't have a mortgage."

"That's not the point. Dr. Chatwin said she was sure I'd be okay."

"I'm sure you will be, too. But we'll make an appointment with the specialist and if we don't need it, we'll cancel."

She crossed her arms. "It's a waste of everyone's time."

"If it is, then there's no harm done." His voice lowered and he shifted the car into Drive. "But you're going."

She stared, not pleased, out the window as they swerved onto the road that would take them home. She loved that

Bishop was a leader, that he wanted to protect and care for her. But she didn't need to be bossed around. She hated visiting doctors and hospitals. How many times did she have to say she was okay?

She stole a glance at his profile, the hawkish nose and proud jutting chin and her arms slowly unraveled.

And another thing…he hadn't come to bed last night. When she'd woken, his side hadn't been slept in. Seeing the covers still drawn, the pillow still plump, had put an unsettling feeling in her stomach, as if she'd already foreseen or had dreamed that he wouldn't be there when she woke. Not that she'd tell Bishop that. He'd blow it way out of proportion. She didn't need to be asked more questions.

But perhaps Bishop needed the green flag from this specialist before giving his consent to her falling pregnant. He liked to have all the pegs lined up before going forward with anything. And he took the whole becoming a father thing ultraseriously which, on a baser level, she was grateful for.

So she would grit her teeth, visit this specialist, get the all clear, and once she had a clean bill of health, there should be absolutely nothing to stand in their way.

Three days later, splitting wood for the fireplace, Bishop set another log on the chopping block and, running a hand up over the smooth handle, raised his axe. The blade came down with a whoosh and a *thunk* that echoed through the surrounding forest of trees.

He'd taken the rest of the week off, and every minute since that doctor's visit, he'd waited, wondering if this would be the day when his metaphorical axe would fall. Every minute inhabiting that house, sharing that bed, he was conscious of living out the mother of all deceptions.

But, if he were being manipulative, it was with good reason. He was a man stuck in the middle of a particularly difficult set of circumstances…locked in a game of nerves where he could anticipate the moves and yet still had little control over how this rematch would end.

Grinding his teeth, Bishop set another log on the block. He was about to bring the axe down when Laura appeared, carrying his cell phone, traversing the half dozen back stairs and crossing the lawn to where he waited near a yellow clump of melaleuca. With her, she brought the floral scent of her perfume as well as the aromas of the casserole and chocolate sponge dessert she was preparing. He'd missed her home-cooked meals more than he'd realized. Hell, he'd missed a lot of things.

"It's Willis." After handing over his phone, she dropped a kiss on his cheek then inspected the blemish-free sky. A frown creased her brow. "You should put a hat on." She headed off with a skip. "I'll bring you one."

He was about to call out *don't bother,* but he liked her looking after him. The meals, the smiles. The love.

His attention on the sexy bounce of her step, Bishop put the phone to his ear. On the other end of the line, Willis didn't beat around the bush.

"I don't know how much longer I can put them off," Willis said, referring to the potential buyers of Bishop Scaffolds. "They want to speak with you, Sam."

Having set the axe down, Bishop wiped sweat from his brow with his forearm. Laura was right. He should wear a hat.

He moved into the shade. "Not this week, Willis."

"Early next week then."

"I'll let you know." He tipped his nose in the direction of the kitchen and inhaled. "Laura's doing beef Stroganoff. You should smell it."

Willis stayed on track. "I've given them as much as I can with regard to figures and projections. But the guy keeps calling. You should at least give him ten minutes on the phone. It's only good business."

Bishop understood Willis's point. He should phone, but he wasn't in the right frame of mind. He was anxious about when, or if, Laura's memory would return, but on another level he was feeling, in a strange sense, settled; he worried he'd tell the buyers he was no longer interested and later regret that he hadn't moved on the opportunity. So it was better, for now, to wait and see what transpired.

Bishop swapped the phone to the other ear. "I'll call him next week."

A long silence echoed down the line. Bishop dug a booted toe in the black soil while he waited for Willis to spit out whatever else was bothering him.

"You want me to be frank, Sam?"

"That's what I pay you for."

"Laura still hasn't got her memory back?"

"Correct."

"I know you want to help, but there's a good chance the past will all come back and you'll be in the doghouse again. Even if those memories don't return, you're still going to have to tell her the truth." When Bishop only stared into the sun, scrubbing his jaw, Willis prodded. "You know that, right?"

"It's not that simple."

"I don't imagine it is. That's why you need to be doubly cautious."

Hell, cautious was his middle name.

But Willis was right. He was getting carried away. Getting tangled up between past, present and possible future. One of them needed to keep their feet firmly planted on the ground.

Willis changed the subject. "Are you coming tomorrow night?"

To his birthday bash? Bishop moved back to the axe he'd left leaning beside the block. There'd be people there from work. People who knew about his divorce. He doubted anyone would have the guts to ask either him or Laura directly about that, or the fact that they looked to be together again. If anyone did…

With his free hand, he swung up the axe and inspected the blade. The sharp edge gleamed in the sunlight.

Bottom line, he wanted to help her remember, right? If things got interesting tomorrow evening and she started to come around too quickly, he'd whisk her away and begin explaining. Not a moment he looked forward to.

But Willis had hit the proverbial nail. He and Laura couldn't live in the past. Not indefinitely, anyway.

"We'll be there," Bishop said. "Laura's excited about it."

"Great. We'll find a few minutes to talk then."

Bishop was signing off when Laura strolled out again, Akubra in hand. She stuck it on his head and told him to leave it there.

Grinning, he tipped the rim. "Yes, ma'am."

"Is everything okay at the office?"

"Everything's good."

"It's been wonderful having you home this week, but if you need to go in, don't stay because you're worried about me." When he only looked at her, she set her hands on her hips. "I feel great, Bishop." Then, shading her eyes from the sun, she asked, "What will we give Willis for his birthday? Is he interested in chess?"

"Not that I know of."

"You've never asked?"

"It's never come up."

"But you have a chessboard in your office. The one I gave you as a wedding gift."

Twenty-four karat gold and pewter pieces. It was the most exquisite set he'd ever seen. But something in her tone set his antenna quivering. These past days they'd spent so much time together, taking walks, enjoying picnics, at other times staying indoors to ponder over the chessboard. Laura had been testy when they'd left Dr. Chatwin's office on Tuesday;

she didn't want to see a specialist. And she'd seemed so off balance that evening on the porch—Monday. But since that time she hadn't shown any obvious signs of feeling foggy, as she called it, or agitated. Quite the opposite. She'd seemed particularly breezy.

And yet subtle things she'd say or do let him know that some connections, or at least curiosities, were still clicking. The thing that struck him most was that, despite whatever connections she might secretly be making, Laura didn't seem any the less in love with him. In fact, her love seemed to grow every day.

As for him…

Laura's next question took him by surprise.

"Have you heard from your parents lately?"

He gave the obvious reply. "They live in Perth."

"I know that, silly. But there is such a thing as a phone."

Some years ago, his parents had moved to Western Australia, a six-hour flight from Sydney. They'd flown back for his wedding and had approved of Laura in every way. He only wished his mother hadn't cried so much during the ceremony. Without asking he knew she was wishing that his brother had been there; she'd made sure to tell him later. Bishop understood the emotion—he felt it, too. But on that one day, Lord knows he hadn't needed it.

He'd vowed if anything so tragic ever happened to him—if, God forbid, he lost a child—he'd keep the memories, the pain and regrets—to himself. But in hindsight, he should have been more open about his feelings after Laura's miscarriage rather than building that wall…pretending it hadn't hurt as much as it had. As Laura stood here now, the mountains a dramatic backdrop and the sun lighting her hair, he knew he ought to have shared more of himself, particularly when she'd stayed shut down.

She'd needed comfort then, not steel.

"Maybe we should invite them out for a couple of weeks,"

Laura went on. "Your mother seems so sweet. It'd be nice to get to know her more."

"I'm sure she'd like that, too."

"You could call your folks tonight after dinner."

"I could do that." But he wouldn't.

"I should probably start getting the guest wing ready."

"Laura, my parents travel a lot. They might not even be home."

And as they walked arm in arm back to the house, she leaning her head against his shoulder and a palm folded over the hand he had resting on her waist, Bishop decided that was the excuse he'd give after pretending to call.

The following evening, he and Laura arrived in Sydney for Willis's birthday bash forty minutes late. For a present, they decided on a dinner voucher at one of Sydney's most exclusive restaurants. As Bishop slid out from the car now, the lights and sound coming from the party venue descended upon him. He'd tried to stay optimistic, but he couldn't see tonight working out well. Someone was bound to say something that would trip a switch and Laura would naturally want to know more. Most likely she'd grow suspicious. Agitated. There could be a highly embarrassing scene.

It wasn't too late to back out.

Instead, Bishop sucked it up, swung around the back of the car and opened Laura's door.

"Willis knows a lot of people," Laura said, surveying the elite restaurant as she slid out. Through the generous bank of streetfront windows, a throng of people could be seen milling, talking and generally having a good time. Wringing her pocketbook under her chin, Laura hesitated.

Bishop's palm settled on her back. "We don't have to go in if you'd rather not."

The pocketbook lowered, her shoulders squared, and she pinned on a smile. He guessed that at some deeper hidden level where memories waited to be restored, she was as worried about this evening as he was.

"I want to go in," she told him, but then rolled her teeth over her bottom lip. "I'm just a little anxious. I don't know many of the people you work with."

Bishop straightened his tie. She'd know fewer of them tonight.

They climbed the stairs, entering through tall timber paneled doors decorated with colorful leadlight, and a DJ's music, underlined with general chatter, grew louder. There must've been a hundred people talking, drinking, laughing at anecdotes and discussing politics or the latest Hollywood gossip. Bishop's gaze swept over the group. No Willis in sight. In fact, he couldn't see anyone he knew. But then a familiar, animated face emerged from the crowd.

Ava Prynne worked in Bishop Scaffolds's administrative section. Tonight she wore her platinum-blond hair in cascading ringlets that bobbed past the shoulders of a snug-fitting aqua-blue dress that barely covered her thighs. When she saw him, Ava, champagne glass in manicured hand, sashayed over.

"Mr. Bishop! I was hoping you'd come."

"I've said before, Ava, call me Sam."

He didn't agree with those formalities in the office.

Ava's gray eyes sparkled beneath the chandelier light and she breathed out his name. "Sam."

Bishop cleared his throat. He hadn't been aware that Miss Prynne had a crush on him until this moment.

Laura leaned across and introduced herself. "Do you work at my husband's company, Ava?"

The blonde's gaze slid across. Her smile disappeared at the same time Bishop's stomach kicked and he bit his inside cheek. *Already it begins.*

Ava looked Laura up and down. "Husband?"

Bishop waited for the answer, then the next question, then

the next. He might feel sick to his gut, but what else could he do?

But before Laura could speak and confirm that the man to whom this woman was so obviously attracted had been married three months, a uniformed waiter with a tray appeared.

"Drink, sir, madam?"

Thankful for the intervention, Bishop grabbed a juice—he was driving back—and collected a champagne cocktail for Laura.

He nodded at Ava Prynne's glass. "Top up?"

Ava's curious gaze, swinging from Laura back to her boss, lightened a little. "Uh, no, thank you...*Sam*." But the smile she had for him fell as she looked back to Laura, then she manufactured an excuse to leave behind an awkward situation. "Katrina from accounts has just walked in. I'll see you both later." Ava and her blue micro dress hurried off.

Laura's brow quirked at an amused angle. "Lucky I'm not a jealous woman."

"You have nothing to be jealous of."

He'd said the words before he'd thought, but it was true. Laura had never had reason to think he had eyes for anyone but her. She still didn't. Ava Prynne, Annabelle...no one compared.

Tables set with gleaming cutlery and fragrant multicolored centerpieces occupied the far end of the room. To their left, waitstaff manned a line of bains-marie filled with steaming dishes. The tantalizing aromas of roast beef, mornay and Chinese cuisine seeped into his lungs.

Ready to set off toward the food and avoid any more awkward introductions for the moment, he tipped his chin at the spread. "The buffet's out."

Her nose wrinkled. "I'm not that hungry yet. Are you?"

"I can wait." In fact, he could wait until they got home. He'd thought they could handle whatever came from tonight but now, whether it might seem rude or strange, God how he wanted to leave. But he could delay…keep them alone and together for a time.

"Would you like to dance?"

Laura's emerald eyes lit up. "You recognize it, too."

"Recognize what?"

"That song." She sidled up to him, toying with the silk knot at his throat. "It's our bridal waltz."

He concentrated and the memories the tune stirred left a warm place in his chest. He cast a glance around for a dance floor, but couldn't find one.

Laura craned to peer over the heads of the crowd. "There's a courtyard through those French doors."

Bishop smiled. More private than he'd hoped.

"In that case," he offered his arm, "may I have this dance?"

They cut a path through the pack and emerged in a private courtyard. Over the fainter music drifting out, the nearby trickling of a fountain could be heard. Above them, the moon was a pale yellow claw hanging amid a quiet tapestry of twinkling lights. Feeling as if they were the only couple on earth, he brought her to the center of the cobblestoned area, instinctively immersed himself in her eyes, gathered her in his arms and began to slow dance.

She rested her cheek against his shoulder. The floral scent that was so distinctly Laura wrapped itself around him. His eyes drifting shut, he grazed his jaw over her crown, soaking up the magic that was "them" again for however long it lasted.

Moving against him, she looked up. Her eyes were dreamy, her lips moist and slightly parted.

From his heart he said, "You look incredible tonight."

She wore a black evening dress, low at the back, with a high halter neck, the ties of which were studded with glittering diamantés. But Laura looked as breathtaking in a pair of tatty weekend shorts as an evening gown. In *anything*. Or nothing.

She was the kind of woman who could never lose her beauty. It was far more than classic bone structure and those large well-lashed eyes. Laura had a quality that defied and superseded simple beauty. No matter how old, she would always glow and turn heads.

"So," she said, with that seductress's smile, "you're not sorry you married me?"

She'd said it teasingly, but a certain light in her eyes hinted that she was digging and not simply for compliments.

Holding his easy expression, he rocked her gently around. "Why would you say that?"

"There're a lot of beautiful women in there."

"The most beautiful is dancing with me."

Happiness radiated from her every pore. It hadn't been empty flattery. He'd meant every word.

Leaning her cheek against his shoulder, she gazed up at the stars.

"Have you ever thought what we'd be doing ten years from now? Twenty?"

He gave an honest answer. "I'm more focused on to-night."

"I wonder how much of the world we'll have seen together. How many different celebrations we'll have had." Her gaze lowered from the stars and met his. "I wonder if we'll be as in love as we are now."

His heart thumped harder. He didn't answer. Hell, didn't know what to say. So, with the slightest pinch between her brows, she rested her cheek against his lapel again.

After an uncertain silence, she asked in a soft, curious voice, "Are you happy, Bishop?"

He fought not to stiffen or clear his throat.

"Don't I look happy?"

She peered up again and warm trust filled her eyes. "Yes. And we'll always be." Her hand tightened slightly on his. "I was thinking, after I see that specialist next week, after he gives me the all clear—"

"Let's get there first," he cut in.

But she plowed on. "I thought we could talk more about having a baby."

His jaw tensing, he looked away. But he'd known that request had been waiting in the wings. Given this romantic setting, how close they felt right now, he shouldn't have been surprised that she'd brought it up.

His palm moved to stroke the smooth dip low on her back. "We'll talk about it when we get home."

"I don't want to stir anything up," she added, "but we need to talk about it again sometime."

He cocked a brow. Was she going to push it now? "Laura, this isn't the place."

She flinched and he cursed himself. He'd sounded dismissive, patronizing, when he knew full well how much having a baby meant to her, probably better than *she* did at this point. He was only trying to delay. Delay long enough for all her memories to return.

Or to consider more that other idea…half-baked and brainless though it was. What would happen if Laura fell pregnant again only this time she went full-term and gave birth to a healthy child? Given her condition, he was well aware the notion was appalling. While they slow danced beneath this moon and he thought about taking her home, however, it was also dangerously appealing.

He'd never wanted a divorce. He should never have left that day.

The music faded and inside someone took a mic.

"Everyone, it's time for the cake!"

Stepping back, Laura toyed with one diamond drop earring, his wedding gift to her two years ago. "Guess that's our cue."

"We'll talk later. Promise."

She gave a wan smile that said she'd like to believe him.

Back inside the crowd was congregating at the far end of the room. A massive cake was displayed on a round table, its decorated top ablaze with candles.

A heckler called out, "Blow 'em out, Willis, or the place'll burn down."

Dressed in a tux, Willis laughed along.

Someone hollered, "Speech!"

The man of the hour held up his hands and eventually everyone quieted.

"First I want to thank you all for coming tonight," Willis said. "The big three-oh is certainly a milestone. But I've enjoyed every step along the way. Best one being the day I met my wife." He held out a hand and the lady in question joined him, her face stained with a blush. "Life wasn't complete until I met you." He brought his wife close and gifted her with a heartfelt kiss.

Someone called out, "You're getting soppy in your old age, Will."

"I'll get soppier still," he called back. "I have an announcement." Oozing love and commitment, he brought his petite wife closer. "Hayley and I are having a baby."

A hoot went up. Glasses clicked while Willis and Hayley embraced like the young lovers they were, with all their future ahead of them.

His heart sinking to his knees, Bishop dared a sidelong look at Laura.

Her eyes glistened with unshed tears. When she caught him studying her, she forced a carefree laugh.

"I'm so happy for them." When she lowered her head, he read her thoughts. *I want us to be that happy.*

Bishop ran a hand down her back. They'd come tonight, had a nice dance. Now, after that announcement, it was past time to leave.

He was about to say they'd go home when Willis appeared

before them, surrounded by well-wishers raising their glasses.

Willis nodded to them both. "Glad you could make it. Laura, you look wonderful."

Faultless in company, Laura resurrected her smile. "Congratulations." She came forward and pressed a light kiss on his cheek. "You and your wife must be so happy."

"We've been trying for a while so, yes, we're both over the moon."

Having received dozens of congratulatory hugs, Hayley joined them. Her face shone like Laura's had when she'd known she was carrying their child—the same rosy tint to her cheeks, the same exuberant confidence knowing that soon she would be the mother of a healthy, beautiful babe.

Willis brought his wife close again. "Hayley, you remember Sam Bishop. And this is Laura."

Bishop held his breath and his gaze darted around at the faces of onlookers. Some murmured behind their hands. Others, less discreet, openly gaped at the boss's stunning companion. He guessed the women might have glimpsed the wedding bands on both their hands.

"I've heard so much about you," Hayley said.

"I'm looking forward to getting to know you and your husband better. He's only started at Bishop Scaffolds recently?"

Bishop held himself taut, but Hayley showed no sign of inappropriate curiosity and only smiled. Obviously, Willis had clued his wife in.

"Willis said you invited us to your home in the Blue Mountains. I'll look forward to it."

"You might be showing by then."

Hayley beamed and touched her belly. "I'm only twelve weeks. The doctor said another month or so before I feel him move."

"You want a boy?"

"I'd be happy with either—" she sent her husband a knowing grin "—but I think Willis would like a son."

Willis's hand covered his wife's where it rested. "What man doesn't?"

Bishop felt Laura's gaze edge over to him and his neck burned. Yes, he'd wanted a son. He'd wanted a family. Still did.

But he hadn't let himself think that way for so long.

Hayley dropped a kiss on her husband's cheek. "I'm going to serve the cake. Would you like some?" she asked them both.

"None for me," Bishop answered.

At the same time Laura said, "I'm good."

And Bishop stopped and thought, *This must be the first time either of us have passed on dessert.*

As Willis and his wife moved away, Bishop found and held Laura's hand. "Would you like to stay?"

"Actually, would you mind if we go?"

She was looking at her shoes and he suspected those tears had welled in her eyes again. She might be happy for Hayley, but she was also envious, and hurting because of it. Her logical side would be assuring her that her husband would agree they should try to conceive while her subconscious might be reliving the miscarriage and heartache that followed. That would explain why she felt so fragile. So ready to break.

Only Laura didn't know that.

"I'll take you home." He threaded his arm through hers and added, "We'll talk."

He couldn't wait for the specialist's appointment. She needed to be told and she needed to hear it from him, no matter the consequences. No matter if she slapped his face and called him every name invented.

But as he began to lead her out she stopped. Her glistening lashes lifted and her needful eyes found his.

"I don't want to talk. Bishop, I want to make a baby. I want to make one tonight."

Eleven

During the drive home, she and Bishop didn't discuss her no-frills request. She'd said she wanted to make a baby...not sometime in the future or next month, but tonight!

Rather he turned on a CD, and when the road didn't demand two on the wheel, held her hand, his thumb grazing the back of her fingers. She wanted to speak with him more about it. It was one thing to insist and another to have her husband's blessing.

The reality was that they'd only been married a short time. They didn't need to leap into this, particularly given the roadblocks Bishop perceived to be in their way—her heart condition, his fear of losing a child. But when Willis had made his announcement tonight, something greater than logic or fear had whispered in her ear. Spoken to her heart. Some inner deliberate voice had embraced her and stated, *Now is the time.*

Call it women's intuition or blind faith. As weird as it sounded, she only knew she had to act.

Their baby would start off smaller than a pinhead but from the moment of conception, the life growing inside of her would be a person with a soul, already loved, so very much longed for. When the good news was confirmed, Bishop would overcome his concerns because, as Willis and Hayley's joy had proven tonight, hearing that you were soon to be parents must be the very best feeling in the world. She couldn't wait to know it herself.

As they moved from the garage into the living room, Bishop took her hand, ready to lead her to the bedroom, she guessed, but she pulled back. Already in her mind she knew how this scene should play out, how and where she wanted to fall pregnant. In the quiet of the shadows, she reached behind, tugged the bow at her nape, and the black evening dress rustled into a silky puddle on the rug at her feet.

Bishop's hot gaze raked her body, drinking in every line, every curve she knew that he admired and loved. In that moment, she felt the heat in the room, in their blood, grow and thicken and beat. Tossing back hair fallen over her eyes, she tried to make out his expression in the shadows. She wanted to know what he was feeling other than fast-rising physical arousal.

Was he concerned? Feeling trapped?

"I'd like to stay out here by the fire," she said.

Bishop lobbed his jacket at a chair while his gaze skimmed over her tingling breasts then dropped to take in her quivering belly and the black silk triangle covering the apex at her thighs. As she stood before him, trembling, anticipating, he removed his tie, purposefully flicked open each button then rolled his shoulders out of the shirt.

Gloriously naked from the belt up, he moved forward and, in the gray darkness of the room, their eyes connected. He reached for her. Warm palms shaped down the column of her throat before arcing out over her shoulders and upper arms. His grip tightened slightly. She heard the groaning rumble in his chest as his fingers fanned to curve around the outside of her breasts.

He stepped closer and then his face was hovering over hers, so close their noses touched. His voice was deep and husky.

"You want that fire now?"

That's what she'd asked for, and yet now that his hands were upon her, she didn't want him to leave, not even to build that fire. She wanted to say they could create their own. Already, flames were licking a blistering causeway through her veins.

But then she glimpsed a vision of Bishop prodding the kindling, a theater of light and shadow rippling over his perfect torso, shoulders and arms. She smiled into his eyes.

"A fire would be good."

His thumbs slid up the underside of her breasts, brushing the aching tips and making her light-headed before his hands slipped away and he moved toward the fireplace. While he collected small logs from the stack, Laura heeled off her shoes and hunted down blankets and pillows. When she returned, Bishop didn't turn or acknowledge her, even as she made their campout bed. As she spread a blanket out over the large center rug, she studied his broad back and her stomach began to churn.

He wanted to make love, she was certain, but was he that agitated over what she'd asked of him tonight? She'd been firm about what she'd wanted. He hadn't said no. She knew he was way less than one hundred percent comfortable with this. She hated the thought of him being angry with her then having that anger linger and, perhaps, burrow deeper and spread. She would hate that at any time, but particularly if she were to fall pregnant.

A shiver scuttled over her skin and she held the second blanket to her chest.

Maybe she should tell him that she knew she was pushing; they had plenty of time yet. Having a child—her own flesh-and-blood child—was important to her. But so important she was willing to risk her relationship with her husband? Risk their marriage? Still, she couldn't agree to adoption when there was every reason to believe she was fertile, and Bishop, too.

Another shiver—more a chill—racked her body. As the warm feeling in her tummy began to wane, she wrapped the blanket around her shoulders. She was about to tell Bishop to forget the fire, that they should head off to the bedroom, or perhaps not make love at all. Earlier he'd said they should talk.

But then he turned to face her.

Balanced on haunches, he smiled, the kind of smile that left her blissfully warm all over. An expression that, in an instant, touched and reassured her like nothing else could.

He wasn't angry. She'd let her imagination run away on her. He loved and supported her in everything, just as she loved and supported him.

He noticed the blanket cloaked around her.

"I didn't realize you were that cool," he said. "I'll get this heat turned up."

Laura slid down onto their "bed" and let the cover slip from one shoulder. Hugging her knees, she soaked up every smoldering movement he made. Arranging the logs, seeing to the kindling. After pushing to his feet and scouting down matches on the mantel, he struck one. A flare went up, illuminating the dramatic angle of his jaw, the *GQ* dimensions of that chest.

Bishop was classically handsome with the rugged features Australian men were famous for. He possessed an air of confidence that was innate but never overstated. She loved the way he laughed and moved and smelled and felt. What would have become of her life if they hadn't met and fallen so instantly, deeply in love…if he ever truly turned his back on her and left?

Her gaze drifted up to their wedding picture. The frame was glowing in the firelight, but the photo itself was dark. She could still make out the happy couple, one dressed in black, the other in white.

Making herself comfortable, she lay back on the pillows.

She was a homebody where Bishop was a highflyer. One was step-by-step cautious, the other more casual. But she didn't see herself and Bishop as different so much as complementary. Perfect foils.

Ideal as man and wife.

When orange flames curled high behind the grill and the logs were crackling nicely, Bishop rotated back. His eyes glued to hers, he heeled off his shoes, unbuckled his leather belt with one deft pull, and stepped from the rest of his clothes. She reached out and he moved closer, kneeling beside her carefully, as if she were a bubble that might burst at any time. His face in the flickering light appeared both tender and intense, the prisms of his eyes black but for the occasional sparkling flash of blue.

With a fluid movement, he spread out beside her. The masculine breadth of his chest rose and fell in a regular hyp-notic rhythm. His body radiated its own perfect heat. Cords, ridging his biceps, wound down to his equally strong lower arms. Still lower, his heavy erection demanded relief.

When he reached for her, drew her close, she swallowed a short breath. They'd made love before, this past week so many times, but what was unfolding here, the prize this particular union might bring, left her giddy.

Her mouth welcomed his and he gathered her close. His hand smoothed over her hair, trailed her cheeks then lifted her chin high so that his kiss could penetrate deeper. For an endless moment, she reveled in the feel of his chest pushing against her breasts, the way he moved enough for the friction and simmering tension to build naturally. Swiftly.

As the kiss eased, she drove down a breath and her arms came from around his neck. Cupping the sandpaper roughness of his jaw, she spoke to his eyes. From her heart.

"Know what?"

"What?"

"I'll love you forever."

Beneath the shifting shadows of his eyes, a fire ignited. Then he grinned, a slow slant of a smile.

"Forever," he said. "Is that a promise?"

"On my soul."

That fire blazed again then his mouth covered hers, possessing her, thrilling her, filling her with a desire that was rare and precious and all theirs alone.

If two people were ever meant to be together, it was them. One wasn't complete without the other, and having a child could only make that need stronger. Nothing would go wrong. Not when everything about them…about this…felt so right.

Reluctantly, his mouth broke from hers. She sighed to her bones as his tongue trailed down between her breasts and his thumb and forefinger toyed with a nipple until liquid heat pooled at her center and her hips tipped invitingly up. He dropped loving kisses over her breasts, his head tilting this way then that as his tongue and teeth worked to create a cadence that set fireworks off in her head.

Her touch wandered down, over the superb landscape of his chest and abdomen, then lower until her fingertips combed through strong, dark hair and curled around a shaft that felt too hard to be human. Savoring the heat and the rock, she gripped him low. As his tongue flicked and teased, she dragged her hand up, the pressure unforgivably firm the way he liked it. On reflex, his teeth tightened and her hips bucked while her nipple burned and cried out for more.

"Do it, Bishop." Already, his skin was deliciously damp. She tried to slip beneath him at the same time she whispered in his ear, "I've never wanted you more."

Every muscle in his body seemed to lock. She ran her hand down his side and her fingers came away wet. As he moved above her, her head rocked back. Mind and body, she was more than ready.

He kissed her thoroughly, a caress that made her tremble so badly, her core throb so much, she worried she might climax then and there. His palm slid from her hip to the mound at the top of her inner thighs. His touch curled between, slid over that most sensitive spot, and she gasped, clinging on and concentrating on the purest of energies smoldering there. His touch swam up, circled around, and again. Laura ground against him as the pulse inside of her beat faster.

He nuzzled her neck. "You want to do this?"

Make a baby? "Yes. Do you?"

He took less time to answer than she expected.

"I do."

He scooped up her hip, captured her mouth with his, and as her leg wound around his thigh, he nudged in, naked and hot. A blissful goose-tingly shudder rolled through her. She bit down on her lower lip and moved beneath him, willing him deeper inside, feeling the ceiling beginning to lift as his concentrated rhythm bit by bit increased.

She was vaguely aware of the hiss and crackle of the fire… the smell of wood and passion smoking. Then the pulsing and glowing deep in her womb was absorbing all her attention. As he murmured her name and his thrusts became urgent, she clenched her inner muscles, clung to his arms, and sent up a prayer that this would all turn out well.

A heartbeat later, the blast went off, and fire and ecstasy consumed them both.

The next morning, rubbing his eyes, Bishop rolled over and stared at the empty space beside him. After they'd made love last night in front of the fire, they'd shifted into her bedroom. *Their* bedroom. Where had she gone?

He elbowed up, sniffed the air.

No smells from the kitchen.

Sweeping back the covers, he set his bare feet on the floor and craned his neck. No sign of life from the attached bathroom, either. He dragged on some trousers, trod out into the hall and looked up then down and up again.

"Laura! Laura, where are you?"

A twinge knotted high in his gut.

But she couldn't have vanished. Most likely she was on one of the verandas or lounging around the setting on the eastern porch. It was her favorite place, particularly in the mornings. His, too.

He moved past the empty kitchen; no breakfast preparation in sight. Past the offices, the library and other rooms. His heartbeat picking up, he strode out onto the porch and flung a glance around. The mountains murmured with the usual soothing noises of the Australian bush—a kookaburra laughing, insects clicking. Everything was eerily calm.

That twinge grew into an ache and he turned back to the house. Perhaps she'd taken the car and gone into town. She was a stickler for having her pantry well stocked.

At a jog, his soles slapped on the timber hall floor all the way to the other end of the house. He flung back the adjoining door.

Both cars were parked in the garage, engines cold. Bishop rotated in a slow, tight circle. The walls started to close in and the edges of his world began to darken. He couldn't shake the thought that had scratched at the back of his mind since he'd opened his eyes and found her gone. A horrible, this-can't-be-happening-again feeling.

His heart in his throat, he sprinted out the door.

Flying down the front steps, he spotted her in that long red negligee she'd slipped into late last night. She was exactly where he'd worried she would be—standing on that footbridge, right on the edge, peering out as if in a trance.

"Laura!"

Panic rocketing through him, he shot off. He didn't stop

until, out of breath, he reached her and snatched her away from any possibility of another fall. His grip hard on her arms, he willed her to meet his eyes. But her gaze—her mind—was a thousand miles away.

He held her face, tilted up her chin. Gradually her gaze tracked back from some faraway spot. But she looked at him as if he were a stranger. Or as if she couldn't see him at all.

"Are you all right? Laura, answer me."

Her brow creased and she shut her eyes tight. After a heart-stopping moment, she shook her head slowly.

"I…I'm not sure." Her eyes blinked open and she seemed to focus more. "I woke before you and decided to take a walk. I didn't mean to…I didn't mean to come this way…this far." The distant look in her eyes cleared more and then she shuddered enough for goose bumps to rise on her arms.

"Bishop, I had the weirdest… I think it was a dream."

"Come inside." He swallowed against the lump rising in his throat. "It's cold out."

But she wound away, edging two steps back toward the railing. As if dizzy, she touched her brow with one hand, gripped the wooden rail with the other, and peered over the edge at the bed of hedges below.

With measured steps, Bishop moved to join her. Her hands were shaking. So were his.

This was it—the moment when all the snippets that Laura had been too proud to mention these past days filtered together and gelled. He'd planned to tell her everything last night. No matter the outcome, he believed she needed to be brought back to the present. But he'd been weak. When she'd told him she wanted to make a baby, he'd remembered the thought he'd had earlier…about her falling pregnant and being able to keep the baby and their marriage this time. To his core he'd known it was wrong and yet he'd gone ahead and had sex with his ex without protection.

Last night at the party had affected him as much as it had her. He wanted a son. He wanted to be with his wife.

Had he fallen back in love with Laura?

He wanted to feel what she had felt this past week without reservation. But this moment, when she began to remember—remember it all—had constantly played on his mind, holding the possibility of total surrender to hope back.

"I remembered a miscarriage," Laura murmured, her gaze turning inward. "I remember pain. And blood. Lying in the hospital and…" She cocked her head as though she were trying to see the memory from a different angle. Then her face screwed up as if someone had pinched her. "I remember… *crying*. But that can't be. I've never been pregnant. I've never lost a child. If that ever happened…"

Stripped of defenses, she found his gaze and unshed tears filled her eyes.

Bishop leaned his hip against the rail. Now the process had begun, the memories would flow like water from a running tap. First the miscarriage, then the growing distance between them, the fall, the arguments, the total disintegration of trust. Of anything remotely resembling faith. He couldn't help but believe that last night, when they'd made love without contraception, had brought this about. What would she have to say when the final pieces settled into place? More importantly…

Last night had they created a baby?

"We'll go sit down." His hands on her waist, he encouraged her away.

"It doesn't make sense, does it?" Wincing again, she held her head. "It's all mixed-up."

He rubbed the back of his neck. He'd never felt more helpless in his life. "Come on, Laura. Come inside."

Finally, she agreed and carefully they made their way back to the house. He took her into his office and helped her as she lowered into the Chesterfield couch, confusion still stamped on her face.

Anxious, she rubbed her palms down the lap of her negligee and sent him a lame smile. "I suppose I do need to see that doctor later in the week."

He found a blanket. After wrapping it around her shoulders, he folded down close beside her. "You'll be okay."

She smiled, but then searched his eyes. "There's something that's been bugging me more than anything." Her lashes were wet and a pulse beat erratically at the side of her throat. "Last week, you said something," she started. "You said that you wished you'd told me more often how much I meant to you. I said it didn't quite make sense." She inhaled, then blew the breath out in a shaky stream. "Bishop, now I want to know. Tell me. *Please.*"

His head began to tingle. Nausea burned up the back of his throat.

You knew this would happen. You thought you'd be prepared.

But he wasn't. He was seriously low on preparedness. All the things he'd rehearsed in his head didn't seem even half-adequate now.

She stiffened as her hands wound into that red silk. "Whatever it is, don't hold back. I trust you. I want to know. I want to know everything."

He took one of her hands in his and held it tight. His voice was deep, but remarkably calm.

"I wasn't sure what to do. But when the doctor said I could take you home…that you'd remember in time, I was cornered."

"Cornered in what way?"

"When we got home, things got more mixed-up for you. Certain things were making less and less sense, right?"

She examined their entwined hands and nodded. "I didn't want to worry you. I didn't think it was a big deal. I'd find clothes, shoes, dishes I couldn't remember buying. I thought the plants around the house had grown or perhaps I'd shrunk. Even looking at our wedding photo…" Her face blanched. "Something didn't sit right."

He siphoned in a breath. Where to begin? He wanted to save her as much pain as possible without coming across as the biggest jerk of all time. He'd slept with this woman when she'd been far worse than vulnerable. Could she even begin to understand?

She sat straighter. "I don't have some degenerative disease, do I? Is that why I fell? From losing my balance? My mind?"

"I don't know how you slipped on that footbridge. Either time."

She shook her head, trying to understand. "*Either* time?"

There was no easy way, so he'd simply say it. "When you fell last week and hit your head, you lost a portion of your memory. More than just the time directly before and after the accident."

Her eyes narrowed. "How much more?"

"This last week, you've been living in the past. Two years in the past."

Her hand slid away from his. Her smile looked slightly hysterical. "Okay. Sorry, but that doesn't make sense. Am I hearing you right? You're saying we've been married over two years?"

"It's more complicated than that. This time two years ago…" He let out a long breath. "You fell pregnant."

Laura felt as if a bowling ball had smacked her in the stomach, leaving her winded and seeing stars.

What Bishop had suggested was ludicrous. *Absurd.* So crazy she wanted to laugh in his face. She could swallow that she'd lost part of her memory. If she'd been pregnant, however, she sure as hell would've known.

Inside her head a squeaky cog turned and, taken aback, she blinked several times.

Hadn't he implied the same thing a few days ago? She'd laughed at him then. Had been more than a touch offended, in fact. And yet now…the way he was looking at her, as if nothing more serious had ever been said, some part of her was inclined to believe him, except for one rather obvious point.

"If we were pregnant, Bishop, where's the child? And if you say we gave her away, that I *won't* believe." His face remained grave and Laura's heart contracted then sank. "She didn't… die?"

His nostrils flared and his gaze dropped away.

An unbelievable anger jetted up inside of her, heating her face and making her want to slap his. Did he truly expect her to believe that she'd carried a baby for nine months, given birth and didn't remember? She couldn't bear to even *think* such an impossibility was true.

Her throat convulsed and the anger turned dangerously close to rage. As well as an unexpected urge to cry.

"You're lying."

He held her arms and his voice deepened. "Listen to me. You had a miscarriage in your second trimester. You were devastated. I couldn't get through to you. Nobody could."

That flash came again—pain, mess, anguish, so powerful and real, it threatened to tear her apart. She searched the eyes of the man she loved…*had* loved?…and like a ball circling then rolling into a shallow hole, the memory fell into place. She and Bishop were no longer married. They were divorced, and had been for an entire year! Much more than that—

All the breath left her lungs. A feeling crept over her, heavy and black, like a tainted, rough knit shroud. She remembered Grace being there to console her. The doctor explaining there was no reason not to try again. And Bishop…

She saw Bishop sitting in his home office, staring at his

computer screen, that Rubik's Cube rolling around in one hand, no emotion on his face.

"I'd been afraid of what might happen if we conceived," he was saying. "With my history, I worried about losing the child after it was born. I never considered a miscarriage. It left me numb, Laura. I tried to tell myself it could be worse even though I knew that sounded heartless. And I wasn't there for you. I tried to be, but I didn't know what you needed, what to say, and whenever I tried to get close—"

"I pushed you away." She looked at him, her eyes stinging. "I was so angry with you. Angry because you were right. Us falling pregnant was a bad idea. I thought I was strong but afterward…" Fresh hot tears sprang to her eyes. "I wasn't. But you were." Her slim nostrils flared. "And, God, how I hated you for it."

More memories fell, raining down now, pummeling her brain, weighing on her heart. She pushed to her feet. "We had arguments." Looking inward, she blindly crossed the room. "We spent more and more time apart."

"You didn't want to try to fall pregnant again, and I didn't want to push."

Then another memory landed and she held her stomach. "I fell." She spun on her heel and hunted down his gaze.

He was nodding. "Off that footbridge. That was the first time, eighteen months ago."

The room began to swirl and close in.

Yes. She remembered. Remembered it all. She'd been walking across the bridge very early. The planks were wet with dew and there was gravel in a patch to one side. She'd slipped—she remembered the sound—and fell straight under the rail and onto the river stones below. But now hedges grew where the stones had once been. Because Bishop had planted them after her fall, she recalled. Just in case…in case she "fell" again.

She studied Bishop, every mesmerizing, anguished inch. A

moment ago she'd been in *love* with this man. Now, not only did she recall the disappointment, she *felt* it. The sensation made her physically ill. Her heart had been shredded and the scars were as fresh as if the wounds had been inflicted only yesterday.

A tear slipped from the outside corner of her eye.

"How *could* you, Bishop? I was hurting so badly, I needed you to prop me up, support me, and when I fell…"

"I didn't know what to think. You'd been so—"

"Unstable?" Fisting her hands, she cursed at the ceiling. "I'd lost a baby. But no matter how down I felt, I would *never* try to hurt myself. I slipped—it was an accident—and at the hospital…" Her voice dropped to a hoarse, pained whisper. "You wouldn't even look at me."

He found his feet. "I was wrong."

Holding her stomach, she asked in a soft injured voice, "Why didn't you say that back then?"

"I *tried.*"

She sent him a withering look. "Don't lie to me, Bishop. Don't you dare lie to me now."

He took two steps forward. "I'm trying to talk to you, for God's sake."

"Don't you think it's too late for that?"

Throwing up his hands, exasperated, he spun to face the wall. "This is why I left—"

"Why I *asked* you to leave."

"—because no matter how long we hammer it out, we'll never get past this."

A realization struck, so strong, so shocking, Laura's knees turned to water and every scrap of strength disappeared out her toes. She thought this situation was bad, but it could get a hundred times worse.

She balanced her sagging weight against the edge of his desk.

"Oh, God, Bishop. Oh, God. Last night."

His back to her, he scrubbed a hand over his face. "I know, I know."

She held her stomach again, lightly this time.

"What if I'm pregnant?"

Bishop turned back as Laura's expression changed from one of shock to outright alarm. He stood tall, ready to take whatever came. Shouts, tears, accusations that he probably deserved.

Her beautiful green eyes rimmed with red, she dragged herself away from the desk and toward him. "You knew... this entire week, you knew. And you had *sex* with me—"

"Made love."

"—knowing how I really felt? You took advantage of me."

"Did I? I've wondered whether some part of you was purposely holding back. You wanted to be with me, didn't you?"

Her face screwed up as if she'd tasted something sour. "What kind of question is that?"

Damn it. "It's a question a husband asks his wife."

"Divorce, Bishop. Remember that word? We're not married anymore."

"We have been this past week." Growling, she pivoted away. But he grabbed her arm and swung her back. "Tell me you weren't in love with me last night, the night before and the night before that."

As if he'd slapped her, her head drew back. "That's not fair."

"I don't care about being fair. I care about you. Laura, I care about *us*."

Glaring at him, she sucked down a shuddering breath as a tear sped down her cheek. More calmly she said, "You have a strange way of showing it."

He released her arm, then set his hands on his hips. "You're taking this badly enough when you're ready to hear it. What would've happened if I'd sat you down that first night and laid out the facts, cold and hard? Should I have done that? Would that have made me less of a jerk?"

She lifted her chin. "Yes."

"Yes?"

The spark of malice in her eyes faded the barest amount. She moved to the windows, set her hand on the jamb and stared out for a long considering moment.

"No." She admitted, "I suppose you could've done that... been brutally honest. Or you could've just walked out of the hospital when you found out I'd lost my memory."

"Or, when your sister phoned, I could have flat-out refused to come at all."

She curled some hair behind her ear. "And you did make that appointment with Dr. Chatwin. Took that time off work. That was amazing, even before I knew you loathed the sight of me."

What did he have to do to prove it to her? "I never hated you."

"Is *couldn't stand the sight of me* better?"

He growled. "Laura, I wanted to work it out."

"I'm sorry, but you didn't do a very good job."

He locked his shoulders and coughed out a mirthless laugh. "Know what? If you want to blame me, go ahead. I'm used to it."

"It's way too late for that."

"No kidding."

She searched his eyes with a laser beam and he wondered what she'd come up with next.

"Why did you do it?" she finally asked. "Why did you have sex with me...make love to me," she conceded, "without protection, when we'd lived apart for over a year? When it was all finally finished?"

"This last week proved we weren't finished. Over these

past days, I came to hope, to believe, that you and I might be able to work things out this time."

Laura pressed her lips together then, as if she were afraid he'd see tears fall, abruptly peered back out the window. When she only continued to stand there, one hand on the jamb the other bunched by her side, he moved closer.

"Tell me what you're thinking," he said. *For God's sake, don't close up again.*

Her throat bobbed on a deep swallow. "I'm afraid to."

"Do it anyway."

She blinked her tear-rimmed eyes before she spoke. "There's some totally crazy, masochistic side of me that wants to be…"

He said it for her.

"Pregnant?"

Looking bereft, she nodded at the view.

He cut the remaining distance between them and threaded his hands around her waist. He waited and gradually she let her gaze edge up. When her eyes met his, he smiled, warm and reassuring.

"We'll work it out."

She didn't look convinced. "You said that once before."

He brought her mercilessly close. "Did you know that when you were in that hospital room, your sister said this might be another chance for us?"

"Grace said that?"

"I know. Hard to believe. I thought she was talking out her ear." His grin faded. "But then I took you home and little by little, day by day, my perception changed."

Her head tipped to one side and he felt her slide a notch nearer to surrender. But then her hands found his at her back and tried to pry them away. "You're doing this on purpose."

"Doing what?"

"Trying to confuse me."

"I'm trying to *un*confuse." She stilled and, despite everything, gave in to a smile. He grinned, too. "And, yes, that's not a word."

With his fingers threaded through hers, he shepherded her back toward the couch. After an eternity, she sat, then he folded down, too, and waited for her to speak…to say what she'd wanted to say for two long years.

Her gaze wandered around the room and he knew she was taking herself back. Remembering.

"You agreed we could try to fall pregnant," she began in a faraway voice. "And it happened straightaway. I was so excited. You seemed happy, too, but you were busy at work, expanding something or other, and you spent more and more time away, staying in the city apartment." Her fingers dug into the couch. "But when you were home, I saw the look growing in your eyes. You like to be in charge of the next move. *Every* move. When we conceived, what you wanted to control most was taken out of your hands." She blew out a stream of air to compose herself before going on.

"I said we should buy some furniture and linen for a nursery. One day in Sydney I saw those symbols I liked in a jewelry store window. I wanted to buy them—the heart, cross and anchor—but you said *next time*. Then, after the miscarriage—" her eyes filled again "—I felt as if some part of you was relieved. That you were proven right in some way and the risk was gone. You had the reins back and you weren't about to let them go again. Then I had that accident," she went on. "Fell off the footbridge. You thought I'd been so upset that I'd tried to hurt myself." Her head lowered. "We didn't make love again after that."

She squeezed her eyes shut and her shoulders winged in, as if something sharp had pierced her chest. Bishop felt the ache in her throat as deeply as he felt his own. He remembered her wanting to buy those little gold symbols. She'd been so animated and committed. Although it wouldn't have made a difference to how things had worked out in the end, he'd been wrong not to get those trinkets. Truth was that he didn't have faith that her falling pregnant would turn out well. He would have tried to deny his pessimism back then, but he'd proved as much by not going into the jewelry store that day.

"When I lost my memory," she said, "you were happy for me to forget about that time in my life, weren't you?"

"It only made you sad."

"But it was a *part* of me. I want to remember, no matter how much it hurts."

"So you held on to the grief and the hopelessness to the bitter end," he concluded, unable to keep the frustration from his voice, "even if it meant killing what we had."

"I needed your support, Bishop," she said, almost pleading now. "Not your cold shoulder. You left…" She shifted in her seat, glanced dejectedly around the room and grudgingly conceded, "But you left because I told you to go." She blew out a long, resigned breath. "Let's face it. I drove you away."

His mouth swung to one side. He'd been disappointed with himself when he'd finally accepted defeat and had walked out. He'd failed and that had been a blow not only to his ego, but to his sense of self; Samuel Bishop always came out on top. Still, he'd maintained that a man would need to be made of high tensile steel to have withstood the ice storm he'd endured all those cold, bitter months after the miscarriage. Now Laura was telling him she'd felt the same way. Isolated. Lonely. Wanting to reach out. Or be reached.

He shrugged a shoulder. "Guess we can share the blame."

She turned a little toward him, hesitated, but then sought out his gaze. "I'm sorry, Bishop. It's too late, but I am. I'm sorry it all turned out so badly."

He ground his back teeth together to stop his mouth from bowing. "Yeah. Me, too."

"Hard part is—" she sat back "—where do we go from here?"

Where, indeed?

After all the direction he'd handed out this week, and her accusation of needing to hold the reins, he offered, "Must be your call."

Her eyes widened. "My head is still spinning. I'm not sure I'm ready to decide on breakfast cereal let alone how I feel about what happened last week."

He thought it through.

Okay. "I think we need sit back and let our emotions settle. See where we are in a few days' time."

"You mean see if I'm pregnant?"

He remained poker-faced to mask the fact that his heart was beating so hard, he thought his ribs might crack.

"If you're pregnant," he paused and amended, "if we're pregnant, then we both have some serious decisions to make."

Laura didn't know if she was more sad or relieved to see Bishop leave a little later that day.

After their revealing talk, they'd agreed they had a lot to think over, and staying under the same roof would only confuse already high emotions. Despite all she'd learned today, at her deepest level Laura was critically aware that she still longed for Bishop's affection. She longed to have his arms gather her in and his innate strength keep her warm. She ached to absorb the comfort and intensity only the man she'd married could bring. Had married…and divorced.

With dawn breaking, Bishop had passed on eggs Benedict. He said he'd best get a head start on the road, although on Sunday, Laura suspected, the traffic would be less than frantic.

As her ex-husband's Land Rover edged down the long drive, she stood on the front veranda, leaning against a column, trying to shake the hollow feeling of being left in limbo. With regard to their relationship. With regard to her life. But she didn't have time for reflection or self-pity. She wanted to know as soon as possible whether she was or whether she wasn't pregnant, and she knew from previous enquiries that some tests could be performed as soon as six days after the event.

Would she be able to get on with her life, rather empty though it now seemed, or was the dream she'd nurtured for so long about to come true? Although, falling pregnant was only part of the equation, as she well knew. She had to carry to term.

She recalled doing lots of research on miscarriages after her loss and being surprised by the number of women who'd suffered the same pain and grief she had. That knowledge had given her comfort—she wasn't alone—but the information had also left her more than a little anxious. Two years ago she'd been so certain she wanted to conceive, and she'd wanted Bishop to be positive, too. And yet after she'd miscarried, it seemed all her courage had deserted her. She'd withdrawn. She'd been unwilling to talk about her crippling sense of failure much less consider trying again.

And now?

Well, now she was almost frightened to hope.

Seeing Bishop's Land Rover about to disappear around that last bend, she pushed off the column, ready to go back inside, but then another car—silver and stately—wound up the path. Grace's Lexus.

The two vehicles stopped side by side; Bishop was no doubt cluing Grace in on the latest. Laura eased out a breath. At least she wouldn't need to explain to her sister. Or not everything. And while she didn't feel much like talking, she did want to hear Grace's rationale in letting Bishop take her home that day over a week ago. Grace had never approved of her ex and yet Bishop had said that he and Grace had spoken about second chances.

A few minutes later, Bishop's car disappeared and Grace's car pulled up. The moment the door flung open, she flew up the steps and wrapped her arms around her baby sister. Laura felt Grace trembling and realized she was shaking a little, too. One minute she was married, the next she wasn't. She'd had unprotected sex with her ex. She could possibly be pregnant. It was a lot to take in all in one morning.

Inside, with that wedding portrait peering over them and dominating the room, she and Grace folded down together on a couch. Laura got straight to the point.

"Bishop told you?"

Grace's pearl drop earrings swung as she nodded. "Briefly."

"Did he tell you…that we slept together?"

"He didn't need to. I can tell by both your faces."

"We didn't use protection."

Grace's eyes widened. "He agreed to that?"

With her heart beating high in her throat, Laura tried to explain how it'd come about.

"I was living in the past. I was the same person I was just after we'd married." She focused inward, to the happiest times they'd recently spent together, and recalled the almost surreal feeling. "Now I realize when I told him I wanted to conceive our own child, I was pressing a replay button."

"You remember the miscarriage?" Grace asked gently.

Laura shut her eyes to try to block out the pain. It didn't work. The memories were raw and vivid.

"Grace, why did you let Bishop take me home from the hospital? You knew how we'd parted. If I'd had any inkling, I would never have gone."

"We could've made up some story, I suppose, that Bishop had to go out of town and you should come stay with Harry, me and the kids for a while. But my children are two years older than you remembered, and I thought you had more chance of regaining your memories here. Besides, you were in love with Bishop." Grace smoothed her sister's hair. "I don't think you ever stopped loving him."

"Bishop said you thought this might be a second chance for us."

"You were never so happy as when you were with Bishop. At least at first." Before Laura could ask the next obvious question, Grace answered it for her. "It wasn't that I didn't approve of the man, Laura. With mum and dad gone, I saw it as my place to let you both know that I thought you ought to sit down and properly sort out how you were going to achieve your life's goals—and face any consequences—before you exchanged rings."

Laura's gaze dropped to her left hand. Through misty eyes the diamonds shot off hazy prisms of light and color. She felt so hollow inside, so different from the sense of contentment she'd enjoyed only yesterday.

"We were both so in love," she croaked, barely able to speak over the rising emotion.

"And now there's a chance you might be pregnant?"

"A slim chance."

"Still… It's a chance for you to take the best care of yourself and for things to work out the way we would've liked the first time."

Laura leaned her head into her sister's shoulder and they sat together in the quiet for the longest time like they used to when they'd been young and Grace would read to her at night. Laura hoped she wasn't pregnant; what if she miscarried again? If she went to term, could she and Bishop ever forget how they'd treated each other in the past or the pain of having pushed the other away? On the other hand she prayed that she was. More than anything she wanted to be a mother.

Laying a light palm on her belly, she thought over Grace's words.

This time everything could go pear-shaped again or maybe, just maybe with some hope, faith and love, things would turn out right.

Twelve

As Bishop braked in front of the Blue Mountains house a week later, he guessed Laura must have heard his vehicle revving up the long drive. Looking remarkably fresh, and more beautiful than he remembered, she appeared at the door then moved gradually out onto the porch.

This morning he'd rung to say that after seven days and nights apart they should touch base. See where they each stood. He hadn't told her about the guest he'd brought along. And he hadn't asked if she'd taken a test.

The test.

While he slid out of the car, Laura remained at the top of the landing. Her lips weren't curved into a smile. Nor was her brow lined with a frown. The knots that had amassed in his stomach during the trip jerked and snagged all the more. But he wasn't unhappy that he'd come. The whole time he'd been gone, he couldn't focus on work. He particularly hadn't been able bring himself to make a decision over the sale of Bishop Scaffolds. He'd thought only of her, wanting to feel her lips beneath his again, needing to hear and feel her warm, seductive whisper at her ear. Not that he expected her to throw herself at him when they said hello now. But later...

Who knew what lay ahead?

She smiled softly down while the light blue dress she wore swirled around her knees in the breeze. "Hello, Bishop."

He had no time to reply before the guest in his Land Rover tipped his hand. Following a single bark, a playful growl then three or four sharp yaps sounded in a row. Laura's expression opened up. After two halting steps forward, her hands lifted to her mouth and her gaze flew from the rear of the car back to him. Her eyes wide, she gave a little squeak.

Feeling as if he wore a big-bellied red suit and long snowy beard, Bishop unlatched the tailgate and edged out the pet carrier. The puppy's brown eyes were full of life and her tail was beating furiously. She was soft and cuddly and, no matter what happened between Laura and him, this dog would make his ex-wife a fine companion.

He scooped the puppy—Laura had called her Queen—out of the container.

As she flew down the steps, Laura's smile split her face. "You didn't tell me."

"Wouldn't have been a surprise if I had."

Meeting at the bottom of the steps, he offered over the wriggling pup. She held out her arms then, sighing, brought the bundle close. Queen immediately set about licking her mistress's cheek, her nose, her ear. Laura laughed like he'd never heard her laugh before, except for that brief time when she'd been pregnant and beyond happy.

"She's just so beautiful."

"And probably hungry." He headed back to the car. "Take her in and I'll bring up her gear."

Five minutes later, Queen's paws were scratching over the timber floor as she scuttled around, sniffing and wagging, while Bishop set up the food bowl, litter tray and bedding. Crouching, Laura ruffled her pup's ears every time she skittered close.

"You like your new home, little one?" she asked.

Queen yapped once then padded off, her nose zigzagging

over the ground. Laura stood and straightened her dress before she sent a coy smile his way.

"Thank you. It feels like Christmas."

He returned her smile. Then he wasn't the only one.

Queen was running around his feet. "She was supposed to be the quiet one but looks like she's got lots of energy. I think puppy school's a must."

"I'll book her in." Smoothing down her dress again, she inhaled deeply as if to steady herself. "I have a surprise, too."

Moving to the fireplace, she found a pharmacy bag on the mantel. While his pulse began to hammer, she revealed a slim box.

"I've had it sitting there for days," she admitted. "The results are supposed to be extremely accurate."

"This soon?"

She nodded. "It checks hormone levels."

"Ah. I see."

With an awkward but glowing smile, she glanced down and rolled the packet over and over. Her gaze crept up and she blew out a long, shaky breath. "Guess you can tell I'm nervous."

Join the club.

He ironed his damp palms down the sides of his trousers. "So you can do it now?"

"It'll show a result in a couple of minutes." Her gaze flicked away. Came back. "I'm *really* nervous."

As the puppy scampered down the hall, he came forward and folded his hands over hers. He eyed the box that held the instrument that would predict the course of the rest of their lives, one way or the other. Scary. And exciting. As long as nothing went wrong.

He squeezed her hands. "I'll wait here."

As she moved off down the hall, Bishop drove two sets of fingers through his hair and paced the room a few times. He dug out a tug toy from Queen's bag and they played around. When five minutes dragged on to feel more like thirty, he buckled and headed for the liquor cabinet. If ever a man deserved a drink, God save him, it must be now.

The test sticks sat on the end of the double vanity while Laura sat on the top step of the spa bath, her hands holding her burning face. The pack had contained two tests. She'd known the results of both for at least ten minutes, but the news was still sinking in. The shock was still wearing off.

When the numbness tingling across her brain subsided and she knew she couldn't delay any longer, she pushed on her thighs and found, to her amazement, that her legs were steady enough to hold her weight. She wasn't crying. She was totally okay with this. *Way* okay. Bishop would be, too. She simply had to find the wherewithal to go out and tell him.

When she reentered the living room, Bishop was standing by a back window, gazing out over the eucalypt-covered hills, swirling a short glass of amber liquid. Hearing her footfalls, his gaze snapped over and those masculine shoulders, cloaked in that heavenly chambray shirt, straightened.

His delayed smile was supportive, but the emotion didn't quite reach his eyes. He was waiting for her to tell him the news, show him the proof. And while she'd never felt more wound up in her life than she did at this moment, now a certain, almost eerie calm settled upon her, like a mist curling over a long, slow day.

He'd stand by her. This time they'd make it work. Because they needed to for the baby's sake. And they'd be happy. She knew they would.

If only she were pregnant.

Sprawled out under the piano, Queen must have worn herself out. Laura padded past, careful not to disturb her. Quivering inside, she tacked on an ambivalent smile and made herself shrug.

"Guess you're a free man."

His smile dropped. He took one measured step forward, blinked several times and then rasped, "No?"

"I didn't think you'd want to see the sticks. No point really."

The breath seemed to leave his body and he visibly slumped. She'd never seen anyone look so dazed.

"It's probably best," she went on, needing to fill the silence. She needed him to speak. To say *something*. Because, in truth, she'd wanted this…to have been a victim of fate and have the choice made for her, and she'd thought he'd wanted that, too.

He ran a hand down the side of his clean shaven jaw and she noticed he still wore the ring. "Are you sure?"

"As sure as I need to be. Both results were clear. I could go to a doctor, but I don't think there's any need." She'd probably get her period in a day or two.

His gaze distant, he lowered to sit on the edge of the piano stool, his foot inches from Queen's sleeping head, while Laura held the breath fluttering in her chest, waiting. But of course it took a while to sink in, thinking you might be headed in one direction then being shunted off in another. Hoping you were going to be a parent, then not. They'd both been through the ups and downs before.

Then he inhaled sharply. The surprise his next words delivered almost knocked her over.

"We could try again."

She gaped at him, wanting to tug her ears. Had she heard right? She said the first thing that came to mind.

"We're not married anymore."

Was he asking her to marry him again?

His brows drawn together, he pushed to his feet. "The other week it felt like we were."

"That's only because I couldn't remember that you'd signed divorce papers."

His brows knitted more. "I wasn't the one to instigate proceedings. You sent the papers, Laura, not me."

"You didn't have to send them back."

He held her gaze for a torturously long moment before he succumbed to a tight smile. "No. You're right. I didn't." But then the sharp glint in his eyes softened and he took another step closer. "I'm sorry the test wasn't positive."

"Are you?"

She'd sounded indignant, but she truly wanted to know, and know the truth. Had he honestly wanted a positive result or was the greater part of him relieved—again—that the risk and possible danger had passed?

His jaw visibly tightened. "I wanted this…wanted *us* to work, but I knew we didn't have a hope unless you were pregnant. That week we spent together…" His chin tipped up as his gaze penetrated hers. "I think we can have that again."

In that instant, her doubts seemed to evaporate and her heart began to melt. She didn't know if she could speak over the emotion swelling in her throat. But the obvious question swooped down.

"How?"

"We can go from here. Work out each move, step-by-step, together."

"But we'd come up against that same roadblock straight out of the grid."

He gripped her left hand and his heat, as well as his will, consumed her. "We can work it out."

She felt herself teetering as her surroundings drifted in then out. She wanted to agree, so much it hurt. But she simply couldn't go the way of denial. Now that she remembered it all, she couldn't put on her rose-colored glasses even if her heart broke admitting what they both knew to be true.

Her voice was hushed and scored with regret. "Bishop, you said we'd work it out the first time."

His eyes grew dark. "You fell pregnant. What happened after that wasn't my fault. Laura, it wasn't *anyone's* fault."

"I know that."

And she did. But that unhappy fact didn't help them now. Or take away her continuing sense of loss. Or her fear it would happen again.

His voice deepened. "Do you still want a family?"

"Yes…but…"

She tried to battle the doubt, but now, more than ever, the memories seemed so frighteningly clear. The threat of it happening again—of losing a baby well into a pregnancy—left her skin clammy and her throat dry.

"Without being pregnant already, I don't know that I can risk that kind of loss again," she confessed.

She'd named that baby. Imagined how she'd look. Miscarriage might seem like a by-the-by word and occurrence to some, but that day she'd lost a child she already loved.

His shoulders rolled back as he measured her with his eyes. "And you won't consider adoption?"

"No." She slid her hand from his. "Or not yet." Drained, she leaned against the piano and admitted, "I'm not sure. I don't know that I ever will be."

A resigned look dulled his eyes. She'd seen that shadow before in the months leading up to the day he left a little over a year ago. She had no illusions as to what that expression meant now.

"There's no point me asking again, is there?" he asked in a flat tone.

Laura held herself firm. She felt as if she were trying to walk a swaying tightrope. She wanted to reach out and draw him near, feel the comfort of his body against hers and give him some comfort too. But what would that achieve? The chiseled planes of his face had never looked sharper. His eyes, seemingly piercing her soul, had never looked more detached.

They'd been through this before, over and over. There was no solution. And like never before she suspected they both knew it.

He'd wanted to know if it would make a difference if he asked again.

Slowly she shook her head. "No, Bishop. It wouldn't."

After a drawn out moment, he glanced down at his drink as if he'd forgotten he'd poured it then he shot the Scotch down his throat. Mentally exhausted—at a loss to know what more to do—she tried to go off topic. Maybe if they talked about something else for a while...

"Would you like another one? Or maybe some coffee."

He crossed to the mantel and rested the empty glass below their photograph. The barbed wire ball rotating at her center scratched and grew. Next week, would she be taking that picture down again?

On leaden feet, she edged close. "I made some scones fresh this morning—"

"They wouldn't go down so well with Scotch."

His voice was graveled and low. When he turned away from the fireplace—from the picture—his gaze landed on the door and a fist rammed through Laura's chest.

He was leaving?

She studied the drawn line of his jaw, imagined his mind turning over. Neither one of them could ignore the truth. No matter how much they seemed suited, how well they seemed to fit, the past would always cast a long, sour shadow over their present and, subsequently, their future, as well.

Garnering her strength, she clasped her hands, lifted one shoulder and let it fall. She hoped her voice didn't come across as shattered as she felt.

"Seems neither of us has anything much else to say."

His jaw shifted and he probed her eyes. When she waited him out, gave him the chance to communicate, his hard gaze fell away and he admitted, "Seems not." Then he jerked a thumb toward the door. "I should probably start back." His gaze found the puppy. "Glad you like the dog."

Her throat closed off as a colossal weight anchored down upon her shoulders.

That was it. He was going. This time for good.

It took all her willpower to pin that smile back in place when it would've been far easier to crumple up and cry. But she wouldn't let him see how crushed she was. Neither one of them wanted a replay of this time last year and they both knew that if he stayed that's exactly what would transpire.

A few minutes later, as he slid into his vehicle and buckled up, she stood alone on the porch. He hadn't kissed her goodbye. Hadn't touched her, not even a token reassuring brush of his hand against her arm. He certainly hadn't told her that he loved her.

He stared down at the wheel, then his stormy gaze dragged over to hers and her heartbeat began to thunder. Would he swing open the door, take the steps two at a time and enfold her in his arms? Tell her that he was staying, no matter what?

But he didn't move. And when he only continued to sit there, staring, the tears, crouched at the back of her throat, squeezed higher. If he was leaving, why the hell didn't he hurry up and go!

Rather than sounding like a shrew and shouting for him to quit the dramatics and end the torment, she tossed out a blithe, "Traffic will be building. Say hi to your folks when you call."

The hard line of his mouth curved with a whisper of a smile and then he nodded. "Too easy."

A moment later, as the vehicle ambled down the drive and Bishop drove out of her life for good, Laura withered onto the top step.

Now she knew why two simple words had set off alarm bells that morning when she'd asked if he could take another day off, and again when she'd assured him her heart condition was under control.

One year ago, when she'd asked to him leave, after he'd thrown his wedding ring into the fireplace then had slammed the door a final time closed, he'd said precisely those words.

Easy, he'd jeered.

Too easy.

Thirteen

Sitting behind the desk in his Sydney penthouse office, Bishop gazed blindly out the window, absently tapping his pen on the blotter. He wasn't interested in the impressive view of the young cityscape, or the fact that it had been teeming with rain for a week. A stack of emails from Willis filled his in-box, telling him to snap out of it. He wasn't interested in that, either.

Samuel Bishop was well-known for his sometimes agonizingly thorough approach to any important problem. Once he made a decision, however, it was the right one and he stood by it. But for the life of him he couldn't find the wherewithal to give a devil's damn about making a decision on anything right now. His old friend logic said it was a temporary malady. The cogs would start turning again soon enough, even if he barely recognized the lifeless face that gazed back from the bathroom mirror. This morning, he'd fleetingly thought staying in bed might be easier.

The knock on his partly opened door pulled him from his thoughts. His secretary knew he wasn't to be disturbed. Clearly Willis wasn't buying. He strode in, the knot of his tie loose, his expression beyond exasperated.

"Sam, I get that you're the boss—"

"Yes, I am," Bishop confirmed, flicking his pen aside.

"—but I need an answer. *Now*. Clancy Enterprises have given us until midday or they're walking away and, believe me, they won't be back."

Bishop swung in his chair, one way then the other. He wanted to say he'd decided to go ahead with the sale. That he wanted a clean start. A new challenge. He couldn't sit around like an ambivalent lump for the rest of his life. Fact was that he'd wanted to sell the company before Laura had taken her tumble. Now that all the twists and turns of their roller-coaster couple of weeks were done, all indicators pointed to going with his previous decision. So why was he torturing himself, sitting here day after day, wishing that this second time around things had turned out differently?

Closing his eyes, Bishop pinched the ache simmering beneath his brow.

Dammit, why hadn't he dug his heels in, kissed Laura senseless then announced that this time he was staying? Because he didn't love her? Or didn't love her enough?

Exhaling, he opened his eyes and swung to face the desk. He leaned forward, forearms on the blotter, fingers tightly clasped.

"Give Clancy the green light," he finally said. "I want this done."

Willis's jaw unhinged. Then he shook his head as if to clear it. "Are you sure?"

Bishop's temper flared. "You said you needed an answer."

Willis's shocked expression faded into one of understanding as he slung a hip over the corner of the desk. "Want to talk about it?"

Was he referring to Laura?

"Thanks, but I'd be happy never to talk about it again." Bishop tipped out of his chair and headed for his chessboard on the other side of the mile-long room.

"Did it ever occur to you that you're still in love with her?"

"You saw me with her exactly twice."

"At the party she was upset. Hayley saw you leaving, too. Later she commented on how wonderful it was that you'd found each other again. That you were both so obviously in love."

Bishop's smile and voice were tight. "Let me tell you something."

Willis folded his arms. "I'm listening."

"I've thought about this. Thought about it in great depth. Just say, for argument's sake, I *did* love her. It wouldn't make a difference to where we stand now. It wouldn't be enough." Wasn't then. Wasn't now.

"So you're going to close down shop and walk away. Again."

Bishop's jaw hardened. "Be careful, Willis."

"Why? Because you might have to admit that you're wrong?"

"I thought you'd be pleased about selling."

He'd told Willis he'd take him along on whatever venture he started next. They'd even talked partnership. Willis had guts as well as business acumen. He talked straight. Bishop could trust him.

Should he trust him now?

Having crossed the room, too, Willis collected a chess piece off the board and inspected its lines. "She gave you that chess set, didn't she?"

Bishop narrowed his eyes. Where was Willis going with this? "It was a wedding gift."

"And you kept it."

"It's a valuable set."

"And it always reminded you of her, right across from where you sit every day."

Bishop opened his mouth to refute it. But the truth was glaringly clear. He'd wanted to keep something of Laura close.

Could he get rid of this chessboard now as Laura would, once again no doubt, shut away their wedding portrait?

Bishop sank in the tub chair while the yellow gold and platinum pieces shone up at him. Elbow on the armrest, he braced his brow on the slope of his index finger and thumb and massaged the ache that had grown exponentially. He had to get it off his chest.

"Last week," he admitted, "Laura thought she might be pregnant."

"*Holy...*" Willis dropped into the chair opposite. "She wasn't?"

Staring at the board, Bishop shook his head. "She said she wanted to try for a baby. I agreed, even though she was living in the past—we both were—back when we were newly married."

"And she hit the roof when she finally got her amnesia files open?" Willis said without a hint of *I told you so,* for which Bishop was grateful.

"At first, she was angry. But eventually we agreed, if she was carrying our child, we'd work things out."

"And when it turned out she wasn't, you left?"

"She wouldn't listen. Nothing got through to her, just like last time."

Willis grunted. "Right."

Bishop's voice lowered. "She was thinking exactly the same thing I was. Without a baby cementing us together, the past would always be there, cleaving us apart. There's too much history. Too many bad memories." His gaze slid from the board. "Too much to forgive."

"And what kind of memories will you have when you hit sixty-five? That's roughly another half of a lifetime of sitting around feeling like crap."

Bishop's hackles went up. "What do you expect me to do?"

"Win, for God's sake! Win for you both."

Bishop's grin was sardonic. "Great speech. But this isn't a game."

Willis shook his head slowly. "I don't get it. With everything else you're like a tiger on its prey. You lock down and don't let go. But when the prize concerns something as inconsequential as your happiness from this point until the end of your days, you can't tell right from left."

Done listening, Bishop went to stand and walk away, but Willis reached over and gripped his arm.

"Listen to me. I know what I'm talking about. Hayley and I broke up for a time. Swallowing my pride and asking her to take me back was the best thing I ever did."

His head thumping now, Bishop gazed down at the chessboard. The pieces seemed to look up at him, so still and cool, as if they were prepared for any contest, the more demanding and extended the better. Bishop digested what Willis had said, then shut his eyes and kicked open the stiff lock at the end of the mental chain that was keeping him back. Then, for the first time since he was a youth, he changed his mind.

"Let Clancy know we're not selling." With a determined gait and a suddenly focused mind, he set off for his desk.

He heard the frown in Willis's voice. "We were talking about Laura."

"And send Meryl in on your way out." Bishop pulled in his chair. "We have a mountain of catching up to do."

"And Laura?" Willis persisted, following.

Bishop reached for a document that had been sitting in his in-box far too long. Seizing that pen, he began to make notes on a site drawing and muttered, "I'll call."

"When?"

"When I do."

Willis huffed. "You know you're a fool if you don't."

Bishop's steely gaze tipped up. "And everyone knows I'm not that." Not a third time anyway. Willis was about to push more, but Bishop held up a hand. "Discussion closed."

As Willis left, Bishop reaffirmed the choices he'd made. He'd decided to keep his company. He'd thought he'd needed a new challenge, but this one was far from over. There was more work to do, more victories to be won, before he could ever consider walking away. Same went for his situation with Laura. As he'd told Willis, he would call…

But not yet.

Where his ex was concerned, he'd seemed compelled to act on impulse. But this time when he made his move, his strike would be well planned. He simply had to find the right time, the right place. Then he wouldn't back down until he'd claimed his mate.

Fourteen

New Year's Eve had always been such a special night. When they were young, Laura and Grace had stayed up with their parents, growing increasingly excited the closer midnight had come. When the hands of the grandfather clock in the dining room finally hit twelve, they'd join in the celebrations happening all over the east coast—blowing paper whistles, lighting sparklers, hugging and kissing, as well as making wishes that hopefully the new year would bring.

Sipping on a glass of fruity white wine now, Laura scanned the busy room, studying the glitter and hype through the slots of her masquerade mask, a band of green and gold sequins covering only her eyes. This New Year's she was at a charity function in Sydney, a celebration she'd helped organize on a professional basis.

The fifteen-thousand-square-foot room boasted a double-tiered layout with the mezzanine level reserved for the crème de la crème. Pink, pearl and iridescent yellow helium balloons hung suspended in the air, their multicolored tails swaying high above the heads of several hundred affluent guests. Magnificent Corinthian columns supported soaring sixty-foot ceilings while the center Wedgwood dome crowned an atmosphere that celebrated an ultra-stylish event sponsored by the socially elite.

Unfortunately, Laura wasn't able to absorb much of the bubbling atmosphere. In fact, she was counting the seconds until she could leave. She hadn't felt much like partying of late.

She and Bishop had said goodbye a final time eight weeks ago. Her ex had acted improperly when he'd agreed they should try for a baby. He shouldn't have taken advantage of her amnesiac state. No matter how difficult, no matter how much he'd thought she hadn't wanted to hear the truth, he should have told her…about the miscarriage…about their divorce.

But she wasn't angry over that. How could she be when she'd wanted to be with him as much as he'd obviously wanted to be with her? The simple truth was that she still wanted him now.

But from the beginning the odds had been stacked against them. They both wanted a family, but in trying to achieve that, they'd only succeeded in carving out a rift that now was impossible to bridge. Their differences would never be solved or puttied up by anything as simple as talking it out; they'd tried that both times around.

Still she couldn't help but wonder…

If they'd fallen pregnant that night two months ago, would she and Bishop be together now, anticipating the birth of a healthy child, discussing getting married again? Or would she have miscarried a second time?

With her memory restored, Laura found it difficult to imagine ever taking the risk and trying to conceive again, and she hated herself for losing the faith she'd reclaimed briefly during that week with her ex. She'd become what she'd once accused Bishop of being—a person who preferred to live life without risk…but also without the danger of adding any new pain to the old.

She only wished she didn't love Bishop so much, but the

truth was she'd loved him the whole time, even when she thought she'd had enough and wanted him gone for good. Sometimes, especially when she lay awake alone at night, she couldn't accept that they were truly finished. It was like trying to believe that summer wouldn't follow spring.

But now, studying the animated effervescent scene buzzing all around, Laura reaffirmed the promise she'd made to herself after Bishop had left a second time. She was done living in the past. She had to build on her strengths and move on with her life. She and Bishop were history and it was best she swallow that pill, no matter how bitter. No matter how painful.

She was gazing absently at revelers on the dance floor, gyrating to a disco tune from the seventies, when someone bumped into her back. As cool wine splashed her hand, she wheeled around. Louis XVI and Marie-Antoinette tipped their powdered wigs in apology then blended back into the thick of the partying crowd. To her right, a butler topped off Casper's and Wendy's champagne. Laura recognized one of Australia's wealthiest media magnates decked out like a spaghetti Western star from the sixties, checking the time on his Rolex.

Tonight Laura was Tinker Bell, complete with pom-pom slippers and gossamer thin wings, although she didn't feel the least bit mischievous or daring. When Captain Hook had asked her to dance a moment ago, she politely declined as she'd done to others many times tonight. Watching the captain from a distance now, she wondered if she might recognize the face should he remove the mask.

Tickets had asked that guests keep their masks in place until twelve. Not until you'd given or had received a kiss were you permitted to reveal your true self. Not everyone had gone along with the adventurous spirit of the request, however. That man standing next to one of the bars, for instance. Indiana Jones. His hat was worn at a forward slope, all but covering his eyes. The adventure-scarred thirties flight jacket suited

his masculine physique...tall, broad, a posture that said
commanding, aloof. Even *arrogant.* Everyone attending
tonight was wealthy or here courtesy of someone who was.
If it was good enough for the majority—top models, champion
race car drivers, *Forbes* businessmen—to abide by the keep-
your-mask-in-place edict, why should Jones think he was
exempt?

Indiana drank from his heavy-based glass then tipped his
hat back. When a pair of bright blue eyes indolently swept the
room, Laura's blood froze in her veins. Then she broke out in
a sweat. Pressing her hand against the nerves jumping rope
in her stomach, she set her glass down on a passing waiter's
tray before it could slide through her tingling fingertips and
smash on the floor.

Bishop?

It couldn't be.

Desperate to see more clearly, she removed her mask,
blinked several times then focused again. At the same time,
the man in the hat flicked a glance her way. Their gazes
hooked. Stuck.

Fused.

She'd given the attendance list a good going over. Or she
thought she had. Had they come close to bumping into each
other tonight? Had they brushed, touched, unbeknownst to
either one of them?

Shaking inside, Laura gulped down a breath and straightened her spine.

Forget all that. What did she do now?

He made the decision for them both.

Removing his hat, holding it at his chest, he crossed to
her. Somewhere in the recesses of her mind, Laura heard
someone call out, "Five minutes to midnight!" And then he
was standing before her, so tall and more darkly handsome
than any man had a right to be. On his hip he wore a coiled
whip. Beneath his eyes lay shadows she didn't remember

seeing before. Had he slept as little as she had these past months?

Beyond nervous, she pasted a smile on her quivering lips.

"Bishop…this is a surprise."

"A pleasant one."

That husky comment would've been enough to unbalance her, but the slant of his kissable mouth, the sparkle in his eyes, left her dizzy.

Sucking in a breath, she shored herself up.

Cool. Collected. Don't let him know how affected you are. You don't want his pity. Let him see you don't need anything from him, particularly the pain of hope.

She adjusted her fairy wing shoulder strap. "I didn't see your name on the attendance list."

His gaze had dropped to her mouth and was now licking a deliberate line over her lips. Her heart raced faster. She thought she'd remembered how deeply he affected her. Now, with no more than a lidded look, she was dissolving into a warm puddle.

"I decided to attend at the last moment," he told her. "I believe you're a functions coordinator now."

It was on the tip of her tongue to ask how he knew. But she deliberately smoothed the questions from her expression and, as calmly as she could, explained.

"I was always into food. Catering. Making things nice. I wrote up a few proposals, did some promotion and got a few gigs, including this one."

Approval shone in his eyes, transforming them into glittering blue mirrors beneath the lights. "Congratulations. I'll have to put our promotions department onto your website."

"So you kept the company?" He nodded and a sense of right filtered over her. "I'm glad. That place was so much a part of you. You always wanted to build it up into all it could be. I can see you taking Bishop Scaffolds all over the world."

"My suit with its giant S printed on the chest is on order."

He chuckled and for the first time in months, she wanted to laugh, too. How wonderful to feel something other than listlessness.

A call from the center microphone went up. "Three minutes. Get your lips ready, folks."

Laura had unconsciously been checking out the beautiful bow of Bishop's mouth. Now the reference to kissing jolted her back. Her cheeks hot, she redirected her attention to a dazzling nighttime view of the harbor and bridge visible beyond the multistory glass wall. Below, a glittering sea of sparklers lit the boardwalks and streets.

"The fireworks should be spectacular tonight," she said, her gaze on the view while she felt his own gaze sizzling over her.

"Spectacular. Yes," he replied. "Not long to wait now."

While the crowd stirred and the excitement around them grew, her gaze joined with his again and they simply looked at each other, soaking each other up, one drinking the other deeply in. She felt herself being drawn up, like early morning dew to the sun, but then nearby someone blew a party whistle, reality intruded again and she dropped her gaze to her pom-pom slipper feet.

Time to move on before she did something foolish like throw herself at him and beg him to take her home.

She rubbed the back of her neck above her fairy wings. "Guess I'd better let you get back to the party." Her expression suitably poised, she nodded a farewell. "Happy New Year, Bishop."

"Take care, Laura."

He touched her arm and the skin-on-skin contact shot a hot flash straight to her belly before it spread drugging warmth down her suddenly unsteady legs.

She cleared her throat and mumbled, "You, too," before, more than a little shaky, she walked away.

Bishop watched Laura, in that sexy-as-sin pixie outfit, as she vanished back into the crowd. Her legs were just as delectable and her smile still melted his heart. If anything she'd grown more beautiful. More desirable.

Over these past two months, whenever his mind hadn't been otherwise completely occupied, his thoughts had tracked back to his ex and the incredible time they'd spent together when fate could have taken them one way but had pitched them in the other instead. But after his talk with Willis, he'd seen things more clearly...well enough to push himself to climb back on top. He'd made the firm decision to keep his company and had dived back into work with fresh gusto.

And then there was Laura.

That day, when he'd decided he would win back Laura's love, he'd also decided to act only when all the pieces were lined up to give him the best chance of success. His nature was to be cautious; every step needed to be the right one. And yet in the past he'd acted impulsively where Laura was concerned. She fired up emotions that flicked a switch in him that demanded immediate action. He'd asked her to marry him too soon, had left when he should have held on and seen the rough times through. Hanging off from approaching her these past weeks had been agony. But the wait would be worthwhile. Tonight he felt the time was right. Soon he would make his move.

As the "one minute to midnight" warning echoed through the vast room, Bishop knocked back the rest of his drink. Then, setting down his glass, he shouldered a path through the elaborate costumes and masks and found a relatively quiet spot against a column near the main entrance. Crossing his arms, he leaned back and absently watched an assortment of guests prepare themselves for twelve.

Soon the countdown cry went up.

"Ten, nine, eight, seven..."

He'd caught up with a few friends tonight and had made a

few new contacts. But he hadn't come here to socialize. Not in that sense anyway. He was here because of Laura.

When they'd touched a moment ago, the sensation had been the same. Almost too hot. Too good. If they met and touched in ten years' time, it wouldn't be any different. He'd still nurse the same maddening urge to carry her away despite any protests. Tonight, if he had to, that's precisely what he intended to do.

The countdown ended. Cheers and cries of *"Happy New Year!"* exploded through the ballroom. Beyond the windows, Sydney ignited in a limitless show of sky-high flares, sparks and luminous color. Crowds clapped and hugged. Inside, streamers flew, whistles blew and everyone seemed to be kissing and embracing.

Bishop waited, anticipating his next move and how the scene he'd envisaged a thousand times would ultimately play out. His gaze landed on a nearby couple. They were young, clearly in love. She was heavily pregnant.

The anticipation in his gut spiked and looped, and rather than that couple, Bishop imagined he and Laura standing there looking that happy. That pregnant.

That in love.

As the couple broke apart and gazed tenderly into each other's eyes, Bishop set his hat aside and moved out. The cacophony of noise expanded to a deafening pitch, but now Bishop blocked it out. On a mission, his heart pounding louder than the fireworks hitting the stars outside, he drove through the tightly-packed crowd until he reached the center of the room. He angled around, focused as his gaze whipped over countless heads and a pulse beat furiously in his throat.

He'd purposely let Laura walk away five minutes earlier. He'd wanted the realization that they were indeed in the same room to sink in. He wasn't concerned he wouldn't find her again, and for one simple reason.

He had faith. At this moment, whether she wanted to admit

it or not, she would be searching for him as earnestly as he was now searching for her.

From the first time they'd spoken, the first time they'd kissed, he'd made up his mind to have her, and marry before anything got in their way. When she'd told him about her heart condition, it made no difference to how he'd felt. He'd work it out. That's what he did. Logically. Methodically.

One maddening step at a time.

He'd married Laura on impulse and despite all they'd been through, it was the best decision he'd ever made. Tonight he intended to tell her just that.

Still searching, he rotated slowly back around and a path seemed to open up through the center of the crowd. At the far end of the room, with her silver wings and fluff ball slippers, stood Laura. Even with a sparkling mask covering half her face, he could see that their eyes had locked. She angled more toward him and he strode up until he stood, determined, before her.

"Time is nothing but a great empty void without you," he said, as cheers and whistles continued to wail all around. But he didn't worry she couldn't hear him. Behind her mask, her emerald eyes were swimming. She'd heard every word.

But when his hands searched out hers, to hold and urge them close, her shoulders thrust back and she wound away.

"We don't need to do this again. Especially not here. We said all we needed to two months ago. There's no point rehashing it."

"You're right. No rehashing. There's been enough of going over old ground. We need to push forward. Get over the past once and for all."

"The only way to get over it, Bishop, is to leave it behind. Leave *us* behind."

"You know neither of us can do that."

"We *have* to. Don't you see? There's no answer."

"I won't accept that."

The breath seemed to leave her and her lower lip trembled the barest amount. "Please, Bishop, don't. I can't do this again."

Blocking out the commotion, he found her hands and held them tight.

"When I left over a year ago, I was angry. Not with you. At how things between us had turned out. You've heard the saying, what you fear most you create. What we were both so scared would happen, did." He stepped nearer and the distance separating them closed more. "We lost a child."

Her shoulders hitched as she swallowed back what he suspected to be a quiet sob. Her heart was there in her eyes as the tips of her fingers reflexively curled over his. "I...I never thought you understood how I felt."

"I thought you'd get over it," he admitted, "and when you did, I wanted to try again. But when you didn't want to—" He corrected himself. "When you *couldn't,* it suited me because at the edges of my mind I kept thinking...what if it happens a second time, a third? What if we go to term and it's my twin brother all over again or there's problems with his heart?" A rock pressed on his chest. "How could I do that to a child?"

She was biting her lip, clearly holding back tears.

"I should have been there for you," he went on, "even when you didn't want me to be." He rotated her hands until their backs rested against the buttons on his chest. "I love you, Laura. Till the end of time I'll love you."

A tear slid past the ridge of her mask, down her cheek, around her chin.

"You love me? Still?"

He nodded, smiled and cupped her cheek. "I want you to give what you always asked of me. Have faith in me, Laura. We were in love again two months ago. I know we can have that again." He brought his cheek to hers. "I'll never stop holding you," he murmured against the shell of her ear as he stroked her back below its wings and willed all the forces of heaven and hell to this time have it turn out right. "I'll never stop loving you, no matter if we live out one lifetime together or ten."

Slowly, he released her. As fireworks ignited the night sky and the party continued to explode, Laura's throat bobbed up and down. Needing to see her face, he found the sequined edge of the mask and slid it off. What he saw left him short of breath. It was there in her eyes, so clear and bright, and he knew what she was going to say before she said it.

"I can't help loving you," she got out. "Even when I didn't want to. I was the one who wanted to take a risk, but when the worst happened, you were the one who stayed strong while I—" Her cheeks wet, she leaned into him. "I gave up. I gave up on us." Her hands knotted in his shirt. "I don't want to give up again." Then she blinked and concern flared in her eyes. "But Bishop, even if we walk out of here together tonight, we still won't have solved our problem."

The dilemma of when and how or *if* they should have a family.

He reached into his top shirt pocket. When his hand withdrew and he opened his palm, Laura's eyes went wide and her hands lifted to cover a disbelieving smile. Gingerly she scooped up the delicate gold pieces. She held them high and the gold symbols caught and reflected a hundred lights. Bishop could see her heart caving, and his did too, as she twirled the pieces so that prisms planed out from a cross, an anchor and a heart.

"We'll try again," he said. "We'll fall pregnant. But only when and if you're ready. And no matter what comes, good or bad, I'll always, always be there right beside you."

That sob escaped and, looking as if she couldn't find her voice beneath a world of emotion, she pressed her lips together and nodded. At that moment, all the commotion in the room seemed to fade. He lifted her chin higher so he could see her eyes…and the open gift of her love.

"Guess that means I have an answer to my question," he said, smiling, too.

"Which question is that?" she choked out.

He cupped her face and searched her eyes until he felt his soul touch hers.

"Will you marry me?"

More tears pooled in her eyes—happy, grateful, as-soon-as-we-can tears. But then she asked, or was it teased? "You don't think we need more time?"

"I only know I can't wait for you to be Mrs. Samuel Bishop again." His lips brushed hers. "I can't wait for the rest of our lives to begin."

While the other revelers were finishing their embracing, Bishop gathered his only love adoringly near. He cherished her...loved her...and with all his heart, he kissed her. A kiss to seal their future and a promise neither one would ever forget.

Epilogue

Sitting in the living room of their Blue Mountains home, Laura and Bishop huddled together on the couch, watching their favorite DVD. With her head on her husband's shoulder, Laura sighed as the camera's eye panned the interior of the quiet church while a hundred guests smiled and gazed on.

On the screen, proud father Bishop carefully handed over his baby daughter for the minister to perform the long-anticipated ceremony. Laura stood beside them, her hands clasped under her chin as her eyes shimmered with more love than many hearts could ever hope to contain. Their baby, Abigail Lynn, had her father's thick dark hair and her mother's striking green eyes. She was dressed in the christening gown her grandmother had sewn and trimmed with white ribbon over twenty-five years earlier.

The minister held Abbey's tiny head over the font and carefully anointed her crown. Cameras clicked and at least one camcorder caught all the action, including the godparents' smiles (Willis and Grace had been honored), and the approval radiating from both sides of the aisle. Bishop's parents had flown in from Western Australia the day before and planned to stay a few weeks. But by far the strongest, sweetest emotion captured that day was the expression on Bishop's face. Gratitude. Pride.

Unbridled love.

The ceremony wound up. She and Bishop, with their baby girl, made their way down the crimson-carpeted aisle, soaking up the best wishes of the people with whom they'd chosen to share this special day. On a close-up, Mum and Dad kissed their baby on each cheek. A moment later the images on the plasma screen flickered to black.

Misty-eyed, Laura reluctantly let Bishop leave her side to remove the DVD from the player. Her gaze wandered to their darling eight-month-old, sitting up by herself on her pink blanket. While Abbey played with her animal friends phone, Queen dozed directly behind, a living, breathing, soft place to land should the baby happen to topple. Bishop ejected the disc while Laura leaned forward to scoop the baby up.

"I'll never get tired of remembering that day." Laura popped her daughter onto her lap and, humming a nursery rhyme, gave her a bounce. Laughing, Abbey raised her arms and squealed, begging for more. "I could play that DVD over and over." Laura rubbed her nose with the baby's. "What about you, sweet pea?"

"Abbey's not old enough to talk." Bishop slid the christening DVD into its labeled jacket. "If she's anything like her mother, God help our phone bill when she is."

"That's what women do," Laura pointed out. "They talk." She spoke to the baby. "And boys flex their muscles and play with balls, both skills, of course, being vital to the happiness and survival of our species."

"I know something else that's vital to our survival." DVD in hand, he made his way back over. "To mine anyway."

Bishop joined them on the couch. Cupping his wife's nape, he brought her lips to his. They kissed, tenderly and with a sincerity that softened Laura's heart and refreshed her belief in all that was pure and good.

Slowly, he released her, but she wasn't ready to let go just yet. Arching a brow, she filed her fingers suggestively through his dark hair. "Tell me more."

"As soon as the baby's down," he murmured, in that deep, seductive voice that made her quiver, "I intend to do just that."

But then he came close again. His mouth was about to capture hers once more when Laura pulled back and looked down. The baby had gripped the edge of the DVD jacket and was giving her first teeth a serious work out.

Gently, Laura pried the jacket away. "No, no, baby. We need to take good care of this."

"That's right, kitten." Bishop stroked his daughter's head. "We have to play it at your twenty-first."

"Twenty-one." Laura held Abbey's little fingers and inspected the tiny dimpled hand. "It'll be here before we know it. Then she'll be moving out, getting married." She studied her baby's soft pink skin, those bright green eyes, and her heartstrings tugged. "I think I'm suffering empty nest syndrome already."

"I know a way to delay it."

"Spoil her rotten so she never wants to leave?"

A fingertip trailed her jaw as his lips whispered over hers. "Have another one."

Laura's breath caught. She never thought she'd hear him say the words. Agreeing to try again to have their first child had been a big enough step, and for them both. But she'd adored being pregnant this time and hadn't suffered one hiccup, not even a single day of morning sickness. More importantly, their child was not only beautiful, she was also brimming with good health. There was no sign of a heart problem, thank heaven, and there was no reason to believe there would be in the future.

So did he really mean…?

"Have another *baby?*"

His smile warmed every inch of her. "Would you like that?"

Laura could barely speak over the emotion—the sheer happiness—clogging her throat. "I would like that very much. *Infinitely* much."

His chuckle faded as an earnest gleam surfaced in his eyes. "Have I told you today how in love with you I am?"

Tipping forward, she nuzzled his bristled cheek. God, how she loved him, too. "Remind me again."

His breath warmed her ear. Warmed her heart.

"You give me direction, give me meaning."

Her eyes stung with another rush of emotion. She pinched the bridge of her nose, uncertain why she wanted to stem tears that came from a place of such perfect bliss. "You're making me all foggy."

"In a good way, I hope."

"The very best way."

So in tune, they looked down at their child at the same time. Just like that, Abbey had fallen asleep on her mother's lap.

"You put down the baby," he said and held up the disc. "I'll put this away. Then I'll light a fire."

"And we'll meet back here."

If they were as lucky as she now believed them to be, history would repeat itself. This time next year they'd have another perfect little addition in their lives.

But as Bishop carried away that disc that held such sweet memories, and she carried their precious bundle to the nursery, Laura caught sight of those two portraits hanging above the fireplace and knew there was no need to guess at the future. They would always be a family who loved and supported each other, no matter what.

No matter what.

* * * * *